Elyn was jealous!

And Nick was oddly unsettled by her tears. The water had soaked through the shirt she wore, and though it lay plastered against her, revealing every soft, swelling curve, he was more intent on comforting her than in taking advantage. "There's no reason to cry. That girl meant nothing to me and I..." He was about to apologize for mentioning Elyn's husband, but she was already upset. Instead Nick pulled her close and kissed the tears away.

Elyn thought that perhaps she was too heavy to lie across him, but he seemed not to mind. If moments earlier his tone had been harsh, now Nick seemed intent on soothing her; and because his concern was nearly as sweet as the pleasure of making love, she lay cradled in his arms. Slowly his kisses awoke the realization that her desire lay just below the surface. It took only a touch or a gentle caress to arouse her. Her lips yielded beneath the light pressure of his mouth, parting to submit, to revel in that possession that was and yet was still to come.

She wanted him now, and nothing else mattered, not pride, not modesty, nothing but the joy that lay ahead...

Also by
DONNA COMEAUX ZIDE

Above the Wind and Fire

Caress and Conquer

Lost Splendor

Savage in Silk

Published by
WARNER BOOKS

Promise Me Paradise

Donna Comeaux Zide

WARNER BOOKS

A Warner Communications Company

*This one is for my sister, Connie, and
my brother-in-law, John Watt.
They are everything family should be—
loyal, loving and supportive.
My love to them both.*

Veracruz, Mexico

February 1914

Prologue

"Have you ever imagined a man other than Alec making love to you?"

Elynora Barford was far too shocked by her cousin Sybil's inquiry to do more than stare. Her dark blue-violet eyes widened before a sweep of thick brown lashes hid their expression. A blush had begun to warm her throat and spread across the soft curve of her cheek. Sybil didn't seem embarrassed. Indeed, Sybil was enjoying the moment immensely. "I was wrong, Syb," Elyn answered finally in a voice tinged with censure. "You *have* changed—for the worse! Why in heaven's name would you want to know something so . . . so intimate?"

Sybil Avery smiled, not at all put out by the younger girl's indignant observation. Age had nothing to do with Elyn's naïveté, though. She had always been an innocent. It was her nature. Syb could still clearly call to mind her cousin's reaction when she had first learned the details of sexual intimacy—from *her*, of course. Elynora had laughed incredulously, rejecting the idea that males and females should fit each other like interlocking puzzle pieces. Now, of course, she knew firsthand that Sybil had not lied. "Darling, we're no longer virgins. Now that you're a married woman too, I thought you would be eager to discuss the subject." She drew the lace collar of her peignoir closer about her slender neck and shrugged a shoulder. "One might even say that you had an obligation to trade knowledge and experiences."

Elyn's eyes widened again. No one had spoken to her of any such obligation, but then, there had been a number of things she hadn't been told. The blush was scarcely off her own marriage of fifteen months, while Sybil had the benefit of six years of connubial bliss. Uncomfortable with the challenge, Elyn answered nonetheless. "I should think such thoughts disloyal to Alec, and certainly if I had a notion of that kind, I'd never tell anyone else about it." Another sip of cream sherry fortified her stated beliefs. "Not even you, who are my best friend as well as my cousin."

"Disloyal? Sometimes, darling, you are a ninny. D'you think Alec doesn't let his imagination wander?" Sybil smirked knowingly and shook her head in dismay. " 'Tis the nature of the beast, love. And if he can do so, why can't you?"

Tiny frown lines played between Elyn's brows; a shell-pink fingernail traced the prominence of a slanted cheekbone. "You don't *know*, do you, that that's what he does?" The question had a waiflike insecurity, a sort of reassure-me hesitancy to it. Sybil's voice had seemed to echo from a well of confidence, transforming her suppositions into facts by their delivery. "Of course he's free to think upon whatever he pleases but . . ." Elynora glanced up, "I shouldn't like to believe that my husband finds my face or figure so unappealing—"

"I can see we've so much to discuss that I shall have to fortify myself first," Sybil broke in before reaching toward the night table for a cut-crystal wine decanter. "You'd think, wouldn't you, that mothers would better prepare their poor girls for the realities of sex?" she continued, freshening Elyn's glass before she refilled her own. "Take, for example,

4

your own dear Aunt Willie. After Arthur and I returned from our honeymoon, I confronted Mother and asked her why she hadn't explained things in greater detail. D'you know what her answer was?''

"What?"

Sybil shook her head, smiling at the memory. "She said I knew as much as she had on her wedding day and why, pray tell, was that not adequate? Adequate—can you imagine? As though it were a game of horseshoes, with only one way to pitch and play! Christ, how ignorance is perpetuated.''

"It's a sin to take the Lord's name—''

"Ignorance is a worse sin." For a moment Sybil's expression was almost fierce; then, as if she had glimpsed her reflection in a mirror, she shook her head in self-reproach. "Perhaps my vehemence surprises you, but I'm a zealot when it comes to my favorite subject. Now . . . weren't we going to try to right your love life?''

"Sybil, I never said . . .'' Elyn's disclaimer trailed off as she caught a glimmer of mischief in her cousin's dark eyes. She raised her chin, determined to steer the conversation away from what she considered a touchy subject. It was, at the least, a weak spot in the armor of her personal knowledge. "I am *quite* happy with Alec.''

"Are you truly? And there is no room for improvement in your relations with him?'' Sybil arched a brow in wonder over the seeming miracle. "I'll tell you how happy you are, how satisfied—but answer one question first. What do you think of when Alec is making love to you?''

"*Really,* Sybil—have you nothing on your mind but physical love? I can see now why Arthur's hairline is beginning to recede . . . you've worn him to a frazzle.'' Sybil's brows met in a determined line, her lips parted. "*I know,* I haven't answered your question,'' Elyn went on. "I don't think of

5

anything." There, it was out, for all Sybil thought she might deduce from the reply.

It was Sybil who looked shocked now, more alarming for the fact that she was not easily rattled. *"Nothing?* Not even what you'd like him to do?"

"To do?"

"Men aren't mind readers, love. One has to lead them, rather like a blind horse, down the path."

The advice seemed sincere despite Sybil's flippant manner. Was she really right? Elyn tried to imagine herself giving directions to Alec and shook her head. Anything she might suggest, no matter how carefully worded, would surely wound his pride. "I couldn't. Can you . . . with Arthur? Truly?"

"I swear it. And, darling, if I did not, he and I would no longer be a twosome. It's that simple. I'm not the type to spend . . . to *waste* my life in an unsatisfactory relationship."

"You can't mean you'd divorce him!"

"Why can't I?"

"It . . . it's just not done, Syb." Elyn shook her head, rejecting the idea that Sybil would take such a drastic step. Marriage was forever, a union sanctioned and blessed by the Lord. There were bound to be minor disagreements, little things that one had to overlook. Like the irritating way Alec fussed over his personal grooming for hours, while she . . . well, she could be dressed and coiffed, ready for any affair within three-quarters of an hour's time. But that was niggling, mean, and petty of her, for she had her own faults. "Not by our kind."

"Blood relatives though we are, my sweet," Sybil replied with an amused arch of brow, "we are not *exactly* the same kind. You may feel the need to accede to all that rubbish over what's proper and what's not, but I . . . well, I am middle-class and determined not to be a martyr to propriety. I have no claim, as you do, to blue-blooded ancestry and no traditions to uphold. I'll not suffer misery simply because Great-great-grandpater Edmund Charles Douglas Somebody happened to be granted an earldom.'' Sybil leaned forward, raised her glass, and smiled. ''There are compensations to being a commoner.''

''You're being a snob, Sybil. I have never, ever said one word to you about my mother's family. Why must you make it seem I sit beneath the family tree and stare up in reverence? I don't care a whit about who preceded me.''

''Good for you, then, love. Not everyone in whose veins flows the royal red can be so blasé. I, for one, have always envied you 'the blood of kings.' ''

Elyn frowned. ''In view of the fact that we did not come by it legitimately, I should think it nothing to flaunt. There are, likely, hundreds of thousands of English with the same heritage but without the documentation. And I place little importance upon such distinctions myself.''

''Ah, how aristocratic to deny the importance of that certain quality for which we plebians long!''

''Stop! Please, Sybil—if you are teasing, it's gone far too long. If you continue to dwell upon it you'll make me think you care less for me than you claim. How ever did we become so enamoured of this subject?''

''You said our kind does not divorce, and I simply reminded you that I don't have to abide by your lofty standards, dear,'' Sybil answered. Then, realizing perhaps that envy had made her tongue unkind, she reached out to pat her cousin's hand. ''If I've upset you, I beg your pardon, Elyn. We haven't seen each other since your wedding. I promise I shall behave myself. Did I ever tell you what Arthur said of you then, as we watched you come back down the aisle on Alec's arm?''

''You did not, but if it was derogatory, I'd rather not hear.''

7

"Why should you suppose it to be? Arthur holds you in the highest regard. In fact, as a matter of a confession, I think he has put you on a pedestal. Don't worry, I shan't envy you that. I would rather be a woman than some form of virgin goddess. That's how he thinks of you, chaste and pure despite your wedded state." Sybil swallowed the last of her wine, staring off into the darkness around the heavily draped canopy bed, musing to herself for a second. "I've a habit of digressing. You'll forgive me, I hope. It grows worse when I have indulged a bit too freely."

"You were about to tell me what Arthur said on my wedding day," Elyn offered. "I've a feeling I shall blush."

"Yes, you likely shall. Don't ever lose that easy blush. Keep it and it'll no doubt wear well on you into middle age. He said, in a voice hushed with respect or reverence, possibly awe, that you looked so sweet, a lamb off to be sacrificed, how ever could you and I be cousins in the first degree?"

Elyn blinked in surprise, then frowned slightly. "That was unkind! It made you appear . . . less than sweet," she said defensively.

Sybil threw back her head and began to laugh. As a fit of giggling consumed her, she leaned back against the heavily carved headboard and wiped at her eyes with the back of one hand. "Oh, oh . . . I am sorry, but you see, my love, I quite agree with him. If I am anything, I am honest, and I have never, since my day of birth, been sweet."

"But I disagree. You've always been sweet to me, Syb. In fact, I've always thought of you as an older sister, since God chose not to grant me one."

"Good. Then I feel free to give you some sisterly advice. If ever, and I know your protests before you speak them, you should find that life with Alec has become unbearable, leave him. God will not strike you with a bolt of lightning; the

8

earth will not shudder in reproach.'' Sybil stared into Elynora's troubled eyes and took her hand. ''No, darling, I'm not encouraging you to break your vows; I'm only saying that the world will not end if you cannot stay the course. And, love, I shall always be here if you should need . . . anything.''

Moved to tears by the obvious affection in Sybil's offer, Elyn found it difficult to answer. She could not foresee any cause that would bring her to take advantage of Syb's help, but then, she had not the ability to see into the future. ''I'll remember that, should the need arise, Sybil. For now, you must accept my word that all is well.'' *Liar, can you not admit that something is wrong?* Elyn reproached herself silently. *A man wed just over a year doesn't keep his young wife awake at night, listening through the darkest hours for his footstep upon the stair. Nor does he finally slumber, fully clothed and sodden, in their marriage bed with the cheap scent of a tavern whore stinking his lapels.* Yet, she couldn't admit aloud that he made her unhappy. To voice her just complaints would only make her miserable; it would not rectify what Alec had done. Perhaps by her tolerance of his misdeeds, he might see that she meant to, as Sybil had put it, ''stay the course.''

Sybil studied the play of emotion on Elyn's delicate oval face and wondered if she had not guessed the truth. At her request, Arthur had taken Alec to his club. The two would be out quite late, affording their wives a chance to catch up on the latest family gossip. Arthur had been secretary to the British consul in Veracruz for the past ten months; it was his first chance to entertain someone from home.

Perhaps more sherry would lessen her cousin's inhibitions and allow her to share her confidences. Sybil reached for the decanter once more, surprised that the level had dropped so over the past hour and a half. Had she had so much to drink?

9

Elyn hadn't. Elynora had no vices, small or large. That's what she needed to make her a bit more human—a tiny vice to make her a little less the angel.

Sybil poured a bit more into her glass, then gestured to Elyn for hers, filling it to the brim when she held it forward. "Come now," she said, patting the spot beside her on the bed. "There *are* things we can discuss that are less...intimate. Your parents, for example. Do you intend to see them while you're in this area? They are somewhere in Central America, Nicaragua, are they not?"

The inquiry had been made out of courtesy. Elyn's parents were a continuing source of amusement to both sides of her family. It was odd enough that Michael Winters made a living from his interest in archaeology. His relatives were fairly tolerant of his penchant for tramping off through an unexplored jungle at a moment's notice. It was Elynora's mother, Alice, who was considered the eccentric. Daughter of an earl, heiress to a great fortune, a socialite who had lost none of the beauty revealed at her debut, Alice Winters had for the last fifteen years followed her husband's lead. They were not, however, in Nicaragua. "Father and Mother are in British Honduras, Syb, and I should love to see them; but Alec won't hear of it. He said I may see them when they choose to meet me in some civilized place."

"Ah, well, he's right about that, love." Sybil felt a giggle bubble up from deep within. "It's bound to happen once in a while, his being right, I mean."

Somehow that seemed amusing to Syb; but since she could not appreciate the joke, Elyn changed the subject, recalling the Russian foretuneteller they had both seen that afternoon. They had ended a day's shopping with tea at the fashionable luncheon room near the docks. "If you'd care to hear

10

something really amusing, I'll tell you what the gypsy predicted for me."

Syb raised a brow. "I know—you're going on a long ocean voyage!"

"No. Though she'd have been more accurate to say that. Can't you guess? What else do gypsies always say?" The sherry seemed to have dulled Sybil's reactions a touch. She stared at Elyn with a blank look and shrugged. "A tall, dark stranger is about to enter my life and change it forever."

"For the bloody better, I hope! Did she say how soon?"

"Very, but I shouldn't credit her with too much accuracy. After all, how much can he change my life? I *am* a married woman."

Sybil's smile seemed mysteriously pleased as she shrugged once again. "My darling, that has never stopped *me* from enjoying myself."

Elyn had made every attempt to appear interested in the one-sided conversation with the gentleman seated to her left, but her patience was wearing thin. Still, his company was preferable to that of the Spaniard to her right, a man who was as slick as his floral-scented pomade.

She couldn't count on Alec coming to her rescue. Her husband had spent the entire evening raptly gazing into the china-blue eyes of a blond socialite from California. Neither of them seemed to care that he was married or notice that his wife was seated directly across from them.

The silver-haired Austrian continued to drone, modestly describing his estates in Mexico and Bavaria. He missed his native land, but then, one must expand life's horizons, didn't she think so? But she must, for here she was, a foreigner in a strange land herself. He liked people, men *and* women, who were bold enough to seek life's adventures, and didn't she

11

know that was why he had retired so young, so he might enjoy the fruits of his labor?

The buzz of his voice was lulling her into a state somewhere near sleep. He never seemed to pause for a breath before rushing on to confide something else. Even the compliments he paid her were dealt out in a nonstop manner. He liked her gown; surely she had purchased it in Europe, for so fine a dress could not be found in Mexico.

Actually, Elyn didn't like the dress, or, more correctly, she didn't care for it on herself. The bright, sequined and beaded crepe fit rather daringly, revealing a bit too much décolletage. Further, the colors were suited to Sybil's brunette coloring and complexion. Syb had insisted she wear the gown; now Elyn regretted the fact that she hadn't been more firm about wearing something of her own.

Did she know anything about metal fastenings? The question startled Elyn out of her musings. She could only stare and shake her head. All she knew, all she *wanted* to know, of bolts and screws could be inscribed on the head of a pin. If it was true that everything happened for a reason, then the last hour must have been a punishment for some long-forgotten sin. No matter, though; if she could just make it through dessert, the guests would gather in the ballroom for dancing. That activity would bring her back to life.

Elyn glanced down the table at Sybil. For someone who had tried her best to wriggle out of this long-standing invitation, she was enjoying herself immensely. Sybil looked lovely, regally understated in black silk. Why had she insisted that Elyn dress like a peacock when she herself had decided to underplay? *God, I sound like a fishwife!* Elyn suddenly thought. The room was hot, despite the open doors leading to a veranda and the overhead fans that circulated the air. She was tired and bored and . . . yes, angry over the callous way Alec had treated her.

Sybil seemed to sense Elyn's eyes on her and looked up to flash a dazzling smile. Despite the fact that she was paying no attention whatsoever to him, Herr Froenich was still rattling on. Elyn raised a brow in his direction and mouthed silently, *So much for Madame Vera's predictions!* Sybil winked and shook her head, indicating the suave young gentleman to her left. Her own fortune seemed on the verge of coming true. If she so desired, and Elyn knew enough of Syb's love life now not to be totally shocked, Sybil had ample time and opportunity to arrange a tryst with her admirer. Arthur had begged off coming, still suffering as he was with a rotten hangover from the previous night's carousing.

Certainly Alec wouldn't notice. Elyn seriously doubted he would notice should she herself wander off to a lovers' rendezvous. She *should* leave. She would never last out the short time between the last course and the dance without coming to some mad, bubbling boil. There were just too many things to set her off. Miserably alone in a room full of strangers, Elyn was not quite sure why she didn't have her husband's attention, or what she'd done to make him lose interest.

Some of the guests were already leaving, drifting away from the dining tables and heading to the ballroom. The dancing would not begin until the host, Don Alejandro Salazar, and his guest of honor, General Miguel Cardenes, had made their appearances. She would take advantage of the milling guests to escape Herr Froenich.

"Alec?" He seemed not to hear her, so Elyn tried to catch her husband's attention once more. "Alec, darling—I've developed a frightful headache. I wonder, might we not . . ." He still hadn't heard her, though everyone else, including the

13

blonde, had. The girl was lovely, really, one of those fresh-faced healthy types who'd never known the torment of even one blemish. Her eyes were a startling blue, her teeth even and white. The silver-blond shade of her hair might have come from a bottle, but otherwise Elyn could find no apparent faults in her rival. She smiled at the girl, trying to appear composed and in control of her emotions.

"Yes, love?" Alec drawled finally in an acknowledgment that stung Elyn by its all-too-apparent lack of concern. "What's the trouble?"

Elyn inhaled deeply. "The trouble is, as I said, that my temples are pounding. I should like very much to leave early—*if* you don't mind."

"Ah, but I do, Lyn. The fun's just about to start." Alec Barford stared at his wife with a vaguely disgruntled look. She seemed out to spoil his evening. He was on holiday; he had a right to enjoy himself. Why ever was she being such a stick? Suddenly it came to him—Elyn was jealous. That was it, of course. Wasn't so much a headache as her not wanting him to enjoy a pretty girl's company.

Well, he wouldn't be rude to the American girl just because Elyn took exception to her looks. Neither would he allow himself to be nagged and browbeaten in public. "Have another glass of wine, darling," he suggested. "The dancing is about to start. A circuit or two of the ballroom and you'll have forgotten all—"

Elynora paled and after a moment's pause rose to her feet, carefully placing her linen napkin by her plate. She wanted very much to toss it at Alec, to cover the silly, insipid expression on his face. "Do as you please, Alec. I shall find my own way home. I should not care to spoil your . . . fun." Other guests nearby had witnessed the exchange and Elyn wanted to sink through the floor with embarrassment. She

14

turned away, eyes stinging with angry tears, ignoring Alec's voice calling after her. At that moment she was close to hating him. It was too late for him to make amends. For once let *him* wonder where *she* was, she thought as she joined the flow of guests passing her chair.

Suddenly a loud explosion of sound disrupted the soft blend of music and conversation. For a few seconds the room was hushed. The string quartet whined to a halt. Another explosion, a bark of gunfire, reverberated through the silence, followed by a woman's scream. The roar of confusion that rose was deafening, almost worse than the sound of the shots. Several more ladies screamed, and there were loud curses from the men. Those who were still seated at the tables came to their feet to stare at the dais and head table.

Those around her seemed to move as one, pressing Elyn against the high-backed dining chairs as they craned to see what had happened. Her own curiosity was second to a panicked feeling that she had to escape the crush of bodies. She asked if she might pass, then pushed her way free of those who hemmed her in. Only when she was away from the crowd could Elynora breathe again. Several deep breaths helped to ease the stifling panic she'd felt. Behind her, a man called out for a doctor; another replied that it was not necessary. General Cardenes and his aide, Colonel von Tobrisch, were dead.

Now, because she could not believe that such a thing had happened, Elyn moved down the length of her table toward the dais, skirting the crowd, rising on tiptoe to peer over their heads. She was sorry, when finally she glimpsed the bodies, that she had been curious. The general's body lay sprawled backward, a surprised expression frozen on his face. The top of his head had been shot away. His aide lay slumped across the table, looking as if he'd gone to sleep. Only the bright scarlet oozing from his back showed any sign of the violence that had struck so swiftly.

Elyn covered her mouth with her fingers as she turned away. She swallowed hard, fighting the nausea that churned in her stomach. All she could see against the backdrop of her shuttered eyes was the floral centerpiece of white camelias next to the colonel's head. Bright drops of blood splattered the smooth creamy petals of the flowers.

If she hadn't had a headache before, Elyn had one now. She backed away, then turned and rushed against the wave of guests still trying to see the victims. Bumped from behind, she nearly fell. Elyn turned to protest, only to find herself caught by the wrist and jerked toward a man who held a pistol outstretched in his other hand.

Briefly, she had an impression of strong, chiseled features in a darkly tanned face, a sense of height and the muscular physique to match it. Her back was against his chest, and his arm was suddenly banding her waist, holding her so tightly that she could scarcely draw a breath.

Two guards had entered the room from the terrace doors behind the main table. They took in the sight of the dead army officers, wheeled to survey the scene, and raised their rifles in the direction of Elyn's captor. Only vaguely, as if it were someone else in danger and not she, did Elynora realize that she was in the arms of the assassin. But for the two glasses of wine she had had at dinner, she would have fainted. Instead, she pried at the man's arm, struggling to free herself before he and the guards exchanged fire.

He backed away toward the terrace doors to his left, dragging Elyn after him. She thought of going limp, but if she did and he panicked, she might be shot in the crossfire that would surely follow. Now a new drama was unfolding for the guests of Don Salazar. All eyes were on the tall man who held her. There were more strangled screams as he inched toward the open doors. Elyn thought she heard Sybil call her name.

One of the guards aimed his rifle, and Elyn closed her eyes. *This is not happening, not to me.* Suddenly, close to the doors, her captor crouched, jerked her to the side, and fired. Elyn flinched as the weapon's recoil shuddered down his arm, causing her own flesh to vibrate. She opened her eyes to bare slits, almost afraid to look. One guard lay on the floor, clutching his right arm; the other had taken refuge behind a potted palm.

That was her last sight of the dining salon at Casa Salazar. Elynora was dragged backward onto a bricked patio that preceded the formal, terraced gardens. There were more guards at the far end of the patio. They fired as the assassin came into a pool of light beneath a lamppost.

The man ducked into the shadows, returning fire to keep the guards busy. The fact that he held one of the female guests hostage hadn't deterred them. A stray bullet struck the lamp above him, sending a spray of glass shards crackling against the brick. Another bullet severed the ropes of a hanging plant; the clay pot crashed to the patio. *Thank God the guards were as good as their* federale *counterparts. None of them could hit the side of a barn at twenty feet.*

It was dark around him now. The flight of steps to his right led down into the gardens, the last well-lighted section of the terrace. He wished again that he hadn't grabbed the girl. The way the bullets were flying, she was a liability. Just protecting her, he would get himself killed. Still, he couldn't free her; she would be safer with him.

"Let go! Let go, I say . . . you're hurting me!" Elynora continued to struggle though it was useless. She couldn't break the man's hold about her waist. His deep, husky voice

17

whispered against her ear, warning her to keep her mouth shut or she'd get them both killed. He was an American, yet his accent was crisp, his speech free of the relaxed drawl of the colonials. Elyn kicked backward and felt a brief triumph as her wedge heel connected with his shin. He loosened his grip on her just long enough for Elyn to try a break across the terrace.

He caught her wrist, jerking her back as bullets whizzed past them. As she tumbled back toward him, he raised his gun and lightly rapped the butt against her temple. He caught her as she fell, easily hefted her limp body across his left shoulder, and raced down the steps, pausing for a second to draw his other gun and fire back at the guards.

When his deep warbling whistle alerted his companion, the wrought-iron gate leading to the street opened. Despite the streetlamps, there wasn't much light, just enough to see the surprise register on Paco's face as he caught sight of the captive.

"Man, I thin' *this* time you have gone loco. You don' got trouble enough already?" Paco, holding the reins to a gray sorrel, shuffled his feet nervously as he gazed past his *compadre* into the gardens. "Leave her, amigo!" he pleaded, then dropped the reins as the American momentarily propped the unconscious girl against him.

A minute later the American reached for the girl and pulled her up into his arms. They were safely off the grounds of Casa Salazar but a long way from the safety of the Sierra Madres and the cabin on the slopes of Mount Orizaba. Paco cursed under his breath as he mounted and followed the westward lead set by his "crazy" friend.

"I know what I'm doing, Paco," he called back, wishing he was as sure of himself as he sounded. "Now let's get the hell out of here!"

*   *   *

Elynora lay on the only bed in the cabin and stared at the rafters. She'd counted them innumerable times in the long hours since her captor had brought her here the night before. There were eight; any way she counted, backward, forward, by two or singly, there were eight boring rafters supporting the roof.

He was outside, splitting kindling for the fire. Each time the ax struck wood, the thin, rough-hewn walls to the left of the bed vibrated. Elyn jerked again at the ropes that secured her wrists to the iron bed frame. Useless. She would lie here, bound and defenseless, until her abductor decided to free her. After twenty-four hours, she still knew precious little about him. His Mexican companion had called him something that sounded like "Neek." Whoever he was, she had no illusions about his character. He was ruthless and dangerous, a coward who had used her to shield his escape, a murderer who had left two victims behind.

She couldn't expect courteous treatment from such a man; yet, other than knocking her unconscious, he hadn't harmed her. Humiliated, yes, but not harmed. They'd arrived at the one-room cabin after a long, exhausting ride through the night. They were somewhere in the mountains, far from civilization and at an altitude that could easily produce heavy snows. Though she was not anxious for his return, it was growing colder in the cabin and the fire had died down.

The thin cotton shirt that had seemed warm enough during the day was not enough to keep her from shivering now, and Elyn wished she hadn't been so careless in wriggling free of the woolen blanket. Last night, soon after their arrival, the American had tossed a shirt and men's pants at her, brusquely ordering her to change into them. Her obstinate refusal to do so had been rewarded with a forced strip. To his credit, the outlaw had not seemed interested in ogling her. The gown,

Sybil's brilliant peacock-shaded evening gown, had been relegated to the fire.

He'd left her alone after that, quietly and efficiently preparing a supper she had refused to touch. The memory of the deaths at Casa Salazar was still too fresh in her mind to allow her much interest in the meal of roast pork and cassava. Nick, if that was his name, had shown no similar loss of appetite; certainly he showed no remorse for the deaths of General Cardenes and his aide.

After supper he had changed from the tailored evening suit that had gained him entrance to the reception and put on a pair of skin-tight pants, knee boots, and a faded red-plaid shirt. Elyn had tried her very best to ignore his presence, and he had made no effort to explain the reasoning behind the brutal assassinations. The only thing he'd volunteered was an assurance that she would be released as soon as he could manage it. His friend, Paco, who seemed disgruntled by her presence, had eaten and then remounted to ride down to the lower elevations and see if the authorities had taken any retaliatory measures against the people.

Elyn tugged once more at the ropes and sighed. Were the federal troops searching for her? Of course they were . . . one couldn't simply kidnap a British national and get away scot-free. But Mexico was a large country with vast stretches of desolate land, and, as Arthur had complained only last week, its government was less organized than a Hampshire fox hunt. They might *never* find her. Her captor had killed twice, with consummate ease, and escaped with barely a hair out of place. Certainly, if she seemed a bother to him, he would think nothing of doing away with her, burying her in some isolated . . . *Oh, God, she should* not *be thinking this way!*

How was Alec handling himself? He would be worried, naturally, but less about her safety than the state of his property. That's all she'd become to him. Once an object of desire, now she was merely an object. Elyn frowned. She hoped he was suffering, imagining the worst, picturing her a helpless captive in the arms of a tall, dark stranger. *A tall, dark stranger*—why did that phrase seem so hauntingly familiar?

Of course, the fortuneteller, Madame Vera. What was it she had predicted? Ah, yes . . . that he would change her life forever. The gypsy had not foreseen death for her; what else, then, could she have meant?

Boot heels clicked against the wooden porch of the cabin and Elynora tensed. As the door opened, creaking on its hinges, she turned her face to the wall, closed her eyes, and pretended to be asleep.

Nick crossed the room and bent on one knee to drop the load of firewood. He glanced briefly at his young hostage, to assure himself she was still bound, before tossing a few pieces of kindling onto the fire. She was too still and stiff to be sleeping, he realized. Playing possum, that's what she was doing, perhaps with the thought that he'd let her be. She needn't have worried. Her presence was a fluke; he hadn't meant to harm her. He'd struck her only to get them both out of harm's way before her struggles got them killed.

He was sorry, but an apology was out of the question. Coming to his feet now with an irritated sigh, he found himself wishing that Paco had returned. Then at least he would know when and where it would be safe to release the English girl. Until then, he hoped she wasn't dumb enough to try an escape. The cabin was six thousand feet below the snow-capped peak of Mount Orizaba but still a good twelve thousand feet above sea level. Used by the shepherds who brought their flocks up the mountainside to graze each spring, it was little more than a bare shelter to keep out the wind and rain. There weren't any villages nearby. The closest one lay in the foothills three miles to the southeast. For miles in every direction, the land was thickly forested with pine and fir, impossible to cross unless one was familiar with the rough-cut paths used by the *pastorados*.

Now Nick carried several buckets of rainwater from the outside catch barrel and filled the kettle. There wasn't much room for privacy in the cabin, but a sawed-off barrel in the corner looked like it would make an adequate bathtub. Maybe the lady would find a little less reason to be afraid of him if she had a chance to relax and clean up.

He walked over to the bed and smiled. Her eyes were still tightly shut, affording him the chance for a leisurely survey. Tall and slender, she was one of those women who would never grow fat. Her complexion, fine and clear, would still look lovely when she was old enough to be playing with her grandchildren. She had even features, and her light brown brows arched above wide-set eyes and thick, tawny lashes. Prominent cheekbones above slight hollows curved softly toward a full, almost passionate mouth. Her chin was stubborn, with nothing weak about it. "You can stop pretending," he said finally. "You're not asleep."

Elynora ignored him but after a few moments her curiosity got the better of her. She opened her eyes just a little and risked a glance up at him. The man's expression was infuriatingly cool and self-possessed. She trembled, and her voice shook with anger. "Go away. Haven't you done enough already?"

The only change in his expression was a slight narrowing of his eyes. They were a clear, deep green, a startling color in a darkly tanned face. The smile stayed and Elyn couldn't help but notice the deep clefts of dimples on either side of his dark, full mustache. They gave him a disarmingly gentle look that made Elyn wonder how he could have killed the two men at the reception.

22

Nick sat on the edge of the bed and Elyn instinctively moved away, as close to the wall as she could manage. He tried to reassure her, telling her he had no reason to harm her, but clearly she doubted him. That skepticism suddenly made him angry. "Look, I don't like your being here any more than you do. For the moment you'll just have to bear with it." Inclining his head toward the kettle of water heating over the fire, he said, "You'll feel better once you've had a—"

Indignation replaced the apprehension in Elyn's eyes. "I'll *not* feel better!" she insisted. "And you can't possibly know what I should like."

"I can venture a guess. How about seeing the *federales* surrounding the cabin?" Nick tossed off the idea without thinking, but it was evident that it had appealed to her, although she shook her head. Her hair, a thick mass of pale brown waves, had tumbled free of the chignon at her nape. A silken coil of it lay across her breast, partially shadowing her expression. She looked very young.

"Why should I wish for that?" Elyn asked, and added resentfully, "You'd only use me to hide behind again. I've no desire to die while you try to escape justice." Her chin tilted up, stubbornly set. "And I shan't bathe while you're about. I'd rather go unwashed."

"Afraid you'll prove too tempting a sight? No need to worry—I'm not interested," he replied; and when Elyn raised a brow, looking surprised, then, almost offended, he added, "I've never found *any* woman worth a fight."

Elynora relaxed her guard somewhat. She should have felt relieved. Why did she feel . . . rejected? "I suppose most of them simply fall at your feet, begging your attentions?"

"I wouldn't say they'd begged. . . ." Nick smiled again and shrugged. "If you've changed your mind, I'll untie you. If

23

not . . . there's no use letting the water go to waste. I could use a good soak myself.''

''In front of me?''

''Why not? You're not exactly a vestal, even if you have the looks of a schoolgirl.'' Nick pointed at her wedding band, and the dimple to the left of his mouth deepened with a quirk. ''Now, Mrs. Whoever-you-are, I am tired and dirty and I am going to avail myself of a little hot water and soap. Watch if you want. . . .'' Elynora's blush started at her temples and pinkened her cheeks. ''No, that wouldn't be 'proper,' would it? Well, face the wall, then.''

He stood and unbuttoned his shirt as he crossed to the fireplace. ''Wait!'' Nick turned and saw Elyn sitting up. ''Have you anything to . . . to drink?'' she asked.

''Water.'' He turned to look over the supplies arranged on a wall shelf near the fireplace. ''I could make coffee, but there's no milk or sugar.'' Elyn wrinkled her nose in rejection. ''I've got *aguardiente*.'' At her puzzled look, Nick explained, ''Brandy.''

''That will do. . . .'' She'd almost said thank you, then had bitten back the courtesy in anger at herself. Why should she thank him for anything? He was *not* her host, he was her . . . kidnapper. One did not have to be civil to a criminal.

He didn't miss the hesitation and what it implied. She *was* a very proper young lady. And he wasn't sure he should have offered her liquor, especially the potent native *aguardiente*. *Hell*, he thought, *if she's old enough to be married, she's old enough to pick her poison*. He poured a small amount into a tin cup and carried it over to her. At the sight of her awkwardly juggling the cup because of her bound wrists, Nick almost untied her. No, that would be all he needed—to let down his guard and find himself naked and wet, staring down the barrel of his own Colt revolver.

24

Elyn took a tentative sip and wrinkled her nose. The brandy was much stronger than she'd expected; it burned her mouth, nearly choking her with the first swallow. When she looked up and found her captor gazing down at her with a bemused expression, she defiantly gulped the rest of the liquor.

"Trying to get drunk?" Nick asked, then shrugged off his concern. He wasn't her guardian. Still, when she held the cup out for more, he warned, "You won't like the way you feel later."

What did it matter to him . . . had he worried when he'd abducted her, when he'd struck her with his gun? "I *can't* feel worse."

Returning to the table where he'd placed the bottle, Nick poured a refill for her and filled a cup half-full for himself. Back at the bedside, he handed her the cup and saluted with his own. "To you, Mrs. . . . I wish I had a name for you."

"I've *several* for you, none of them pleasant. If you must, you may address me as Mrs. Barford." Elyn took another sip of her drink, irritated further that he wasn't decent enough to untie her hands. "I cannot deal with an . . . an outlaw on a first-name basis."

"Quite. I understand perfectly, madam. There *is* a certain protocol to follow, rules that can't be breached." She was every inch a well-bred lady, a model of decorum even under stress. Except for the fact that Queen Victoria had been dead for quite some time, he might have been fooled into thinking he'd snatched the old girl herself. Certainly this lady didn't need his sarcasm—that was insult added to injury. The brandy *was* strong, helping to wash away a slightly sour taste, a taste his conscience had sent to plague him. But he'd done worse in his time with Zapata's ragtag army. No doubt there were darker sins yet to be committed.

25

When the water was steaming, Nick carried the kettle to the makeshift tub and dumped it in, adding a bucketful of cool water before he tested the temperature. Still too hot. He carried the bucket back to fetch more cool water from the outside barrel.

Five minutes later he had stripped and climbed into the tub. There wasn't much room. His knees jutted above the water, but at least it was warm and relaxing. He reached for the soap he'd brought in from his saddlebag. It was little more than a sliver now, worn down from the fat, musk-scented bar he'd found in the stores of a hacienda raided months ago. His one luxury, and soon it would be gone. *Son of a bitch, but he was tired of it all, the hiding and raiding, the deaths and the torture.*

Elyn heard the water splash and gritted her teeth. She had listened to the rustle of his clothing as he undressed, had heard him whistle a cheerful tune, and had clenched her fists in impotent fury. Why was she so angry? The man had left her alone. It wasn't as if he'd ripped the clothes from her back and tossed her into the tub. Maybe that was why she was angry. No, that was ridiculous. She had a strong desire to turn and steal a glance. His shoulders were broad and solid, he . . . *She should never have asked for the brandy.* It had affected her judgment, altered her perceptions. Her head seemed to buzz, and she felt languid, careless. The water splashed again. Elynora sighed and turned her head.

Nick had washed away most of the grime and dust. Now he lay back, arms stretched along the perimeter of the barrel, relaxing his six-foot-four-inch frame as much as possible within the squat tub. His arms were as muscular as she had imagined, covered by a thin mat of dark hair. Though it was an unfair comparison, Elyn couldn't help measuring him against her husband. The outlaw was taller, and his chest—as

26

much as she could see—was well muscled and seemed to taper to a narrow waist. Alec was slight, far more slender and fair, with the light hair and coloring of his Scots mother.

As if he'd sensed her observation, Nick opened his eyes and turned his head toward her. For the briefest moment, before she could cover her interest, their eyes met. He didn't smile but the corners of his mouth curled up in amusement. Elyn's face flamed with embarrassment. She could think of no logical explanation for her boldness. It must be the strain of being held captive. And hunger. Did starvation not affect the mind's workings? She *was* awfully hungry.

Nick was surprised to find that the young Mrs. Barford's curiosity had overcome her modesty. That didn't necessarily make her an unhappily married woman, but he wondered now whether she had ever seen her husband naked. Probably not, he decided. "If you've changed your mind," he said, "I'll draw another bath."

Predictably, in answer.Elyn turned her back to him and faced the wall. A few minutes later the water sloshed as he rose. She tried to think of something else, anything to keep her from picturing him standing there, naked and . . . Elyn shifted restlessly, wishing she hadn't been so stubborn in refusing to bathe. He was warm and clean, while she still felt the dust of the road like a film upon her skin. And, as an icy wind howled beyond the cabin walls, she was beginning to feel a chill that would have been assuaged in the luxury of a warm bath. Somehow modesty no longer seemed important.

Later, after Nick had prepared a meal of bacon, biscuits, and coffee, Elynora put away her pride and joined him. She consumed the food with a ravenous appetite that at another place and time would have been embarrassing. Still, she had adapted, and she had learned two valuable lessons: modesty belonged in drawing rooms and places frequented by polite society; and pride . . . well, one could not *eat* pride, nor was it nearly as comforting to wrap about oneself on a cold night as a woolen blanket. When she had finished the simple fare and not a crumb was left upon her tin plate, Elynora felt quite satisfied with herself and much stronger for having relinquished those two emotions. The coffee, laced with more of the strong, pungent *aguardiente,* had both warmed and relaxed her.

Nick had freed her hands for the meal. After exacting a promise that she wouldn't try to escape, he allowed her to remain free of the bonds that had restrained her movements for so long. As on the first night, they shared the bed. The thin, worn blanket covering her was Elyn's only protection, but thus far it was a barrier the outlaw had respected.

About midnight, when his breathing had been regular and even for some time, Elyn made her escape attempt. Though her word had been given, she rationalized that she need not honor an oath sworn to a man who lived his life outside the law that made civilized beings out of people.

The only problem she faced was the difficulty of crawling over him without disturbing his sleep. She tried scooting down but the end of the bed was blocked by a trunk turned on end. Elyn waited awhile longer, to make sure he was soundly asleep. If she failed this time, she wouldn't have another chance; he would tie her again. Finally, she dared to make her move. She inched toward him and came up on an elbow. There was just enough of a glow from the fireplace to outline the shape of his body. He was on his side, facing her.

Elynora studied her captor for a moment. His face looked very young in the soft, reflected light. Very young and extremely handsome. His dark hair was parted in the center and waved away from a face that had clean, aristocratic lines. He might have been a lord in Parliament rather than a rogue who had murdered, kidnapped, and likely stolen as well. There was a virile scent emanating from him, something rich and quite attractive, which reminded her again that he had bathed while she had not.

But that would be remedied as soon as she reached civilization. In minutes she would be out the door and away on his horse. She wasn't sure where to go, but there must be a path down the mountainside, a town somewhere below in the foothills. She sat up, arching her left ankle over his legs just below his knees. It seemed the easiest spot to cross. Elynora held her breath the entire time, afraid that at any moment she might wake him. Long, agonizing seconds passed and he remained still.

Her foot had just touched the earthen floor when Nick moved. One moment she was almost free; the next she was flat on her back, pinned by his body. To further her humiliation, his knee rested between her legs, effectively stilling any attempt she might make to struggle free. His face was only inches above hers.

"Going somewhere?"

Elyn was furious. He'd been awake the entire time. "I . . . I was . . ." She found it impossible to think of an excuse with his body pressed against hers. "Move your knee," she said. "*Please?* I was . . . I needed to use the . . . facilities." A pleasant word to describe something nonexistent. Apparently shepherds cared little for the amenities.

"And you didn't want to disturb my sleep. How thoughtful."

"You weren't sleeping. You knew—"

"Knew what? That you had to answer a call to nature?"

"No!"

"That I couldn't trust you to keep your given word?" Nick clicked his tongue in mock dismay. "Mrs. Barford, I should have made you swear on something sacred, like your marriage vows.''

"That wouldn't have made a difference." For a moment Elyn was shocked by the admission, but it was true. An oath taken on the sanctity of her relationship with Alec would not have made the slightest difference. She wanted to be free. Tears had suddenly sprung to her eyes. She was too angry to be frightened.

He had ignored her request for him to move. The pressure of his body against her hers was light. She wasn't so much physically stressed as emotionally distraught. "What's wrong with your marriage?"

"Nothing. And it's none of your business!" The tears were beginning to slip down her cheeks. She couldn't have stopped them if she'd wanted to; they felt right, somehow. "You've only aggravated the situation by stealing me away," she insisted. "I shan't be able to face Alec. He'll never believe you haven't—"

She had stopped in mid-sentence, as he had reached out and gently brushed away the fall of tears. "Haven't what— made love to you? Does he have any reason not to trust you?"

"Me? How dare you imply . . . It's *you* he wouldn't trust. I am the innocent in this af . . . in this ordeal."

"I wasn't implying anything," he answered calmly, in so reasonable a tone that Elyn would have liked to scratch at his eyes. "Only, if *I* were your husband—"

"Well, sir, you are not!"

"Amen to that, but if I were, I'd believe you. Now why wouldn't he?"

"Should you, in his place? I think not. If your wife were carried off by a desperate—"

"Who was desperate? I was in control every minute."

30

Elyn ignored him as if he hadn't spoken. "By a desperate, ruthless killer, a man who had the gall to dine with his victims—"

"I didn't eat that much. Never do before a killing." Nick came up on an elbow and glared down at Elyn. "I think we have a few things to clear up, and since you're so damned restless, I can't think of a better time. Why do you think I shot those two?"

He was suddenly angry; Elyn could feel it in the tenseness of his muscles. "I don't know—and I don't *want* to know. There are no excuses for murder. A man who could cold-bloodedly execute two unarmed men—"

"Would think nothing of raping a defenseless hostage," Nick finished. "I've had nothing else on my mind."

The sarcastic denial was too much for an already-frustrated Elynora. Without considering the consequences, she raised her hand to strike him. They were both surprised when her palm connected with his right cheek. Elyn sucked in a deep breath, waiting for some form of retaliation.

Nick rolled onto his back and rubbed his cheek. He didn't like it, but for all he'd put her through, he'd deserved the slap. "Get some sleep, Mrs. Barford," he said quietly. "We could both use the rest." He shifted, slipped an arm beneath his head, and closed his eyes. "Here's a promise *I* won't break—I'll get you back to 'civilization' as soon as humanly possible."

His reaction deflated Elyn's anger, leaving her stripped of the justification she'd felt in striking out at him. He was infuriating, a man out of character with the vicious killer she'd thought him to be. "Why *did* you shoot them?"

Nick's first instinct was to answer sarcastically, but the girl seemed genuinely puzzled. "It isn't important. They weren't friends of yours. Go to sleep."

"No. I want to know. You owe me that much for—"

31

"Ma'am, I figure that slap made us even. I don't owe you a damned thing."

Elyn's mouth formed a thin, frustrated line. She'd tried to understand his reasoning. Her opinion of him didn't seem to matter. "I shan't sleep if you don't explain," she said. "And if *I* can't, neither shall you!"

Nick started to laugh. At the moment, he wasn't sure he hadn't done her husband a favor by taking her hostage. "Let's just say that Cardenes enjoyed his work too much. And von Tobrisch took the little strutting cock and turned him into one of the government's best strategists. Together, they killed a lot of people."

"Haven't *you?*" Elyn wasn't sure why she was so defensive. She hadn't known the general or his aide. "They weren't the first men you've killed—you did it too efficiently to be a novice. And you're not Mexican. Were you hired by the rebels?"

"Honey, when it comes to murder, I'm not in the same class as General Cardenes and his henchmen. And the rebels are too damned poor to hire anybody."

"Then why? Why you and not one of them? If it was done in vengeance, *they* had more reason—"

"I had my reasons. Who says you have to be Mexican to know the government's a cesspool of self-serving bastards? Pardon me, ma'am, but all it takes is the sight of a few *campesinos* strung up because a rebel troop came through their village to water the horses. Or one look at the eyes of a young girl who's had twenty or more *federales* take turns—"

"Stop! *Please,* that's enough," Elyn protested. Her stomach churned with nausea. "The rebels, Villa's soldiers, have been brutal as well." It was a weak justification for what he had just mentioned.

"Mostly in retaliation. And the ones they tortured or killed

32

weren't innocent women or children." Nick sighed. "Don't let it keep you awake. The *peones* aren't your class anyway."

"That wasn't necessary. I'm not insensitive. How could I know . . . I was only visiting Veracruz on holiday." Elyn thought of the horrors he had described and fell silent. Until she felt the dampness on her cheeks, she wasn't aware that she was crying again. "Killing the general won't bring those people back to life. Despite his death, nothing's changed."

"Uh-uh," Nick disagreed. "There'll be one less vulture preying on the people. For a while, at least. And maybe, just maybe, it'll make the others less secure. I'm satisfied. Now all I have to do is figure out how to get rid of you."

Elyn wiped away the tears with the back of her hand and rose to question his intent. "Get rid of? You . . . you wouldn't . . ."

"It's a temptation, but no, I didn't mean to kill you. For God's sake, quit crying! I can't just dump you anyplace." His tone of voice implied that that, too, was tempting. "Between the rebels and the government troops, you wouldn't stand a chance of getting back to your husband without losing that virtue you're so worried about."

"I don't recall asking to go with you!"

"No, you sure didn't, but I'm only human—I make mistakes, too. Now go to sleep. Christ, it must be past one A.M.!"

"I am not tired. *You* go to sleep."

Nick sighed again. "That means I won't get any sleep either. You'll just try to get away again. I've got an idea. Why don't you just climb on me now and get it over with?"

Elyn's tone was frosty with hauteur. "I didn't climb *on* you, but *over*. There is a vast world of difference between the two."

"Care to try it my way?"

"I beg your pardon?"

"Well, since we're both staying up . . ." Nick was smiling. "If you're going to be accused of a sin, you might as well get some pleasure out of it." He rolled toward her and reached out to brush a strand of hair out of her eyes.

Elynora found his reasoning somewhat convoluted and quickly set him to rights. "The difference is that I could scarce hold my head high with a guilty conscience. Whatever Alec may think, *I* should know the truth. You seem to have forgotten I'm here against my will."

"That can change."

When she opened her mouth to protest the arrogance of that statement, Elyn found herself drawn against his chest. Trapped between the wall and his body, both unyielding, she struggled briefly, digging her nails deeply into his skin, before his lips gently came down on hers. She wriggled, trying to free herself, but as Nick continued to press light, teasing kisses against her mouth, a subtle languor seized her limbs. She didn't want him to stop. In fact, she had ached to know the feel of his body against hers for some time.

He pulled her even closer and cradled her head against the hard, bunched muscles of his upper arm. One hand circled her neck while the other softly stroked her breasts through the thin material of her shirt. His fingertips brushed against a nipple and Elyn panicked. "I *can't*," she whispered. "He'll know it . . . *I'll* know!"

Nick tugged at her shirttail, then slipped his hand beneath it to caress the warm, plump curve of a breast. Despite her soft, whimpered protest, the tension flowed out of her. A shiver rippled across her skin as his mouth touched her throat just below an earlobe. Her nipples hardened and stabbed against his chest. "Tell him you had no choice." He nibbled at her ear. "I wouldn't let you alone." Nick drew back and smiled down into her eyes. "Wasn't your fault; you didn't encourage me; you were just another victim."

"Bastard." The word had more potency because it was so foreign to her vocabulary.

"Who? Your husband—or me?"

"Both." There was no use resisting. If she struggled, it would be denying what she wanted as much as he. Nick closed the distance between their lips, parting her mouth with his, stabbing his tongue within. Elyn's breath caught in her throat. A range of emotions troubled her . . . a blend of delight and wonder at the response his kisses had evoked, a sense of curiosity over what was to come, fear, and a desire to pull back before it was too late. "I don't even know who you are," she whispered, more to herself than to him.

"Nicholas Ro . . ." He had been about to say his full name, then had thought that the less she knew of him the better. "But everybody calls me Nick." He didn't give her a chance to ask any more. His lips found hers and stirred a whispered moan from her while his fingers deftly caught at the waist of her pants and tugged them down.

Only barely aware of what he was doing with her, Elyn lay back and forgot who he was, who she was, forgot that somewhere not a hundred miles away she had a husband waiting to hear some news of her. None of it seemed to matter.

The storm had begun innocently enough, a few snowflakes falling from an ashen-gray sky. Sometime during the night of their third day at the cabin, the snowfall had become an isolating blanket of white. By dawn, more than a foot of snow covered the landscape and frosted the boughs of the tallest pines.

When the snow continued to fall without any sign of

cessation, Nick carried in more firewood. He had several cords cut and stockpiled under a lean-to next to the cabin. It wasn't the supply of fuel that worried him but the danger of running out of food. Paco hadn't yet returned, and now with the snow continuing to drift and accumulate, he wouldn't be able to make it through the pass. After breakfast Nick decided to go hunting. With any luck he'd bring back a few rabbits or some game birds.

For a reason she couldn't fathom, Elyn was more afraid of being left behind than she had been of being kidnapped. She hadn't the clothing or footwear to venture out in the icy temperatures, though, and Nick ruled out any chance of her accompanying him. It was impossible for her to admit that she was loath to see him go, even for a short time, and so, before he left, her resentful petulance precipitated a full-fledged fight.

"Look, I don't have time to sort out why you're so foul-tempered—"

"Ah, well, being abducted always brings out the best in me!" Elyn snapped back. She crossed her arms and for the moment ceased her angry pacing to glare at him as he stood by the half-open door. "You're letting in a draft. . . ." She raised her brow and added, "Close the door, *if* you don't mind?"

Nick scowled and turned to leave, mumbling under his breath. What Elyn could catch of the statement sounded like, "Warmer out there, anyway." When the door slammed behind him she stared at it for a moment, and almost ran to fling it open again and call out a warning to be careful. Instead she whirled toward the fireplace, drawing her fingers through her tousled hair as her eyes clouded with tears.

She was mad—or soon would be. He knew perfectly well how to survive, most certainly better than she. And why, in

God's name, should she care if anything happened to him? He was, after all, the man who had stolen her away from family and friends. He was a coward and . . . and a seducer.

He was also charming and warm and none of the things he should have been. Perhaps it was the place to which he'd brought her, so isolated even before the blizzard. Or the fact that she had already been disillusioned with Alec and angry at him before the abduction. Or even . . . No, she was trying for excuses when all along she knew the underlying reason for her fitful temper.

Nick was incomparable—the single most attractive man she had ever met. Handsome . . . yes, he was handsome. She couldn't deny how very much the lean, hard lines of his body made her heart catch in her throat, made her shiver in the anticipation of his touch. And yet it wasn't so much the heavy-lidded looks that spoke of his desire or the knowing way his hands slid along her curves. She found him so complete a man . . . intelligent, educated, mannerly when he chose to be, and always, always in control.

Nick would admit to her nothing of his background—not where he was from, not how he'd been reared, no details with which she could round out what little she knew of him. She would have liked to share part of herself, incidents from her past; but those memories were better left to that other world, where she was a proper and well-bred upper-class matron. He had asked, after they had become intimate, if he could use her first name. Elynora, even Elyn, belonged with that other young woman, and so, to suit the new her, she had told him her name was Nora.

She didn't love him. Who could love a man, no matter how attractive, after five days—and after so violent an introduction? Now, though, as she puttered about the cabin, straightening what little mess there was, touching things he had touched, his shirts, his razor case, Elyn suddenly realized what made him so special to her.

Despite the silly, girlish flirtations of her youth, the minor infatuations, despite her fifteen months of marriage, Elynora had never *wanted* a man. Only now was she beginning to understand what Sybil had talked of, what other women had always sought within or without the bounds of matrimony. She felt like a child who had suddenly seen the world the way it was. The most amazing aspect of the discovery was that she was alone with it. There was no one in this place so far from civilization to criticize her newfound pleasures or to deny her the chance to explore them fully.

There was no way here, other than the rise and set of the sun or the shadows cast upon the snow, to tell the hour.

Nick would be gone for hours. Elyn sat on the bed. There was nothing to occupy her, nothing to do but wait.

She lay back and closed her eyes. At once she saw his face, firelight reflecting off its planes as he bent over her. The stiff wiry mat of hair covering his chest scratched at her breasts; his weight pressed lightly against her naked flesh. She . . . had better think of other things or know a frustration too great to contain.

Elyn rose and crossed to the kettle to fill it with water Nick had earlier brought in from the barrel. She would bathe in the hottest water she could stand and exorcise those feelings that could not be satisfied without him.

An hour later she emerged from the bath softer and cleaner but no more in control of her thoughts than before. She searched for and found a clean flannel shirt of Nick's, far too large but warm and somehow comforting, before she settled on the bed to wait.

The minutes dragged on into more than an hour. She rested, curled beneath the covers for warmth, trying to focus her thoughts on something other than her desire. She felt very alone and vulnerable, almost abandoned after what had seemed like an eon. To keep herself from dwelling on the possibility that something had happened to Nick, she rose and wandered about, looking for something to do.

She couldn't help herself when, in folding a blanket that lay on the floor near the table, she discovered his saddlebags. It was wrong to pry, she reasoned, but if he had anything to hide from her, he should have been more careful with the bags. And he shouldn't have left her so long with nothing to do.

She carried the bags to the bed and sat cross-legged to examine them. As he was wearing several layers of clothing and she had on one of his warmer shirts, there was little clothing within the saddlebags. Again she smelled that distinctive scent, and dug into the bag to find a thin wafer of soap. That he should value and keep close an item of personal hygiene revealed much about his upbringing. His friend Paco had not been so discriminating.

In an inside pocket sewn so close to the leather that she had nearly missed it, Elyn found two worn photographs. One was a family grouping, quite a large family with a very regal dowager type seated in the middle of nine children of various ages. This must be Nick's family, but she could not decide which of the boys was he. She envied him the brothers and sisters, for she'd had none of her own to share her lonely childhood.

The other picture seemed more recent. A dark-haired girl was seated beneath a rose arbor, and she couldn't have been more than seventeen. Elyn turned it over, wondering if she could be one of his sisters. On the back was an inscription, in a legible, very pretty handwriting. *"For Nick Douglas, with my love and devotion, Always, Cecelia."* This could have

39

been a sisterly inscription, but something about it . . . Elyn turned the picture over and frowned. The pose looked a trifle too flirtatious to be that of a sister. She turned the picture to face the other and returned them to the pocket where they belonged. Somehow, some way, she would find out the true nature of the relationship.

Other than the pictures and a few articles of clothing and personal items such as a toothbrush and shaving kit, there wasn't much to give Elyn a clue about Nick's character or background. He traveled light, he wasn't tied down to anything or anyone . . . or was he? Suddenly it struck Elyn that Cecelia could be his wife. He wore no wedding band, but that proved nothing. Some men didn't care to . . . especially those who pursued extramarital affairs.

Not only was *she* sinning, perhaps he was as well! Of course she didn't *know* that to be true. She'd ask him, as soon as he returned, whether he was married. For now, she must put away the evidence of her snooping, for if he should come in and find her going through his things, she had no doubt he would thrash her soundly—and enjoy it too!

When she had arranged the saddlebags back beneath the blanket and positioned it exactly as she'd found it, Elyn again found herself with nothing to do. Earlier she had poured out the water from her bath. Now she thought she might heat water and surprise him with a relaxing bath when he returned from the cold. She added more kindling to the fire and bent over to stir some life into the embers with the poker.

Nick had prepared himself for another bout with Nora Barford's temper, steeling himself, before he returned, to keep a rein on his temper. She had, after all, plenty of reason to be irritable. Outside the cabin he dropped his game bag, which contained two rabbits and a brace of doves; a greater prize in the form of a young wild pig was strapped to his saddle.

He wasn't prepared for the sight that greeted him on opening the door, or for the effect it had on his senses. Nora was wearing one of his shirts and little or nothing else. All he saw was an expanse of long, shapely legs and just the bare edge of her derriere as she bent near to the fire. He stood there in the doorway, a slow appreciative smile spreading over his face before the draft of chilly air alerted her to his presence.

Elyn tensed as the icy air frosted her skin with goose bumps. She was afraid to turn, afraid that despite the storm and the cabin's isolation, someone other than Nicholas had opened the cabin door. When she did glance over her shoulder, she breathed a sigh of relief and set the poker she had intended to use as a weapon to the side of the fireplace. "You startled me," she explained, then blushed as she glanced down at her bare legs.

Then she looked up and straight into his eyes, staring guilelessly with her velvet blue eyes, seemingly unaware of how desirable she appeared. Nick could only continue to stare. Even when he reached back and shut the door with one foot, his eyes never left her. Absently, he pulled off over his head the snow-covered blanket he'd used as a poncho and then stripped off his coat. "You're not angry anymore."

She shook her head. Her hair, clean and still damp, had been pinned loosely to the top of her head. With the motion, some of it came loose and tumbled down her back. Her skin was still glowing from the hot bath, and she gave the appearance of a flower that had suddenly blossomed. Even the fullness of her mouth seemed touched by a rosy blush. Her posture, the artless attitude of innocence awakening, and everything else about her spoke of a desire that modesty forbade her to voice.

She should have dropped her gaze, should have moved to cover herself with more than his shirt. She should have . . . But she was delighted with the look her appearance had brought to his eyes. And Elyn wanted nothing to interfere with what she wanted, with what she had made him want.

Nick smiled. "Sure you're not too hot, dressed like that? Not that I'm complaining, mind. In fact, I can think of only one thing that would improve your style of dressing."

Elyn arched a brow and half-smiled. "Such as . . . ?"

"We'll discuss that after I show you what a great hunter I am. Don't move—I'll be right back." Much as he would have liked to ignore his catch and accept the invitation in Nora's eyes, Nick couldn't chance leaving the game unattended. There were wolves in these mountains, and with the blizzard, hunting had been made extremely difficult.

Behind her the kettle was beginning to steam. It would soon be ready for his bath. She almost hated to allow him the leisure time to wash. Though she allowed herself some vivid fantasies while he was gone, the reality of seeing him again, of knowing that he had recognized her needs and responded to them, made her desires that much sharper. Nothing else seemed important.

What was he doing for so long outside? With a great deal of effort, she lifted the kettle off its standard and managed to carry it over to the bath. It was more difficult to empty the awkward, heavy pot than to drag it over. The next kettleful he would . . .

The door swung open and Nick stomped the snow from his boots before entering. He dropped a burlap bag inside, then swung a rope from over his shoulder and deposited a blood-smeared animal on the blanket next to the doorway.

There was so much blood that Elyn had a hard time trying to decide what it was that he had killed. "It should last some time," she offered in an optimistic tone, "whatever it is." He looked so proud of his skills that she had to say something.

"It's a wild pig. They don't often stay this high in winter," he explained, and made light of what was really an extraordinarily fine day's hunting. "Luck, I guess. Anyway, we'll be having roast pork again." Nick grinned and rubbed his hands together as he took several steps toward her. "Now, as I was saying, you look awfully warm in that shirt. . . ."

"Do *not* take another step." Elyn had just caught sight of the blood soaking his shirt and coat. Pig's blood, whether it was that of a suckling or of a boar, had a strong, distinct odor. "Your bath is nearly ready. If you'll drop your clothing over there," she pointed to a far corner of the cabin, "I shall wash them for you."

Nick looked down at his shirt and grimaced at the dark maroon stains. "That bad, hmm?" He was beginning to catch the scent now. Nora nodded. "Say nothing more, m'lady. I'm happy to oblige." He started to unbutton his shirt and glanced up with a crooked, teasing grin. "Hell of a way to get me out of my clothes, ma'am. All you really had to do was ask—" He ducked just in time as a tin cup whizzed past his ear.

He had taken off his boots and socks and dropped his shirt in the indicated corner when Nora asked for his help. She was holding the kettle handle with both hands, struggling with the weight of the iron pot full of steaming water. There was water in the tub already. He frowned and came up to her with a scowl. "There's nothing says you have to wait on me, Nora. You might have hurt yourself, scalded your—"

"I wasn't waiting on you, and I *was* careful. I'm not quite used to doing for myself, but I assure you I'm not *completely* incompetent." Elyn's one try at preparing a meal had been an utter disaster and Nick's attitude had been humiliatingly patronizing. Now he was implying...

"I know just what you're thinking," he said, and canted his head as he took the kettle from her. "And you're wrong. I'm not implying you're helpless—"

"Only that I can't do a simple task any—"

"I never said that."

Elyn's bottom lip curved in a charmingly stubborn pout. "You didn't have to—I can read minds as well as you can. I know what you think of me—I do—and I'm not nearly as helpless or dependent on—" She had come within a hair of admitting her infatuation. She'd had no brandy to muddle her reactions or to spread oil upon the waters of her inhibitions. "Take your bath, please," she said in a tiny, forlorn voice. She could trust herself to say no more.

"Will you join me? Oh, not *in* the tub—that'd take some doing. Why don't you come talk with me? I've had only squirrels and rabbits for company today." Nick smiled, a quick, vulnerable gesture that made him all the more appealing. "And you had no one to talk to. I must be better company than the walls."

"By far," she admitted, and followed him as he carried the hot water to the tub and poured it in. Out of habit, she turned away as he finished disrobing and stepped into the bath. Admittedly, she would have preferred to watch, for she found nothing in his form that was not appealing. Late though she was in discovering in herself a bent toward sensuality, Elyn had taken to the newfound freedom like a duck to water. She wanted nothing more than to revel in the physical bond they shared, to luxuriate in the male-female magnetism she experienced each time he was near.

When he held the sliver of musk soap out to her with an

unspoken request, Elynora could not refuse. She did, however, chasten him for expecting such indulgences. "Someone spoiled you," she asserted, and remembering the photograph of the blonde named Cecelia, she managed to work the name into the conversation. "Likely your mother began the task, then Cecelia carried on. Was she your fiancée?"

Obviously Nora hadn't spent the entire time sleeping, Nick noted. Actually, Cecelia had been a parental arrangement that had failed, a reason he'd gone off on his own and ended up in Mexico; but Nora, already trying to disguise an avid interest in the subject, was better left in the dark. "Cecelia was a . . . friend," he answered, managing to imply that she'd been much more. "We had some good times; then again, we argued a lot." Nick grinned. "Making up again was always worth the fight."

Elyn paled slightly, jealous of this unknown girl who had apparently enjoyed a serious relationship with Nick. "Really? I don't care to discuss your past. I care very little *what* you thought of the girl. . . . I was merely curious as to her identity." *And why you still carry a picture of her. And what you really felt for her.* It was horrible to be so envious. In her entire life, Elyn could not remember a single instance when any man had been worth such petty concerns.

"Hmm . . . curious enough to go prowling through my saddlebags," Nick commented. "Nora, have I asked anything about your husband?" A constrained silence met his inquiry and he looked up to find her staring past him, at nothing in particular. Maybe she wanted him to ask. "All right—fair's fair. Tell me a little about him."

Elyn started to rise and threw the soap into the bath. "I don't care to and you may—"

To save her the later embarrassment of realizing she had cursed, Nick caught her wrist and tugged. Though he hadn't

45

meant to, the action brought her tumbling toward him; she landed with a splash in the bath.

Instead of sputtering angrily, suddenly Elyn began to cry. She hadn't wanted to think of Alec; little as he meant to her, he was a reminder of the vows she had broken. It was her fault for mentioning Cecelia. Neither name should have come into the conversation. She was, Elyn suddenly realized, unreasonably jealous of anyone in Nick's past. But why should she be, when theirs was only a temporary affair, a coming together because of time and the isolation of the winter storm? She shouldn't be, and yet the matter stood: Elyn was jealous.

Nick was oddly unsettled by her tears. The water had soaked the shirt she wore, and though it lay plastered against her, revealing every soft, swelling curve, he was more intent on comforting her than on taking advantage. "There's no reason to cry. She meant nothing and I—" He was about to apologize for bringing up her husband, but she was already upset and the tears had come soon after his first mention. Instead, Nick pulled her close and kissed her tears away.

Elyn thought that perhaps she was too heavy to lie across him, but he seemed not to mind. If moments earlier his tone had been harsh, now he seemed intent on soothing her; and because his concern was nearly as sweet as the pleasure of making love, she lay cradled in his arms. Slowly his kisses awoke the realization that her desire lay just below the surface. It took only a touch or a gentle caress to arouse her. Her lips yielded beneath the light pressure of his mouth, parting to submit, to revel in that possession that was and yet was still to come.

She wanted him now, and nothing else mattered, not pride, not modesty, nothing but the joy that lay ahead. Elyn rose and pulled at his hand. He was clean of the hunt, but if he hadn't been it wouldn't have mattered. He came up out of the water, ignoring the torn piece of blanket she'd handed him for a towel.

Nick bent his head and softly whispered her name over and over as she leaned against his naked flesh. His hands were at the buttons of the shirt, impatient to bare her flesh as well, so impatient that he tore off several buttons in his haste. Without an awareness of the action, they were suddenly on the blanket in front of the fireplace, hungrily exploring each other's bodies.

No man's touch had ever elicited such a feverish response, and she doubted . . . no, she *knew* that no man would again. It was partly that realization that fueled Elyn's desperate need to lie in his arms as much as possible. She seemed insatiable and wondered that her strange new cravings did not make him turn from her in disgust. Yet there was nothing in his own ardent lovemaking that revealed anything but delight and appreciation.

When his mouth sought and found her breasts, her nipples had already frozen hard with the call of passion. The warmth of his lips, the gentle, insistent suckling, the stirring of something deep and primitive within her drove Elyn wild. She wanted their lovemaking to last forever and still she yearned for that moment of release.

Nick drew back for a moment's breath, more than a little awed by the tigress that had emerged from so shy a kitten. Nora wasn't vain about her looks—a rare quality in a girl so lovely. She had no idea now, though, how breathtaking she was. Stretched out before the fire, wearing nothing but a mantle of soft golden light and shadowed hollows, she was beautiful . . . and she was his. For the moment, for the next few days, they belonged to each other.

He trailed his fingers lightly down her belly, caressing

circles on the tender flesh of her inner thighs. Her breasts rose and fell more rapidly with every contact; she was willing and abandoned, the perfect female, a partner to his desire.

It would have been infinitely pleasurable to draw out the minutes, to spin hours of them into a long, golden night of making love, but such was his longing that Nick could no longer stay his needs. Nora was ready, so ready, to receive him. She moved pliably, malleable more to their mutual desires than to his manipulations, welcoming him between her slender thighs.

They seemed made for each other. He entered and became a part of her. She felt him slip within her and, before feeling replaced thought, wondered at the miracle that melded them into one sentient being, intent upon the same sensual reward.

Everything about the union was fever-pitched. They came together as related elements of the same sweeping storm, thunder and lightning clashing, yet so close, so fiercely loving. Elyn held him, her fingers closed possessively on the damp curls at his nape. She wanted to absorb him, to keep forever the instrument that dealt such exquisite pleasures.

And Nick, in sensing that flare of selfishness, knew an exultation that carried him beyond the tightly reined control that had seen him to this point. He drove forward again and again, still locked in that feeling of oneness, yet separate enough to feel the return of the delight he gave her.

Elyn cried out, something between a whimper and a scream. Every nerve of her body was attuned to the white heat radiating from her thighs. For what seemed like minutes, nothing registered. She was either dying . . . or being reborn, completely sensate, a body seeking release from the pain of too much pleasure. Then, as a gentle, drifting feeling buoyed her body, she *knew* she had died, knew beyond any doubt that she existed in some otherworld. What she felt, the breathless

48

surge of energy and well-being that followed each wave of relaxation, were reflections of paradise. Why had she been transported to heaven, though? Elyn could not imagine; she knew only that hell was ten thousand miles in the opposite direction.

Even as she came back from that tranquil place beyond herself, Elyn found herself wishing she might stay, linger there for a day beyond forever. Could one ever tire of such a heaven, or was it only the passage toward it that made the destination so sought? She opened her eyes in a languid, lazy gesture and found Nick studying her. His face was only inches from hers. He looked . . . sated; that, and pleased with himself as well. "You look as if you're about to crow with pleasure, as does the cock at sunrise," she commented and allowed a smile to tip the corners of her mouth. "Am I mistaken or are you the vainest of men?"

"You've confused vanity and pride, love," he answered, amused that Nora had come back from total abandonment with so saucy a wit. The sleepy look had left her eyes, she was the playful kitten once again, and he liked her more for the intelligence that enhanced her natural beauty. "A vain man recounts his accomplishments for an audience of one," he explained; "a proud man doesn't have to speak at all . . . others do it for him."

"And you're proud?"

"Shouldn't I be?"

Elyn thought a moment. He *had* driven her wild, made her feel more a woman for all her naïveté. He was skilled—and had every right to be proud. Why was it so difficult for her to admit that he had given her such delight? Was she guilty of the same vanity of which she'd accused him? She was; the silent admission brought a blush to her face. "You should," Elyn finally admitted, then gazed up, into a pair of green eyes

49

that crinkled at the corners with a tolerant good humor. "I cannot say what I felt . . . what *you* made me feel . . . only that I traveled to a place where I have never been." That was as much as she could say without embarrassing herself and him.

Nick smiled, pleased by the compliment. He came closer, pressed his lips to a pulse that raced at her temples, kissed her brow and finally her lips. "Let's go traveling again."

Elyn's ordeal was over, or would be shortly when the train from Veracruz stopped at the rural station of San Lazaro, on the outskirts of Mexico City. Ordeal, indeed. For just over a fortnight she'd lived a dream, stepped into one of Sybil's fantasies. But fantasies weren't reality . . . reality was boarding the train and going on to the capital; reality was leaving Nick behind and returning to Alec.

She glanced down at her clothing and smiled. The gathered cotton skirt and brightly embroidered peasant blouse made her look a different person. She wore sandals, showing off a pair of slender ankles that had tanned a gold-pink. A lace mantilla covered her braided hair. Elyn hadn't worn braids since middle school.

Nick looked uncomfortable, his hat slouched low to shadow his face. He was taking a risk, waiting at the crowded station. When he could have merely taken her down through the mountain pass and put her on an eastbound train for Veracruz, he had insisted that it was too dangerous. Instead they'd waited for Paco's return. When the rebel hadn't shown by the ninth day, Nick had decided to take her west, skirting the train route from Veracruz to the capital. There were any number of stations along the way where he might have put her on an eastbound train. She suspected—or did she simply want to believe?—that he was also delaying the time when they had to part.

Did he feel awkward? When they'd broken camp this morning, he had been unusually curt. On the way to the station, with his arms encircling her waist, the silence between them had formed a wall no less impenetrable than stone. They had begun as strangers, evolved into lovers, and had now come full circle.

In the distance the train whistle shrieked. It would be another five minutes before it puffed into the station. No one, least of all Nick, cared that it was already late. He glanced at Nora and found her staring off across the fields that bordered the platform. She'd changed. Hell, so had he. Two weeks ago he'd wanted to be rid of her. Now . . . now he wanted to keep her. That was a laugh. He could just see himself saying, "Look, forget your husband. Stick with me and we'll have a great life—dodging bullets, living off the land." She wasn't a *soldadera,* and even if she wanted to stay with him, she couldn't. He wouldn't let her.

He didn't know what to say. A plain old "goodbye" didn't fit the bill, and if he said more, well . . . the less said, the better. The train was pulling up beside the platform now. San Lazaro was little more than a whistle stop. As soon as the passengers had boarded, the train would be on its way.

He took a step closer to Nora and touched her arm. "Remember what I told you—the quicker you get to the embassy, the safer you'll be. A woman alone's fair prey for . . ." He'd told her several times what to watch for. "And tell your husband to take better care of you. Mexico's full of outlaws." He flashed a quick grin and tugged down the brim of his hat. "Can't tell us good guys from the bad without a scorecard!"

The platform had cleared, and the engineer had given a warning blast on his whistle. There were only seconds left. Elyn glanced over her shoulder and saw the conductor raise his thick, dark brows, questioning whether she meant to board. She raised her hand, waving the ticket she held, then turned back and impulsively threw her arms around Nick's neck, burying her head against his shoulders. She didn't want to leave him, wanted instead a thousand more nights in his arms and an equal number of days to study everything about him.

Finally she lifted her head. The tears that threatened to betray her feelings were, by an exercise of willpower, held in check. She would not humiliate herself or embarrass him, and she did not care to leave him with a memory of her eyes puffed by maudlin weeping. Elyn smiled, studied his features for a moment, then stood on tiptoe to kiss him. She wanted that much, the imprint of his mouth on hers, the remembered texture of his skin touching hers, when, later, this would all seem a dream.

"Señor, the train is already late. You put the lady on board or she stays."

Nick barely heard the conductor, though he had come up behind them. All he knew was that he didn't want to let go of Nora. And from the way she pressed the length of her slender body against him, she felt the same. "Come on, the train's leaving," he whispered, then trailed soft, nibbling kisses down her throat. Since neither of them seemed able to separate from the other, he had one choice—to delay the parting yet a little while longer and travel on with her into the city, danger be damned.

In a second, one of the poor ragged boys who haunted the station had caught the centavos thrown by Nick and sworn on his mother's life to keep a watch over the sorrel until the señor returned. Yes, he would water the stallion and even find him something on which to feed. The promise of an equal amount of pennies on Nick's return that afternoon was enough to assure the boy's loyalty.

The cars were crowded but the conductor managed to find them a seat together near the back of the last car. Though the señor had spoken a flawless Spanish, he had the look of a gringo; and hadn't the *policía* said that a tall Americano was wanted for the murder of an important general and his aide? Ignacio Rualdo scratched his chin, trying to remember if the *capitan* had given any more details of the fugitive's appearance. Tall, undoubtedly one of the rebels who plagued the country, not an unhandsome fellow; this could indeed be he.

Was there not something about a girl? The gringo's accomplice, a *soldadera?* No, not an accomplice, a captive . . . *sí,* an Anglo, a woman he had kidnapped. Ignacio walked down the aisle, taking tickets, glancing occasionally at the couple. The girl, despite her attire, could easily be English. The color of her hair was hidden by the mantilla draped across it, but surely her fair skin was of the English, so white and fine. She was very beautiful. Rualdo's mouth suddenly went dry; he tried hard to remember if there had been mention of a reward. In these hard times, no one was his brother's keeper . . . it was every man for himself. His sympathies might secretly lie with the rebels, but none of them helped feed his family . . . or drape his mistress in fine laces.

He smiled broadly when he took the girl's ticket, and certainly his bow was most polite when he accepted payment from the young Americano. Neither seemed to notice his interest. They were too absorbed in each other to see beyond each other's eyes. This girl, fair as the English rose, could not be a captive. No captive ever gazed so sweetly at her captor. On the platform they had kissed, then there had been a sudden change of plans and the gringo had come aboard with her. They made a handsome couple. She wore a wedding band on her left hand . . . perhaps they *were* only another young couple, parted by the day's politics and then, for a brief time, reunited. It would do no harm to check with the authorities when the train pulled into the central station.

In that split-second decision to accompany her into the city, Nick had communicated much. He felt the same as she, and though neither of them could say as much in words, their rather ambiguous relationship was at least that—a relationship. He was committed to the rebellion; she was, legally, tied to Alec. If either were free . . . but they weren't. It was useless to discuss a future; they had no future together.

As the train approached through the suburban areas on the outskirts of the capital, Nick grew increasingly irritable. He should never have come aboard. It would have been better to finish it in San Lazaro. What had possessed him to think . . . ? It didn't matter now anyway. He'd just delayed the inevitable, put off saying goodbye for another twenty minutes. He stared morosely out the window. It was covered with a dirty gray film, but he could just barely make out the stark colonial outline of Santiago Tlatelolco. Nick had memories less than pleasant of the military prison, enough so that he didn't care to make a return visit. Again he regretted having boarded at San Lazaro.

Once the train had pulled to a stop under the eaves of the Mexican railway station, Elyn insisted that he stay in the station and out of sight as much as possible until he was able to board a train for San Lazaro. And equally obstinately, Nick argued that he would see her safely away in a carriage bound for the British embassy, several blocks off the broad main boulevard known as Paseo de la Reforma.

Exiting the station, Elyn was nervous, afraid that at any second some alert policeman would recognize Nick's description and shout out a command to surrender. Nick himself was cautious but not alarmed. His regard for the skills of the Mexican civil authorities matched his opinion of their military counterparts. Both were unorganized, corrupt, and, approached in the right manner, quite open to bribery.

Nick called to the driver of one of the closed carriages for hire and bargained with him for a few minutes before they settled on a price. He would wait, he told Nick, while the señor said his goodbyes. Nick helped Nora into the carriage and slipped in beside her, then drew the shades. "Don't get out anywhere but the British embassy," he warned. "I'll be gone within the next half-hour, so it doesn't matter what you tell the consul."

Elyn looked at him with wide, wounded eyes. "I won't say anything. You know—"

"How's that going to look? You're not thinking, Nora. It doesn't matter about me." He grinned, and in the shadowed recesses of the carriage Elyn could see the flash of his even, white teeth. "Say whatever comes to mind. My reputation is compromised already." Nick reached out and lifted her chin with his fingertips. "You're not smiling. You could leave me with that, a smile."

Elyn brushed away his hand, angry and at the same time shaken by this final moment. There was so much she wanted to say, so much she couldn't. "I don't *feel* like smiling," she snapped, then silently cursed the petulance she heard in her voice. "I . . . I'm sorry, I don't . . ." She stumbled, unable to pull the phrases together in her mind before she spoke. Her hands were trembling, her lips tightened into a line, and she turned away, drawing a deep breath to compose herself. It was awful to behave this way, so lacking in self-control.

Suddenly Elyn was in his arms, and blindly, instinctively, she turned her face to him. They kissed, and she didn't care

55

that her face was wet with tears. The emotion passing between them seemed to vibrate the very earth; distantly Elyn felt the carriage give a lurch and heard the alarmed whinnying of the horses. In the single-mindedness of the moment, it seemed that the whole of nature was attuned to the lovers' farewell.

Then, as suddenly as Nick had entered her life, he was gone from it. He pulled away, opened the door, and stepped down, not even looking back before he closed the door and called out a terse command to the driver. It was Elyn who was unable to make a clean break. She touched the shade, startling when it shot up, and leaned toward the window to gaze at the station. For a moment, before the carriage was lost in the congested traffic, she caught a glimpse of a tall, lean figure entering the station. He hadn't glanced back.

Inside, Nick headed for the ticket counter. He was frowning, preoccupied. "San Lazaro," he said to the clerk; then he glanced back at the entrance and added, "One, please. How soon—"

"Track three, in . . ." the clerk consulted his pocket watch and nodded, "fifteen minutes. But they're boarding now." He pushed the change across the counter and made an attempt to cover a yawn. It was ten o'clock and already he wished for the siesta hour.

Nick pocketed his money and looked around the station. Across from the ticket counter was a kiosk that sold newspapers, candies, and fruits. He hadn't had much of a breakfast, hadn't wanted to. None of the fruit looked too clean, and besides, his appetite wasn't any better now than it had been this morning. He wandered over, passed on what was probably a stale lot of candies, and decided on a cigar. As he reached out for a thin, Cuban cigarillo, the headline of a newspaper caught his eye. ASSASSIN STILL AT LARGE, HOSTAGE BELIEVED DEAD.

It set Nick back a minute to realize that the story was about him. At first his frown deepened as he picked up a copy of the Veracruz paper and read on. Finally, because the reporter had made him out to be the greatest blackguard in Mexican history, he began to see the humorous side of the story. He chose a cigarillo, paid for it and the paper, and wandered toward the train platform, still reading about his evil deeds.

According to an entirely fictitious set of "facts," he had killed more than two people at the dinner reception honoring the general. One of the guards claimed to have wounded him, and he was supposed to be Villa's right-hand man. *That error should please Zapata,* he thought, pausing to turn the page to the continued story inside the paper. The small picture next to the story brought back his frown. It was a photograph of Alec Barford, a distraught-looking but nattily dressed Alec Barford, husband of the young woman taken hostage. In the text, he was quoted as appealing to "the assassin's sense of decency and fair play" and asking that he not take his political differences out on an innocent. That part was true enough, but the mention of decency and fair play made Alec sound like an idiot. He certainly didn't deserve Nora.

Across the main hall of the station, two men had been observing Nick. They stood in the doorway of an office behind the ticket counter, watching to see what he would do. "I told you he would be back, did I not? Left his horse in San Lazaro; of course, he must return for the animal."

"Silencio, Rualdo!" The *policía* spoke sharply, more than a little irritated by the conductor's prattling. At first he had not believed there was anything to the claim that General Cardenes's assassin was here in Mexico City, here in Thomas Castillos's little corner of the world. Now, with visions of a long-deserved promotion and perhaps a raise dancing before his eyes, Private Castillos wanted to move cautiously. He

would not have such a chance again. "You will let me think in peace or there is no reward for you."

"Think? How can you stop to think?" Ignacio could see his fine, fat reward drifting away like a cloud of smoke. "You must *act*, else the fugitive will get away. Catch him and we will both—"

"Receive our just rewards, Rualdo," the policeman finished. "But you see, *I* am in charge, while you . . . you are only a train conductor, a ticket taker."

"I know well what I am," Ignacio said through clenched teeth, "and if you don't want to be nothing more than a private forever, walking around, arresting nobody, stay there and think! I will go after the outlaw and all the reward money will be *mine*." He started to elbow past the policeman, but Castillos stuck out his arm.

"We go, but you follow my lead," he insisted. "And keep your mouth shut or you will warn the criminal!" In the course of their argument they had lost sight of their quarry; now they both scrambled toward the boarding area, brushing past porters and passengers, studying the crowd beginning to line up before gate three.

"There—there he is!" Rualdo shouted; then he staggered slightly as Private Castillos punched his right shoulder and hissed an order for silence. Several people, including a tall man with a dark, thick mustache, had turned at the sound of Rualdo's call. Only the tall stranger reacted. Suddenly there was a gun in his hand; suddenly he was backing through the gate toward the tracks, balancing catlike on the balls of his feet, watching for any signs of interference to his sides and behind him.

"There is no escape, señor," Castillos called after him, his own gun drawn, though he was hesitant to use it in a crowd that included women and children. The outlaw didn't know

58

that, of course. Thomas raised his weapon and aimed at the figure some forty feet away.

The policeman wouldn't shoot; his hesitation in raising the revolver and his nervous glances toward the passengers translated as official caution. One never knew who was important; one might even kill a senator's relative or somebody with connections. Nick continued to inch backward. Once on the train he'd be able to slip back through the cars and probably get away through the city streets bordering the tracks. For a second he thought of Nora. Thank God she was safe. The whole thing would have played out differently if she'd still been at his side. He allowed himself a smile as he ducked to the left and up the steps of one of the first-class cars. When he died, it wasn't going to be at the hands of a paunchy, aging *oficial* in the city police. The attempt at capturing him was almost an insult.

Private Castillos paused only a minute to glower at the conductor's stupidity before he started after the fugitive. He brushed past the line of passengers, who by now had emerged from a stunned silence to a sudden-found panic. One woman screamed and fainted directly in his path, a child began to cry, and there were a few curses from the men, one of whom grasped his arm as he passed, indignantly demanding to know what was happening.

Thomas Castillos pulled away, shouting a warning that the man was obstructing justice. Suddenly he was free and falling, surprised for the moment by his own strength as he lurched away from the gentleman passenger. It seemed the ground was rushing up to meet him. An angry rumbling sound issued from the earth; it seemed to twist and quiver beneath his prone body like the throes of a dying animal. More than he had been when the outlaw had pointed a gun at him, Thomas was scared.

Ignacio had been thrown against one of the cars. He lay crumpled next to it, his head bleeding near the right temple. Around him, passengers frightened by the near violence of the police confrontation screamed in earnest. Babies wailed and men ducked glass falling from the vaulted framework thirty-five feet overhead to grab their families close.

The earth tremors continued. The train cars rocked and swayed from side to side as a wave of force swept along the track, buckling the metal and ripping stakes from ties. The air was choked with the dust of plaster and dirt, the tinkle of glass breaking against the wooden platform sounded out of place, almost orchestrated. For a few minutes the earth quieted and the moans and cries of human misery replaced the rumbling and splintering. People wept, blinded by a cloud of dust so thick it was impossible to breathe, and what air they could breathe was tainted by the smell of blood and sweating fear.

The second earthshock came without warning. There was no distant grumble, no sense of the earth beginning to vibrate. It was quiet; then, as if a bomb had exploded, the ground shuddered, slamming those who could still stand off their feet. A protesting whine of metal shrilled, a seesaw noise that terrified those trapped in the station into silence. Of them all, only Ignacio Rualdo made sense of it, and he was praying loudly, asking forgiveness of a God whose judgment he would soon meet.

In his office at the British embassy, Vice-Consul David Withers Endicott frowned in general at his overburdened schedule and, more specifically, at the phone receiver. His superior, Sir George Atkins, had picked one hell of a time to take his vacation. First young Mrs. Barford had shown up, out of the blue, and then, not much more than an hour ago,

60

an earthquake had ripped through the northern quarter of the capital.

Thank heavens it hadn't leveled the entire city. He hadn't been here then, but the consul had described the last quake, back in, what year was it . . . ah, yes, in 1911. Early June, right after the elections; two hundred people or more dead in that one. Nasty business, earthquakes. Never see 'em in a civilized country. Certainly not in England. Course, he wasn't in the foreign service to see England. One had to put up—Suddenly there was a blast of static on the line, jarring Endicott from his musings.

"Yes, yes I'm here, Avery," he replied. "Can you hear my voice?" Endicott raised his tone a bit and tried again. "Better? Good. We've had a deuced time of it, old man. Lucky you are where you are, eh? Yes, as I was saying, your cousin-in-law, Mrs. Barford, is doing well. No, physically she seems in fine fettle; we have had a doctor in. She was understandably upset by her ordeal, but you may assure Mr. Barford we're taking the best of care with . . . I say, Avery, are you there?"

The vice-consul laid the receiver on the desk top and sighed. It was likely to be this way all day. First the lines worked, then they didn't.

Across from him, Elynora Barford rested on a chaise-longue. She looked peaceful enough, but Lord, what a bother she'd been not a half-hour past. Not that she hadn't a right to some hysterics; it was her timing of them that had thrown him. Delayed shock, the doctor had said. She was sedated now, sleeping, but even the drugged rest seemed bothered by stress, as if the sedative had not dulled all her senses.

She'd appeared at ten-thirty, and because of her attire he had almost not believed her claim that she was the kidnapped Mrs. Barford. Still, her accent was clearly British, and he could do little but invite her in and listen to what she had to say. It seemed the chap who'd abducted her had put her on a westbound train somewhere between Veracruz and the capital. She hadn't been harmed; the outlaw had been a gentleman. She was none the worse for wear despite an ordeal of two weeks' length. Something didn't ring true, but David hadn't the presence of mind to decide what exactly, and then . . . then all hell had broken loose with the advent of the quake.

The embassy had only been shaken a bit. It was sturdily built and far from the area hit the hardest. At first the reports of damage had been greatly exaggerated. Power lines had fallen, causing some damage from fires, and phone lines were down in parts of the city, but other than some structural failures to the north, Mexico City still stood.

David lifted the phone and heard a squawk, then a different voice came on, a man who identified himself as Alec Barford. "Yes, sir, Mr. Barford. David Endicott here. No, sir, we're safe here. The quake was centered around a business section to the north. Yes, bit of luck, that. Your wife narrowly missed being one of the fatalities. It seems the outlaw put her on the train, the national line, westbound. Next to Buenavista Station. She was already with us here when it started. I understand the station's a bloody awful mess. Trains knocked about like toys . . . Yes, the roof caved in. They'll be days digging the bodies out. Yes, quite. Well, the main thing is, she's back safe and, I think, sound, all things considered."

Barford's voice rose in alarm at the idea that his wife's mind might have been harmed by her ordeal.

"No, I didn't mean to make you think . . . well, she's naturally been through so much, sir. The doctor's been here and she's resting. He said she ought not to be moved for several days, and we've quite adequate, even comfortable lodgings. I can't say when the rail lines will operate again. The main thing to remember, Mr. Barford, is that your wife's come through this safely and will soon be with you again. Yes, if the phones are working later, I'll ring through to Mr. Avery's office and you'll be able to speak directly with her. It's no bother, sir. We're here to serve any of our citizens visiting Mexico. Thank you, sir, and may I say how pleased we are that it all worked out so well. Yes, goodbye.''

Endicott hung up the receiver, quite satisfied with the conversation and the way in which he'd handled matters. Avery would no doubt see that he was given credit for a job well done, and his career would likely profit from this minor crisis-of-the-moment. Barford had been worried over his wife's emotional state but had calmed at a reassurance that she was doing well.

David rose from his desk chair and walked around to study the lady's face. A nurse sat at her side, occasionally stroking her brow when Mrs. Barford seemed restless. He had a great many questions, not all of which could be asked politely. Where had she spent the past fortnight? Did she have any knowledge that would help the police or the army, both of which were searching for the rebel, locate his hiding place? Most curious of all had been her reaction to the news of the rail-station disaster. Elynora Barford had arrived at the embassy in a calm if subdued mood. She'd seemed fine until the reports of damage to the station came in. That had begun her hysteria, and David had had everything he could do to restrain her from leaving before the doctor arrived. She'd wanted to go back, but she wouldn't say why, just that she had to go.

The doctor saw nothing unusual in her agitation. Once he understood the circumstances of what she'd been through, he sedated her, staying until she was quiet. She was experiencing delayed shock and a strong association with the place where she'd first been free of the danger of captivity.

It sounded complicated to David, but he hadn't the knowledge the doctor had. And it would have done no good to mention it to the lady's husband. Now that she'd experienced the hysteria, Dr. Fallin had said, it was out of her system; she would soon be back at her husband's side, and life would go on as it had before her abduction.

"I have been patient, Elynora, to this point," Alec Barford complained, "but a man can only be patient for so long. You've refused to tell the federal authorities anything of this villain who abducted you, you have *not* cooperated with the police. You haven't even told *me* what transpired in the fortnight you spent as his captive."

"I don't wish to speak of . . . that time, Alec. Why do you persist when you see how it distresses me? Have you no thought for my feelings, for what I have been through?" Elyn hadn't thought Alec's presence would be so burdensome, but it seemed again to be a reinforcement of the gypsy's predictions. Nick *had* changed her life, and she could not pretend it would ever be the same.

From the moment she had returned to Veracruz, Alec had played the role of the model husband, concerned, devoted, attentive. If she cared, Elyn might have wondered over the transformation. She did not, though, and found it instead an irritation to be petted and cosseted by a man she didn't love . . . perhaps had never loved.

Did she think, now that Nick was gone so absolutely from her life, that she might have loved him? Elynora wasn't sure. These past three weeks, since her return, she had dwelled too much upon what might have been. Even if Nick had survived the earthquake, she could not have divorced Alec. Her family would never have allowed it, and Alec, would never have freed her. It was unthinkable that she might have pursued so socially damning a course, and yet for Nicholas . . . no, she could not have, even for him. It was bred into her—duty, conformity, propriety; whatever name it was given, she could not have chosen to break the vows she had taken on her wedding day.

Still, the time spent in her lover's arms seemed more the reality than the dream. It was so unfair, almost a cruelty too harsh to bear, now that she had known such pleasures as a gentle touch, an intimate look across a room, that she should be deprived of them for all the long years ahead. *And* consigned to the prison that was her marriage to Alec. Perhaps . . . perhaps she had sinned too greatly, and this, then, was to be the penalty she must pay.

"But I will persist—I must, Lyn, or go mad!" Alec was saying. "I, of all those who love you, would not press a cause that makes you so pale and distraught, but I *will* have it from you. *What happened in those weeks that you were gone?* D'you not think I was mad with worry? What I imagined . . . No, I cannot tell you what. You must set my mind at ease."

"You were hardly tormented when I saw you last that evening, Alec," Elyn replied, amazed that the shy, under-standing wife in her had vanished. It was some other woman surely, more bold than herself, who called her spouse to task for his inconstant love. "And *if* you worried, I shouldn't think that you had to endure it alone. Perhaps your dinner companion, the young blond American . . ."

"Elynora!" Taken aback by the startling confidence, the almost unconcerned attitude his young wife now showed, Alec could scarcely recall the lady she had mentioned. "After you were carried off . . . why, I had no thought for a harmless flirtation with any woman." Alec had begun to pace before

Elyn's chair, his hands nervously clenched together behind his back. "My wife had been ruthlessly abducted, stolen away while I stared in helpless confusion. Can you know what I felt? Less a man for not protecting you better, my love. Now I ask, no, I *beg* you to tell me what he . . . what that bloody rogue did with you. If he hurt you, by God, he could not hide in the deepest pit of hell!"

Elyn looked up, not at all impressed by her husband's theatrics. "How very fierce you are, Alec. By some miracle you have been transformed from a pursuer of virtue to a protector of it. You'll have to live with your curiosity as well as your desire for revenge." She glanced down but not before Alec caught a brief glimpse of some emotion akin to pain deep in her velvety eyes. "You can exact nothing from my abductor; he is dead."

Alec stared at his wife. She appeared more lovely than ever, more desirable. Elynora held her head high—there was a certain assurance in her posture that she had not previously shown. "You think to use him to make me jealous, is that so? To make me suffer remorse for the way I've treated you? Well, I am sorry for my . . . inattentiveness. And for what seemed to be a flirtation. It was nothing, I swear." Alec took a deep breath and paused in front of Elyn. "Can you say the same of your weeks away from me?" Incredibly, he was down on one knee, grasping her hands within his damp, sweated palms. "Say you are mine still," he pleaded, "untouched by any other man. Say it, Elynora, and I *shall* believe you."

Silence greeted his plea. Her life would have been so much easier had Elyn lied, had she masked her feelings and spoken the words Alec longed to hear. She looked at him directly, then turned away, unable or unwilling to comfort him no matter what the consequences.

Alec stared at Elyn, refusing to believe that another man might have possessed what belonged to him. He tried to comprehend the reason for her silence. She was ashamed. Of course, the bastard had assaulted her, and Elynora, for she'd ever been so innocent a girl, was too shy to speak the truth. Yes, that must be it; he'd press her no further. It all made sense now, why she had said nothing, why she'd insisted upon separate bedrooms. Alec raised her hands to his lips and pressed a tender kiss on the soft white skin. "Say nothing, then, sweet. I know, your silence speaks eloquently, fully of what you endured. He attacked you, the cur gave you—"

"No." Elyn stared at his fingers, so despising his touch that her feelings were apparent though she'd said nothing. When Alec jerked his hands away as if their contact with her flesh had dealt him a shock, she looked at him. "It wasn't that way. He wasn't an animal and I . . . I didn't resist—"

Alec struck her without thinking, his right palm slamming across her mouth, cutting off the words he didn't want to hear. Her head rocked back and her eyes closed, and though his ring had cut the corner of her mouth, she made no move to wipe away the trickle of blood that appeared. She may have believed it was deserved; she may not have cared.

There is no rage quite so righteous as that of a husband who believes himself betrayed. Elynora had hurt him, deliberately tried to dishonor his name. For a moment he considered the possibility that she had lied to avenge his treatment of her that night and on other nights. But she hadn't. Written on her face, in misery that had nothing to do with the physical pain of a swelling cheek and a bruised mouth, was the truth. Suddenly it was very clear to Alec. He recalled Elynora's dazed appearance on her return, her quiet, withdrawn mood, her refusal to share a room with him. Elynora was in mourning, grieving for a man she'd barely known and hurting silently because she could not admit, to anyone, that she'd loved a bloody rebel bastard.

Elyn thought the worst was over when Alec slapped her. The truth was out. In an odd way, the physical pain was welcome. For the moment her attention was drawn from the dull, empty ache within. She expected that each of them would have to find a way to deal with what had happened. Time would . . . Suddenly she was on her feet, drawn upward as Alec caught and jerked her right wrist.

Reed-thin and fair, even pale, Alec was livid with fury. His expression was maniacal, his eyes fixed upon her features with such vengeance that Elyn cowered. He said nothing, and when his palm again slammed against her face, striking her cheek, the blow propelled her backward. She went limp, but Alec held on to her arm. Elyn dangled like a lifeless doll until he finally released her and she crumpled to the floor, coming down hard against knees that were protected only by the thin material of her cotton gown.

She was not physically afraid of Alec. And emotionally she already hurt too much to feel anything but a vague sense of pity; for him, for her, for Nick—it wasn't clear who deserved the emotion. She raised a hand and ran her finger lightly across her cheek. Her eye was beginning to puff, and a scratch from his ring streaked across her cheek. Elyn covered her eyes with her forearm, wishing only that he would tire of his righteous posturings and leave her. Through the sound of her own weeping, she barely heard the whispered rustle of his silk dressing gown.

Alec stood staring down at her as he loosened the drawstring tie of his pajamas. He wanted her more than he'd ever wanted anything and he meant to have her. If taking her would hurt her, he would only be returning a measure of the pain she had dealt him. In fact, his own pleasure would be heightened if she begged him to cease. He would erase the memory of her outlaw lover and show her which of them was more the man.

When Elyn felt the cool rush of air touch her legs, the sensation confused her. Alec had said nothing more and the vilification she'd expected had not come. She wiped quickly at her tears, wincing as her fingers brushed her swollen cheek. Alec was suddenly on the floor near her, a strange gloating expression in his eyes as he shoved her nightgown higher to bare her hips and belly.

No! Oh, dear God, no! Reality was enough of a punishment. She couldn't take this, Alec's revenge for his suddenly discovered pride. Elyn twisted away, but his hand shot out, grasped her hair, and jerked her back. Her head slammed against the floor with a sickening thud; for minutes her vision was blurred and her temples throbbed with a dizzying pain. When the fog cleared, he was kneeling between her legs, fondling her as he had never dared to before.

Elyn tried to close her legs, to use her knee to push him back. Alec seemed possessed of some greater strength than his slight frame allowed. He was fueled by hatred or jealousy, whatever mad emotion ruled him at that moment. She hadn't a chance to stay him from his intent, and with that realization Elyn ceased struggling.

Alec felt her resistance ebb and cursed her aloud. She had outguessed him, and she meant to rob him of the pleasure he had every right to exact from her. She was a bitch, a whore; the names tumbled from his lips without thought. He fell on her with the full weight of his body and for seconds was content to kiss her, to stir some fight from her by using his mouth as an instrument of punishment. Elyn tried to escape, to turn her head to the side, but Alec caught a handful of hair at each temple to still her struggles.

In his mind's eye, Alec pictured his wife lying beneath the nameless, faceless outlaw, even as she now lay beneath him. He let go of her hair with his right hand and reached down to guide himself toward the warmth between her thighs. For the moment, he was swollen and hard, excited beyond any desire he had ever experienced, ever thought to experience.

She was his, by right, to possess, she had no way of resisting, and yet, momentarily, the sound of her weeping broke through the wall of his anger. In that pause, so brief, he felt himself go limp, felt the strength recede.

Alec collapsed heavily atop Elyn, impotently jerking his hips against her. It was useless; she'd stripped him of pride and honor and now his masculinity. He wasn't aware he was crying. Elyn was quiet now, staring at him without any emotion. He wanted her love back, the way it had been. *Why couldn't she see that was all he wanted?*

He rolled away from her, started to speak, and gave up. There was nothing he could say, no excuse she would accept. He rose, pulled on his nightclothes and robe, and walked to the door. There he paused, fingers whitening as he gripped the doorknob. "I *loved* you," he said and let the accusation hang in the air. For what it was worth, he had loved her.

"Let me send for ice or you'll—"

Elyn shook her head, though the movement renewed its ache. "It will heal, Syb. I can't risk waking the entire house. And I desperately need your help, only you must swear to keep a secret of what I ask. Promise." Sybil hesitated only a moment before she nodded. "I knew you would!" Elyn exclaimed, and the rush of gratitude in her eyes was almost painful. She caught her cousin's hand and held it tightly, then squeezed it hard as if to draw courage for what she must say.

"I am leaving Alec. Tonight, before he can stop me. Tonight, before I can reason myself from doing so."

Sybil reached up and just barely touched the puffed discoloration surrounding Elynora's left eye, wincing in pain herself at the obvious tenderness of the spot. "Let me at least dampen a cloth with cool water," she said as she drew away her hand. Then she rose and crossed the room. "Are you sure, my love?" she asked as she pulled a washcloth from a drawer and dipped it into a basin of water on her lavinette. The question was asked mainly to give herself time to think. Clearly, Elyn had been given reason to decide upon so drastic a course.

She returned with the cool, wet cloth and held it out to Elyn. "You do it; I can't bear the thought of hurting you. Somehow I knew it would come to this. Alec's been brooding for weeks. He's a cad for what he's done, but—"

The cloth felt wonderful against the heat of her eye, but Elyn took it away to answer Sybil before she'd finished. "No, I don't think there's a chance we might reconcile. Sybil, I *am* surprised. Didn't you tell me, not so long past, that you'd divorce Arthur if he made you unhappy?"

"Well, I did . . . but that was *I* talking, darling. Oh, I don't give a fig for the scandal, but have you thought what your grandmother would say?" Elyn's grandmother was the doyenne of the family, a veritable dragon who liked to control everything that affected her loved ones; and, despite the modern times, she was a proper Victorian lady. "Is there no way to patch things without . . . you know . . . ." Sybil mouthed the word *divorce*.

Elyn stared at her cousin. Where had all the fine brave sentiments concerning independence and feminine worth gone, and all the bold assertions about women's rights? Her disap-

71

pointment must have shown, for in a moment Sybil touched her arm.

"One rarely has to back up advice with action, love. I'm afraid I've run off at the mouth a bit much. If I influenced you to take this step . . ."

"This," Elyn said, pointing to her swollen, left eye, "was influence enough. There's nothing left between Alec and me, nothing to rebuild upon. I don't love him, Syb, and furthermore, he knows it. I am not the stuff of martyrs, I'm afraid."

"But where will you go?" Suddenly Sybil's face brightened, then her eyes narrowed like those of a cat who's cornered a mouse. "I know—you needn't tell me if I've guessed right— but it's back to that dashing rebel, isn't it?" She waited for some sign that she was right and instead saw Elyn catch her bottom lip between her teeth. She was treading on dangerous ground, poking her nose where it didn't belong. "All right, I apologize. My help doesn't hinge upon knowing your destination. What d'you want of me? Anything, just ask it."

"I'll need money. I hate to ask you, but Alec has charge of every penny. I shall return whatever I borrow, Syb." Sybil was her only hope, but the chance that she would turn her down was nearly nonexistent. "I thought . . . well, I must let Mother know what's happened, so I thought I might take passage to Honduras. She'll stand by me, I know. After all, she defied Grandmother to marry Father."

"Hmph—that was to marry, not divorce."

"Sybil."

"I know, I know, that doesn't help a bit. Well, I knew you'd offer to return the money; but if you do, I shall take offense and disown you. If I didn't help when you needed me most, I wouldn't love you as much as I'd claimed. You'll want to leave as soon as possible, to avoid trouble with Alec." Now that she was growing accustomed to the idea,

Sybil seemed excited by the chance to execute a secret plan. "You'll have to hide somewhere until . . . I know the perfect place, a villa belonging to a friend, Marita Guerro. She's an angel, no one's truer. She won't say a word and . . . oh, I *am* going on, aren't I? You'll be happy to be rid of me, no doubt. You *are* sure about this?"

Elyn nodded. It was, at the moment, the only thing she was sure of. She didn't know what her future held, where she would live, whether she might meet someone else and remarry. Everything seemed cloudy, nebulous, except for the decision that she would not spend her life married to Alec Barford. That she would not do.

London, England

May 1921

Chapter One

"Ah, might I fetch you something . . . perhaps a liquid refreshment?"

Despite a growing irritation with her grandmother's meddling, Elyn sensed Colin Burney's painful sincerity and wished again that she'd not agreed to the arranged evening out. "An iced tea would be lovely, thank you," she answered, smiling, a little awkward in the role of the older woman.

Colin was simply too young for her. Oh, he was a nice enough chap, not unattractive. If Elyn had been sixteen, she might have been thrilled with his invitation to a tea dance benefiting the Ladies' Society for Veterans' Aid. The fact was, at twenty-six she felt a great deal older than her twenty-year-old escort.

Quite properly he had called for her at home, bringing a bouquet of flowers, roses, in one sweating hand and a large box of sweets in the other. Grandmother had beamed her approval with the smugness of the Cheshire cat, reinforcing Elyn's belief that the date was predestined to failure.

Even at the age of seventeen or eighteen Elyn had disliked associating with young men her own age. She'd had little patience with their raw, unfinished look, with the insecurities that made them seem awkward and graceless, with their lack of the self-assurance that could only be garnered with time

77

and experience. She'd wanted someone to look to in moments of uncertainty. For that matter, her tastes had not undergone any vast change.

"Elynora? Miss Winters?"

Colin's voice startled her, for she hadn't expected him back so soon. He stood in front of her, a puppy, all feet and hands, holding a frosted glass of tea that, even as they watched, dripped onto her favorite blue crepe. Immediately he looked horrified, as if he'd committed the most unpardonable of sins. His hand jerked away the drink, and he groaned as more of it spilled, splattering her dress.

"My word . . . oh . . ." Colin was nearly petrified, rooted to the spot, his gaze transfixed by the spreading stain. "L-let me fetch a . . . a towel," he stuttered. "Clumsy of me. I *do* apologize. What . . . what can I do?"

"Colin, it hasn't ruined anything. I'll just go off and rinse the spot with a little water." Elyn spoke slowly, pronouncing each word with care so that it penetrated. It suddenly occurred to her that she was using the same tone with her young escort that she employed with six-year-old Jackie. "You're not to worry," she insisted. "No harm's been done." He didn't believe her. Colin's complexion had flushed a dull ruddy shade, emphasizing a healing blemish that heretofore had gone unnoticed. Elyn looked away, frowning. Her grandmother would hear a choice word or two of this . . . disaster in the morning!

"Can I not do *something*, Elynora?" Colin pleaded and uneasily shuffled his feet.

She knew, without benefit of evidence, that his palms were sweating once more. "There's nothing to be done, Colin. Believe me, I shan't hold a grudge. People would not be human if they didn't make mistakes. D'you think I've never spilled something—on myself or someone else?" He looked

78

up, disbelief battling with a hope that she was telling the truth. "Yes, it is true—I am not quite perfect. You may do one thing for me. . . ."

"Name it, please. Anything, there is no task too—'"

"Colin?"

"Yes, miss?"

"Call me Elyn. I shouldn't think we can't be friends even if we aren't meant to be more. After all, we've at least one thing in common."

"I cannot think what," he replied dejectedly. "I've made a muddle of the evening. My grandmother will—"

"Do nothing. Your grandmother, sweet as she is, and mine both deserve a good dressing down for their romantic intrigues. That's rather what I thought we had in common."

"They meant well, miss . . . I mean, Elyn."

"No doubt they did, Colin," Elyn agreed and patted the chair next to her. "Sit down, relax, *please*. Good intentions or not, they were interfering. You cannot let someone else, no matter how you love her, manage your life, Colin. Long after your grandmother is gone, *you* are the man who'll have to live with the choices you made."

"I . . . I wish that . . . that we'd been right for each other, Elyn. I do so admire your spirit!"

"Well, Colin, I'm sure there must be a girl out there," Elyn nodded toward the dance floor, "who has more spirit and fewer years than I. You'll never find her sitting here." Colin looked hesitant; he thought it improper to leave her. "Go!" Elyn insisted, giving him an encouraging push. "It will give me time to dry . . . and to think what I shall say to Grandmother."

"No. No, no, no. Absolutely not!" Elyn stomped her foot in exasperation, ashamed of her temper and yet justified by her grandmother's meddling. "If I marry again," she went on, *"I'll* choose my prospective groom, thank you! I shan't be pushed into a relationship that could affect my happiness— as well as Jackie's."

Anne, countess of Westford, stared at her granddaughter with an exasperation that equaled or possibly surpassed Elyn's. "Come now, you've been divorced for how long . . . seven years?"

"You *know* it hasn't been that long. Jackie's not yet seven."

"Well . . . five and a half or six years, then. What difference does a year make? You have been unmarried for too long. Jackie needs a man's influence now that he's older, and you—you need someone to talk with, someone with whom you can . . ." Anne paused, searching for the most persuasive phrase, "share the more intimate moments of life. In other words, darling, your bed has been empty too long."

For a moment the blunt statement threw Elyn. If there was anything of a delicate nature to be said, Grandmother usually spent hours talking around it. "I have spent most of my life sleeping alone," she replied finally, "and I've yet to meet a man who made me feel I wanted to change that habit. Furthermore, I can't quite understand your attitude. *You* never remarried."

"True enough, but I was much older when your grandfather died." The countess's somewhat severe expression softened, and she reached out for Elyn's hand. "You have been without a man since your divorce . . . you weren't even twenty."

"Grandmother, I never had a man. Oh, I don't mean physically—I have Jackie to show I'm not a virgin. I mean . . . oh, what do I mean? Alec was a baby. I couldn't trust him, I couldn't lean on him, he was never there when I needed him." Elyn squeezed her grandmother's hand and sat on the settee beside her. "Don't you see, I can't afford to make another mistake. If I marry again, I shall have to stick with it, whether or not I'm happy, whether or not he makes a good father for Jackie."

"I understand your caution, dear. I even admire it. What I cannot do is condone your behavior. You can't be so afraid of failure that you allow it to control your life. And if you cannot decide, then I feel impelled to help you with the problem."

Elyn withdrew her hand from her grandmother's. She might as well have been talking to a wall. "I haven't a problem, nor have I asked for your help. Grandmother, I am well over the age of consent, I have been married and divorced, and I have borne a child." Her voice was rising steadily, a sure sign she was losing this battle of wits. "I don't need you to find me a husband!" Lord, why was she so nervous? There was nothing her grandmother could do to make her marry against her will. *Or was there?* "I simply refuse to accede to your plans," Elyn asserted. "I will *not* cooperate."

Anne frowned at her granddaughter's obstinacy, though it was only a reflection of her own determination. "You've no choice in the matter, Elynora. Within the next six weeks, I shall present a number of suitable young men for your consideration. You *will* select the one with whom you are most pleased, and you *will* marry him."

Elyn stood, infuriated now by the old woman's imperious attitude. "And what if I care for none of them, Grandmother? This is 1921, not 1821 . . . no one is forced into an arranged marriage. It's against the law."

The countess let out a deep breath. "I had hoped it would

not come to this, my dear; however, I am determined to see this matter finished to my satisfaction. Now, you will do as I ask or risk losing custody of your son.''

Beyond fury now and with an oddly terrified feeling in the pit of her stomach, Elyn tapped a foot and glared at her grandmother. Despite her advanced age, Anne's mind was clear and free of the cobwebs of senility. Or it had seemed so until this inflexible decree had been issued. ''I can think of no reason, Grandmother, why I should lose custody of Jackie. And to even hint at such a possibility reveals a cruel side to your nature. For my part, this discussion is finished. I'll forget your . . . threat, just as you must put aside your desire to manipulate my future.''

Elyn was at the door to the drawing room when Anne said, ''I had hoped you would not call my hand on this, child. And I still want very much to settle this just between the two of us. No one benefits by a public scandal. Still, if you remain stubborn, I will—''

''Will what?'' Elyn turned to face the dragon, her heart beating so rapidly that she felt faint. Behind her, one hand clutched tightly at the door handle, the other was clenched into a tight ball at her waist. ''Exactly what do you think I've done? In my wildest dreams, m'lady, I cannot imagine what trespass was so odious that it would warrant depriving me of my child or him of me.''

''I did say I did not want it to come to this, my girl, but I know far better than you what is best for your welfare.'' The countess of Westford leaned heavily on her ornately carved oak walking cane and with some effort rose to her feet. She took a moment to steady herself, then crossed cautiously to the fireplace. Above the mantel hung a picture of her father, the third earl of Westford. The artist's style was dark and somber and suited Henry Fitz Morough's bejowled intensity.

She and he were really quite alike, Anne thought as she stared up at the painting. Both of them had always been sure of what they wanted in life and how best to obtain it. Now what Anne wanted most was to see her granddaughter remarry a man of whom *she* approved. Jackie would be the next earl, but what if something happened to him before he was grown and had children of his own? Anne would not chance losing the family title. She must have more male heirs from Elynora; it was a necessity.

"I am waiting, Grandmother, though for the life of me I cannot say why. This nonsense—"

Anne turned to face her granddaughter with surprising agility. "It is not nonsense, child, and may I remind you to whom you are speaking? I never allowed you to address me in that tone of voice when you were younger, I shan't allow it now." For a moment Anne's face was flushed with righteous anger, then as she realized she'd lost her composure, her much-vaunted composure, the grande dame inhaled deeply and sighed. "You are puzzled. Let me remind you of a period some years ago when you were seeing a gentleman by the name of Stephens. Does that name elicit any remembrance, my dear?"

Elyn's brow furrowed as she wondered what lay behind her grandmother's question. Of course she remembered. Leslie Stephens had filled a void in her life, an emptiness of spirit that all her maternal devotion to Jackie had not eased. Leslie wasn't the first man she had dated after the divorce, but when he had come along, with his unorthodox views and roguish charm, he had made the others pale in comparison. Oddly enough, it was his politics that had brought them together and, finally, ended the brief romance they'd shared. Leslie's real love was socialism and in his devotion he'd become fanatical. For a few brief weeks Elyn had thought herself in love with him. He believed in equality, in freedom for all classes, in beauty, in truth. Unfortunately, he also believed that all his lofty ideals were meant to be realized in a very short time. He was a revolutionary, bent on toppling the existing structure of society before his "utopia" could supplant it.

"I'm afraid I still don't understand," Elyn answered, and indeed, her violet eyes were wide and puzzled. "What has this demand of yours to do with Leslie? I haven't seen him in years."

"Did you know that Mr. Stephens was a Bolshevik?"

Elyn's frown deepened. "A socialist, Grandmother," she corrected. "There *is* a difference."

"None that I can see," sniffed Anne. "Both mean to change the order of the civilized world, and that, my darling, can only bode evil for our class. That is enough to condemn you, in my eyes and in the view of a court of law, as being unfit to raise young Jonathan. I should think that I'll not even have to mention your affair with him."

"Affair?" The two nights she'd spent with Leslie some five years before could hardly be termed an affair. She had in no manner compromised her son's morals or hurt anyone but herself. She had found no fault with Leslie's lovemaking; in fact, he had seen her through a most difficult transition from shy young divorcée to woman. They had been discreet; there was no way for her grandmother to know . . . unless . . . "You can have nothing but gossip, mere rumors to support your claims, Grandmother," Elyn answered, holding her chin high in rejection of the shame the countess sought. "What happened between Leslie and me—and I admit nothing—was no business of yours."

"You are wrong, child. It was I who raised you when your parents practically abandoned you in favor of traipsing after the filthy, unholy relics of some ancient savages. Who saw that you were properly raised, that your moral and social education was as complete as your schooling? Everything you are you owe to me, and I'll not have it said that I taught you to be loose with your favors! A woman, a *lady*, does not share a bed with a man unless she is wed to him in the sight of God. There is no excuse for your conduct, *none!*''

Past anger, beyond fury, Elyn felt an icy chill settle over her, cooling her temper and sharpening her mind. ''I shan't allow you to stand in judgment over me, Grandmother. You've no way of knowing what I did with Leslie; and as far as his politics are concerned, they are what ended our relationship. I've never espoused socialism, though I think the class system of Britain is far too inflexible.''

''You've only proven my theory, Elyn. He influenced you against your own kind. If all the Leslie Stephenses in this world had *their* way, we—you and I, and Jackie as well— would be sharing this house—''

''Mansion, don't you mean?''

''. . . With all manner of factory workers and . . . and common clerks and such!'' Elyn's sarcasm had only added fuel to the countess of Westford's indignation, and she stood her ground as well as any soapbox speechmaker in Hyde Park. ''Mock me, Elynora,'' she asserted, ''but I shall have the last laugh! You have been morally indiscreet and politically incautious. I've proof of it, sound enough to influence a custodial suit in my favor.'' The countess smiled, confident that her ''persuasion'' had gained her Elyn's cooperation. ''Unless you have decided to be reasonable.''

In all her life, Elyn had ever been respectful and obedient to her grandmother's wishes. Now, as the reed-thin, regal old dowager smiled at her, she had a desire somehow to prick the puffed hauteur of Her Ladyship's smug content, to deflate the woman's determination to ruin her life. "I don't think you've any proof at all, and I shan't allow myself to be browbeaten by your empty threats to take Jackie away. He is my son and he will *stay* mine. Whatever evidence you think you possess to the contrary, I in no way compromised my ability to raise him. Grandmother, have you forgotten the age of this 'indiscretion'? Or the fact that your righteous indignation is overly late in showing itself? What—did you brood for the past five years and suddenly decide I was unfit to keep Jackie?" Elyn sensed, in her grandmother's sudden air of discomfort, that she had hit upon a weak spot in her armor. Why, indeed, had she waited until now to broach the subject? What was so important now that she had had to employ a long-held bit of gossip to try to force Elyn's hand? A glance at Henry, third earl of Westford, and another at his daughter's face were enough to confirm a nagging suspicion. . . . "You're afraid for the title, aren't you?" The realization and its acknowledgment in Anne's pinched expression brought Elyn's hand up to cover a laugh, a near giggle at the preposterous idea.

"You want more than just an arranged marriage for me, don't you, Gran?" Somewhere between incredulous amusement and shock, Elyn felt as though she were dreaming. "Am I to be some kind of breeding animal, m'lady?" she asked. "Have you considered the chance that I might have only girls? You've already Jackie for your heir. Why should you want . . ." Her voice trailed off softly as she looked inward and remembered a long-ago conversation with her own mother. It had been something about "wanting to live my own life," and at the time it had seemed an ordinary desire for her mother to have. Now, considering her grandmother's calculating manipulations, that desire took on new meaning. Everything, from the emptiness of Elyn's childhood to the strange reluctance of her parents to visit England, took on new complexities. Had her parents "given" her up to Anne's care because she had attempted to regulate their lives, to influence them to produce male heirs for Westford? "I think, Your Ladyship, that you have already unduly influenced my life." Elyn turned away and opened the door, pausing just a moment. "And I swear you shall not have your way . . . not this time."

"I will!" the countess insisted petulantly, her shrill, angry voice following her granddaughter into the hall. Anne banged her cane on the shiny parquet flooring, frustrated by the seeming failure of her ambitions. "I shall disinherit you, missy," she yelled as an afterthought, a threat likely not even heard except by the servants. Once more in anger, Anne slammed down the tip of her cane. She had, perhaps, made a mistake in attempting to coerce Elynora. The girl was one of those who balked and became more stubborn when threatened.

"I should have played on her sympathies, made her feel guilty," she mumbled to herself as she made a slow progression back to the settee. *Damn my age!* she thought as she carefully settled her spare frame on the seat. And damn the withered limbs that seemed to take some special joy these days in not obeying her commands to move! Nothing paid attention to her anymore, nothing but the servants, and they, after all, were paid to. Her control of the events that shaped the lives of those around her was slipping, and she did not care to give it up just yet. She would find some way of bending Elynora's will to hers . . . there must be some way.

Upstairs, in her room, Elyn was lying on her back, gritting her teeth to hold back a flood of frustrated tears. Above her, the pale green canopy of velvet seemed a constant, something that had always been above her except for the brief period of her marriage. Now she almost hated the sight of it. Instead of signifying the warmth and security of Elyn's childhood home, now it seemed to mock her and the recent revelation of the darker side of her grandmother's character.

Grandmother wouldn't have her way, for by gaining it she meant to make losers of Elyn and her son. It was true enough that Elyn had shied from remarrying . . . but then, who wouldn't have, after Alec. The chance of repeating her vows to honor another man, only to find disappointment as she had with her first husband . . . Elyn thought that perhaps it was better to remain free. Jackie seemed not to mind having only a mother. He had long ago given up questioning why his father demonstrated no interest in him and seemed to be satisfied with one indulgent mother and an equally doting great-grandmother.

She had decided, in the last year, that Jackie needed the discipline of a good school and the company of other boys, and so she had sent him off to Gryrdale Academy in Suffolk. Her first apprehension over letting him board at school had quickly vanished. Jackie had settled in and was thriving. Jackie was a born survivor; he would make his way no matter where she sent him.

Elyn sighed, wishing she were as self-sufficient. This thing with Grandmother had her worried, though she knew, absolutely believed, that there was nothing substantial in the threat. Magistrates did not separate mothers from their children, no matter how wealthy or influential the person initiating the custody suit. It was *not* done. Still, if there was the smallest chance . . . Elyn sat up. She would ring Blake Harvey—no, better still, she would go see him. Blake had handled her divorce and been her solicitor since. He knew the ins and outs of domestic law and would certainly know if such a suit could even be brought before the bench. As she swung her legs over the side of the bed, Elyn smiled to herself. This time Grandmother had chosen the wrong person to try to intimidate. What had worked on Elyn's mother wouldn't work with Elyn. She loved Jackie too much to lose him.

Chapter Two

"Well, Nick, it might not be done in America, but I can assure you that the practice continues here. Why, my own marriage—and no one has been happier—was arranged by your great-grandfather and your great-uncle James's father. Once they'd come to proper terms, you see, we proceeded with a quite lovely courtship and wedding." Aunt May took a sip of her afternoon sherry and smiled. "I daresay, should your parents have kept to so civilized a custom, the world would not have suffered as calamitous a conflagration as it recently did."

Nick Rowan raised his wineglass to cover his amusement. Of all his grandmother's relatives living in England, her sister, Aunt May, was his favorite. She was very conservative and strictly orthodox in her beliefs, but, just often enough to keep him unsettled, she would pop up with a statement that was either very original or thoroughly irreverent. In any case, she was consistently entertaining, and he made it his business to drop in on her when he was in London. "I don't think the matrimonial customs of my father's generation had much to do with the war, Aunt," he answered. "It seems to me the kaiser wanted to expand—"

"Oh, tish, dear! One must use one's head and read the underlying reasons for discontent. Passion has replaced companionship; the bed has supplanted two cozy chairs set before the fireplace. People are so concerned with..." Aunt May raised her handkerchief to her brow, a little nervous with the turn of conversation, "with their bodies; they've taken to thinking with them instead of using their brains. I do love you, Nick, scamp that you are, and hope fervently that you'll take some advice from one who cares."

"What's that, Aunt? I'm all ears."

"Don't be cheeky, Nick! You must have some scnsc, else you'd not have remained a bachelor so many years without falling for a pair of shapely legs and a... an ample bosom. You must be compatible with your chosen spouse, there must be something more between you than... than..." Her nephew was laughing at her—oh, not openly, but she could see the amusement in the fine crinkles that framed his sea-green eyes and in the dimples that showed on either side of his full, pleasant mouth. "Oh, you *are* a devil, Nicholas Rowan! How can anyone be serious with you?"

"I'm sorry, May. You know I love you. Besides, I was only teasing. I think this matter between Colin and... what was the girl's name? Elynora Winters? I think it's singularly important. You have to know, though, that my sympathies are with your grandson. Colin isn't old enough to settle down, especially with a ready-made family." Whoever she was, Miss Winters *had* to be unappealing. She had money, breeding, connections; to his mind, she couldn't be good-looking as well. It was against the odds.

"Colin's mind is as closed as yours. He never gave the dear girl a chance. I honestly don't know how I shall face Anne. She is absolutely my dearest friend. Of course, Colin is a trifle younger, but age doesn't—"

"Six years *does* make a difference, Aunt. If you want the truth, she probably felt uncomfortable with him. After all, she's been married . . . she's traveled, I assume . . . she's had a child. Colin, much as we love him, probably looked like a baby to her. It was a mismatch from the start.''

May refused to give in. ''It was not!'' She leaned forward and touched her grand-nephew's hand, then whispered, ''Swear not to tell a soul, Nick?'' When he nodded, she continued, ''*I* was four years older than Uncle James. Even he didn't know, and you may believe me, it never made a whit of difference.'' Her nod seemed to ask, *What d'you think of that, eh, lad?*

''Well, you're the exception, love. Anyone who couldn't get along with you would be a damned fool.'' May frowned at his language but she couldn't cover a blush at the compliment. ''Seriously, May, we're twenty years into a new century. Colin wants to choose his own bride, when *he's* ready. Let him have his freedom for a while—he's only . . . what, twenty?''

''Aye, twenty, Nicholas, but a very mature twenty.'' She gave his hand a push. ''You've been a bad influence, Nick, what with your wanderings and loose ways.''

''Me . . . loose?'' For a moment May almost regretted chastening him. So it must have been with his parents, when he was young, for they never had gotten a hold on him. ''Despite all my faults—or maybe because of them, May— you love me. You know you do.''

''Oh, you're incorrigible! I can't for my life think which family you favor. Certainly it's not the Bruces. We've always been so proper . . . and dull.''

''Oh, I don't know . . . I heard a rumor about Grandma that'd curl your—''

''Don't tell me, I can only guess,'' May insisted. ''Pamela always had a wild streak. I believe, I do, that my parents breathed a sigh of relief when she married your grandfather, poor as he was.''

''Wasn't poor long.''

"No, had the devil's own luck...and charm. Only met him once, soon after he'd made so great a fortune in gold."

Nick couldn't suppress a smile. "Silver."

"Yes, whatever. I knew it was a metal. He brought her back home in style, did Gordon Rowan, and treated her like a princess. *I* was jealous."

"No...not you," Nick protested. "You're far too sweet to envy anyone, much less your own sister."

May nodded. "Yes, yes, I was. She was older and prettier than I, and she knew her own mind. I've always admired that quality." For a few moments Aunt May was lost fifty years in the past. The slight smile that curled the corners of her mouth for those moments made her look like a girl again. "And I wished I had met Gordon first. He was ever so breathtaking, so handsome."

"You were better off with Uncle James. I've heard more stories about Grandpa...he was no angel, May."

Nick's great-aunt smiled, and he recognized that certain twinkle in her eyes, a look that usually preceded some sharp witticism or irreverence. "It isn't the angels who populate a lady's daydreams, son. I'd wager, were I the type, that you've more of Gordon Rowan in you than *any* of his sons or grandsons have."

"Now the question lies—is that meant to be a compliment or not?"

"I'll let you puzzle that out. That should give you some pause. D'you know, now that I think on it, your sister Amanda also favors the Rowans. The rest of them, they're all Bruces or Douglases. What *is* Amanda doing now? Last I'd heard, she'd had twins."

"She's working on another, due in the fall sometime. As passionately as she's always done everything, that's how she's taken to marriage. She'll go on for hours about how happy she is."

"And knowing her," Aunt May said with a laugh, "she had plenty of eligible young ladies to parade before you! And you ran, even at a hint you might be caught. How old are you now, Nicholas Rowan?"

"Thirty-one, Aunt, and still enjoying my freedom, thank you. And to save you the bother, you can skip the lecture on loneliness and the joys of holy matrimony."

"Well, when *will* you settle in? Dear boy, if you wait until you're forty, you'll be an unbearable husband. All of your bad habits will have—"

"May, darling, I don't have any bad habits."

"Of course you do. You're vain, slightly arrogant, too independent, and . . . I could go on but I shan't. You know yourself, Nick. Haven't you *ever* been tempted to give up your precious freedom?"

"Nope." Nick grinned. "Not even once." A face suddenly appeared before him, a tantalizing flash of his past, two wide velvet eyes set in a delicate oval. As quickly, it vanished. "Actually, it's a near profession—evading girls with marriage-minded mothers."

"Well, when she comes along, the right one, you must let me know immediately. I should like to be the first to congratulate her . . . and to see what makes her so special. Domesticating a Casanova must, of necessity, require a certain mettle." Laughter tinkled from the older woman. "And I don't mean silver or gold, m'boy!"

"Can I let *her* know first?"

May waved a finger at him. "There you go again—you're too fresh, Nick. You must let her know first. I don't suppose it's occurred to you that this young woman, whoever she might be, could possibly refuse you?"

He shrugged. "Anything's possible. Still, if I wanted her badly enough, she'd be mine."

"Oh, Nick, you've enough confidence to pledge half of it to charity! Give some to your cousin Colin. I think it was his lack of it that made Elynora refuse his suit."

"I doubt it. She's older, more experienced, she's been divorced. That was a surprise—I'd have never thought you would allow your only grandson to court a divorcée."

"My dear boy, she's not just *any* divorcée. Elynora Winters is the only granddaughter of my dearest friend. Why, her pedigree extends back to Saxon England, possibly before it. So she's divorced. People *do* make mistakes."

"How modern you are, Aunt—when you want to be."

"And how critical you can be. I think you're getting stodgy in your advancing years."

"Stodgy?" Nick choked on his swallow of wine and sputtered the word.

"Stodgy," May insisted. "The young lady is as fine as *you* will ever find. Very pretty, too, and almost . . . Well, you obviously think I'm going on about her because I'm biased."

"Why would I think that?"

"But I'm not. It's the truth, she *is* beautiful. Very English in appearance, fair complexion, blue eyes—what I call periwinkle."

"So why hasn't some peer of the realm snapped up this living goddess?"

"According to her grandmother, Elyn's too particular. And likely, too, the child is afraid of making another mistake. Poor thing, must be a lonely life, rearing a child by oneself, shouldering all of the responsibilities . . ."

"What responsibilities?" She was leading up to something, and though he wasn't sure what, Nick suspected it somehow involved him.

96

"Heavens, there are so many when one is a parent!" May gave him a vague smile, patting his arm in an almost patronizing manner. "Why, there's moral guidance, proper etiquette, schooling . . . and to be a parent alone?" She shivered delicately and shook her head. "Twice as difficult. At least she doesn't have financial worries. Her mother left her money, and of course when Lady Anne passes on, Elyn and the boy will inherit everything. The title is Jackie's; until he was born, Anne was very worried that it might pass out of the family."

"What about her ex-husband?"

"Anne's? Anne is a widow, darling."

"I meant Elyn."

"Yes, I see . . . Alec his name was, and though I barely knew him, I can say I didn't like him, not a bit. Always had a pinched look, you know, as if someone had just fed him a pickle. They were divorced not long after the boy was born. He has never shown the slightest paternal interest in Jackie. An all-around cad. Remarried, last I'd heard, and to some vulgar little shop girl. There's no accounting for taste, is there, m'boy?"

Something jangled within Nick's head, a distant sound like the muffled buzz of an alarm clock. He shifted, uncomfortable with whatever had made him recall a time better left forgotten. Nora's name had been Barford. Was it possible . . . No, a thousand, ten thousand to one, the odds were against it. "Was Winters her married name?"

"No—heavens no! Elyn dropped that as soon as she was free of *him*. Her mother, naturally, was Lady Anne's daughter, only daughter, and her father is . . . or was Michael Winters, an archaeologist of some note." May suddenly realized that she'd been going on and on, "prattling" James had always called it. Her nephew's thoughts were somewhere

97

else. He seemed very distant, his eyes set upon some sight or memory that both pleased and troubled him.

Elynora. May had called her Elyn but "Nora" was a possible diminutive. She was divorced from a man named Alec. He was almost afraid to ask what her married name had been. Nick looked up to find May studying him with a curious look. He smiled at her and said, "I know what you've been angling for, May, and though I'm reluctant to mix in other's business, I'll talk to the young woman."

Nick's smile had broadened, baring an even row of white teeth. Even though she disliked mustaches, much preferring a full beard clipped neatly in King Edward's fashion, May thought Nick's gave him a particularly dashing appearance. She had nearly given up hope for poor Colin . . . he really was too young, but perhaps Nick would be able to turn the tide to favor her grandson's suit. Certainly, if anyone could charm a woman, of any age, it was *this* one. "Oh, Nick, if you would—you've no idea what this would mean to me!"

Nick waved away her thanks. "There's no one else I'd do it for, Aunt—and I haven't done anything yet. Mind, I won't press the lady into agreement. Colin would be miserable if she really didn't want him."

"I know, but you might persuade her to . . . to at least consider him. He's a *handsome* lad. And never would he give her a moment's worry. Well, you know him. I shall leave everything to you. Do come back to me, though, with something encouraging."

"I'll try, Aunt May. That's all I can promise."

Later that evening, after dinner, May caught Nick's arm and drew him aside. Her cheeks were flushed with conspiratorial excitement. "I've spoken with Lady Anne," she whispered, enjoying both the matchmaking and the need for secrecy. "Elynora has gone away for several days, but while she's gone, Lady Anne would like very much to speak with you. She's quite single-minded, Nick, and perhaps between the two of you . . . well, who can say what might be the outcome? You'll go, won't you?''

Nick would have much preferred to meet Elynora herself. Now he had to put aside his anticipation and face her grandmother, who, from what he'd gathered from talking to his aunt, was a rather formidable type. It was not exactly what he'd hoped for, but if Elynora Winters *was* the same Nora Barford he'd known . . . well, he would play it by ear. He wasn't sure what his reaction would be if he came face to face with her.

Promptly at ten the next morning, Nick arrived at Lady Anne's Belgravia townhouse and was shown directly to the gray drawing room, where, the butler assured him, the lady was awaiting his call. Though he had only a fleeting impression of the surroundings, Nick recognized the understated quality of the furnishings. Everything from the rich patina on the main staircase to the pink-and-gray Aubusson covering a good deal of the polished oaken floor quietly whispered of "old" money. Colin apparently hadn't seen what he was refusing along with the heiress.

The old woman seated near the fireplace merely raised her head when he was announced. It was several seconds before she nodded a dismissal to her butler and deigned to look at her guest. Immediately it was clear that Anne Fitz Morough-Whyte had never been strikingly good-looking. It wasn't simply a matter of the bloom of youth having faded; the woman had an arrogance in her expression, especially in her eyes, that Nick had seen in few men. She was used to power and did not like to be thwarted. He could well imagine that the lack of warmth between her granddaughter and Colin had upset her. Of course, she, the countess of Westford, would not show her emotions.

Though it ran against his grain, Nick made an attempt at a bow and murmured something like, "M'lady . . . my pleasure." The rudiments of English etiquette always escaped him. He was, after two generations, too American to believe in kowtowing to a title. When she nodded, indicating a chair opposite her own, it was again an imperial gesture. Whoever the granddaughter was, even if she wasn't Nora, he felt an instant appreciation of her endurance. Lady Anne certainly couldn't be pleasant to live with.

The countess leaned on her cane as she studied him quite openly. This time, rather than a nervous and perspiring young lad, May had sent a man—a quite handsome and, it seemed, very composed gentleman. Usually, even the strongest of hearts turned to pudding and caused their owners to quiver under Anne's scrutiny. He, Nicholas Douglas Rowan, only returned her gaze with a veiled hint of sardonic amusement. He *was* cool, this one, but she very much wanted to see whether he could manage to remain unperturbed under fire.

"So, young man, you are May's grand-nephew . . . from the colonies. What is your impression of the mother country?"

"I've visited before, Lady Anne, and always enjoyed your . . . sceptered isle. However, I'm afraid I've never thought of England as my mother country. There was some disagreement over whether it should remain so, settled almost one hundred fifty years ago . . . in the 'colonies' favor. We like to think it gave us a certain amount of independence."

Her first reaction was irritation, but the more Anne considered Rowan's answer, the less she found to dislike. He had called her challenge. Again, this was no mealymouthed boy. She nodded, allowing him a smile. "I stand corrected. I do

100

vaguely recall the disagreement of which you spoke, though on this side of the Atlantic we called it treason.''

"It would have been if we'd lost," Nick replied, grinning. "But, fortunately, we didn't.''

"Amazing, is it not, the difference winning makes? I make a practice of always winning, no matter what I set my mind to. Would you agree with that resolution, Mr. Rowan?"

"Please, call me Nick. I feel we're friends already, m'lady," he answered, though he knew as well as she they were more adversaries than allies. "And I see nothing wrong in your philosophy, except . . ."

"Go on, please. Though you shan't influence my actions in the least, I should like to know your opinion.''

He shrugged. "All right. There's nothing wrong with winning unless it means walking all over your opponent. I'm afraid I don't care for the inflexibility of 'always winning.' Each challenge has its own diversity. I prefer to take my victories from sources rather than people." The old woman had canted her head. Some of his ideas puzzled her. "If I play a game of cards and win, I've challenged my fellow cardplayers' skills. I've won over people. If, however, I bet a five-pound note on King's Cross to win at Epsom, I'm victorious over no one in particular.''

"Except the poor man making book on the race."

"There's a subtle, barely discernible difference. It's a victory with personalization. Besides, the bookmaker is in the business of taking risks.''

"Your philosophy is as interesting as mine," Lady Anne admitted with a smile slightly less chilly than the previous one. "However, I'll still take mine. Nothing gives one so . . . complete a feeling as the exercise of power, the subjugation of yet another opponent.''

"I don't see the world as full of opponents, m'lady. And I think I enjoy my life more than you do yours."

"This is something that you cannot know, Mr. Rowan." Her guest started to speak, but the countess waved a hand. "I know, you wish me to be less formal. I prefer not to address you by your given name . . . at least until I have what I want from you."

The lady had a way of tossing off intriguing statements and watching for a reaction. "Okay, I'll bite. What is it you want?"

"I should like to ask you a few very personal questions."

"For the purpose of . . . ?"

"Ascertaining whether you are a suitable match for my granddaughter. I know your connection with May's family certifies your stock, however . . . every family has its black sheep."

"I'm that, all right," Nick said, far too quickly to be convincing. "Back home in Colorado, ma'am, everybody calls me Black Nick." The very mention of marriage had made him nervous, and though it didn't show on the surface, his speech had suddenly taken on the broad tones of a rustic, the colloquialisms of the range cowboy. "I think there's been a major error here somewhere. I came to throw in a little support for Colin. I never tossed *my* hat in the ring."

"That's true, but your aunt and I discussed your eligibility and decided, pursuant to my approval, that you may—how did you so quaintly phrase it—ah, yes, 'toss your hat in the ring.' You are a bachelor, are you not?"

How could he deny it? Aunt May had no doubt given her a complete rundown. "I am, but I—"

"Good." Anne nodded her approval, and went on before her guest could make any further protests. "Your age is

... thirty-one? Is there some reason you have failed to marry?''

"Perhaps I didn't choose to." Nick was beginning to do a slow burn. He couldn't quite understand whether the lady was sincere (in which case she was crazy) or if she was trying purposely to goad him into anger. She didn't look crazy, but then the insane never did. He decided to humor her. "Ma'am, I don't know how much clearer I can make this. . . . The fact is, *I ain't interested.*" That should do it. Lady Anne might not be all there, but she'd never want her granddaughter to marry a foreigner who didn't speak the King's English. "And furthermore, just to set the record straight, I didn't fail to marry, I succeeded in *not* getting married."

"This is not an accomplishment, Mr. Rowan. Have you no wish for children? Sooner or later, everyone does."

"I'm perfectly happy with my nieces and nephews, thanks." The countess certainly was determined. "Look, there's something I can't figure out. Maybe you can clear it up for me." He was keeping his tone reasonable, low and even, just in case. "Why are you so adamant about finding a husband for your granddaughter? She's not ugly . . . and I assume she has the usual social graces. Why has she 'failed' to remarry?"

The old patrician's expression altered with amazing speed. He had touched on a sore spot. For more than a minute, Anne fought to regain her composure, and in that time it was clear how much she meant to triumph over her granddaughter's desires. Whether the young woman wanted to get married, whether she was ready to marry again, Grandmother wanted her wed. *Why?* What was so important? Suddenly it occurred to Nick that Elyn could be carrying another child. That would be reason enough, to save the family honor.

"Why doesn't Elynora want to marry?" Anne had just soothed the anger called up by Rowan's impertinent questions when he asked another. It was none of his business . . . and she was tempted to toss him out; but something, perhaps the fact that he was the most attractive of all the prospective suitors, made her rein in her temper.

Once again she was calm and spoke in a clear, even tone. "I don't know how you came by that impression, sir. Elyn is hesitant only, anxious to find the proper husband. She worries over making another mistake." Now that she was thinking calmly once more, Lady Anne tried to gauge her offer from the American's viewpoint. The social strata of the peerage seemed not to matter to him. His family had money, though not, she thought confidently, as much as she. What could she offer to catch his interest? Suddenly she had it and looked up with a genuinely pleased smile. "You haven't seen a photograph of my granddaughter, have you? No? Well, I think you will be pleasantly surprised. Come, give me your hand, that's a good fellow."

She thought a picture of Elynora would do the trick; he had gathered that much from the sudden brightening of her expression. His right hand was tightly gripped by a bony, age-spotted hand, and he supported the lady's elbow with his left. In her tight-lipped, almost pained expression there was a bitter acknowledgment of the one foe she had not been able to vanquish. Despite her wealth and position, Lady Anne, countess of Westford, could do nothing to stop age from drawing her closer to death.

Anne led him slowly across the room, annoyed at the strength and resilience she felt in his hands. He was strong and young and handsome. Yes, this was the one she wanted for Elyn. Oddly enough, he was also the one she felt least confident of entrapping. Pausing before the grand piano in the west corner of the room, Lady Anne slid carefully onto the bench seat. "There, take up the silver frame; no . . . yes, that's the one. That was taken on Elyn's thirteenth birthday. She went away that year to a finishing school in Geneva. Now, the ceramic-glazed frame. Ah, well, not a good choice, but you can see how she matured. That was her wedding picture, something like seven and a half years ago. I must see if we can have Alec brushed out of the photo.''

Nick barely heard her voice. The first photograph had revealed a pretty girl, a little thin, undeveloped. The wedding picture . . . for a moment his breath stopped, as he imagined the girl another year older and wearing a bright, multihued evening gown, a dress he'd tossed into the fire because he thought it didn't suit her. It was Nora all right. He wanted to laugh, finding her after all these years . . . divorced, available. For a second he entertained the idea of turning to her grandmother and shocking the old lady by asking for Nora's hand. But he didn't, because it wasn't fair to Nora . . . or Elyn, Elynora—whatever she preferred to be called. And he wouldn't be playing fair with himself either. He needed to get away—away from this sour dragon of a countess who smelled of lavender, away from the house where Elyn had grown up, and where, though it was unlikely, she might suddenly return and find him, unprepared after so many years. When he saw her again, and he was sure he would, he wanted to know what he was going to say and do.

There was a third picture, in another silver frame. This one was more recent, taken outdoors somewhere in the country. Nora leaned against the thick, straight trunk of a magnificent, aged oak. She wore a pale dress of some thin cotton material, a summer dress, and laughed at the wind that threatened to whisk away her broad-brimmed, beribboned hat. She held it on with one hand; the other held a small boy close in front of her. Her son. She hadn't had a son when he'd known her.

''Well, Mr. Rowan . . . or perhaps I should call you Nick

105

now. D'you *still* think I'm trying to strike so poor a bargain?"
Anne was quite pleased with her ploy. By his expression, the
young man was very taken with her Elynora.

"I think, Countess, that you shouldn't be bargaining at all.
I think the young lady's capable of finding her own husband—
without your help. And I think you'd better reconsider before
you lose her . . . and the boy. She doesn't look like the type
who takes commands well." It wasn't the answer she was
looking for, nor was it what she'd expected. He decided to
leave before she began some kind of harangue. His bow was
short and sweet, more mocking than courteous. "Ma'am, it's
been a pleasure . . . of a kind. I'm sorry to have to refuse your
offer, tempting as it is. I'll just see myself out."

Obviously stymied by her failure, Anne stared at him
open-mouthed. She was incredulous, flabbergasted, and, for
once in her life, speechless. He was at the door when she
finally found her voice. "Can't you tell me why, young man,
out of common decency?"

"That's just it, ma'am . . . common decency."

Chapter Three

If time had given Elyn an emerging independence, it had dealt less kindly with her liberated cousin, Sybil. The blithe woman-about-town lived in a two-story brick cottage in Ealing, on the edge of London's vast metropolis. Though she dearly loved her four-year-old Edward and looked forward to the end of what had seemed like an interminably long second pregnancy, she now considered herself a captive of domesticity. It mattered little that she had a full-time maid, a cook, and a live-in nanny; she was trapped by duty, burdened with responsibility, and hysterically bored.

Oh, for the old days, for the long nights of dancing and endless flirtations. She and Arthur had been quite happy, he with his nights at the club, she with a variety of discreet liaisons. That had all changed drastically, due to a brief visit home between tours of duty. Though Sybil did not resent Elyn for it, she believed her enslavement was indirectly Elyn's fault.

Arthur, the same Arthur who had sworn he hated children, who called them monsters behind their mothers' backs, had fallen in love with Elyn's son at first sight. At first his adoration of Jackie had amused Sybil. The boy was large and healthy, with pale golden hair that would no doubt darken to a light brown, like his mother's. His eyes were a deep green, and for a while Sybil had occupied herself trying to think who in the family had had that shade.

With a sudden and alarming rise of ardor, Arthur managed to be with her constantly, every minute it seemed until she was ready to scream for a moment's solitude. He had, after eight years of compatibility, developed an insatiable passion for her. In the morning, after lunch, after tea—no time was sacred. The attention was flattering but one could have only so many headaches. Seven weeks later, when they embarked for Arthur's new post in Rio, Sybil was pregnant.

Now the instigator, free as a robin herself, was coming to visit. Sybil couldn't blame her, really, for all Elyn had done was produce a beautiful child, but she did envy her her freedom. She might have had it herself, now that Eddie was over four, had Arthur not decided he'd like to try for a little girl. Part of her boredom arose from the forced inactivity attending her gravid state. After this, there would be no more, Arthur had promised her, had sworn on his own and Eddie's lives.

A horn tooted, raising Sybil out of her doldrums, and she glanced up to see Elyn's bright yellow Citroen convertible pull into the drive—yet another sign of her cousin's liberation. Sybil couldn't drive. If she wanted to go somewhere, shopping or out to lunch, someone had to take her.

Elyn came up the walk smiling, her arms full of packages. Halfway to the porch, she paused, puzzling over the grim expression on Sybil's face. "Is something wrong? Eddie isn't sick—"

"He's industriously healthy," Sybil interrupted, crossing her arms and resting them on the rounded fullness of her belly. "You must promise me, Elyn, after the baby's come . . ."

"Yes? What is it?"

"You must teach me to drive. Promise?"

"I swear, on my honor." Elyn laughed and, relieved that the request hadn't been as dramatic as Sybil had implied, continued to the porch and gave her cousin a peck on the cheek. "For the baby," she said as she handed over a box tied with pink and blue ribbons. "That's from Jackie. He said to give you his love."

"He's so much a little gentleman now. How is school coming?"

"Fine, but then I thought it would. He's very sociable." Elyn pulled another, flatter box from a bag and handed it over. "That's for the expectant mother—from me. I do remember what those last two months were like. It should make you realize things *will* return to normal."

Sybil felt her irritability give way to genuine pleasure. How could she have spent time resenting someone who brought her gifts and, even more appreciated, companionship? So Elyn's figure was slender and shapely, so she seemed a free spirit, able to come and go as she pleased. What mattered was that she cared enough to come by, out of her way, really, to visit. "I know they will, only now that time seems very distant," Sybil replied as she began to tear off the pretty, flowered wrapping paper. At her first sight of the gift, she gasped in delight and pulled the red silk blouse from its surrounding bed of tissue paper, exclaiming over the row of delicate oyster buttons that lined the shirred bodice. "Oh, Ellie, it's . . . it's gorgeous!" She held it up to herself, frowning at the way it draped over her jutting belly.

"I thought you could wear it with your navy skirt, the pleated one," Elyn said. "Hems are up this year—not that I have the courage to wear anything cut above the knee. Grandmother would have a stroke." She frowned at the mention of that impossible woman, though Sybil was too busy opening the baby's gift to notice. The crocheted cap and sweater was done in a soft yellow, because, though everyone was wishing for a girl, pink would have been presumptuous.

"It's darling, really, my love—you've such fine taste! And you spoil us famously. I don't know how to thank you. Can I get you something, tea . . . or coffee? A sandwich?" Already a bloom had come to Sybil's complexion, and her eyes sparkled with interest in something other than her own self-concern. When Elyn said she would have tea, Sybil rang for Sonya, the maid, and asked her to bring the service out on a tray.

"So, how are you feeling physically?"

Sybil shrugged. "Fat," she said, and added after a glance at her stomach, "and lumpy."

"Shouldn't be much longer . . . what, seven weeks, is it?"

"Seven, yes. I'm just so damned bored! There's nothing to do, no place I can go without looking like an elephant escaped from the zoo."

Elyn laughed. "*I* think you look lovely, though I do recall how awkward I felt—"

"Auntie Elyn!" The childish voice came from the door. Edward stood there, an escapee from the nanny, blackberry preserves covering his small fingers and smeared across his chin. Before his mother could shout a warning, he bounded out the door and into Elyn's arms. "What *did* you bring me?"

Sybil shrieked, and both the toddler and Elyn jumped before a pointing finger revealed the source of Sybil's displeasure. The front of Elyn's green lawn summer dress was fingerprinted in dark purple blue. Edward hung his head, bottom lip trembling, guilty. "Agnes! Agnes, come at once!" The nanny would come, there would be no visit with Elyn, no present. A tear slipped down Edward's cheek.

Elyn was smiling. She wiped away the single tear and

lifted Edward's chin with a fingertip. "It doesn't matter, love. I—"

"It *does* matter, Elyn!" Sybil broke in, annoyed with the too-lenient dismissal of the boy's guilt. "You'll never get the stain out. The dress is—"

"I can dye it. There's nothing wrong with a dark blue summer dress—with white shoes, it's very smart. There, you see, no problem. And I did remember, but you must give me another kiss first." Edward ignored his mother's frown, threw his arms around Elyn, and kissed her full on the mouth. "Oh, that was a good one!" Elyn laughed, as much at the sudden comeback from tears as at the to-do Sybil had made of a slight mistake. "There, dig in the bag. Yes, that's yours. I hope you like it."

"Agnes!" Sybil turned in her chair, as much as she could manage, and glared toward the door. "Where *is* that woman? I can't imagine how she's going to manage two. You haven't the name of a reliable woman, have you, Elyn? I shall go mad with Agnes."

"I never used a nanny. Agnes may be in the—"

"Yes, mum?" The nanny appeared at the door, flustered at having been caught off guard. "Oh, Edward, what've you done?" By the look on Mrs. Avery's face, there was no use explaining that she'd just gone off to the loo for a second. Edward seemed not to be in too great a trouble, though. He had a new toy, a large, carved wooden duck with a pull string. The boy tugged at the string and found to his delight that the duck's beak opened and closed as it rolled along.

"Quack. Quack, quack."

Sybil closed her eyes. "Agnes, if it's not too much to ask, could you take him in? And do wash his hands."

Edward quacked again, then smiled up at Elyn. Before her

employer made a further fuss, Agnes grasped a sticky hand and tugged Edward and his duck after her into the house.

Elyn, too, was in trouble. "I *don't* think it's amusing," Sybil said and sniffed. "The time has come for Edward to realize he cannot rush forward and ruin someone's frock with his messes. He must learn to be neat. Jackie was never a mess."

That was true. "Jackie's a perfectionist. He's tidier than I." Sybil glared, not sure if Elyn was pulling her leg. "No, truly, he didn't inherit it from me. Must come from his father's side of the family."

Sonya brought the tea then, as well as a plate of biscuits to explain away the delay. She waited to see if there were any further requests, then bobbed a curtsy and retreated.

Sybil served Elyn, then poured herself a cup of tea and took a biscuit, staring at Elyn with a thoughtful look. "Did you know, darling," she finally commented, "that you never say 'Alec'?"

"For good reason: I've put him out of mind."

"No, dear—I mean, when you refer to Jackie's father. You always say, 'his father's' this or that, never 'Alec's.' I just now noticed. I don't suppose . . ."

"Suppose what?" Sybil was staring off, one arm resting on the slope of her belly. She seemed to be concentrating. "Contraction?" Elyn guessed.

Sybil nodded. "A brief one." It was over; she glanced at Elyn and opened her mouth, then hesitated. "May I ask you a very personal question?"

"Of course. I think . . . well, *ask;* I may not answer."

"Is Alec . . . is he . . . oh, dear, I can't ask!"

"You needn't, then. The answer is no, he isn't."

"Are you sure? Well, of course, you *would* know. . . . I did rather suspect. Ellie, are we talking about the same subject?"

"Yes. And Alec knows. That makes three of us."

How can she be so calm? . . . Well, she's known for years, ninny! "I *thought* Jackie was too good to come of him." Sybil smiled, pleased with the admission. "I . . . I'm glad for you, love. Should I not ask who . . ." Sybil's fair brows furrowed, then her whole expression brightened. "It was the bandit, that dashing fellow who stole you—"

"He's dead," Elyn said quietly, guessing what the next question would be. It had been some time since she'd thought of Nick.

"Dead, but . . . how, when?"

"In the earthquake . . . you remember. He brought me to a rail station just outside the capital, then came into the city with me. The station was nearly destroyed."

"You know for sure he's dead?"

Elyn nodded. "I couldn't ask the embassy to search the ruins. If they'd found him, he'd have been arrested . . . they would have tortured him for what he'd done. A captured rebel was reason for celebration." Sybil wondered then if she'd erred in broaching the subject. Elyn spoke in a monotone, devoid of emotion. "The roof of the station collapsed, you see. Next to it, the Buenavista station was almost untouched. One man, I think, survived."

"Oh, God . . . don't cry!"

Elyn blinked, puzzling over Sybil's distress. "I'm not . . . please, Sybil—it's *been* seven years. There's nothing to cry over now."

Sybil was dying to ask more. She weighed her concern for Elyn against her curiosity and decided glumly that she would keep her questions to herself. "If you want to talk about it . . . now or ever, you know—"

"I *do* know, darling. Some other time, perhaps. There are more-current troubles to discuss, I'm afraid."

"Such as?" Sybil raised the teapot and questioned Elyn with a look.

"No, thank you. Such as my grandmother."

Sybil finished freshening her own teacup and looked up, wrinkling her nose. Lady Anne was infamous for her interfering ways. "What's she done now?"

"Decided I must be married and put the whole thing on schedule. If she has her way, I shall be engaged before you have the little one."

Sybil's mouth rounded in shock. This time the old bat had gone too far. "What audacity! Has she chosen for you, or do you get to pick?"

"Oh—my choice, but the field is limited to babes with the proper pedigree and blue-blooded, balding widowers."

"I'd like to have been there when you told her no."

"No, you shouldn't, it was an awful row. I lost my temper and she . . . well, she threatened me." Now Elyn truly looked as if she was about to cry.

"Threatened? How so?"

"She said she'd take Jackie from me." Elyn's hands were tightly folded in her lap. She looked absolutely miserable.

"She can't! It's impossible. There's no way . . . is there?"

"There may be, but I doubt it. I've spoken to Blake about it; he seems to think it's all bluff and smoke." Elyn gnawed at her thumbnail, her eyes fixed on the teapot, seeing nothing. Finally she looked up. "D'you know what I've done that's so terrible? I slept with a socialist." She would have smiled at Sybil's perplexed look had it not hurt so much. "Yes, twice, to be exact. Somehow she found out; perhaps she had me followed. I don't know, but she seemed to think it made me unfit to raise her heir."

"Who was he, anybody I know?"

Elyn shrugged. "No. You hadn't come back from Mexico

yet. I was . . . testing my wings." She smiled, a sad, lopsided smile. "For what the affair will cost me, I should remember the man with more fondness. I can scarcely call up his face."

"So, what will you do? You can't let her bully you."

"I know." What could she do, though? Her choices were limited. Perhaps she should take Jackie from school and leave. But where could she go? And Jackie was happy. She didn't want to drag him about all over Europe. It was, after all, her problem. She was an adult. "I just haven't had time to think. It all began last week; I suppose because I hadn't been cooperative, she suddenly presented an ultimatum. I am to choose one of the men of whom she approves in the next six weeks . . . or lose my son."

"I should investigate it further, Elyn. You know what a stickler she is for family honor and avoiding scandal. I don't think she'd go through with a suit that might discredit the Westford title." Sybil shook her head and reached for another biscuit. "Christ, I'm glad she's not *my* grandma. Makes me glad I was a Winters." Sybil bit into the biscuit, then gave a glance at her too-plump figure and left half. It would be a while after the baby came before she would be able to wear the new silk blouse. "Speaking of Winters, is there any word of your father?"

"No, and that is another sore point between her and me. Grandmother insists he's dead." Sybil's dark eyes widened, then narrowed as she frowned. Elyn shrugged. "She could hardly endure speaking to him when he came to visit. Now that Mother's gone, she no longer has to keep up a pretense of civility."

Sybil crossed her arms under her breasts and sighed. "You don't think he's dead, do you, pet? I know it's been over six months, but still . . . Mexico has thousands of miles of unexplored territory. Why, there are places in the Yucatán highlands where white men haven't traveled since the conquest.''

"I know, I told her that. She wasn't listening. Grandmother only hears what she cares to. I want to search for him. We certainly can afford to mount an expedition, and there are plenty of available guides."

"What a coldhearted bitch she is!"

"Sybil!"

"Well, love, the truth *is* the truth, isn't it? I should think you'd admit it by now. The woman is totally selfish and self-serving. Does she care that you want to pick your own husband? No. Does she care that she's cruelly threatened you with the loss of your only child to gain her way? No. And naturally you're concerned about your father. A girl only has one. But she's written him off, because it doesn't matter to her if he's alive or dead. That, in my book, is a bitch.''

Somehow it was difficult to think of the countess of Westford in those terms. Not that she wasn't a bitch. Everything Sybil had said was true. It was just . . . Elyn had been strictly brought up, nurtured in the belief that no matter how harsh any of her grandmother's decrees might be, they had been formulated for her benefit. Ingrained in her training had been a strong bond of loyalty that now, despite the most trying of circumstances, was still sturdy enough to draw an instinctive defense from her. "I rather feel sorry for her, myself. The lady, at the age of seventy-six, has yet to learn what we knew before we'd left the nursery . . . that anyone who must always have her way soon enough has no one left to have it with. I think she is lonely."

"She acts as if she doesn't need a soul in the world. Well, everyone has her day of reckoning. Haven't you enough funds of your own to finance the search?"

Elyn nodded. "From Mother's money. Somehow I think

116

she'd have considered it money well spent. D'you still have friends over there . . . in the embassy?''

''Hmm . . . we haven't quite kept up a correspondence, but I can give you several introductions. I don't know that I care for the idea of your personally accompanying the search party. The revolution is over, but the country's still unsettled. Talk to Arthur first. He should be home on leave next week; you'll have a chat with him then.''

''How does he like his post?''

''Madrid?'' Sybil cynically waved a hand. ''Once you've seen one Spanish capital, you've seen them all. God, how I wish Arthur had majored in some other romance language. Anyway, he'll be home for a fortnight, then he's back there for the next five months.''

''Pity he can't be home for the baby's birth.''

Sybil looked at Elyn askance. ''It was enough, my darling, that he was home for its conception. He'd just be in the way. I don't even miss him that much, except that it's so damned boring here, with no one to talk to and nothing to do but sit and wait.''

Elyn stared at her cousin for a moment. Sybil seemed to need cheering even more than she. A weekend in the city would do her good, do them both good. ''Syb? Why don't you come back with me? I could use some moral support, and we could go shopping or attend the cinema. I'm sure Agnes will watch over Eddie. Surely the house can get along without you for two days.''

Sybil sat erect, brows raised in interest. There was no reason why she shouldn't spoil herself with a little fun on the town. She could use a few things from Harrods, and a moving picture at the Gardens would be quite entertaining. ''You've twisted my arm . . . I'll do it! I wonder if they've a Fairbanks showing. I do so like him.'' She inched forward on

117

the white wicker chair and slowly, supporting herself by its arms, rose. "Don't you move a muscle, I shall just run off..." she glanced down at the awkward bulge of her stomach and grimaced comically, "waddle off and pack an overnighter. On second thought—you'd best come with me, else we'll waste half our weekend!"

Chapter Four

"It's a bloody disaster, but something about it challenges me," Freddie commented and turned to flash a grin at Elyn. "Yes, by Christ—I *shall* play Pygmalion to this shabby trollop of a room!"

Elyn closed her eyes for a second, praying for patience. Mr. Wilfred Parks—"Freddie" to those fortunate enough to secure his services—was society's current darling. If he insulted one with a string of blue epithets, the more his value as a source of titillation. Thus far, with her, Freddie had behaved himself. He had even dropped his affected Cockney accent and speech to address her in the King's plain English. For some reason known only to Freddie, she was ahead of the others.

"Let me just jot a few notes," he continued. "You're not the frills-and-lace type, eh? Which way did you want to go, then? French decadence, or perhaps heavy Spanish? Queen Anne? No?"

"*No.* I rather thought something on the quiet side. Tapestries, oils, a Persian carpet. Soft colors, mauves or roses . . . perhaps with a pastel green?"

"Ah, earnestly English . . . well, nothing wrong with that."

Freddie scribbled a few lines, then glanced up. "I've the feeling you're the independent sort, couldn't give a damn what the rest of us think, eh?'' A slight, introspective frown furrowed the designer's brow as he cocked his head to one side. ''Sound a bit hostile and bitchy now, don't I? Don't let it frighten you, love. All a part of the expected role, I'm afraid.'' He winked at her and added, ''Actually, I'm a ravin' heterosexual.''

''Good for you.'' Elyn took a step back and lifted her chin, smiling despite a slight unease. ''Mr. Parks . . . Freddie, I don't mean to seem rude, but quite frankly your sexual preferences are none of my business. As long as I don't return home to find the flat all done up in fuchsias and burnt oranges, I shall be perfectly happy. I trust you . . . your sense of aesthetics, rather, implicitly.''

Freddie bowed, managing to make the gesture graceful. ''I shall do my utmost to live up to your expectations. Fuchsia and burnt oranges, did you say? I'll keep that in mind for use on some old biddy I take a dislike to! Now, I expect by next week I should have some preliminary sketches done. If it's not inconvenient, could you come by the studio for a look-see at my swatches? Say around half-past-ten a week from Thursday? If you like what I've done, I'll treat you to lunch.''

''That seems fair enough. What if I don't care for your designs?''

''Heaven forfend! We shan't look on it negatively, but if that slim chance should occur, *you'd* have to take *me* to lunch. I take failure badly, so says my psychoanalyst. Have you gotten yourself one yet? No? I can recommend mine quite highly—he's all the rage with the foxy set.''

Even if he was flirting, Elyn found Freddie Parks most amusing . . . and relatively harmless. She might even enjoy a lunch date with him. Certainly she wouldn't be bored. ''If ever I *do* need one, I'll ring your doctor first,'' she promised with a laugh. ''I'm sure there are more than a few of us who

120

could use a bit of analyzing, though it might be opening a Pandora's box of problems."

"How bloody true, though I shouldn't think so in your case, Miss . . . look, I cannot continue to call you Miss Winters. I refuse, it's too formal. Elynora, isn't it?" At a nod from her, Freddie continued, "Then I shall call you Elynora. Lovely name, quite . . . it suits you. Well, I'm off, I am." Freddie tucked his clipboard under his arm and gallantly caught up her hand to kiss. Elyn smiled, surprised by the gesture. The interior designer shrugged nonchalantly. "You've inspired me, my dear. Oh—by the way, two of my men will be by later to take measurements, if this afternoon's not inconvenient. They can't make it before three. Will that suit?"

"Perfectly. I shall be in all afternoon. Anytime before half-past-five is fine."

"Good. They shouldn't bother you long. Both know what they're about, pop out the old tape measure and talley-ho! You've been most gracious, Elynora. I'm looking forward to a quite satisfactory relationship . . . purely business, of course."

"Naturally." Though not classically handsome, and inclined to somewhat bohemian tastes in clothing, Freddie Parks was quite charming. More so, certainly, than some of the men of whom her grandmother approved. Though it would deal the dear old thing a fit, Elyn could not see herself matched with this slightly eccentric interior designer. She held the door open for him and, with a smile, said goodbye.

"Naturally . . . yes, well, I'm off. If you think of anything special you'd like to incorporate, ring my studio." He seemed reluctant to leave and dawdled in the doorway. Finally he turned back to Elyn and smiled, his shyness at odds with his earlier flamboyance. "I don't suppose . . . you've probably already made plans, but . . . would you care to attend a performance of *King Lear* tonight? Royal Theatre production, it is, and I thought—but you're likely busy, right?''

''I thought you didn't care to be negative?'' Elyn replied. She hadn't plans, but there was so much to do before the trip. She had yet to call Arthur, or book passage on one of the liners bound for New York . . . and she desperately needed clothes. ''If I hadn't so many tasks to attend, I should be delighted to go with you,'' she explained. ''There are ever so many things to see to for the trip. You do understand?''

For a moment Parks studied Elynora's face. She wasn't refusing him because he wasn't of her class. He believed her—certainly anyone with a sea voyage and intercontinental travel ahead of her *did* have a thousand and one chores to do. ''Of course. Well, some other time, perhaps when you return home. Ta.''

After she'd closed the door, Elyn nearly changed her mind. She needed something to divert her attention from her own problems—and heaven knew, Lear certainly had enough of his. Had she used the trip as an excuse? No, it wasn't Freddie Parks she was trying to avoid; it was men in general. An awful way to feel, and to be sure, the responsibility for it lay directly at her grandmother's door. Maybe Elyn *did* need to see a psychoanalyst. No, what she needed was to be away from Lady Anne, and, to that end, taking this flat had been the first part of her therapy.

She turned and studied the room. It was not the ''bloody disaster'' Freddie had labeled it. The furnishings were simply old, dated, purchased some twenty-five years before, when her parents had bought the row house on Earl's Court Road. Again, refugees from Lady Anne's manipulating ways. They had been away too often to put it to good use, and for much of the past fifteen years it had been rented to Miss Eunice

Quist, now gone to to her reward. Elyn had nearly forgotten that she owned the building.

She should have moved out of Grandmother's years ago and made a separate life for herself and Jackie. Should have ... two of the most definitive words of regret. It had been easy, all too easy, to drift, to be welcomed back into the secure pattern of life under her grandmother's roof. A new baby, a young, inexperienced mother, and so many responsibilities.

In exchange for security she had given up her freedom, but, in light of the current confrontation, at too high a cost. Elyn crossed the front drawing room, absently tugging at the buttons of her blouse. She had time for a bath before Freddie's men arrived to measure the flat. Yes, a warm, scented bath would do wonders for her peace of mind.

In a few minutes the bath water had been drawn and a cube of lavender bath sachet had dissolved. Elyn stepped into the deep enameled tub and sank into water that rose above her shoulders. Luxuriating in the silken feel of the bath, she lay back, eyes closed, smiling.

Suddenly the telephone rang, startling her from a near-sleepy languor. She frowned, almost deciding not to answer it. She could not ignore it though; a small maternal voice inside her urged her to answer. One never knew when the school might call about Jackie. A few seconds later she was standing beside the telephone table, juggling the receiver in one hand as she tried to slip an arm into her robe.

"Yes?"

"Elyn? You sound breathless—is my call inopportune?"

"Blake? Oh, not really, I was only ... Blake, is anything the matter?"

"Yes and no—how's that for resolution? I felt I had to call and tell you of a conversation I had with a friend, an

123

associate really. I won't give his name, but he *is* a justice and knows about these things.''

"What things?"

"Why . . . your problem with Lady Anne . . . about the custody of your son. Hasn't been resolved yet, eh? No, I thought not. Well, to sum it up, he feels, my friend, that the matter is not something you'd want to test legally. I am sorry to—''

"Why?" Elyn interrupted. "I haven't done anything—''

"I'm afraid the fact that you admitted sleeping with the man—''

"Blake, I never said that . . . not to you, anyway.'' The house was warm, but Elyn suddenly felt chilled, as though an icy draft had swept down the hall. She gathered the collar of the robe closer about her neck.

"I assumed, Elyn. Was I wrong?" He waited for a few moments and heard nothing. "I see. Well, that in addition to Stephens's record . . .''

"What record?" Elyn was growing more confused with each passing second. Leslie hadn't been a criminal—at least not when she'd known him.

"He is believed to have been a part of a socialist anarchy group operating out of Antwerp before the war. The Yard has since opened a file on his activities in England.''

The cold that frosted her skin with goose bumps and sent a shiver rippling along her spine originated from within. One brief period of pleasure years ago had come back to haunt her. "You don't think . . .'' Elyn was afraid to put her fears into words. "Blake, there can't be anything on me in the files. . . . Oh, God, what shall I do?''

Blake Harvey took a deep breath, held it, then slowly exhaled. "I can't tell you, I can only offer my advice. I *have* taken care of all your legal affairs for the past eight years. I shouldn't push your grandmother on this, Elyn. She seems to be on rather firm ground here. Legally, she can't use her knowledge to force you into an arranged marriage; however..."

"However?"

"However, it would be difficult to prove coercion. The alternative to refusal is to risk losing your son. It's a sticky situation. You've not been given much of a choice."

"To say the least."

Elyn sounded defeated. Blake pressed for a definite answer. "What'll you do, then?"

"I honestly don't know. . . . Yes, of course I do. There are no choices left to me; I must do as she wishes or . . ." Elyn's voice trailed off, then came back strong and bitter. "The woman has gambled and, it appears, won."

"Do let me know your decision. And, Elyn?"

"Yes, Blake?"

"If it's any consolation, I think you've no choice. You have decided in favor of Jackie's welfare. I know how very important he is to you."

"More than you could guess, Blake. He's my life."

"What can I say, then, Elyn? Only that I wish the news had been more encouraging. If there's anything I can do to help, anything at all . . . just give the office a ring. And, Elyn, I'm sorry it had to be this way."

"I know. Goodbye, Blake." Elyn's tone was dull, vastly different from the breathless energy with which she'd answered the phone.

Blake Harvey frowned at the receiver, then hung it up and rang for his secretary. He had one more task to do before leaving for the day. "Miss Stock, please call Mrs. Harvey and tell her I'll be detained in town this evening. And make a reservation at my club for dinner and overnight." The older woman scribbled a notation, then bobbed her head and retreated to her own cubby.

Harvey reached for the telephone again, then hesitated briefly before he dialed the number of Lady Anne's Belgravia house. He'd been sincere when he told Elyn he was sorry. All things considered, it had been relatively easy to convince her that she hadn't a chance against her grandmother. After all, he had her trust. And he wouldn't have betrayed it for simply any reason.

Suddenly Lady Anne was on the line, her dry, papery voice rustling an irritable inquiry. "Well, young man—what've you to report?"

Blake liked neither the use of the term *young man*, for he was an established solicitor of excellent reputation, nor the idea that he should have to make a "report." "I am pleased to be able to say that your granddaughter believed me, Lady Anne."

Lady Anne's sigh of relief was audible; her tone revealed a triumphant pleasure. "Good. What did she say?"

"That she wasn't sure what she'd do. I should venture to say that within the next week you should hear a confirmation of your request of her. You see, she feels that she has no alternative but to submit to your greater wisdom."

"False flattery will get you nothing, Mr. Harvey," Anne snapped. "It is only results that win my approval, and you have, it would seem, produced some results. I shall instruct my secretary to forward a check to you tomorrow."

Harvey smiled, then nervously wet his lips. "And the bonus, m'lady?"

"If my granddaughter agrees to an approved match within the month, sir, then you shall have your bonus fee. I should not be too greedy. After all, you're receiving moneys from both parties in this matter—a most unethical practice. You shall hear, no doubt, if Elynora has agreed to marry. Pray, do

126

not contact me before then. I've no stomach for a man lacking in principles. Good day.''

Harvey nearly called Elyn back to confess his part in the sham. The old lady deserved a good dressing down. He should have given much to see her thwarted, but he had, unfortunately, already spent the money the countess was to send him. If not for that small fact, plus the desire for his bonus of 250 pounds, he would gladly have set her back on her heels.

Blake Harvey's call had utterly destroyed Elyn's anticipation of a relaxing bath. The water was cold, and she was even colder. She kneeled down and pulled the stopper from the drain, hypnotized by the swirling waters and the steady gurgling of the drain. He could be wrong . . . but Blake was never wrong. He was too methodical, too excellent a lawyer to err on such an important matter. And there was nothing left to do save to accede to her grandmother's wishes.

Elyn wriggled into her slippers and padded down the hall to her bedroom. She could take Jackie out of school, take him along to Mexico. Then if Grandmother wanted to start something, she'd find it a good deal more trouble. Everything would have to be handled through Mexican . . . No, she couldn't. Jackie was quite happy where he was. She sank onto the edge of the bed, despairing. Why did it seem as though all the light had gone out of life? Was it truly so horrible a fate—to make do with a loveless marriage? There were plenty of women— not so many now, but in the days of old—who had not only endured but prospered under the same circumstances.

But not Elyn. As far as she knew, she had only one life. Was she willing to hand control of it over to a ruthless, selfish woman? Hadn't she a right to find the man, if there was such a creature, who could make her happy? Elyn struck a tightly balled fist against the covers. *It wasn't fair, it just wasn't fair!*

Why— The doorbell suddenly tinkled, interrupting Elyn's stream of indignation. Still furious, she flounced to her feet and stomped toward the front door. By the clock on the mantel, the men from Freddie's studio were two hours early. They would simply have to return, at her leisure.

"Who is it?"

There were several moments of silence before a deep, resonant voice replied, "Nick Rowan."

"Who? I'm afraid the name isn't... Are you with Mr. Parks's studio? He said you'd not be by until at least three."

"No, ma'am, I'm not. I'm an old... acquaintance of yours."

Something about the man's accent, the way he'd used the word *ma'am* instead of *madam* or *miss,* was familiar, but the name Nick Rowan meant noth... "What did you say your name was?"

"Nick... Nick Rowan. Could we... uh... speak face to face? It might clear up your confusion."

She only barely heard him. Something had clicked. Elyn leaned against the door, eyes closed, remembering... remembering a lean, handsome face set with cool green emeralds of eyes, a tall, broad-shouldered man she had loved and lost. It couldn't be; Nick was dead. Elyn turned and with a trembling hand reached for the latch. She was half-afraid to open the door, afraid it was he, afraid it really wasn't. "Nick?" She opened the door a crack, looked up, and found herself staring into a pair of amused green eyes. "Oh, my God!" Elyn shrieked and promptly shut the door.

Chapter Five

Nick stared at the door. For a second, before she'd slammed the door, he'd caught a glimpse of Nora's face. It was a start. For the past two weeks he had vacillated, trying to decide how best to approach her. It was never a question of whether he should see her again, only of when and how to present himself. "Elynora?" That sounded oddly formal, especially after what they'd meant to each other.

He tried again, leaning against the doorjamb. "Nora?" No one else seemed to call her by that name, but he was comfortable with it. "Surprised you, hmm? Turning up after all these years. Bad penny, I guess. When I found you were living here, in London, on your own, I thought . . . Look, could we talk face to face?"

The answer came quickly. "No!" Elyn thought for a moment, glanced down at her beloved, frayed bathrobe, and explained, "I . . . I'm not decent."

Nick smiled. It didn't seem at all like seven years had passed. "You were always decent," he said. "Even naked." Her gasp was audible even through the door.

Elyn leaned her head against the cool, polished surface of the door. Incredibly, Nick was only inches away, alive after all the years she'd thought him dead. "Why aren't you dead?" she asked.

A puzzled frown lined Nick's forehead, and he cocked his head and stared at the door. "Disappointed? I mean, I'd like to be obliging, but that's carrying things—"

The door opened a crack. "I'm *not* disappointed, it's only that you've shocked me," Elyn answered defensively. "You've no right suddenly to make an appearance on my doorstep seven years after I thought you'd died." He still looked puzzled. "In the earthquake . . . at the station!" She was angry, though unsure of the reason. Perhaps it was that he seemed to have the advantage over her. He had somehow found her—but how? And he certainly knew more about her than she did about him. "Where have you been all these years? Never mind—do come in, but don't look at me, please. I was not expecting company." *Especially you.* Her hair was a mess and she wore no make-up; she must look awful. Of all the people in the world to see her so . . . why did it have to be he?

Elyn couldn't face him, much look into his eyes. Nervously she pulled the wide floppy collar of her chenille robe around her neck. In contrast—oh, but this was horrible— Nick Rowan was impeccably attired in a tweed walking suit and seemed markedly cool, calm, and collected.

Obviously Nora had just come from the bath. Nick took a step closer, catching a scent of something familiar and sweet . . . lavender. "You look beautiful," he said. She did, despite the shapeless, worn robe, despite the tangle of waves curling damply across one shoulder—she took his breath away. He hadn't quite prepared himself for this gut-wrenching reaction. He'd seen her several times in the past week, even followed her on the day she'd moved from her grandmother's, but nothing had prepared him for this schoolboy feeling of infatuation at being so close.

Elyn had a million and one questions, but she could ask

130

nothing dressed as she was. "Please," she said, gesturing toward the front drawing room, "sit down. Do make yourself comfortable. I shan't be but a minute. I—" She made the mistake of glancing up and stumbled over what she meant to say. "I think all I've stocked on the bar cart, there," she pointed across the room, "near the window, is a half-bottle of Scotch and perhaps some . . . some rye." It was impossible; she couldn't think *and* look into those deep, sea-green eyes of his at the same time. "I've just moved, you know. I'm surprised you found me."

"You shouldn't be," Nick replied. "Once I'd seen you, a pack of wild dogs couldn't have stopped me. Can I fix you something while you're changing?"

"Yes . . . no, I'd best not." Elyn remembered very clearly another time when he had offered her a drink . . . Mexican brandy, that strong and potent liquor, *aguardiente*. The eroticism of those memories now returned to haunt her. "Excuse me, please," she said in a soft, trembling voice. "Make yourself comfortable." She sounded inane. Of course he would—he already looked more at ease than she. Elyn turned and made a hurried exit, quite painfully aware that his gaze never left her until she was out of his sight.

In her room, Elyn closed the door and leaned her back against it. He was alive, Nick was alive and here, in her very own home! The fact that he'd survived the devastation was in itself amazing, but the chance that he would accidentally see her and then trace where she was living . . . the odds against its happening boggled her mind.

She couldn't keep him waiting; there were a million questions to ask. What had he been doing since they'd parted, why was he in London, how long would he be staying? Elyn opened her wardrobe and frowned. Suddenly the dresses and skirts and blouses that had been quite appropriate for any of

131

her recent social engagements seemed unsuitable. She had nothing to wear, though the huge antique wardrobe was full of clothing. Well, she couldn't very well ask him to wait while she shopped for something that would please her.

Elyn chose a white linen skirt and a white cotton midi-blouse sprigged with tiny embroidered wildflowers. She tried on the outfit, fussing this way and that in the mirror, and finally decided that, whether she was perfect or not, she must soon make an appearance. She sat on the bed and drew on her stockings and garters, then began a search for her shoes. In the week since the move, she had not fully organized herself. The truth of the matter was that she didn't know where anything was to be found. It had come as a sudden and abrupt shock, after years of being pampered by servants, actually to look after her belongings herself.

Nick had finally tired of waiting. He had gone through a shot of Scotch, refreshed his glass, and poured one for her before he wandered around, studying the lay of the house. Apparently Elynora had finally had her fill of Grandmama's interference. She was either renting the flat or had purchased it. He wondered how independent she was of her grandmother's influence. The furniture was older but in good shape; some of the carpeting needed replacing. Could she afford it, with a child to support? He knew so little about her.

In the bedroom, Elyn was close to tears. Everything was wrong. She had searched high and low for the white pumps to match her outfit. She'd found a pair of red calf high-heeled shoes, a navy pair, too, riding boots, slippers . . . everything but the elusive white pumps. Now the matter was out of her hands. She could only take the shoes she'd found and match her clothing to them. In a fit of temper, she tossed a boot across the room and started for the wardrobe, then paused.

She hadn't checked the bed. It was an unlikely spot but it was possible.

Nick came down the hall and paused before the only closed door. The flat was large and a circuit of the rooms had revealed that it was adequately furnished, with the added benefit of a large, well-cared-for garden behind the house. "Nora?" There was no answer to his call, but he rapped lightly and said her name once more before he tried the door.

Elyn heard the door creak just as she managed to reach and retrieve the second of the pumps from beneath the bed. Nick had tired of waiting. Dear, and what an awkward position in which to find her. She saw a pair of Italian, hand-crafted leather shoes appear before her and sighed, then brushed the hair out of her eyes and straightened. He was smiling, leaving Elyn somewhere between irritation with herself and with him. She held up the pumps by the heels. "Just found them. I shan't be much longer." Nick cocked a brow and grinned, and Elyn found herself justifying her predicament. "Don't *you* ever lose shoes?"

"Not under the bed. Need a hand up?"

"No, thank you. I suppose you think this is amusing? I only wanted to . . . to look nice. My maid always kept track of such things. I haven't quite had time to get used to life without her." Still sitting on the floor, Elyn wriggled her feet into the shoes, then struggled to rise as gracefully as possible. Why did she feel so ill at ease? She saw the extra drink he carried. "Good, you made me one despite myself. I'm glad. I could use a drink. Scotch, is it?" Elyn crossed to her dressing table, more to escape the proximity of Nick's body than for any practical purpose. She didn't want him that close; no other man had ever made her feel so . . . vulnerable to the threat of surrendering body and soul. "I'll just take a brush to my hair and pin it, then you shan't have to wait any longer."

"Why are you afraid of me?"

Elyn glanced at him in the mirror and arched a brow in surprise. "Afraid? Does it seem I am?" Without realizing, she gripped the edge of the table, her knuckles whitening. "You're mistaken, I believe. I've no reason to be afraid. I am..." To calm herself so that a trembling tone did not betray her agitation, Elyn picked up the brush and began to pull it through her shoulder-length waves. The action was soothing, allowing her time to organize her thoughts. "I am only shocked, still, to discover that you truly are alive. For so long I have thought of you as gone. Now, to find you living and breathing and... and here. You must give me time to think." He started toward her and Elyn half-turned. "Stop! Please, stay there. Don't come nearer, else I shan't be able to think at all. Sit on the bed.... Tell me, what brought you to London?"

Nick sat reluctantly, still puzzled by Nora's attitude. "My grandmother has relatives here," he explained. "I see them every two years or so."

"Is that where you're staying... with your relatives?"

"Yes, but I don't want to talk about—"

"Are you here for long?" It was rude of her to interrupt, but Elyn was shy of what he might say. Blake Harvey's phone call had rather thrown a kink in her plans to leave for Mexico. Now she had to solve that problem before she was free to search for her father. "I was planning a trip to Mexico," she went on nervously. "Have you been back since the revolution ended?"

"I'm not on a time schedule and I pretty much do as I—" Nick broke off in mid-sentence, his curiosity too strong to contain. "Why Mexico? I thought you didn't like that country."

Elyn put down the brush and searched the top drawer for hairpins. "I really didn't, but this wasn't exactly to be a pleasure trip." As she sectioned her hair and rolled it into a chignon, Elyn explained about her father. "My grandmother seems to have given up on him, but that's neither here nor there. He's *my* father—and I intend to find him. He's not dead; I would know if he were."

"Has something happened to change your plans?" He had no way of knowing how effective Lady Anne's measures had been, but she seemed most determined. He waited, wondering if she would tell him she had gotten engaged.

"No . . . well, in a way, something has temporarily set them back. I may be . . ." Elyn looked up, meeting his eyes in the mirror. She couldn't say it; the words would not form. "I may be getting married before I leave." There, she'd said it. Saying it would, no doubt, be easier than going through with it.

"Oh? You don't sound certain." Nick surprised himself with the bland tone in which he'd spoken. His heart was racing, and every nerve was taut, hanging on her answer.

How could she explain herself? She had accepted her grandmother's plan but had not yet chosen one of the proposed suitors. She expected it would be the most pleasant of them, but not young Colin. If by some chance she was able to find a way out of the marriage, she did not want *his* life ruined because of her. "I can't discuss it now . . . you must forgive me but—"

"It's none of my business, I know."

"I never said—"

"You didn't have to. Let's drop it." Nick took a large swallow of Scotch. "Where was your father when he was last seen? I might be able to help you there."

Elyn was finishing her lipstick, blotting the pale rose shade, when he made the offer. She stared at him, then half-turned, breath held in, hoping. "North of Mexico City,

135

near the pyramids of Teotihuacán. There is a village called—''

"San Juan; I've been there. It's not a populated place."
Nick rubbed his chin, trying to remember as much as he
could of the area. "Course, it's no jungle either, where a man
could get lost and never show up. Was he with a large
party?"

"No, not really. He'd an assistant named James Wyley, a
photographer, a cook, several Indian servants . . . I think that
covers everyone." She concentrated for moments. "Yes,
that's it. Not more than eight or ten altogether. Does that
make it easier or harder to find them?"

"Harder, I think. The more people missing, the greater the
chance they've left clues behind. They just completely
disappeared?"

Elyn nodded. "I know it's a rough land, full of . . ." She
had been about to say *outlaws*. Nick looked at her and
together they smiled. "You know I didn't mean *your* type.
Looking at you now, all proper in your day tweeds, so
gentlemanly, I can scarcely believe . . . That time seems like a
dream." She realized suddenly how nostalgic she sounded, as
though she wanted to return to that simple, otherworld existence. Elyn sighed, then remembered her Scotch and raised
her glass in a toast. "To your resurrection."

Nick lifted his glass, then watched her take a sip. "You
handle your liquor better now."

Elyn smiled and shrugged. "Seven years is a long time.
I'm older." She canted her head, eyes closed, still smiling.
"Did you know, I always thought Douglas *was* your last
name. I suppose you meant me to, else you'd have enlightened
me."

"I have another toast," Nick said, and she looked up, eyes
wide and curious. "To your marriage . . . and happiness. *Are*
you going to be happy, Nora?"

That form of her name—only he used it, only he could have given it that intonation. The question was startling, prompting Elyn to consider something she wanted to ignore, at least for the time being, with Nick Rowan here. "I expect I shall be happy . . . or, if not, satisfied. That's the trick, you see. If you believe you're satisfied, you shall be. I am a master hand at appearing to be satisfied."

"Who is he? Not that I'd know him. I'd just like to find out what kind of man attracts you."

Elyn frowned. Nick was leading the conversation deeper into a subject she didn't care to discuss. "I never said he was attractive. I really don't want to—"

"You've got one divorce behind you. Trying for a record?"

"I don't care for your tone *or* your questions. You've no control of my life, and if I am content to—"

"Are you, though . . . content to slip into another unhappy marriage? You said you were older, Nora. A mature woman wouldn't allow herself to be caught up in something that doesn't make her happy."

"You don't understand. There are reasons. . . I can't tell you, but you must believe I know what I'm doing." Elyn stood and took a moment to straighten her clothing. When she looked up, he was watching her again, almost as if he could read her thoughts. "Come, take a walk in the gardens with me," she said. "I've still so very much to ask you. Can you stay for supper?"

"You mean you've learned how to cook? I wouldn't miss it for the world!" Nick laughed. He started to rise, then changed his mind as she came up to him. "You don't really want to stroll in the gardens, do you? I saw them out the window . . . that's enough of a look for me." He stared up at Nora. She hadn't changed, physically, in the seven years. She looked as young and fresh as she had then . . . and he wanted her as much, possibly more.

Elyn sensed his desire even before she saw it warm his eyes. Nick wanted her, and she . . . though she hadn't consciously named the unsettled feeling within, Elyn now recognized her own desires and retreated from them. She liked being in control of herself, of her emotions, and this overpowering need to make love to him stripped her of all sense of self-control. Elyn turned away, the better to resist him . . . and herself.

Nick caught her arm. Nora stubbornly refused to face him, so he stood, circling her to catch her shoulders with both hands. "Look at me, Nora," he said and tightened his hold. "We aren't strangers . . . and we aren't a couple of kids who have to sneak and hide." She seemed to have shut him out. There was a very distant, shuttered expression in her eyes. He sighed. "Do you want me to leave?" His hands slid up along the slender column of her neck, fingers knitting together to cradle her head.

"No . . . yes—oh, I don't *know!*" Elyn raised her hand to curl her fingers around his and tug. She couldn't think logically with him so close. He reminded her of a time when she had been, all too briefly, happy. She longed to recapture the feeling of that time, but the circumstances were not the same. She was no longer a young girl, a captive. Responding to him now, of her own free will, as a woman . . . there were no excuses to explain such behavior. But, Elyn suddenly realized, there was no one to whom she owed an explanation. She was free to do as she pleased in the privacy of her own home. As Nick had said, they weren't strangers.

Finally, as she reached out to touch his cheek, Elyn looked up into his eyes. "No, I don't want you to leave. Whatever that makes of me, I will accept. Only, tell me the truth. . . ."

Nick brushed her lips in a soft, yearning kiss. "What, my love? Anything."

"Oh, do stop a moment!" His lips had found the spot, just behind and below her ear, that sent shivers down her spine. "*Now,* before anything happens, I must know if . . . if you are married. I can forgive myself for loving you, but never for loving another woman's husband." She held her breath for moments, waiting. It would seem impossible that so handsome a man, so charming a rogue, had not been snatched up by now. She wasn't sure of his age, but he was older than she.

He didn't hesitate. "No, I'm not. Never have been. And I'm not engaged, promised, or otherwise bound." Nick bent his head and kissed again the place that made her tremble. Up close, she smelled even more lovely.

Elyn closed her eyes and smiled. Impossibly, against the odds, he was free, and for some reason more complex than simple morals, she was deliriously happy. Her arms rose to circle his neck, every atom of her being was attuned to one goal, one purpose. She seemed to melt against him; she wanted to be one with him again. The years, long empty years without him, had not passed. It was yesterday and Elyn was safe, secure in the arms of the only man who had ever made her feel a woman.

They were both impatient. Nick's hands swept over her and she clung to him, carried along in a rising tide of passion, a passion so strong it coiled deep within her and sent little shivers of pleasure rippling forth at the slightest contact with his body.

Somehow their clothing seemed to disappear. It didn't matter that her blouse lay crumpled on the floor. What

139

mattered was the feel of his hands, rougher than the texture of her skin, caressing her bare flesh. Suddenly, with the same magical ease with which her clothing had disappeared, Elyn was lying back on the bed, clad only in camisole and knickers.

Nick lay next to her, the tips of his fingers brushing her skin, playful and teasing at first, then more possessive as they caught and tugged at the thin lace strap of her camisole. Exposed to the cool air of the bedroom and, as well, to Nick's admiring gaze, her breasts firmed, her nipples rising to dark rosy points. She closed her eyes and a Mona Lisa smile curved her mouth.

Nick reached out to cup first one breast, then the other, his thumb brushing lightly at a sensitive peak, stirring a soft, barely audible sigh from her. Elyn moved restlessly, sensitive to a gentle assault of caressing hands, yet impatient for what lay beyond the loveplay. Despite the years that had passed, his touch was familiar. He knew the curves and hollows of her body far better than she.

He moved higher now, his body half-covering hers, and Elyn tensed at the sudden, heated contact, then relaxed. For long, lazy minutes, Nick kissed her, thrusting his tongue against hers in a battle that finally dragged a moan from her. Memories, called up at his touch, returned to heighten the pleasure of reality. Remembering how skilled a lover he was, Elyn's anticipation was multiplied a thousandfold.

Nick would have liked to lie next to her longer than forever, drinking in her ripe beauty, renewing his claim upon her after so many years. She was so fragile and delicate, and yet . . . there was something of the survivor about her, something strong beneath the obvious femininity. That he wanted her had come as no surprise; that his desire to possess her, body and soul, had grown so much in the seven years of separation *did* surprise and even alarm him. Was he ready to commit himself to her? Could he take the chance of losing her again?

Nick groaned low and hoarsely. He moved, covering her body with his, then Elyn felt a gentle probing between her thighs. A moment later he was in her, deeply buried in one smooth thrust that curled her toes with pleasure. His mouth came down on hers, more roughly now, as if to brand her with his lips, with the heat of his kisses.

Elyn raised her hips, communicating her need in an ancient, unspoken language. She was on fire, and her nerves strained for that moment of consummation that would bring release. Nothing else, nothing in the whole world, mattered. In answer, Nick began to move; he plunged forward again and again, drawing soft, whimpering sounds from her. She was crying, impossible tears of sheer joy cascading down her cheeks. The first wave of feeling hit her with a dizzying force, radiating out from the pit of her stomach, spiraling in successive ripples across her skin, threatening to drown her in its wake.

Arching his hips, he slammed forward against her. She tossed wildly, digging her fingernails into his back, clawing and straining for the last degree of sensation. Sweat beaded his forehead; his entire body was slicked with it. He slowed his pace, drawing out the feeling, then began to pump against her in rapid strokes that swept him over the edge. He swore; at another time and place, the fierceness of his expression might have been frightening. The pounding of his heartbeat echoed the pulsing force of his orgasm.

Afterward, he stayed deep within her and both were too contented to speak. Elyn didn't want to move; she wanted to be one with him forever. Finally, though not without a certain reluctance, he rolled to one side, stretched, and, with eyes closed, smiled. A few moments later, Elyn was nestled close, her head resting on his shoulder, eyes wide as she studied him.

"I shall miss you terribly," she said with a sigh.

Nick turned his head to look at her and cocked an eyebrow. "Am I going somewhere?"

"Eventually you must return to . . . wherever you call home. I don't even know where that is. It is an odd contradiction to know someone so intimately and yet . . . know so little of his life. Where *do* you—" Elyn stopped in mid-sentence and listened. From the front of the house, the doorbell sounded, a muted but insistent ringing. Elyn sat bolt upright, one hand to her mouth. "Oh, my God! I totally forgot. The men from Parks!" Suddenly she realized her nudity, aware that her hair was damp and tangled, her face flushed. She raised her fingertips and touched her cheeks to find them hot, as though fevered. "I should tell them to come back or—"

Apparently she'd made an appointment, but whatever it was could wait. Nick caught her arm and pulled her back beside him. "You can't go explaining anything in the buff," he said, and then added in a mock British accent, "It just isn't done, m'dear!"

"But I told them to come and now . . . oh, dear. D'you really think I should pretend not to be here?"

He nodded. "I don't think you have much choice unless you want to explain me away. And I'm not getting dressed—not yet, anyway. What are they here for?"

Elyn explained about the renovation and the need to see it started within the next few weeks. "They should be finished by the time I return, otherwise I should have to put up with carpenters and tradesmen making a racket all day."

"You're really serious, aren't you—about this search for your father?"

Elyn raised her head and looked at Nick, then sat up. "Of course I am. Why shouldn't I be?"

"Don't get your dander up. It's just—well, the odds are against finding him. If he hasn't been seen in . . . how long?"

"Seven months, twenty days."

"If it's been that long, he's either hiding out on purpose or . . ." Nick hesitated. He didn't want to deflate her hopes.

"Or what?"

"Or he's dead. There are a lot of men in Mexico who'd slit a throat for a pound of coffee. I'm sure your father had money with him, tools that could be sold, supplies. . . . Chances are, kid, he was robbed and—"

"But there's been no trace of his personal belongings; nothing has turned up in all these months. I *am* going . . . and I *will* find him, even if . . . if—" Elyn couldn't bring herself to say it, to pronounce the words aloud. He wasn't dead; he was alive and she would prove it!

If determination counted for anything, she would find her father. Nick reached for and caught her hand, pulling her back into the circle of his arms. "I believe you. Exactly how are you going to manage this on your own?"

"Oh, I shan't be alone. I'm going to hire a guide. My cousin's husband, Arthur, is with the foreign service. He was posted in Veracruz when you ab . . . when you and I were last together. He still has contacts there and—"

"You want someone you can trust? Someone who knows that area?" Elynora nodded, eyes suddenly wide and interested. "Then forget about calling Arthur. I've got the man for you." She puzzled over this, head canted as she stared at him. Her lips started to form the word *Who?* and Nick smiled. "Me."

"You?"

"Me. Unless you have some objection?"

143

"No, but . . . how can you take the time? You must humor me, Nick Rowan, and remember that I know next to nothing about you. I don't know where you live, what you do, whether you've family. All I do know, after seven years, is your full name and the fact that you're not married." Elyn's smile was a bit exasperated. "Precious little, considering our relationship."

"You may have a point. I'll tell you everything . . . well, almost everything, if you answer a question for me."

"That sounds fair," Elyn agreed, then wrinkled her nose at him. "You first, though." She was dying to hear about his life. There were so many things she wanted to know.

Nick grinned, a one-sided grin that deepened his dimples. "Let me see, where do I start? I was born in Denver, that's in Colorado. Know where that is?" Elyn shook her head. She knew woefully little of the United States. "In the mountains, the Rockies. It's a nice place to grow up. Air's a lot cleaner than London." He studied her face for a moment and smiled again. "I'll take you there sometime. Early summer's pretty." He was staring into her eyes; for a second he looked as though he were going to kiss her, then he made a visible effort to shake off what seemed very like a trance. "Where was I—ah, what I do for a living. That's hard to say, really. A little of this, a little of that. You might call me a jack-of-all-trades. Now, what else do you want to know?"

Wishing that he had kissed her, and wondering why he hadn't, Elyn stared at him, afraid of what she felt. There was an indefinable tie, something intangible yet strong that seemed to interweave their lives. She wanted him, and he wanted her, but how much . . . and for how long? Everything was such a muddle. "Have you any brothers or sisters?" A moment later, Elyn shook her head and answered her own question.

"Of course you do. Silly of me. I remember now, I saw a picture of them, quite a large family. How many brothers?"

"Five—and three sisters. I'm the youngest. How about you?"

Elyn shook her head. "No, unfortunately. Oh, I always wanted a brother or sister, but I'm afraid my parents never quite got around to it. I envy you. Are you close to them?"

"One or two. The eldest was twenty-two when I was born. Now, are you still curious, or may I ask *my* question?"

"Do I have to answer?"

Nick nodded. "Truthfully." Elynora arched a brow, then smiled, as if to say she had nothing to hide. "Okay. Tell me about your marriage plans. Who's the lucky guy?"

Elyn was not ready to answer. How could she explain about the arrangement—or the reason she must go through with it as her grandmother wished? She hadn't even had time, since Blake's call, to consider which of the approved men she would choose. "Well, we haven't set a date." That much was true. She couldn't meet his eyes. "You don't know him, Nick—I can't see why you should want to."

"I told you I was interested. I'm curious about the kind of man you find acceptable for marriage. What's his name? He must have one."

Nick hadn't taken his eyes from her face. He reached out now to caress the side of her cheek lightly with his fingertips. Elyn caught his hand, staring for a moment in frustration before she looked away. She couldn't think logically when he touched her, and he knew it. "His name? Of course he has one. It's . . ." Why couldn't she think; it was dreadful to go blank. "It's Colin . . . Colin Burney." There, she'd pulled a name out of thin air.

"Colin Burney? Of course he'd be English. Not titled?"

Elyn shook her head. "Why did I think a title might be

important to you? My mistake. So, how old is he—your age?'' Again she shook her head. "Older, then?" Nick wasn't sure why he was being so persistent. He wanted her to admit her problem without his revealing that he had already learned of it. "He's younger? Nora, you're not robbing the cradle, not you? There's no need to—you have to have a legion of suitors chasing after you. You're young—" he traced the shape of her mouth, set stubbornly now, with a fingertip, "and beautiful. If there was half a chance, I'd . . . no, forget that.''

"What?" For long moments, while she held her breath, her heart pounded, surely loud enough for him to hear. Did he mean . . . no, it was her imagination, her desire taking shape.

"It doesn't matter. You're engaged, right? You're an adult; you've made a choice of your own free will. I haven't any right—" Nick frowned. "It was *your* choice?"

Despite her best intentions, Elyn desperately wanted to admit the truth, to lay her problem directly in his lap and let him take care of it. He had nearly guessed; could she not . . . ? No, much as she wanted to, she couldn't. It wasn't fair . . . to him, at least. "Yes . . . my choice," she said finally in a dull, distracted tone. "It is, you see, best all around. Jackie is of an age now to miss having a father. It never quite mattered before, but now he's in school. . . ."

"And Colin . . . Burney, was it? Will he make a good father?''

"He's very nice, a little on the quiet side, rather shy—"

"You're not answering my question. Let me ask one more. If you were making a choice based on what *you* wanted, who would you choose—Colin Burney . . . or me?"

Elynora's eyes widened, and she stared at Nick, afraid he was teasing her, afraid she had heard incorrectly. *Dear God,*

146

she prayed, *don't let this be a jest!* She couldn't quite trust her voice; surely it would emerge in a wavering, awkward tone and betray her feelings. "I...I don't know what to say." This was the love of her life, the father of her child, a man who could make her melt at his touch—was she mad to hesitate accepting what was tantamount to a proposal? "Truly, Nick, you've...startled me so, I cannot think."

He was smiling. This was no spur-of-the-moment decision. For the past two weeks he had considered her predicament. It wasn't fair for Lady Anne to have her way at the cost of her granddaughter's happiness. But more than that, from the first second he'd seen her—no, from the moment he'd seen her photograph—he'd wanted her again. There was no reason why he shouldn't have her. "Just say yes, that you'll marry me," he said. "I'll see to the details."

"Are you sure?" Why on earth was she trying to talk him out of it? "You'd be giving up your freedom...and...and it will not be easy to become the father of a six-year-old."

"I'll handle Jackie. You're not to worry about anything—except finding a proper dress to be married in." His hand curled around her neck and he pulled her close, pausing when their lips were perhaps an inch apart. "You *have* said yes?"

Elyn nodded, then closed her eyes as his mouth touched hers in a sweet, gentle kiss. There was only one answer she could have given, one answer, she was sure, he would have taken.

Chapter Six

It was very like a fairy tale come true, this sudden, whirlwind marriage of hers. Though the wedding band on her left hand affirmed the fact that she was, indeed, Mrs. Nicholas Rowan, Elynora still thought she must be dreaming. She was too happy—did anyone have a right to such joy? And jealous—afraid she didn't deserve it, afraid that somehow it would be snatched from her.

As he had promised, Nick had seen to the details of the wedding—and with amazing efficiency. It was a pleasure to have someone take charge of her life and make decisions for her. By early the next morning after she had said yes, he had arranged for a license, found a Church of England minister, and even ordered baskets and baskets of white roses for the chapel. All she'd had to do was shop for a pale green froth of organdy and lace, complete with a wide-brimmed, ribboned hat.

They said their vows in the chapel of Saint Edward, near Whitehall. In great contrast with her first wedding, held with great pomp and splendor in the magnificence of Saint Paul's, the ceremony was simple, elegant, and quite solitary. If anyone else had been there, Elyn should not have noticed . . . she saw only the tall, handsome man standing to her left. And though Nick had responded to the Reverend Mr. White's ceremonial inquiries with a strong, sure voice, his eyes had never left her face.

The day passed as beautifully as it had begun. They lunched at a quiet restaurant in Belgravia, very near to her grandmother's house, then spent an hour or so on the river, heedless of the hired boatman's tourist monologue—two lovers drifting in a world of their own. Back at the flat, they made love and sampled Elyn's cooking, made love again, and dressed to go looking for a restaurant nearby.

She would never be a cook, but Nick was an excellent chef. He was, as well, much neater than she and more organized. It didn't matter. All that mattered was the days and nights of togetherness, the idle hours spent in each other's arms. Time passed, the world continued to revolve, but Elyn wanted endlessly to lie beside her husband and know nothing more.

Try as she might to avoid it, life, in the form of her grandmother's imperious summons, had intruded on their honeymoon. Relayed through Lady Anne's secretary, the message was short and direct. Would Elyn please present herself at two the next afternoon for tea in the gardens?

Elyn had expected to hear from Anne sooner or later, and though she would have wished a longer, more peaceful honeymoon, she had no reason to be leery of a confrontation. She had thwarted Grandmother's schemes, chosen her own husband, and there was nothing the old woman could do. Absolutely nothing.

Absolutely. Still, Elyn had insisted Nick accompany her. He had to meet Grandmother sometime, and what better time than now, when she was showing her true colors?

Now, standing before the house that had been her home since birth, Elyn was more nervous than she would admit. Perhaps she had made a mistake in bringing Nick along before revealing her surprise. She still hadn't told him of the threat her grandmother had used. It certainly said little for her family's morals, to admit that so close a relative would use coercion to gain her way. Elyn took a deep breath to calm the racing of her heart. She was grown, married, and quite able to make her own decisions. So why, with Nick holding her hand, did she feel intimidated, almost guilty?

Nick felt her hand tremble and gave it a reassuring squeeze. "Are you ready, Mrs. Rowan?" He was there, to protect her if necessary. The old woman was a dragon; she had tried her best to bend Elynora to her will and had lost. She would be shocked to see him—too shocked, he hoped, to reveal his previous visit. And she had not really lost, not completely. He had been granted her approval. Everyone had reason to be satisfied with the turn of events.

Tucking her arm in his, Nick walked Elyn up the long flight of marble steps. Once inside the mansion, they were escorted to the gardens and announced. Lady Anne, attired in a regal white damask day gown, was seated at a small table, hands resting on her cane, gaze fixed on some spot beyond the garden setting, past the river Thames flowing behind it.

When the butler announced them as Mr. and Mrs. Rowan and the old woman turned her head, it was difficult to tell whether she was shocked by Nick's appearance or by her granddaughter's presentation as his wife. To give her her due, she barely flinched, recovering her composure immediately to nod at them with a semblance of a smile.

"Grandmother," Elyn said, and more out of habit than affection she kissed the cool, weathered cheek Lady Anne offered. Then, straightening, she held out her hand to Nick and he came forward. "Grandmother . . . I should like to present my husband, Nicholas Douglas Rowan. We were married two days ago, at Saint Edward's."

The silence was thick, heavy with expectancy. Anne's eyes, more blue than her granddaughter's, swept down, then up Nick's figure to come to rest on his face. She smiled, and though he had never felt less like smiling, he matched the lady's pleasant expression for Elyn's sake.

She offered her hand, white and bony but surprisingly soft and smooth, for him to kiss. Though he had never considered himself a moralist, Nick found himself hard put to kiss it. Instead, he clasped her fingers and bent in a short bow, murmuring something about the introduction being his pleasure.

Lady Anne was exceedingly pleased with Nick Rowan. Of all the men she had considered for Elyn, this one had impressed her most, but she hadn't thought there was a chance that he might change his mind and pay court to her granddaughter. Now, two weeks after he had denied any interest in meeting Elynora, he was her husband. "Please...do have a seat, join me," Anne insisted now, gesturing to the other chairs. "Elynora, my pet, will you pour, please? You are a tea drinker, Mr. Rowan? So many Americans prefer coffee. Myself, I find it too strong a taste, one that lingers after it should."

To do as her grandmother requested, Elyn had to take a position to Anne's left, leaving Nick an open chair to the lady's right. He was no longer smiling when he settled his large frame onto the delicate wrought-iron seat.

The old lady was up to something. Of course she recognized him, but the fact that she hadn't even acknowledged their previous meeting...What could she possibly gain by telling Elyn he'd been here before? To calm a growing unease, Nick refused both tea and the little fancy-cut watercress sandwiches and made an excuse for an early departure. "We can't stay long, I'm afraid. Elyn and I have an appointment with her decorator. We're refurbishing the flat on Earl's Court.''

"I do believe my granddaughter mentioned that last week. She did not, however, mention you. How recently did you meet?''

Elynora had just taken a sip of tea. She looked up into Nick's eyes with a stricken expression, not sure how the question should be answered; then finally she swallowed, choking as the hot, sweet beverage slipped down the wrong way.

Nick reached out for her hand and asked if she was all right; then, reassured by Elyn's nod, he answered Lady Anne in a bland, unconcerned tone. "Actually, we're old friends. Elynora and I met in Mexico, some years ago ... at a party given by a mutual acquaintance. Isn't that right, darling?''

It was hardly an accurate description of their original meeting, but the truth was too bizarre to reveal. Elyn nodded, reaching for the silver carafe to freshen her teacup. Thus far, Nick was holding his own with Grandmother. He could, with Elyn's blessings, continue. For once, she had an ally, someone to intercede with Grandmother on her behalf. It was a delightful feeling.

"I should never have guessed. And you just happened to run into each other again ... how romantic. You seem to have swept my Elynora off her feet.''

"Yes, I have," Nick replied, then added an implicit warning: "And that makes her *my* Elynora now, doesn't it?''

"Yes, it would seem so. I offer you my congratulations, young man, for your ... how shall I put it ... for your good common sense. This alliance with my only grandchild assures your future security. And, as well, Elyn seems quite smitten by your charm.'' Lady Anne's smile was somehow unpleasant, almost smug, as she went on, "All in all, everyone, including your dear aunt May, should be satisfied with the union. You have told *May*, haven't you?'' Still playing her game to the hilt, Anne lightly rapped Nick's hand with the edge of a folded fan. "Shame on you! I see you have not. Well, love does make one forgetful, eh?''

Nick's eyes darkened in displeasure, but he made no attempt to deny her grandmother's words. Suddenly, for Elyn, the beauty of the past few days was tarnished. The utter and complete trust she had given Nick seemed foolish.

So, he had found her because her grandmother had arranged the entire affair. All the sweet words of love he had whispered returned now to haunt her with an empty, false sound. Nick had married her because she was an heiress. He was just one of those "eligibles" the countess had chosen as a proper mate for poor little Elynora. And who was Aunt May? As far as she knew, her grandmother had only one friend by that name, the same May who was Colin Burney's grandmother. Elyn bowed her head. She wanted to die, simply to fade away from the company of these two . . . conspirators.

The wounded expression on Elyn's face made Nick want to pull her into his arms. Her grandmother had won, or nearly so. Elyn was married to a man of whom the countess approved. So why, with her desire realized, did she have to gloat? He didn't know how to comfort his bride, nor did he wish to explain in front of her manipulating grandparent. "Elyn? Let's go. I—''

"How are you related to Colin Burney?'' Elyn asked, wanting to hear the truth from him, to see if he showed any shame at his part in this masquerade.

Nick opened his mouth, then shut it, silently cursing the day he had come to see Lady Anne. He could have found

Elyn on his own. "Colin's a cousin, second cousin really. May Burney is my grandmother's younger sister."

"My dear Elyn, I can't see why you're upset," the countess interjected, all innocence though she was quite aware of the havoc she had wreaked. "Mr. Rowan is acceptable to me, and now there's no need, absolutely none, to become involved in a battle over Jackie. Everyone is happy."

Everyone was not happy. Only the countess of Westford, wrapped in a cocoon of selfishness, was happy. Elyn fought to contain her emotions, to keep from crying though her heart was broken, but a single tear burned a path down her cheek. She swiped at it with a trembling hand and rose, turning blindly toward the house.

"Elyn? Wait—" Nick stood but Elyn had already run to the terrace door. "Son of a bitch!" He cursed under his breath but his words were audible enough for Lady Anne to express dismay over his language. "That's how I *feel*, m'lady," he snapped and turned away to follow his wife.

Inside the house, a long empty hall loomed ahead. Nick hadn't noticed much of the house as they'd been escorted to the garden terrace. It was a big house. She could be anywhere. Again he cursed; then, catching sight of a maid emerging from a room down the hall, he called to her and asked if she'd seen Elyn.

"Miss Winters?" Nick nodded, not bothering to correct the name change. "No, sir, I ain't, but beggin' your pardon . . . last I 'eard, she's not livin' 'ere no more. 'As a flat of 'er own in Earl's Court." The maid self-consciously pushed a strand of hair behind her ear and looked away, then spotted the butler coming toward them. "'Ere's Mr. Plim, our butler. If any'ne'll know, 'twill be 'im." The girl waited until her superior came abreast of them. "Mr. Plim, sir. Could you be of 'elp to this nice young gentleman? Looking for Miss Winters, 'e is."

"She's no longer Miss Winters, she's Mrs. Rowan . . . my wife," Nick explained. "Have you seen her?"

"Why yes, sir. Miss Elynora has . . ." Plim paused a moment and directed a stern look at the curious maid. "Sara, please go about your work. Her Ladyship doesn't pay you to be idle." Only when the girl was gone did he continue. "As I was saying, sir, the young lady has retired to her bedroom. She was . . . if I may be so bold . . . more than a trifle upset."

"How do I find her room?"

"It is the third door at the top of the staircase, sir, but I don't think—"

"Excuse me, Plim, I know you mean well, but the lady *is* my wife." He started down the hall, and the butler cleared his throat.

"Excuse me, Mr. Rowan? I am being presumptuous, but I've known Miss Elynora since she was a child. She doesn't like to cry, sir . . . or have anyone see her at it. If you'd care to wait in the solar, I'll bring you a refreshment and—"

"Thank you, no, Plim. I'm going up. Third door?"

"Yes, sir, third door," Plim answered, though a worried frown lingered on his face.

It wasn't difficult to find Elyn's door. Pausing by it for a moment, Nick heard the sound of a furious sob, followed by a series of sniffles. He knocked.

"Go away . . . whoever you are."

He tried the door, found it unlocked, and opened it. Elyn had been lying on her stomach on the large canopy bed. At the sound of the door, she lifted her head and glanced back over her shoulder. "*You,* especially! This is *my* bedroom, and I want you gone from it."

Nick moved, but only to shove the door closed with the

back of his heel, then assumed a casual stance, arms folded across his chest, ankles crossed. "You're forgetting something, Elyn. You don't live here any longer. Miss Winters no longer exists."

"A mistake I'll soon rectify, you may be sure. You lied to me, Nicholas Rowan, and that's reason enough for an annulment. Now, leave my room before I call Plim."

"And what will Plim do? Elyn, be sensible. He's an old man—I outweigh him by forty pounds and stand a good six inches taller. Why should he get hurt because we're having a minor disagreement?"

"*Minor?*" Elyn squealed, offended with all her heart by the cavalier attitude of a man she was already beginning to think of as her *ex*-husband, "Minor, Nick, is not deceit and betrayal. Minor is not entrapping a woman in a marriage to better your lot in life!" He looked so cool, so controlled, while her own sputtering fury made her even more helpless with rage. "I trusted you, you . . . bastard!"

"Ah, I love an English accent. Even the word *bastard* is said with such significance, such fine delivery." Nick unfolded his arms, straightened, and strolled over to the bed. "Fortunately, I don't take offense easily. It's good only one of us is thin-skinned."

"Stay away!" Elyn warned. As he approached, she rolled and came up kneeling, poised at the opposite side of the bed, ready to slip off if he made a move toward her. "I know how you are—a kiss or two and everything's all better. Well, it shan't work on me. Don't you dare touch me."

"Wouldn't dream of it," Nick answered. "You don't mind if I sit, though?" He didn't bother to wait for a reply; he was going to sit whether she objected or not. At the moment, Elyn looked like a little girl. Her cheeks were tear-stained, and her bottom lip pouted. "Look, Elyn . . . we're both adults," he began. "Why don't we discuss this calmly, without resorting to name-calling or accusations?" Nick paused for a deep breath. Lady Anne had certainly set him up. "I admit that you might have had some reason to be upset about—"

"*Some* reason? I discover you've lied to me, that you're only a part of my grandmother's schemes—ooh, Nick Rowan, there is no name for someone as despicable as you! You are worse—"

"Why?"

"Why?" Elyn stared at him, unable to believe he could question her right to repudiate such a betrayal. "Because . . . because you knew ahead of time that I felt something for you, and you . . . you took advantage of my feelings. That makes you worse than the others. At least there was some honesty to be found in an arrangement where both parties knew what was expected."

"Why did I have the impression I was saving you from a fate worse than death?" Nick questioned. He was beginning to lose patience with Elyn's refusal to understand. "Your dear grandmother made it seem a good deal more stealthy than it was. I came over originally because I was interceding on Colin's behalf." That wasn't completely true. If he was going to be honest, he should tell her the whole truth. "Actually, I had an idea it was you. My aunt had said a few things that led me to think . . . well, I was curious enough to dig deeper. And I'm not sorry I did."

"Of course not; I can imagine the terms Grandmother offered." Elyn was too wounded to look beyond her feelings. Nick neither looked nor acted as if he'd needed money. His family, if not as well connected as hers or as wealthy, certainly was comfortable. "I don't suppose you'd tell me what the final settlement was, even if I asked."

"We never got around to discussing terms. I hope you can

believe that; but it's not really important after all. What matters, Elyn, is that we're man and wife, and nothing, save either of our deaths, is ever going to alter that. Nothing."

"I have divorced once and—"

"You didn't love him."

Elyn wanted to lie, just for one tiny second, to see if it would hurt him. It was painful to realize that he had the power to move her either to sorrow or to happiness by his actions, and distressing to think she might not hold the same power over him. But she could not lie, because he would know. Elyn shook her head. "I did not. But that has nothing to do with us. You are not the man I thought you to be. Suddenly you seem to want to control my life, and I'll not be—"

Nick had stretched out on the bed and was listening with a contemplative air to her assertions. "The Bible says that the husband is the head of the wife, as Jesus was the head of his church."

Elyn's mouth dropped open, her eyes wide as she stared. Something about the reference frightened her, coming as it did from a man she knew only as an outlaw, a rogue with barely a conscience to his name. They were strangers. She had married, given up her independence for, vowed to honor and obey a man she scarcely knew. "You are, Rowan, the last man I ever expected to hear quote the Holy Scriptures."

Nick cocked a brow and half-smiled. "I don't know why, love. I studied for the priesthood."

"You didn't." Fascinated by the confession, Elyn forgot that she wanted to stay her distance from him.

"I did...converted when I was eighteen, went off to a Franciscan seminary in New Mexico. It gave my mother a heart flutter she has to this day. Claims I nearly killed her." The corner of his mouth quirked and a dimple showed to the left of his mouth. "She had me all set to marry the daughter of a friend of hers. Anyway, I guess if I'd have stuck with it, I'd be a monsignor by now."

She could never, in her wildest dreams, have imagined a man less suited to the clergy than Nicholas Rowan. Elyn gazed at him, half in wonder, half in disbelief, unable to accept this new aspect of her husband's personality. She imagined him in a dark coat and clerical collar, ministering to his flock, preaching from the pulpit, giving absolution, and, try as she might to ignore her thoughts, all she could see was how handsome a priest he would have made. "What happened . . . why didn't you be—"

"Become a priest?" Nick slipped his arms beneath his head and smiled to himself. "I would have made a good one. My grades were high, I was dedicated, admired even, for my sincerity. Maybe it had something to do with the Yaquis. When I was nineteen, we took a supply train loaded with medicines and food over the border, to the Yaqui reservation. Seeing how they lived, or *survived* might describe it better, how many had been taken as slaves, how many would rather die than be taken . . . that was a far greater poverty than I'd have had to live with as a priest."

"Is that when you went to Mexico?"

Nick shook his head. "The revolution hadn't started yet. And I was still too wrapped up in theology, the word rather than the deed. I stayed at the seminary until I was twenty-one, almost twenty-two, until I started doubting my vocation."

"After so many years?" The expression on Nick's face was troubled, the memories clearly disturbing even now. Elyn was touched by the confidence, and yet she was almost suspicious of it, as though it might be a trick to win him his way.

"Hmm . . . it was getting close to graduation, commitment. I questioned everything, especially the vows. After what I'd seen in Mexico, a vow of poverty seemed a joke. It didn't mean going hungry from one day to the next, or sleeping under the stars without a bed or blanket. And celibacy...damn, that was the one that really threw me. The more I tried to ignore it, the more I thought about what I was denying myself...years and years of abstinence, cold and empty, ahead of me.''

Elyn tried to imagine Nick alone and leading a life of physical and spiritual devotion to God. The image was jarringly out of character with what she knew of him. He wasn't a thin, dried ascetic. Nick Rowan was a very physical, very sensual man who needed...well, it was true...who needed a woman—and not just any woman. Despite the aura of command surrounding him, Elyn was fascinated by him, by the way he made her feel. "And two years later, you were able to kill two men, without hesitation...or guilt. Nick, you mystify me. I don't know quite what to make of you.'' Elyn was less tense now; she slipped next to him, resting her head against her hand as she studied his profile.

Nick turned his head and smiled at her. "I'm not so complicated, honey,'' he said. "Most anything I do, I do 'cause I want to...or because I think I'm right. The devil may take me for killing Cardenes, but hell, I'd do it all again!''

"Including kidnapping me?''

"Especially that. Otherwise we wouldn't be married now. We belong together, Elyn. I'm not losing you a second time.''

Touched by the warmth in his eyes, by the declaration of devotion, Elyn felt a blush warm her cheeks. She lowered her lids, her fingers fidgeting with the bedspread. Finally, she glanced up again with very puzzled, violet eyes. "You don't even know me,'' she said softly.

"And you don't know me,'' Nick answered, reaching out

to raise her chin with his fingertips. Very gently, he traced the lines of her face, from the curve of a cheek to the delicate arching of a brow. "This face has been a part of my dreams for years. I know enough, Elyn, to want to spend the rest of my life beside you." He leaned forward and brushed her lips with his, then, sensing her response, kissed her more deeply.

Elyn lay back, staring up at Nick. He was her husband, he loved her, he said, and . . . suddenly she could not think of the reason they had fought. She didn't care . . . it wasn't important. "So, I am yours," she said with a slight smile, for admitting she belonged to someone, someone she desired as well, was an entirely pleasant sensation. "And it seems I am to allow you to lead me through life. Where, then, are we going next?"

"Away from here. After we've set the countess back on her heels." Elyn's eyes widened in surprise. "She likes to play with people as though they were puppets, make them dance to the tune she pipes. The lady hasn't gained a grandson, she's lost a granddaughter. I don't intend to let her continue pulling your strings, love. She's got enough venom for five rattlers—and she can spend it on someone else."

As much as she adored the feeling of being protected, time had made loyalty to Grandmother Anne a habit, one that, no matter how annoying her misdeeds, was difficult to break. Elyn was torn between guilt and a desire to be free of the old woman's meddling. She burrowed her head against her husband's shoulder and shook her head. "I can't, Nick. She . . . she's stronger than I, she'll—"

"She'll never try to interfere in your life again, Elyn. I won't let her. The more you let her have her way, the more she takes advantage of you. There's a secret to handling people like your grandmother." Nick swept the hair back out of Elyn's eyes and smiled. "She meant for you to be upset.

She didn't slip and say any of that by accident. And if she intends to upset you, don't let her. It's that simple. She can't bother you if you don't let her.''

"Then I shan't let her . . . but I can't do it without you.''

"I'll hold your hand. The only thing you have to remember is to stay calm and smile. Believe me, it'll drive her crazy.''

Chapter Seven

Though she had motored through Suffolk many times on her way to Jackie's school, Elyn had never taken the time to notice the scenery. The countryside was lovely, really, a patchwork of small, quaint villages set among gentle hills greening now in late spring.

This was, of course, the first time she had viewed the passing countryside from the passenger seat of her Citroen. She glanced to her right now, studying Nick's face in profile as he maneuvered the motorcar along the road to Lavenham. Although he was handling the car quite well, certainly he was no better driver than she. Indeed, he had taken several curves at what Elyn considered breakneck speeds. His assertion, at the beginning of their journey, that as the older, more experienced driver, he should assume responsibility for their safe arrival in Lavenham had spurred Elyn to a spirited if futile defense of her own abilities. Had she not driven for some six years without one accident? Had she not motored along the same route to the school time and again—without incident?

She may have, Nick had answered adamantly, but now that she had a man around to help ease the burdens of being a single parent, she could take life a little easier. Even if she didn't care to? Even if she didn't care to. Certain tasks were traditionally masculine, he explained, and though she had done admirably well on her own, there was no longer a need to be anything but a wife and mother.

Traditional, indeed! The assignment of certain perogatives to gender galled Elyn. She *had* done admirably well on her own and would continue to do so, despite Nicholas Rowan and his imperatives.

This time, and this time only, she had given in, seemingly acquiesced, but with a certain innate self-knowledge, Elyn realized she would find some way of wreaking vengeance on Nick for his high-handed manner. She was not in the best frame of mind to defend her rights. The entire week, since she had known of Nick's decision to go up to Gryrdale and meet Jackie, Elyn had been nervous and unsure, afraid of that one critical moment when she introduced Jackie and Nick.

Would they like each other? At the moment, that uncertainty seemed to rule her entire life. They were, after all, flesh and blood. Perhaps they would each recognize something in the other and . . . No, that was a vain hope. Relationships grew of affection and knowledge, not kinship. Elyn stared off through the windscreen, simultaneously dreading and anticipating the first meeting of father and son. Perhaps she should tell Nick; he might feel more at ease in his new role knowing there truly was something of him in the boy.

Absently Elyn gnawed on her lip, her eyes fixed unseeingly on some distant spot. How could she phrase so shocking an admission? She couldn't, at least not now. Later, perhaps, when both Nick and Jackie had come to know each other a bit. It was cowardly of her, but waiting would do no harm.

They were approaching the turn-off to Lavenham. Elyn glanced over at Nick and started to remind him of it, then paused. She would say nothing. Motoring, after all, was strictly a man's domain.

"I see you've finally decided to be gracious in defeat," Nick commented a short while later. He had been watching her from the corner of his eye for some time. Some ten minutes before, a deep, introspective, almost nervous expression had been replaced by an enigmatic smile. "I knew you couldn't stay mad at me for long." He raised his arm and rested it along the back of the seat, taking his attention from the road for a brief moment to smile warmly into her eyes. "You don't have to sit so far away, you know. No law against a husband and wife showing some affection, hmm?"

"None that I know of, but then I shouldn't care to be accused of distracting you from your driving." Elyn just barely contained a self-satisfied smile. She should tell him soon, before his inadvertent detour took them too far out of their way. Still, it was a moment of supreme pleasure, to be so right. She did not feel the least bit guilty, either.

"I'm not that distractible. Basic difference between a man and woman—the ability to do more than one task with a good deal of attention for both." Nick raised his hand to the nape of her neck and toyed with the soft, downy curls there. "Admit it, you've enjoyed the ride from London, and I've gotten us here safe and sound. Or nearly. How far is it yet to Lavenham?"

Elyn made a valiant effort to keep a straight face. "About twice as far, I imagine, as it should have been had I driven."

"Oh? And what's that supposed to mean?"

"Simply, that some nine miles back we passed a cross-roads. You should have turned left."

With a screech of brakes, Nick parked the car, shut off the motor, and faced Elyn with a fierce and vengeful glower. "Would it have been too much trouble for you to mention the turn?" he asked. Elyn looked all innocent and wide-eyed, wounded at the sarcasm in his voice. She started to speak, but

Nick forestalled any attempted excuses with a curt, "I know, I know—I was driving and—"

"And I'm *only* a wife and mother," Elyn finished for her husband, feeling smugly superior and quite virtuous. She was only acting in accordance with his wishes. "I know my place, darling—even if you had to remind me of it. You've my solemn promise, I shall never interfere in any area you deem to be masculine."

"You know the roads better than I do, Elyn," he retorted. "Couldn't you at least have given me a hint—"

Elyn recognized his effort to make her feel guilty, but she would not allow him to shift any of the blame onto her. "It wasn't my place to say anything. You're the head of the family. I'm nothing but a second-class citizen. In truth, I'm surprised I haven't been made to ride in the boot."

"That might not be a bad idea. I hadn't thought of it but . . ." Nick smiled. "Let's concentrate on making it to Lavenham now. Jackie will be waiting."

Touched by Nick's consideration for her son, Elyn stared down at her hands. She was embarrassed at her thoughtlessness. A mile or two down the road, she broke the constrained silence to say, "I'm sorry," so softly that Nick asked her to repeat herself.

Elyn gnawed on a thumbnail, debating whether she should say it again. "I said I . . ." Oh, but this was difficult! She glanced quickly to the side and found him, thankfully, watching the road ahead. "I was apologizing for my behavior. I should have warned you when we came to the crossroads. It was small and mean and, *yes* . . . petty of me!"

Nick managed to keep a straight face as he nodded and said, "Yes, it was." Even without looking, he could tell that Elyn had bristled. He went on, before she could erupt into another flare of angry words. "But I have an apology of my own to make. I was slightly . . . overbearing."

"Slightly? *That*, my darling, is a gross understatement of fact."

"All right," Nick admitted with a sheepish grin, "I wasn't exactly diplomatic. You can probably drive a car just as well as I can."

"Better."

Nick's grin widened, showing a dimple in profile. "Maybe better. I just don't take to the idea of being chauffeured around by a female. You'll have to excuse me for being old-fashioned, but where I come from, the men usually get the privilege of escorting the ladies. You have to learn to give in a little."

"So do you. I know quite a lot about compromise. I've been married before."

"Not to me you haven't. And Barford's a dead issue. I assume you had good reason for dropping him. Unless you still harbor some feeling for him . . ."

"You know I don't. I loathe him. I—"

"He is Jackie's father. I'm sure there must be some tie, emotional or otherwise, to the man who fathered your child."

There it was, the perfect opening, a chance to tell the truth. Nick had a right to know. Why was it so hard for her to talk about it? "You'll miss the turn again if you don't watch. Just up ahead, to the right, and Lavenham is some fifteen miles farther." Elyn held her breath, waiting for him to pick up the conversation, to press on about Jackie's father, but Nick concentrated on the road, lapsing into a silence that lasted nearly to the boundary of Lavenham.

Once an important wool town, Lavenham's former prosperity remained in the solid, timber-framed houses lining the street, in the guildhall and the wool hall, and in the church

169

beyond the village. It was one of the loveliest villages in East Anglia, a storybook town, serene with studied grace. Elyn loved it so much that she had come for visits more often than Jackie might have wished.

And now she was here once more, this time to present him to his new stepfather, a task that, even as Nick drove through Lavenham and on up the road toward the academy, sent a chill rippling along Elyn's spine. They were so close now to that one agonizing, awkward moment from which there was no retreat. Elyn glanced at Nick. He seemed unperturbed by what was to come, was even, if she was to judge by his expression, quite relaxed and even-tempered.

"Relax, darling," Nick suggested as if he'd read her mind. "If you've told me the truth about Jackie, you have nothing to worry about."

"The truth?" Elyn puzzled for a moment before she understood his meaning. "You mean about Jackie's temperament?" For a moment she was offended, but the feeling fled as quickly as it had come. "I assure you, no matter what his feelings, he'll behave as a gentleman."

Nick sighed, wishing there was something, anything, he could do to make this coming meeting easier on Elyn. He reached out, taking one hand from the wheel to squeeze her hands, which were nervously twisted together in her lap.

"Give it a chance, Elyn," he said reassuringly. "He may think I'm the greatest thing since Santa Claus. Most people like me on sight."

"*I* didn't!" she retorted, softening her words with a smile.

"Ah, well, how many kidnappers are well loved?" he teased back, and she laughed aloud when he halted the Citroen before the Gryrdale gates and asked her, purely rhetorically, "I was irresistible though, wasn't I? Come on, admit it."

170

By the time the gatekeeper had unlatched the towering wrought-iron gates, Elyn was feeling more secure with the knowledge that Nick truly wanted to love Jackie and be loved by him in return.

The school sat on fifty acres of well-manicured lawns and rolling, wooded hills. Formerly the estate of a London clothing manufacturer, it was a squat, almost ugly Victorian manse with little to recommend it save its immense size. Elyn had always thought that the family must have been pleased to get rid of the place and retire to some simpler, more pleasing dwelling.

Mr. Quartermain, assistant to the headmaster, Mr. Fields Petry, was waiting at the bottom of the stone steps leading to the entrance of the main building, known as the Hall. A young man not nearly as sober as his superior, he was, in addition to his administrative duties, in charge of the academy's athletic program, and was trim and muscular beneath his black scholastic robes.

As soon as the Citroen pulled up to the curb, Quartermain was at her door, helping Elyn out of the car, bowing over her hand, stumbling for a second and using her maiden name before remembering that she was now Mrs. Rowan.

David Quartermain stared at Elyn, wanting her no less now that there was no chance under heaven that she would consider his suit. Not that there ever had been. It was, he thought, a general failing of human nature to desire what one could not possess. From the first moment he had met Lady Elynora, at a tea to welcome the new boys and their parents last fall, David had been mad for her.

She was as beautiful now, or perhaps more so, as she'd been on that afternoon. The stiff organza of a midnight-blue cloche hat forced the fine curls and tendrils of her ash-brown hair forward to frame a delicate face highlighted by an air of quiet dignity. She was a lady, one of a vanishing breed as far as he could tell, what with the war and the new freedoms it had granted women. None of them, or very few anymore, no matter what their rank in society, knew how to maintain that cool, polite repose, that gracious mien that had to come of something within.

"M'lady, we feared you'd met with an accident on the road. If you had not appeared, I'd instructions from Master Petry to go searching."

Although Nick's expression was casual, he noted the concern in the young man's voice and in the way he seemed to hover around Elyn. She seemed slightly embarrassed with the solicitous display of courtesy, as if she wished to extract herself but couldn't do so politely.

"No need for any worry," Nick insisted and came around the car to offer Elyn his arm. Her expression, before her long, thick lashes veiled it, was grateful. "My fault completely. I'm not as familiar with the roads, took a wrong turn." He introduced himself then and offered his hand in a firm grip that was meant to leave little doubt in Quartermain's mind as to who was in control of the situation.

So . . . this was the American. Not a bad-looking chap, but a trifle overpowering in that typically colonial cockiness. Petry had commented on the suddenness of Lady Elynora's wedding, and his remark had caused at least one sleepless night for his subordinate. There'd been no announcement of an engagement, no banns published that he knew of. "Yes, well, the roads can be tricky when one isn't used to the way. Master Petry waited past the time you were due and then went on. He thought you might care to join him for lunch on the study terrace. With young master Jonathan, of course. Shall we go along directly?"

"We'll follow your lead, sir," Nick answered for them, and tucked Elyn's arm more tightly in the crook of his arm.

They found Fields Petry seated at a rectangular dining table, set for lunch, on the terrace. He rose as he caught sight of Elyn, smiled broadly and crossed to greet her, then offered his hand in a hearty welcome to Nick. His voice, no doubt from years of experience in His Majesty's Fusiliers, seemed to thunder as he issued an order to his second in command to retrieve young Master Barford from the schoolroom.

"Please, do be seated. The young gentleman should be with us shortly. A fine lad, your son, madam. Quite a popular boy, even with those in the older forms." The headmaster rattled on, independent of need for a partner in conversation. "Never had a chance to visit the States, m'self, sir. Been all over the empire, but never to our former colonies. Mustn't refer to them as that still, eh?"

Nick was saved from answering by the return of Quartermain. Behind him, nearly obscured by the schoolmaster's voluminous robes, stood Jonathan David Arthur Fitz Morough Barford, looking like an average little boy though he was destined to be the earl of Westford. Although he stood straight and tall, Jackie's momentary uncertainty showed in the wide-eyed glance he gave Nick before smiling at his mother.

"Come, lad, greet your dear mother properly," Petry's voice boomed. "Good, very good, nothing wrong with a show of affection. Mothers are the backbone of the nation. Where would we be without 'em, eh, what? Indeed, yes, where?" Petry chuckled to himself over something only he had found amusing, then looked up and gestured to the boy. "Come, Jackie, and give your new father the respect he deserves."

Jackie approached Nick warily. All eyes were on him; he could do little but make a correct bow and say politely, "How

173

d'you do, sir.'' Despite a dream in which his new stepfather had appeared as a short, bulbous ogre, the reality—this tall, well-formed man with a smile that reached his eyes—lessened some of his fears. Still, the man had come between Jackie and his mother, something no one else had ever been able to do. Too, it seemed as though he had moved quickly, in stealth, for Mother had not mentioned even so much as his name on her last visit a month ago. She looked anxious, Mother did, when he glanced over at her for a second.

Nick found himself quite impressed with Jackie's civility, with the obvious control of speech and mannerisms that made the boy seem twice as old as his six years. His table manners were irreproachable, and he responded to questions about his school activities and studies with clear and lucid explanations. Nick tried to remember himself at the same age, but all he could call up was a vague image of a shy, tongue-tied urchin with dirt-smeared freckles and large green eyes...eyes rather like Jackie's, now that he thought of it.

About halfway through the meal, Nick noticed that Jackie seemed restless, unable to find a comfortable position in which to sit. As the luncheon progressed, his agitation increased. Not for the first time, Nick silently swore an oath. It was damned hard for him to talk to the boy with Petry around. He didn't want to go back to London without discussing, in private, their new relationship.

"The pie was excellent...the entire meal was, Mr. Petry," he said finally, complimenting the shepherd's pie that had been the main course.

"Well, I shall tell cook how pleased you were, sir," Petry replied. "Though we are out in the country, we at Gryrdale do try to maintain the amenities. Rounds out the lads' social education, it does, to be exposed to a variety of gastronomical experiences."

"From what I've seen so far, the education at Gryrdale is quite well rounded. If I could make a suggestion..." Nick turned and smiled at Elyn. "Darling, why don't you catch up on Jackie's progress. He and I'll take a walk, get to know each other a little better."

Elyn stared at Nick for a second, caught her lip between her teeth, and then hesitantly faced her son. Thus far, Jackie had been the perfect gentleman. Was it expecting too much to send him off alone with Nick? She sensed Jackie's resentment of this sudden marriage and was afraid it would flare openly in some form of rebellion.

"I really should return to class, sir. We're doing an experiment this afternoon. On the properties of magnetism." This, suddenly, from Jackie, whose face was bright with the hope that he could wriggle free of his stepfather's plans.

"Stuff and nonsense, boy! Surely you can miss one experiment to spend some time with your father," Petry said, pleased to have the chance to show how amenable he could be. Even if this Rowan chap was an American, he seemed a good enough sort. "Jackie, show your father our playing fields," Petry added. Then, beaming, his fingers laced together over the broad expanse of his stomach, he addressed Nick. "Mr. Rowan, we've quite recently graded the land and planted new grass on the rugby field. I should be quite pleased to have your son show it to you. And take your time, do. I shall have a pleasant chat with your lovely wife."

Elyn appeared no more pleased than Jackie but she rallied to offer Nick a wan smile when he paused to cup her shoulder in a reassuring gesture. After mouthing the words, "Be good," she blew her son a kiss and turned her attentions to the headmaster. Whatever would be, would be.

Nick held Jackie's hand, at least until the two had descended the terrace steps and turned left, out of the headmaster's sight. Then Jackie pulled his hand away and stood his ground, chin stubbornly tilted in a gesture that reminded Nick of Elyn. "I am *not* a child, sir," he said, "so you needn't treat me as one."

Nick contemplated the boy with one raised brow. "You have my sincere apologies, son," he said, and gestured to the stone-paved walkway, muttering under his breath, "Why did I think he was *only* six?"

"Sir? Were you addressing me?"

"No, Jackie, I was talking to myself. It's something that comes with age." Nick smiled and glanced down at the boy. "You'll see—give yourself a year or two." He was talking over the kid's head, more to keep his own sense of humor in a trying situation than for any other reason. They had continued walking and the path had brought them abreast of the rugby field. Dutifully, Jackie pointed out the recent improvements, then asked if Nick knew anything about the game.

"Not really, but it's close enough to football. How about you?"

Jackie shook his head. "I'm too young... I mean, they really don't stress team sports, sir, until the older forms."

"I see. Well, you'll be involved soon enough. Maybe I can help when the time comes." Nick's offer was met with silence. "I'd like to help." Jackie stared at his feet, reaching down to pull up one of his gray kneesocks and flick an imaginary dust mote from his gray knickers. "Who knows, by then we may even be able to talk to each other."

The boy looked up, wondering at Nick's sense of humor, not sure how to take him. "I've no problems talking to you, sir," he asserted, then walked a few steps farther and glanced back over his shoulder. "Ask me anything you like."

"All right—when's your birthday?"

"Why, sir?"

"Because I'd like to get you something when the day rolls around."

"You want to bribe me."

"Why would I want to do that?" The boy was precocious, almost annoyingly smart.

"Because, sir . . . my mum wants us to get along."

"I think she has every right to expect that we will at least *try* to get along, Jackie. I don't have to like you—I *want* to like you. We might not be instant friends, but we've got a lot in common already."

"Like what?"

"Your mother. You love her. I love her. We both want her to be happy. You make her happy because she's proud of you and . . . because you're very special to her. I think I can make her happy, too."

Jackie turned away to face the field, but not before Nick saw a film of unshed tears turn his eyes a liquid sea-green color. "We didn't need anybody. Everything was . . . was fine the way it was."

"If it had been, your mother wouldn't have married me, would she? Perhaps you think there's only so much love to go around. Jackie—come here. Please?" But the boy wouldn't; he wouldn't turn or even acknowledge Nick.

Suddenly his school cap was lifted from his head. Jackie whirled, hands curled into tight balls of fists at his sides, more angry than was warranted. "Give it back! You've no right—"

Though he wasn't sure he was handling the boy correctly, Nick's expression was cool and controlled. "You can have your cap when we've finished our talk. Now that I have your attention, I'd like to know why you think I'm taking your mother away. She's a very nice woman, Jackie, a very warm, loving person. She'd like for all three of us to be a family. I'd like that, too. How about you?''

Jackie didn't want to answer. He didn't feel very old right at the moment and he didn't want to understand. "She's *my* mother," he insisted.

"Yes, she is. I'll make you a deal." Jackie glanced up quickly, squinting out of one eye, wary again. "I don't want her for a mother. I already have a mother, who, incidentally, would be crazy about you. Elyn can't be my mother, right? So I'll let her be your mother, all yours, if you let her be my wife. Deal?" It was, in retrospect, not the best proposition. If the boy were allowed to run their lives, everyone would be miserable. Nick sighed. This job of being a father was going to be rougher than riding with Zapata. "Okay, this is my last offer—I'll throw in the cap, too." He grinned, hoping for a break.

Jackie considered the offer and found no reason why it would not benefit him. Still, he couldn't appear eager. One couldn't bargain well from that standpoint. "It's October sixteenth, sir," he said and held out a hand for his cap.

"What is October the sixteenth?"

"My birthday. You did want to know. And I should like a horse, if you please."

"You mean a pony?"

Jackie settled his cap back on his head, adjusted its angle, and folded his arms across his chest. "You've a bit to learn about being a father, sir. I got a pony for my fourth birthday. I *am* going to be seven."

For a few moments Nick was lost in his thoughts, his forehead wrinkled in concentration. "Seven . . . yes, that *is* old. I can see this is going to be an expensive relationship."

"It's all right, sir. We've money, lots of it. I should think you'd know . . . uh, never mind, I—"

"Go on with what you were about to say."

178

"Oh." Jackie was stuck. He didn't care to finish but he couldn't disobey. "Well, sir, Bunny said . . . he said it shouldn't surprise him should you turn out to be a fortune-hunter, after Mum's money."

Nick stared past the boy, a pulse ticking at the edge of his clenched jaw. This wasn't the first time someone had suggested he was some sort of gigolo who'd swept Elyn off her feet. It was especially irritating because here in England he was a fish out of water—everyone knew Elyn's worth and nothing of his. At home he'd been considered an excellent catch. "Who's Bunny?"

"Oliver Lloyd Bunham, Viscount Fitch, sir. I room with him."

"That kind of talk hardly does justice to your mother. She's a beautiful lady. You can assure your friend Bunny that I married her because I love her. Viscount Fitch doesn't know what he's talking about. I have my own money, and if anyone buys you a horse for your birthday, it'll be me."

"Yes, sir."

"Let's walk a little farther. And, Jackie?"

Jackie had extracted a hand from a pocket to offer it to Nick. "Yes, sir?"

"Why don't we forget about calling me sir. It makes me feel old. At least for now you can call me Nick. Agreed?"

"Yes, sir . . . I mean, Nick." The boy smiled, dimpling, then asked suddenly, "D'you know any Indians?"

The unexpected question stopped Nick in his tracks. He started to chuckle and ended up laughing. "A few, son, mostly Mexican Indians. Why—are you interested?"

"Oh, yes. I've read about them. I think though . . ." Jackie hesitated as if he was afraid to give his opinion, then gathered courage and went on, "I think they're not as bad, the

179

Indians, as everyone makes them out. It wasn't fair, you know, to take their land.''

Nick was touched by the boy's compassion and again found himself searching through faded childhood memories, looking for a similar maturity. He had developed compassion, but much later, certainly not as young as Jackie. "I know. There's a great deal in life that isn't fair, though.''

A group of older boys, remarkably restrained, almost constrained, came onto the rugby field. Several of them waved at Jackie. One with special exuberance Jackie identified as Bunny. Ahead on the path, still with a clear view of the football practice about to begin, an iron and oak bench was set beneath a lime tree.

"Come on, we'll sit awhile and watch,'' Nick suggested. He thought little of it when Jackie said he much preferred to stand, thanks. "How do you like Gryrdale?'' Nick asked a few minutes later. Jackie shrugged, concentrating his attention on the field. Nick tried again. "I'd like to know if you're happy here, son.''

Jackie turned with a puzzled expression. "Happy, sir? Why, yes, I suppose I am. I've never been to another school, you see.''

"Schoolwork's not too hard?''

"Not at all . . . except . . . I am an awful dunce at printing. I try hard, I do, but sometimes the letters turn out backwards.''

"Maybe we can get you extra help on that.'' Nick looked back at the field where the boys were still behaving like puppets. There was none of the general rowdiness and jesting usually found among a large group of nine- or ten-year-olds. "What about discipline here?'' he asked Jackie. "Are they very strict?''

Jackie's face flushed a dull red. His bottom still stung from this morning's thrashing. He would not discuss the subject with anyone, especially not his new stepfather. There were rules and traditions to follow here, and one of the most important, one he'd learned his first week at school, was that one took his punishment in silence and discussed it no further. It had always been so; the older lads had confirmed it; why, it had been so even when Master Petry was a Gryrdale boy. "Not bad, sir," he mumbled finally, hoping desperately that the subject would be dropped.

Nick frowned. Jackie had sat very stiffly during lunch, as though he was in pain. He stood now to his left, slightly in front of Nick, facing the field. Nick reached out, caught the boy's arm, and tugged him backward. Jackie plopped down slightly off balance, landing hard on his bottom. He stood up again directly, his expression a mixture of surprise and pain, hands automatically reaching for the distressed spot. "All right, the truth now," Nick insisted. His suspicions confirmed, he was determined to find out what was going on.

"Please, sir, I'd really not like to talk of it," Jackie pleaded. "It doesn't hurt so awfully—I'm just being a baby."

"When . . . and why were you punished?"

Tears came to the boy's eyes. He struggled with his conscience and found it intolerable to betray his tradition. Still, he didn't like being caned. "It was this morning, sir. My . . . my manners at breakfast were improper. I d-did deserve it."

What could a boy this small have possibly done at breakfast to deserve a beating? Nick was angry, but it was a cold, tight anger, coiled within him. He would have words with Mr. Petry before they left today. They would either come to an agreement about the use of discipline or Jackie would leave the academy. "Jackie, I want a straight answer, the truth, and I'll know if it isn't. What did you do wrong?"

"I . . . sir, I'd rather not. . . ." The struggle within him was nearly as painful as the beating he'd suffered. Jackie didn't know what to do. "I was asked to . . . to pass the salt cellar, and because . . . because I was too ab-absorbed in my own self, sir, I didn't hear. M-Master Pinckney had to ask three times, and then I—then I spilled the salt before I got it to him."

"How often are you punished?" Nick asked, incredulous that so small an offense was so severely dealt with.

"Not so often," Jackie lied. Then, in a newfound desire to trust and be trusted by this man, he admitted the truth. "No, sir, often enough. At least once a week, more often if we do something that—"

"Hold it right there," Nick interrupted. "You're saying the boys are all disciplined with a cane, on a regular routine? Without having done anything?" And silently he thought, *Jesus . . . and I considered* my *father strict.* "You can't be happy here. It's almost time for the school year to end. . . ." He was thinking aloud, sorting through his alternatives. "Okay, I may get in trouble with your mother but . . . how'd you like to meet some Indians face to face? Mexican ones." Jackie's eyes widened, deepening in color. He didn't have to say anything; it was obvious that the suggestion delighted him.

"Sure. Elyn can't object, and we'll have some time to get to know each other," Nick said, nodding, convincing himself as he talked, ignoring the small voice in his conscience that warned him he should have spoken to Elyn first. She wouldn't object, when she found out how things were really run around here. "Now listen up, fella—here's what I want you to do. When we get back to the terrace, you head for your room. Pack your clothes and anything important. We'll send for the rest. Meanwhile, I'll handle your mother and Mr. Petry. Agreed?"

Nick, whether he recognized it or not, had won himself an ally. Jackie was freed from the discipline of Gryrdale and his studies for the remainder of the term, and he was off for a strange new land to meet real Indians. Somehow, every desire he had had come true. And this friendly giant from America, this man who was to be his father, was responsible. Jackie nodded, praying he wasn't dreaming.

Elyn was relieved to see Nick and Jackie finally return. They certainly looked as though they'd gotten along, to the point that there seemed to be an air of conspiracy between them. Seeing them together . . . she couldn't help but feel a strong tug of emotion. Father and son. The impossible, or what she had always considered impossible, had come to pass. They looked like they belonged together. Like his father, Jackie would be tall, his shoulders broad, his posture straight. And his eyes, perhaps the clearest evidence of his heritage. How could Nick not know instinctively that it was his own son's hand he held?

Elyn turned away, leaning back against the iron railing at the edge of the terrace, light-headed, though for the life of her she couldn't decide whether it was love or anger that had left her weaker. She had, very quickly, to decide what to do about Jackie finishing the term at Gryrdale. Mr. Petry had retreated to his study to await her decision.

Their discussion of the disciplinary measures employed at the school, prompted by Elyn's concern over Jackie's agitation at lunch, had rapidly escalated to a quarrel. It was Mr. Petry's position that as long as Gryrdale turned out a proper young gentleman, prepared to go on to university, it was no concern of the parents, and never had been, how such a product was produced.

Oh, he had admitted quite readily that the boys were physically chastised for the slightest infraction of the rules, for any minor breach of etiquette, and sometimes for moral reinforcement. Moral reinforcement, indeed. It made Elyn blush now with shame at the thought of the nine months Jackie had already endured here. She could not let him continue, and yet . . . what was she to do? She and Nick were leaving for Veracruz within a fortnight. Taking Jackie to Mexico, especially with the expedition into the countryside to search for her father, was out of the question. Yet she couldn't, or didn't care to, leave the boy with Lady Anne.

"Hello, Mum," a small voice called, and Elyn glanced over her shoulder to return Jackie's enthusiastic wave. He broke from Nick then, running up the terrace steps to fling himself against her. "Nick knows Indians, real ones . . . Yankees!"

Nick came up the steps chuckling and corrected Jackie, "Yaquis, son, they're Yaqui Indians. *I'm* a Yankee." He grinned and ruffled the bangs falling across Jackie's forehead. "Now go do as I asked."

"Yes, sir!" Jackie's eagerness to please drew a puzzled look from his mother. To her he added a polite, "Pardon me, please," and then bolted toward the Hall and his room.

Elyn watched him go, then turned back and smiled in wonder at Nick. "You've won him over completely—and I thought he might . . . resent you. I've underestimated your powers of persuasion. Thank you, darling." Elyn stretched on her toes, hands balanced lightly against his chest, to kiss him. Suddenly his arms were around her; the gentle kiss she offered in gratitude was returned with a passion that left her feeling weak and helpless as a kitten. When he finally broke the kiss, it was she who expressed reluctance at the separation. She clung to him, nestled safe and secure within his arms, a shelter that protected her from harm.

"Elyn?" he said finally.

"Hmm?" Her voice sounded lazy and content.

"Why didn't you tell me that Jackie was my son?"

She had been listening to his heartbeat, its strong resonant sound as reassuring as the feel of strength in his arms. Now her entire body was suddenly tense. "I . . . tried to. It was not something I could easily say." She lifted her head. He didn't appear angry. "There was a moment—on the way here—when I thought I might . . . Nick Rowan, don't look at me like that. I'd have told you, only . . ." Elyn turned away, unable to meet his eyes, "only I was afraid." There, it was out, the truth as she knew it, for she'd searched her soul and come up with no other reason.

"Afraid? Of me? But—"

"No, never of you." Elyn faced him again, raising her fingers to trace lightly the outline of his mouth. "I thought . . . you knew how important Jackie is to me . . . I thought you would see it as . . . as some sort of desperate lie, to make you want him, too." Talking now of her feelings, Elyn found it difficult to speak directly to Nick. She turned away and leaned back against his chest.

"Jackie has been mine, only mine, since birth," she went on. "No, even before then, from the time I knew I was to have him. When I came back to Veracruz, I had nothing. I believed you were dead, lost to me." Elyn closed her eyes. Thinking of that time was painful, though it was more than seven years past. "I couldn't bear to be in the same room with Alec. I thought *he* should be dead, not you. I left him and I swear—on Jackie's life I swear—I never slept with him again, not after you. I should have killed myself if . . ."

"Shh . . . it's all right, baby." Nick had responded automatically, without thinking. Now his lips softly touched her temple, and his arms circled her to comfort, to protect.

"I had already begun divorce proceedings when I discovered

I was carrying Jackie. My first reaction was hysteria. My grandmother, who had opposed the scandal of a divorce, would not have allowed me to bear a child out of wedlock. I actually considered ways of commiting suicide. Then . . . then I realized that though you were lost to me, I still had a part of you. From that moment, I very jealously guarded my health, my emotions. Everything centered around my baby. I even became calculating about his future.''

Nick nuzzled the silken waves at her crown with his chin and smiled. ''You—calculating? I can't picture it.''

''Have you never been around someone under the influence of the maternal instinct? We should easily kill for what we protect. At any rate, I spoke to Grandmother, reaffirming my decision to divorce. She was quite adamant that I should not.''

''But you won.''

''Only after I informed her that my emotional well-being was directly tied to attaining my divorce. And should I lose my baby, she should lose her only chance for a male heir to the empty Westford title. We were divorced three weeks after Jackie's birth. I believe he gave up all rights in exchange for a settlement.''

''Bastard,'' Nick muttered under his breath. ''Has he ever seen the boy?'' He was curious to know if Alec Barford believed Jackie was his.

''Once. He came to Jackie's fourth birthday party, accompanied by his second wife, Molly. Alec had been drinking, I'm sure of it. He brought a small stuffed tiger as a present and insisted repeatedly that Jackie address him as 'Father.' My cousin Sybil had just had her son, and Arthur, her husband, was home on leave. He threw Alec out, but not before they exchanged blows. Jackie was nearly hysterical.''

Nick's jaw was clenched. Hearing about it long after the

fact, he was no less incensed then he would have been at the time. "He hasn't bothered you again?"

"No. I think he was too humiliated. He did ring me back later with a rather sullen apology, but I'm afraid I hung up on him."

"If he contacts you again, I'll handle it. Right now, my love, we have another problem to deal with." Puzzled, Elyn glanced over her shoulder, and Nick turned her about gently but firmly with his hands at her shoulders. "I made a decision—without you—but I think when you hear the circumstances, you'll agree. I'm taking Jackie out of Gryrdale. I had a long talk with him, and I don't care for the way they measure out discipline around here."

Elyn stared up into her husband's eyes, wondering how they'd managed to come to the same conclusion. "What shall we do, then, about Mexico? I don't care to—"

Nick shrugged. "We'll take him along. He won't be a problem. I told you about that place I have near the capital. My housekeeper has a girl just about his age. She can teach him Spanish. I wouldn't feel right going off and leaving him with strangers, Elyn. He *is* my son."

Elyn smiled. "And you're the head of the family. So, my darling, go and beard the dragon. Mr. Petry is in his study. *I* shall wait for you in the car."

Chapter Eight

Thrilled to be out of school and with the promise of a future adventure, Jackie had been most amiable. On the drive to Ealing, he alternated his attentions between watching the scenery and studying Nick. He liked him, though he suspected that his lot might have improved had he withheld his approval. At least for a while, at least until he knew more of the man.

That his mother loved Nick there was no doubt. In all of Jackie's young life she had loved only him. Still, as Nick had said, there was no limit on the amount of love Elyn had to give. Nick seemed no threat to his security; he seemed even to have improved it. As yet, his new stepfather had issued no undue authoritarian commands, except indignantly to pull Jackie from the academy and Mr. Petry's responsibility, an act with which Jackie and his mother heartily concurred. It seemed that he had found an ally in Nick. Jackie prayed silently now, as his mother bent to kiss his brow, that nothing would happen to change that.

"I shall only be downstairs, darling," Elyn promised and rose from the cot that had temporarily been set in Eddie's room. They were to stay the night at Sybil's and then drive on to London in the morning. Downstairs, with the children fed

189

and tucked away, the adults had finished their own supper and retired to the living room to relax.

His mother seemed hesitant to leave, and with more than his usual independence Jackie reassured her. "I have been sleeping at school for nine months, Mum. Eddie offered me his own teddy but I am too old for such things."

There was a mild rebuke in the reminder, an unspoken assertion that he was quite fine, thank you, and she was not to worry. "Indeed, love, you are," Elyn answered and reached out gently to stroke her son's cheek. "However, you may indulge me and stay mine for yet a while. I don't want to lose you before I must."

"Oh, you shan't, Mother," Jackie said, and very quietly continued, "but you've got him now, d'you not?"

"Jonathan David Barford!" Elyn exclaimed. "You know you have your own place in my heart that no one can take." Her eyes filled with tears. Her son *must* not become jealous of Nick. "Jackie, darling, there are things you cannot understand, some matters I may never explain, yet I do not care to see you troubled or uneasy." Elyn searched her mind for a way to explain how Nick fit into the scheme of things as they had been, as they would be. "You have always been my prince, a good and valiant champion, none better in all the world. But ours is a kingdom, is it not? And home from the wars has come the king, home to his rightful place. His return does not make you less a prince or diminish your prowess as a knight. I love you both. I always shall." She held out her arms and he came into them, hugging her close with all the frail might that only a child can muster.

Elyn held him close to her for minutes, feeling his love, letting her own surround and reassure him. Finally she drew back and fixed upon him what she hoped was a stern look. "Now, Prince Jon, it is well past the time your royal self

190

should be asleep and dreaming of some gallant deed. Have I your word of honor to go directly to sleep?"

Jackie lay back and smiled at her. "Yes, m'lady . . . as you wish. I can never refuse you a thing."

Elyn was smiling as she left the room and walked toward the stairs. Halfway down them she met Analise, one of the two maids, an au pair girl from Lorraine.

The girl paused, curtsied, and spoke in a shy, halting English. "Madame, I am coming to find you. The telephone rings. From London, it is for you."

Who could be calling her from London? Indeed, who knew she was at Sybil's? "Did they say who . . . Never mind, dear. In the study?" She would find out soon enough just who had rung her, and there was no use taxing the poor girl's knowledge of English.

In the living room, Sybil was comfortably settled in a high-backed, upholstered chair, her swollen feet propped up on an ottoman. In one hand she held a Scotch on the rocks; a cigarette dangled from the other. She had been watching Nicholas Douglas Rowan all through the evening meal, fascinated by both the man and the story, surely concocted, of how he and Elyn had met, fallen in love, and married.

Despite their recent introduction, Sybil felt there was something elusively familiar about him, something she could not quite put her finger on, yet she knew absolutely that she had never been introduced to him before this afternoon.

"Freshen your drink, old man?" Arthur asked now.

Nick nodded and rose to deliver his nearly empty glass to his host. He turned then to see if Sybil's was empty and found her staring at him with a puzzled frown. Suddenly her expression altered, her features sharpening as she hunched forward slightly, her hand clutching at the rounded bulge of her belly.

He was at her side immediately, even before Arthur realized anything was amiss. "Is it over?" he asked as the tension in her posture seemed to flow from her. She nodded and took a deep, rather ragged breath. "How long?"

Sybil held out her glass, saw she still had a good swallow of Scotch left, and finished it off before handing it to Nick with a silent plea for a refill. "Since this afternoon. Not regularly and nothing to be concerned over." She smiled at him and started to ask how a lifelong bachelor knew anything of childbirth, then she caught sight of Arthur's face. He had gone white and seemed rooted to the spot. This same man who, in the course of his career in the foreign service, had thought nothing of socializing with prime ministers and royalty now seemed panicked at the imminent birth of his child.

"Darling, before you say a word, I am fine," she insisted. "All I need at this point is another Scotch."

"Not bloody likely, m'dear!" Arthur swore, and when Sybil seemed about to protest, he cut her off with a fierce and obstinate look. "That's my child about to come. You've had enough and shall have no more. Why on earth didn't you say something before now?"

Sybil shrugged. "We were expecting company. As little chance as I have had lately to see interesting people . . . to see anyone, my love, I was not about to change my plans."

"You mayn't have a choice anymore, sweet." Some of his irritation had evaporated, but Arthur was the typically harried expectant father. He wasn't sure what to do and that made him very nervous.

"Do be a dear and go fetch my slippers, won't you?" Sybil sighed a little impatiently. "I believe they may be under the bed on my side. Ah, there's a good lad, I knew you would, darling." Arthur somewhat reluctantly headed for the stairs and the master bedroom. He wasn't sure why she needed her slippers, but this was a time when one indulged the slightest whim.

Sybil listened until she heard his footsteps on the stairs, then grinned almost wickedly at Nick. "They're in the closet, near the back. It should take an hour to find the things. And in the meanwhile, cousin, you can answer a few questions."

Nick retreated to the bar cart and picked up the whiskey Arthur had poured him. "Such as?"

Again Sybil shrugged, lowered her eyelashes, then glanced up. All her life she had been a flirt, and she could not break old habits. A smile curved her lips as she speculated aloud, "Where *have* I seen you before? I never forget a handsome face."

Nick swallowed a sip of whiskey and smiled back. "I never forget a beautiful one, so we couldn't have met."

Sybil swung her feet down from the ottoman and patted it. "Come closer and sit with me while I puzzle this out." For a minute or two she rubbed her temple with the tip of an index finger, concentrating. "For some reason I connect you with Veracruz. Have you never been there?"

"Not for quite a while." Sybil was on the right track but Nick doubted that she could, after seven years, recognize him as the rebel who had kidnapped Elyn. "I'm a— Are you all right?" Again Sybil had leaned forward, rigid for a full minute this time. She nodded, took a breath, and looked up with a weak smile.

"That one was stronger than the rest. I think before the night is out I shall have to leave for hospital." She was recovered now and patted the warm, strong hand that had covered hers in concern. "I rather like you, Nick, that's why I'm going to confide a secret very few people know. You've heard of Alec and his shenanigans of course. Did you know that Elyn fell in love when she was in Mexico?"

"Did she? While she was married to Barford?"

193

"Yes. It was tragic, an affair doomed from the first, but how I envied her!" Sybil watched him closely, sure that there was a connection between Nick and Elyn's lost love. He seemed interested, but perhaps a bit more blasé than he might logically have been on hearing of a past rival.

"Why, Sybil? You and Arthur seem to be perfectly matched, happy as anyone—"

"Why? Because Elyn loved more deeply and passionately in that short span of time than I shall in all my life. Very few women find what she found."

It was strange to hear about Elyn's "lost love" and know it was he Sybil was talking about. He had an instinctive urge to confide the truth, but he knew it was better to stick to the story he and Elyn had devised. "But it ended tragically?"

Sybil was vaguely disappointed, having hoped for some confirmation of her suspicions. Could he be Elyn's rebel from so long ago? Perhaps she would never know. . . . Still, she would like so very much to think so. "He died," she explained, and sighed. "I never thought to see her happy again."

"Jackie made her happy."

Sybil wrinkled her nose and shook her head. "It's not the same, you know. Mother love is satisfying. Loving a man is . . ." she smiled ruefully and shrugged, "loving a man. I'm glad she's found you."

Nick grinned. "Well, I'm glad you're glad—with one small correction. *I* found *her.*"

Sybil grinned back, then canted her head and studied his face. "Did you know, Nicholas Rowan, that you've the most gorgeous pair of green eyes? Oddly enough, so does Jackie." She could have sworn he paled then, and she might have pressed the point had Elyn not returned with a worried Arthur at her side.

Elyn's expression was dazed, her complexion pale as alabaster. Arthur slipped an arm around her shoulders and appealed to Nick. "Your wife's just had an awful shock, old man. A call from London . . . shall I tell them, love?" Elyn nodded, still seeming preoccupied. Nick came up, reaching out gently to take hold of her shoulders. "It's Lady Westford," Arthur said in a subdued whisper. "She's been taken ill. The doctor doesn't seem to think she'll live out the night."

"Well, finally," Sybil said, and then remembered that Elyn had always loved the old woman no matter what she'd done. "Oh, I *am* sorry, dear," she went on, hoping the apology sounded sincere. "Still, she *is* old, isn't she then? It's only to be expected after a certain—"

"Syb, don't go on so," Arthur protested, leaving Elyn to join his wife. "Elyn feels bad enough, I'm sure, without your prattling on."

As he settled on the arm of the chair, she twitched her nose in disdain and whispered, "What's wrong with the old bat?" Respect for the dead and dying aside, it would have surprised Sybil less to learn that someone, one of the many enemies the countess had made in too long a life, had stabbed her. Somehow, it seemed unsuitable that she was simply expiring.

"I'll tell all I know once you're tucked safe in bed, my darling, a place you shall stay until the doctor rings me back."

"You called him?" Sybil fairly shrieked, drawing a startled look from her cousin. "Oh, Arthur, how *could* you have? It might be hours yet—"

"Second babies don't take as long and I—"

"How d'you know that?"

"Because I've read up on all the latest on the subject. I *am* the child's father—in case you've forgotten, sweet. And your husband, as well. I shan't hear another word of protest."

Sybil glared up at her husband and opened her mouth in rebellion, but Arthur cut her off. "Tut! Not a word. Now come, I do think we might allow Elyn and Nick some privacy. If you wish, I'll carry you."

Rarely had Arthur been so assertive. Though Sybil had no desire to be packed off to bed, she was tired, and it did seem as though she'd be going off to hospital sometime in the night. Bad timing on her part, or the baby's, to go off just when something truly interesting was about to take place.

Arthur helped her to her feet—no easy task when her point of balance was so uneven—and walked her to Elyn's side. There Sybil reached out and grasped Elyn's hand, then raised her head and kissed the taller woman's cheek. No matter that Lady Westford would soon be going to the reward she'd earned on earth, Elyn had loved her and would grieve.

"We all must go sometime, love," she offered then, and for the life of her, she could think of nothing more that would not sound completely insincere. Perhaps some tea might help. "I shall go off and tell Mariette to bring tea—"

"You'll go up the stairs like a good girl," Arthur corrected her, "and *I* shall have the tea sent. If you'll be wanting it. I expect you'd rather leave for the city immediately. Leave Jackie, do. It's no good for him to be around doctors and dying, and nurse will watch him should we have to . . ."

For the first time Elyn seemed aware of her surroundings. She blinked several times, as if clearing her mind of a fog, then glanced down at Sybil's rounded belly and up into her eyes. "It's time . . . oh, tonight of all nights. And I thought we might be here for Arthur. I'll stay if you wish."

"Nonsense!" Both Sybil and Arthur spoke simultaneously and smiled at each other before Sybil turned back with a grin. "See how it is to be married for so long—can't even keep a thought private till it's spoken. No, Arthur shall be a brave

196

soldier about all this—while I fight the battle! I'll be fine, truly. You're to worry over nothing but driving carefully, hmm? Do let us know if Lady Anne's condition changes, and of course Arthur shall ring you immediately anything happens here.'' Sybil held out her arms and hugged as much of Elyn as she could manage, then held her breath for a minute as another, more intense pain clutched at her belly. ''I th-think I shall let you carry me,'' she said to Arthur, and winked at Elyn before her husband caught her up in his arms. ''I shouldn't care to have it here. Especially if it's a girl, she'd never forgive me!''

Chapter Nine

Aunt May couldn't stop crying. She had wept softly through the funeral services at Saint Edward's, through the elegy at the gravesite, and through the luncheon for the immediate family. One might have thought that May, rather than Elynora, was the close relative. Though Elyn had privately known several sad periods of reflection on her grandmother's sudden passing, outwardly she was composed and tranquil.

Now all that was left was the reading of the will. Within a half-hour Lady Anne's solicitor would arrive. There were few who didn't know that Elyn and Jackie were the principal heirs. Elyn would benefit immediately from her inheritance, while Jackie's property and moneys would be held in trust until he attained his majority.

The family—and with Nick's marriage, May Burney had become a part of it—had gathered to wait in the library. Except for the sound of May's sniffling, the room was silent. Everything kind that could be said of Anne Mary Elizabeth Warren Fitz Morough-Whyte had been said.

To Jackie, in his first contact with death, May's tears seemed to indicate that Nana had gone somewhere awful . . . that perhaps, even as they sat in the library, the flames were already tormenting her soul. He sat quietly, wide eyes troubled and darkly green, with his small hands folded in his lap.

Occasionally he would raise a thumb and bite at his nail, but for the most part he was subdued.

Elyn exchanged a look with Nick, a silent plea for help. She found Aunt May a dear, but her nerves, and Jackie's, could not last the hour. "Do something," she whispered, "anything!" Then, before he could answer, she thought of an idea herself. "Tell her Jackie needs fresh air. Ask your aunt, *please,* to take him out in the gardens awhile. See how peaked he looks—it will do them both good."

Nick had to agree. The boy looked nervous, and it was no small wonder. It wasn't just May and her display of grieving. The funeral had been an elaborate affair, dictated by the lady's position in society. Elyn had imagined it would be a small gathering of family and friends. In reality, over two hundred mourners, many of them peers of the realm, had come to the services, slightly fewer to the graveside.

"I'm sure you could use a little exercise, Aunt," Nick suggested, and turned to his left to ask a favor of Jackie. "Son, I'd like to stay with your mother. Would you be kind enough to escort Aunt May through the gardens?"

Would he ever! Jackie's eyes brightened at the chance to escape the confines of the stuffy library, though he'd have much preferred going alone. Still, he would do whatever Nick wanted. "Yes, sir!" he replied; then, remembering that he must maintain a certain decorum on this day, he made his expression solemn. Rising, he approached Aunt May and with a quite correct bow offered her his arm. "The honor would be mine, Aunt."

May wavered, still wrapped in damp grief. She wasn't a fit companion for the little lad, the way she felt. He looked so anxious to escape, though, that her heart went out to him. Jackie had been good for a very long time. She glanced past him now and, for the first time since she had heard of Anne's illness, really smiled.

"Quite the contrary, sir," she insisted, "the honor is all mine. Come along, then, do . . . I shall show you a very rare specimen of rose growing in Grandmama's gardens." May reached out, touching his cheek for a second, thinking what a handsome boy he was and how lovely it was that he and Nicholas had taken to each other. Though she was quite spry for her age, she accepted his arm, slowing her pace to match the stride of his little feet, telling him as they walked about the Kashmiri rose her husband had brought home from India.

When Aunt May and Jackie were well clear of the library, Nick slipped an arm around Elyn's shoulders and pulled her close. Though he couldn't quite understand the motivation for his aunt's grief, he respected the honesty of it. With Elyn, however, he couldn't quite tell how she was feeling. She'd been close to Lady Anne, and yet, in the past year, Elyn had discovered firsthand just how ruthless the woman could be.

"Want to talk?"

Elyn turned up her head and snuggled closer, glad he was there beside her. "Not really . . . not just yet, anyway," she answered. Truthfully, she wasn't sure what she was feeling. Grandmother was gone, so suddenly that there hadn't been time to talk, let alone settle the differences of the last few months. By the time she and Nick had driven back to London, Lady Anne had lapsed into a coma and died. No deathbed drama, no last-breath remonstrances. If Lady Anne could return to say anything, Elyn was sure it would be a claim that she'd been cheated of her due. Elyn smiled to herself. Yes, she could see her grandmother, ever so strong-willed, doing just that.

"At least you can still smile," Nick commented. He was worried about her. Elyn was far too calm, almost contemplative. He couldn't help but feel that somewhere down the line the emotions she was holding in would erupt. "Sure you don't want to talk about it?"

She shook her head. "I'm quite fine . . . really, surprised only that I feel so little. I owe her gratitude . . . even love. She reared me almost by herself, but she also threatened to take away my son and my freedom. For that I should perhaps despise her. I don't, you know—despise her, I mean. But neither do I love her. I don't feel anything." Elyn stared at him, perplexed. "Should I?"

Elyn had turned to him for an answer he couldn't give. Nick sighed heavily, wishing, although it wasn't a very decent thought, that the old woman had chosen to die after they'd left for Mexico. "I can't tell you how you should feel, honey. There's no right or wrong except in being dishonest with yourself. You didn't have a chance to have it out with her, to clear the air. For all the money she left, she also left a lot of guilt behind." He raised a brow. "If I didn't know better, I'd swear she planned it that way."

"That's silly, darling. She didn't *know* she was sick. There are things I do wish I'd done differently. It's sometimes a great difficulty for someone older to admit she might have been wrong. I should have gone to her before we left town. I shall always regret that. Ah, well, it cannot be undone now. What time have you?" Her own watch had stopped running, oddly enough, at the hour they'd buried Grandmother.

"Twenty past one. Why?"

"Oh, just anxious to have Munroe come and be done with the reading."

Nick grinned. "Shouldn't be any surprises to that. You going to keep me in the style to which I've become accustomed?"

Elyn twitched her nose. "Only if you can behave.

202

Otherwise—it's out on your ear!" She reached up, touching his face, gazing into his eyes. "I honestly don't know how I should have borne all this without you, love. You are Gibraltar—and I love you for it." He started to kiss her, and though she would have loved to linger in the security of his arms, she touched his lips lightly with hers and drew back. "Do be a dear and do me one quick favor. Before Mr. Munroe arrives and we're stuck, take a peek out the terrace doors. Dear as she is, I don't want Aunt May weeping all over poor Jackie. As long as they both look comfy, let them have their walk."

"Of course, my dear. Be back shortly."

"Plim," Elyn asked as the butler entered the room, "could we have some ice, please?" He nodded, and once he had dutifully retrieved the silver bucket from the bar cart, he seemed to hesitate. "What is it?" Elyn asked. "Has Mr. Munroe come, then?"

Plim shifted uncomfortably. "No, madam. He has yet to arrive. It is . . . Mr. Barford insists he is to be allowed to attend the reading of Her Ladyship's will. Says he's a legal right to do so. Shall I admit him?"

Her first instinct was to toss Alec out. Of all the people she had no desire to see, he topped the list. What legal right could he have to hear the will? None that she knew of, but straight away she would find out what he'd meant. "Do show him in, please," she replied absently. Nick would be back any minute. God, if they chanced to meet . . .

When Alec Barford entered the library, Elyn was standing before the bar, her back to him. It gave him the moment's advantage, to study her before she became aware of his presence. She still looked damned good to him, more the pity. The news of her remarriage had, after so many years, come as a shock. Until he'd heard, he had hoped . . . well, it never would have worked again, even if he was in the process

203

of a second divorce. "Hello, love. Mix one for me while you're about it, won't you?"

Elyn nearly dropped the glass she was holding and juggled it for a second before turning to glower at her ex-husband. "You gave me a fright, Alec. And no—I shan't fix you anything. You won't be staying long enough."

"Ah, but I shall, darling. Make it a Scotch—on the rocks. Decadent habit, no? Picked it up over in New York. Ice in one's liquor—actually an improvement; providing you drink it fast enough, you don't water down the potency." The butler returned, offering Elyn the ice bucket and asking if there was anything else he might do. "Well, old boy, she'd like you to give me the old heave-ho, but I think Ellie'll change her mind. Leave us, my good man."

"Thank you, Plim. That *will* be all for now. I'll ring if I should need you." Elyn waited until Plim had made his exit and the library doors were closed. "Don't order my servants about, Alec. It's bad manners. And if you call me Ellie once more, I shall personally throw you out."

Arrogant bitch. She hadn't changed, except to put on a few more airs. "Yes, m'lady," Alec answered with a mocking bow. "You might as well give me my drink. I *am* staying."

"There's no reason for you to stay, Alec. I'll give you a Scotch, but then you must be going. You're no longer a part of the family. It seems to have been difficult for you to accept that fact."

"There you're wrong, sweet. I married before you, long before." He didn't miss the fact that she had made only a single drink. "Aren't you joining me?"

"No, thank you. I like to have all my wits about me in a conversation with you. Now tell me, please, why I should allow you to stay for the will."

Alec took a sip of his drink and searched the left breast

pocket of his suit coat, producing a worn, folded paper. "My invitation, so to speak, to the proceedings. Care to read it or should I just . . . " Elyn held out her hand and he shrugged, crossing the room to hand it to her. "Suit yourself, love. No one trusts anyone these days."

"I didn't trust you when we were married, Alec. I've had no reason to change my opinion." Elyn studied the paper. It appeared to be a legal document, a part of her divorce settlement agreed to by her grandmother and Alec. It was dated some five months before Jackie's birth, while the other documents had all been signed and attested to after he was born. She looked up to find him smugly grinning at her. "I never saw this, Alec."

"A matter for Grandma and me. You were very pregnant at the time and in no mood to negotiate. Read on."

It seemed that her grandmother had promised him the sum of ten thousand pounds if he irrevocably assigned guardianship of their unborn child to Elyn, forfeiting all claims against property that the child might inherit in the future, such sum to become due at the death of the countess of Westford. "Why this extra money? You received a healthy settlement at the time of our divorce."

"Oh, it was a matter of timing. I told the lady that since you wished to be quit of me, I would see to it with dispatch." Again he had that smug look. "She didn't like that idea at all. You see, she was hoping you'd produce a male. If you didn't, the title was almost surely gone. However, should you be so astute as to bear the right sex, why, everyone would be pleased. Except if the father had already flown the coop, there might be talk, questions about possible extramarital affairs and parentage. That just wouldn't do, couldn't be chanced, so as insurance I had to stay the race. I agreed to wait until the child was born, while she . . . agreed to what you're holding."

"And you get the prize for taking advantage of two women." Barford jerked around at the sound of Nick's voice, spilling Scotch on his suit. Quickly enough, too quickly for any amount of character, he recovered.

Alec raised what was left of his drink in a salute. "In some circles, I'd be a genius. You must be Elyn's American. Didn't hear you knock."

"Could be 'cause I didn't. *I* belong here." Nick had already sized Barford up and dismissed him. He'd met his kind before, a weasel despite the outward appearance of manners and good tailoring, a bum at any level of society. "Can I see that, Elyn."

Alec had been prepared to despise anyone Elyn had married, but for a few seconds he actually hated the man. It wasn't only the way Elyn looked at him and trustingly handed over the document. It was that he couldn't find anything seriously the matter with her new husband. He looked as though he'd fit wherever Elyn went, as if he could handle any problem that came her way, and, worse, as if he now meant to try to handle Alec.

Nick studied the paper for a minute, then shrugged negligently. "I could claim I never saw this and have you thrown out." He smiled humorlessly. "The reading would be over. It really doesn't make a hell of a lot of sense for you to be present, Barford. You'll receive the settlement, but I suggest you leave. Now, before I lose my patience with your greed."

Alec's fair complexion had reddened, and he sputtered for a moment before finding his voice. "What utter gall! *I'm* greedy, am I? Well, who married little Miss Moneybags—and just in the nick of time? Aren't you sitting pretty now? Why—"

Elyn stood very quietly in the background, watching the scene play out, knowing full well that Alec hadn't a chance.

206

Nick crumpled the settlement, casually reached into his pocket, and produced the silver lighter she'd recently bought him. Alec stared, unable to believe his eyes.

"You leaving?" Nick held the lighter beneath the wad of paper. Still disbelieving, Alex stared, his mouth opening and closing. He looked so like a trout out of water that Elyn raised a hand to cover a helpless smile.

"You wouldn't dare!" Alec said at last, his voice lowering a half-octave with each word. Then, as Nick sighed and almost reluctantly flicked the lighter, Alec squeaked, "You're insane! Elyn, stop him, for God's sake . . . *please!*" A corner of the paper caught, a tiny flame that quickly spread. "All right, all right, you bloody lunatic, I'm going . . . just save the damned paper!"

Nick tossed him the baseball-sized wad and managed to keep a straight face as Barford juggled the smoldering paper, alternately blowing on it and trying to tamp out any sparks that might erupt into flame. Finally, when at last the paper seemed out of danger, Alec gingerly unfolded it. There was a small hole in the center, too close to the printed sum of ten thousand pounds, and a bottom corner was missing. Alec looked up and glared at Nick. "Even if you'd ruined it, the settlement's in the will. There isn't a thing you can do about it. It's mine."

Striking the lighter again, Nick stared at the flame for a moment, then smiled at Elyn. "I think I set the wrong object on fire. If he doesn't leave—"

"I'm going," Alec insisted. He couldn't believe Elyn's husband was mad enough to do as he'd threatened, but neither could he take the chance that he might actually follow through. "Ellie, I'll expect to hear from Munroe within the week. See that there's no problem or—" Already backing away toward the double doors of the library, Alec hastened

his retreat as Nick once more flicked the lighter. "You've gone and married a bloody lunatic, Ellie!" he yelled just before he slipped into the hall.

Elyn could no longer hold back. Even as the door slammed behind Alec, she doubled over, clutching at her stomach, giggling so hard that her eyes teared. "If . . . if . . . for no other . . . reason in the world than *that*," she managed to say, "I love you! God forgive me, but I have waited years to see him suffer his due, and in five minutes you've seen to it!" She wiped her eyes and suddenly started giggling again, remembering how like a fish Alec had looked. She came up to Nick then and leaned against him, still smiling as she laid her head on his shoulder. "He's right, you know. You are a bit of a madman."

Nick kissed the top of her head, then tilted up her chin with his fingers, seeking her mouth. "Hmm . . ." he said, "mad about my wife, that's all." As his lips touched hers, Elyn stretched, reaching up to encircle his neck with her arms.

A full minute later, a polite clearing of a throat interrupted their kiss. Nick merely looked sheepish as he drew back, but Elyn blushed to the roots of her fine brown locks. "You must excuse the interruption, my fault entirely, should have knocked louder. Much louder." The solicitor seemed nearly as embarrassed as Elyn.

"Mr. Munroe . . . I hadn't expected you. . . ." Elyn glanced at her watch; it was several minutes past the agreed upon time. "Well, you've arrived as punctually as usual. Forgive me . . . us. Darling, this is Grandmother's lawyer, Jameson Munroe. Mr. Munroe—my husband, Nicholas Rowan."

Munroe held out his hand. "I've been wanting to meet you, sir. Congratulations—to both of you. I hope you'll be very happy."

"I'm sure we will be . . . for a very long time to come."

"Good, very good. Well, shall we begin. I think, if memory serves me correctly, that we shall need Mr. Plim, a Miss Halleran, a Jeanine Parks, and a Mr. David Tennby present." Plim, standing vigilantly by the open doors, immediately went off in search of the other household staff who had been named.

When everyone had been assembled, the reading commenced. Anne, countess of Westford, had been more generous of spirit than she'd been given credit for. Each of the servants, depending on the length of their service, had been allotted a large pension. Aside from this, there was a special bequest of twenty-seven hundred pounds for Mr. Plim's "loyalty and discretion."

Aunt May had come in during the preliminaries, having left Jackie to expend his considerable energies on the gardens. Once the smaller bequests and donations to charities had been seen to, Mr. Munroe asked that the room be cleared. "Except for Mr. Rowan, his wife, and his aunt, of course," he added.

Now, with his audience of three, the solicitor proceeded to read the disposition of property. Lady May Burney, to her credit taken totally by surprise, had been left a country house in Surrey and an adequate trust to administer its upkeep. "Of course," Munroe continued, "it will come as no great surprise that one-half of the Westford legacy shall pass, on attainment of his majority, to Master Jonathan Barford, as shall the title that has belonged to his ancestors."

Jameson Munroe looked up over the rim of his spectacles, neither expecting nor finding any disenchantment with the boy's inheritance. Then he cleared his throat once again. What lay ahead was difficult to announce. Though it made a negligible difference in the distribution of the late countess's fortune, it had been important enough to Lady Anne to have a codicil added to her will. It might make a vast difference to the happiness of the newlyweds. Well, he could not avoid it, could he?

"I would beg your indulgence and patience with me on the next section of the will. I shall precede its reading by telling you, Mrs. Rowan, that your grandmother quite recently changed the terms of her legacy to you. She said nothing of the reason, though I gathered your relationship with her had been subjected to some stress." Though she was not frightened, Elyn's expression, indeed the entire posture of her body, had become tense, almost apprehensive. For the second time in that hour, Nick slipped his arm around her shoulder, a protective measure that lately was coming as naturally as breathing.

"Have I been disinherited, then?"

Munroe took a deep breath. It was an odd situation, he thought, but then the rich were eccentric. "In a sense . . . yes." Elyn sucked in a deep breath, paling with the shock. "Let me explain. It isn't as alarming as it sounds. The half of Lady Anne's estate that was to come to you will still be at your disposal."

"Now you have me thoroughly puzzled, Mr. Munroe," Elyn said. "Please explain further." Elyn wasn't the only one disturbed by the change. May was biting a thumbnail, something she hadn't done since . . . before her late husband had come courting. And Nick was silently cursing the dead woman. Respect aside, she had been a cunning old crow, a devious . . .

"You see, it shall be there, I can only imagine, for your use, accessible at your husband's signature. Lady Anne has designated Nicholas Rowan as the beneficiary of the other half of the estate."

Everyone looked at Nick. He had heard the statement but its content had barely penetrated. "Me? Why should she

210

leave me anything?'' Nick turned to Elyn; he could feel the tension in the taut muscles below her neck. "Elyn, I swear . . . you *know* I knew nothing of this." Then, to Munroe, "She didn't even like me. When was the will changed?"

"Oh, it was about three . . . no, four weeks ago. The Lady Anne called me and asked that I come to see her. Must have been soon after your marriage. Perhaps the countess was more fond of you than you realized. At any rate, as I said before, the money will remain for Mrs. Rowan, though it will technically be in your name, sir."

Why would Anne go to expense and effort to make such a change? For the life of her, May could not puzzle out what motive her friend might have had. Certainly it was good fortune for Nick. With the money his parents and grandmother would leave, he was an extremely wealthy young man. Still, it didn't quite seem right. All it could do was possibly cause strife between the couple, and that would be a sin. They were so happy and so well suited to each other. Anne could not have meant to drive a wedge between them . . . surely not that.

"I'm sure there are more details to hear," Elyn said, her voice a lot higher than normal but steady enough. She looked . . . controlled, tightly wound, a trifle dazed. "I should like to go off for a while by myself, if you don't mind." She turned to look at Nick, even offering him a slight smile. "You don't mind, do you, darling? This concerns you now. You must stay and listen carefully. I shall want to hear all about it . . . later."

Elyn started to move from the loveseat, but Nick's hand tightened at her shoulder. "Elyn, we have to—"

"I'm fine, really. No need to worry. Please . . ." She patted his hand, then very purposefully stood. "Aunt May, I'll see you later, at supper." Elyn approached the silver-haired old woman and bent to kiss her cheek. "You've been a darling through it all." On the way, she paused at the desk. Munroe had come to his feet when she had. She shook his hand, thanking him for his courtesy and patience.

Munroe wanted to offer some brief word of comfort but he could think of nothing that would not insult Mr. Rowan and his aunt. He couldn't very well say that it should have been all hers, which was only the truth. Still, Rowan loved her, that was plain to see. "Does it make so great a difference, Miss Elyn?" he asked softly.

And more softly, as she turned away, Elyn answered, "Yes."

"Miss Elyn." He stopped her once more, his hand upon her arm. "Perhaps there's something in this letter that might explain. . . . It's from your grandmother. She left it with me with instructions that it be passed on, sealed, to you."

It seemed to Munroe that Elyn took the envelope reluctantly, almost with distaste, but she carried it with her nonetheless on her way upstairs.

Nick started after her, but his aunt called him back. "Let her be, Nicholas. She's had a shock; she needs time. And you can help her now by listening to Mr. Munroe. I'm sure there is more, is there not, sir?" Munroe nodded.

For twenty minutes more, Nick stayed, listening to an incredible list of properties. There were farms, country residences, homes abroad, and stock holdings, some of them majorities, in some fairly large companies. And above it, the sum of four hundred thousand pounds in cash and bonds. He'd had no idea of the extent. Nick doubted that anyone had, except for the lawyer and Lady Anne. "Did the countess inherit all that?"

"No. In fact her father nearly went bankrupt. She took some of her groom's money, I understand, and eventually made enough to save the earl. That's likely how her husband got the title after him.'' Munroe shuffled the papers in front of him. There was still a bit to go over. Rowan seemed a likable enough chap. And he believed, because he'd watched the man's expression, that the turnabout inheritance had shocked him as much as it had his wife. ''Shall I go on, sir?''

''No. I've had enough for today. I would be happy to continue your retainer, Mr. Munroe. Why don't I bring Elyn in sometime next week; we'll go over everything in greater detail. You know we're leaving for the Americas in twelve days?'' The solicitor nodded; he'd heard. ''Then I can expect you'll take care of settling everything? You'll be given an address in Mexico City. Whatever needs to be done . . .''

''Of course, I should be pleased to pursue the settlement in any manner you see fit. And I shall be at your disposal day or night. Plim, of course, knows how to reach me.'' Munroe gathered the will and its thick sheaf of attendant documents, carefully fitting them into his briefcase. ''And may I say, sir—I wish you and Mrs. Rowan every good fortune.''

''Thank you, Mr. Munroe . . . we may need it.'' Nick shook the solicitor's hand and walked with him to the library doors. ''I'll talk to you next week, then?''

''Yes, sir.'' And because he'd nearly forgotten her presence, Munroe looked back over his shoulder to smile apologetically at Lady May. ''A good day to you, m'lady.''

Nick sighed heavily as the door closed on the man. How long should he give Elyn? Maybe she didn't really want to be alone; maybe . . . Damn, he was trying to second-guess her and getting nowhere. He looked at his aunt. ''I'm going up to Elyn. You'd better say a prayer that she didn't take this the wrong way. Your friend really did it up right.''

''Oh, now, she might have had reasons you can't . . .'' As much as she wanted to excuse Anne, May couldn't think of a good motive for the altered will, a change that could only disrupt Nick and Elyn's marriage. She lifted her shoulders and let them fall in a gesture of surrender. "What matters now is Elyn. Go to her, m'boy...go on. I shall rest a moment only and then gather myself to see how Jackie is faring." As she thought of the boy, May smiled, then looked up at Nick and winked with a hint of her usual good humor. "Or better yet, see how the gardens have fared...if the trees still stand. He's all boy, very like you at the same age, as I recall."

As Nick made his way to their rooms, he went over his "defense" again. *He* knew he was innocent, everyone else had seemed to accept it, and yet...it seemed so incriminating to be a millionaire suddenly while the real heir was left nothing. For all the long years she'd been obedient to the old woman's whims, under her thumb, really, Elyn deserved—had earned—her inheritance. And now it was his.

He'd underestimated Lady Anne. The important difference the alteration of the will would make was becoming more apparent to him with each passing minute. Elyn would resent the loss of what should have been hers; she would resent *him* every time she must ask permission to spend what had rightfully been hers. The money would become a point of contention, and what he decided to do with it might well determine the fate of their marriage.

Nick paused outside the large sitting room to their suite, listening. It was quiet, almost too quiet. He frowned, still concentrating. What was Elyn doing...thinking...feeling?

Inhaling deeply, he reached for the doorknob, pausing at the muffled sound of what seemed to be a sob. With more force than he'd intended, Nick thrust open the door. Another choked whimper greeted him, drawing his attention to the balcony and a table and chair where Elyn sat, half-hidden by the open doors.

Her shoulders were slumped as she huddled in the grip of some strong emotion, both hands covering her mouth and nose. Nick didn't know what to do or say. His instinct was to reach out and comfort her—but what if the effort only made her hysterical? Indirectly he was a part of the reason for her upset. Next to her on the table sat a glass half-full of some dark amber liquid. Whiskey? Elyn hardly ever touched liquor. He cleared his throat once, then again, pronouncing her name.

Startled, Elyn glanced over her shoulder and saw Nick. Above her fingertips, her eyes crinkled, a blue-violet color magnified by a layer of moisture. There seemed to be no attendant frown lines between her fair brows to indicate either rage or resentment. She took away her hands, and a soft rose blush crept over her cheeks. There were slight indentations around her mouth, as if she had been smiling or . . . laughing.

"Are you okay?"

Elyn nodded, wiping away the tears that had gathered at the corners of her eyes, still chuckling every few seconds. She stretched, suddenly feeling free of a burden that had seemed to last most of her life, then reached for her glass and found Nick studying her warily. "Care for some, darling?" she asked.

"No, thanks. And I think you've had enough. We have to talk and—"

"Enough?" Elyn stared at him, looked at the iced tea in her glass, and started to laugh again. It had been a day to remember—and it wasn't yet over. "Here, darling, fortify yourself," she said and handed him the glass.

Nick hesitated, took a sip, and made a face. "Why didn't

215

you say you were drinking tea?" He felt foolish. No, *dumb* was more like it—he felt dumb.

"You didn't ask." She wasn't angry. In her present mood there was very little that could even irritate her. Elyn straightened in the padded wrought-iron chair and patted the seat next to her. "All's forgiven. Come sit down . . . we do have some matters to talk of."

Nick came around her chair and sat down, puzzled but relieved by Elyn's ebullient mood. She wasn't crying—at least not in frustration—and she didn't seem angry or resentful or . . . or anything he'd expected. Again, he had to ask, "Are you sure you're feeling all right?"

"I, my darling, have never felt better in my life. I feel absolutely liberated and, really, far too happy on so sad an occasion."

Nick put his fist to his mouth, resting his thumb against his teeth, thinking. He started to speak, wagged a finger in his wife's direction, and gave up trying to verbalize an extremely frustrating frame of mind. Then he tried again. "Elyn, I thought I'd find you crying. And I thought I'd have to talk myself out of the hole your grandmother dug for me. The way you're acting, you're making me very nervous." Nick sat forward, bracing his elbows on the chair arms, staring at Elyn. "I don't like being nervous. I can't think of another situation in the past ten years that's made me so uneasy. Explain, please."

Elyn let out a whispered sigh. She'd been so concerned with her feelings that she hadn't considered poor Nick. Now she reached out to touch his hand and smile. "I've puzzled you, poor darling," she said sympathetically. "I didn't mean to . . . I just hadn't thought . . . well, of what you must have gone through down there. How did the rest of it go? You must be feeling overwhelmed, hmm?"

"To say the least." He'd come up expecting to offer sympathy and instead had found himself the recipient of it. Not an entirely unpleasant sensation, having Elyn so concerned. "I probably have a good start on an ulcer."

Elyn restrained an urge to smile. Nick looked more like Jackie at the moment, a trifle sulky, but endearing. "Then I shall have to make it up to you, shan't I? Later . . . this evening, perhaps?" His expression brightened appreciably, as she knew it would. "Did Munroe apprise you of the exact worth of the estate?"

Nick nodded. "He did. You can't guess—"

"But I can . . . I know exactly what Grandmother was worth. At least once a year she managed to update the latest figures and work it into a conversation. I think the last time was Christmas. At that time, everything came to slightly less than a million pounds. Of course that includes properties, rents, royalties, all sorts of sources of income. You'll have to learn all of that, of course, or hire someone to oversee—"

"I don't want it."

"Of course you do. Who wouldn't want control over a half-million-pound estate? Why, even after the death duties are paid, we'll be able to live quite comfortably on the balance."

"I'll put it all back in your name."

"Nonsense! Why should you?"

"Because it's your money. Because I don't want it. And because I don't want it coming between us. That's final."

Elyn shook her head, then half-stood and inched her chair closer to Nick's before she reached for his hand. "The only way it'll come between us, my love, is if you allow it to." Nick's mouth had that stubborn set she'd come to recognize. The expression didn't come often, but often enough. "I am *happy* my grandmother did as she did."

217

"You are?" Nick asked warily. He raised a brow, canting his head as he studied Elyn's expression. She seemed sincere. "Why?"

"Oh, there are a number of reasons, the most important of which is that I was feeling terribly guilty. I had put away every rude or selfish act she'd ever done, buried them, and resurrected every instance when I had been unkind or too fresh, disobedient, willful. . . . It seemed she would control me much beyond her own existence, that she might, perhaps, influence me forever."

Nick was beginning to understand. "And what she did made you realize—"

"That she had spent her last efforts virtually trying to destroy my happiness. I do think it was that last effort, that reach beyond the grave, that opened my eyes. I am through with her now. She can no longer hurt me; she is much smaller in stature than I remember." Elyn leaned forward, stretching to kiss Nick, smiling against his lips. "So. You keep the inheritance. I haven't lost it, unless you didn't mean what you said about never letting me go, about being married forever."

Nick's hands came up to frame her face. There wasn't any need for him to reaffirm his promise. The way he held her and looked into her eyes said more than words. "I meant it." His mouth touched hers gently, softly, saying he loved her without speaking.

His hands slid down her shoulders; without breaking their kiss she was on his lap, curled in his arms, safe where she belonged, where it seemed she had always belonged. Her arms twined around his neck, clinging, Desire for him, always close to the surface of her skin, had flared with the kiss, the feel of his hands on her, sure and confident. Finally she drew away, laying her head against his shoulder, content just to be held. Eyes closed, she smiled and mused, "If you

218

dared, ever, to take a mistress, Nick, I think,'' Elyn opened her eyes and smiled almost wickedly, ''no, I *know* I should do something awful and violent . . . to you both.'' One thick dark eyebrow arched. ''Slowly. Something excruciatingly painful.'' Nick's smile lasted a second, showing a flash of dimples, doubting but indulgent. ''You don't believe me?'' Elyn pouted slightly.

''Of course I do. I'll just tell what's-her-name that it's off, that I can no longer keep her in—'' Elyn dug her fingernails into his neck; he flinched. ''Can I pension her off?'' Elyn's fingers tensed once more. ''All right,'' Nick said in mock exasperation, ''final offer. I'll let her keep the winter underwear.''

''Remind me never to be *your* mistress. You're too dear with a penny.''

''Ah, well then, you'll just have to be my wife. I'm much better to wives.''

And Nick was so intent with proving just how good he could be to a wife that he never thought to ask what was in that sealed letter.

Chapter Ten

Although Nick had described the townhouse in Mexico City to her several times, Elyn was still breathtaken by its beauty. Casa Aventura was one of a number of "mansions" set in an exclusive area on the hills near Chapultepec Park. The homes, though each had been altered to suit the style and taste of the owner, all seemed to affect a colonial, almost Moorish flair of architecture.

Casa Aventura, for example, was surrounded by a tall wrought-iron gate. For the most part, only the spikes at the top of the fifteen-foot standards were visible. The rest of the ironwork had, over the years, been interwoven by thick, lush wistaria vines, blooming now with lovely purple blossoms and a musky, sweet scent.

The house itself was whitewashed stucco, with a two-story arched entry lined with bright blue tiles and a wooden balcony overlooking the walkway to the heavily carved front doors. Nick said he had wired ahead. His housekeeper, Señora Maria Consuela Machado, would have their rooms ready. The woman had a child, a small girl close in age to Jackie, with whom he might be able to spend playtime.

A servant had met them at the train and loaded their many pieces of luggage (mostly Elyn's) into a quaint cart that had seen much better days. By now the capital city was a mix of the old and new. Side by side, carts, carriages, and motorcars shared the recently improved highways, though by far the automobile was taking precedence as *the* method of transportation.

Another servant, a grizzled, stooped old man, hailed Nick as the cart approached the driveway of the casa. This was Juan Estaban, who had been the caretaker and overseer of Casa Aventura since before the War of Revolution; only he knew all of its rustic history. He bowed over Elyn's hand and complimented Nick in Spanish, apparently on his choice of a wife. There seemed to be some small discussion of Señora Machado and what her reaction would be, but Nick, with his usual nonchalance, seemed to shrug it off.

It was only when the door opened and Elyn actually saw Maria Consuela for the first time that she understood why the old servant had commented on the presence of Nick's bride. Maria Consuela, or Connie as Nick affectionately called her, was not the old, plump, matronly type Elyn had expected. Though she was indeed a mother, she was no more matronly than Elyn herself. A trifle older perhaps, possibly in her early to mid-thirties, Connie Machado was a voluptuous, light-eyed woman who looked more like the mistress of Casa Aventura than its housekeeper.

And it appeared, once the introductions had been made, that Connie was as shocked to meet Nick's bride as Elyn was to meet her. They appraised each other; there was no other word for the minutely detailed study each gave the other. Neither came away satisfied.

For her part, Connie saw a young woman of obvious breeding, a woman who had now every legal and moral right to act as Nick's hostess. The woman—girl, almost—was truly beautiful in that fair English way that would appeal to Nick. He was, despite the fact that he would never admit it, an Anglophile, a lover of the English culture, of its heritage, its history, its people. They were, after all, his people. Even though she herself had Irish blood, which showed in the lighter skin and blue eyes of her grandfather Ryan, Consuela knew immediately, instinctively, that Nick Rowan had found what he had sought all these long years.

Elyn stared at the woman who was supposed to be a servant and knew at once that she had been more, was more, to Nick. She had that air of command, that assurance that a polished housekeeper, or even the most perfect of butlers, had not. Elyn risked a quick sideways glance at her husband and found her suspicions confirmed in a way that made her heart feel leaden. He looked nervous. Nick was always self-assured, but at the moment he looked as though he would rather be ten thousand miles away. Elyn wished she were, too. How could he do this to her? And she was not alone in feeling betrayed. Connie, too, seemed pale with shock. He hadn't told Elyn of his Mexican mistress; neither had he told his Mexican mistress of his English bride. *The cad.*

Nick knew he'd have to pay for this meeting in more ways than one. First, Elyn knew—or had guessed—that he and Connie had been lovers. Second, he would have to end the affair with Connie. For years now they had given each other the physical release each had needed, and now, for her anyway, it was over. He should have written—anything, a personal note, something to warn her . . . anything.

Jackie came running in, saving the day at least for Nick. The boy was happy to be in a place where they might settle in. "Dad," he nearly shouted, "there was an old man who promised to find me a horse to ride!"

In Spanish, Nick told Connie the boy's name. He didn't have to add that he was the boy's father; it was becoming evident. Each day, as the boy's skin tanned slightly darker, turning a golden brown with the tropical sun, he looked more and more like Nick.

Connie now understood more than she had at first. Even before Veracruz, her husband, Serafino, had fought with Nick. Fino had told her of the woman kidnapped by his friend, of how he had released her here in the capital. Now she was back. Somehow he had found her, her and the son she had borne him. This Consuela could understand, the ties of blood—at least it was more of an excuse than taking a wife on a whim. Nick had never done anything on a whim. The boy was his son, and of course the mother went with the son. And there were ties between men and women who had known love, such ties that lasted, that still bound her to Fino, though he was dead these many years. How, though, could she give up Nick Rowan? She knew his body as well as . . . better than her own. Would this woman, this girl, be able to match the happiness Consuela had given him?

Her own child came running now. Serafina, named after her father but called simply Sera, was a shy thing. She was sweet and gentle, a child who had never caused her mother a moment's worry. Now, as her large hazel eyes stared at Jackie, there seemed to be trouble brewing. Señora Rowan stared at the child, noting the dark wave of the girl's hair and the green flecks in her eyes, and looked away. It never occurred to Nick, or for that matter to Connie, that Elyn might think the little girl was theirs. Only Elyn, with her heart feeling like it would break with the weight of hurting too much, thought of the child's innocence and wanted to turn from the knowledge of her existence.

"I think . . ." Elyn put her hand to her temple and felt a film of sweat frost her forehead. She never perspired. For one thing, she was cold-blooded; for another, it wasn't ladylike. Now, though, ladylike or not, she was not only sweating, she

224

felt as though she might faint. And in front of *her*. Elyn made a supreme effort to regain her composure, though the attempt only made her more pale and damp. "I should like to be shown to our rooms, if you please."

Nick translated again, and requested that a basin of cool water be sent up so the señora's face might be bathed. Connie seemed to be taking his surprise marriage in stride; perhaps she had simply stoically resigned herself to the inevitable. Then again, she might be biding her time. He was sure there would come some moment of confrontation, at least a time when he had to explain what had brought him back so suddenly wed.

Later, after Elyn was comfortably settled in a heavy old Mediterranean bed, Nick left to check on Jackie's progress. Before he went, however, Elyn asked him about Connie. She could put it off no longer. "Why didn't you tell me? . . . I think, knowing your past, I might have survived with less shock, Nick, had you told me she was your mistress."

Nick was seated next to her on the bed. He dampened the cotton cloth again with water, wrung it out, and patted her forehead with it. "There you go again, making me out to be some kind of Don Juan, a Casanova who has ladies in every port." He smiled but Elyn wouldn't, or couldn't, return the gesture. "Look, we've been friends for years. Connie's husband, Fino, and I used to ride together even before we joined Zapata. I owed her a lot. I'll tell you about it sometime. For now, do me a favor—I don't ask for one very often. Let's drop the subject."

And Elyn did drop the subject. Truthfully, she was afraid to hear that there was more involved than lust, or to have Nick admit that Sera was his. So Elyn settled in, somewhat uneasily, to the daily routine of life at the casa. Breakfast was served later than was usual in England, perhaps nine in the morning. For the first week or so, she wandered about, trying to familiarize herself with the layout of the large house. It centered, as did most of the Spanish-style haciendas, around a courtyard. Often, especially in the afternoon when everyone seemed to take advantage of the siesta hour, the gardens and their adjacent patios were the only place where it was possible to catch a brief waft of a breeze.

Elyn had gone shopping for and wore at home the simple, loose cotton clothing similar to what Nick had bought her years before. A cool embroidered blouse worn off the shoulder and a wide skirt that circulated air around her heat-chafed thighs were the most appropriate apparel for the climate. Early in the afternoon, before the heat intensified, she would watch Sera and Jackie practice riding in a small corral adjacent to the main house. They were both surprisingly good. Connie said as much one day, and in the simple statement, Elyn heard a deeper meaning, an implication that perhaps both children had inherited their equestrian skills from the same source.

Again she tried to reason with herself, to explain away her vague feelings of resentment. There were other worries, more real, to deal with. Now that they were here in Mexico, Elyn *had* to find Michael Winters. She tried, still, to think of him as her father but now she knew otherwise. As one of her final cruelties, Lady Anne's note, delivered by Mr. Munroe at the will reading, had informed Elyn that Michael was, in reality, her stepfather and no relation by blood. Now it was essential that she find him alive; or she would never learn the truth about her real father. Of course, she wanted to find him for his own sake. If Grandmother had been the cold strength of her life, then Father had gentled the old woman's authoritarian ways with warmth and quiet affection.

Elyn knew she should have shared the note and its revela-

226

tion with Nick, but something, perhaps a sense of shame, had held her back. He had said he would do everything he could to find Winters. To reveal this sordid bit of information—that Michael Winters had been only a convenient substitute groom for Elyn's already pregnant mother—was too painful and too difficult for her to deal with at the time her grandmother's vindictive will was read. And later, there seemed little to be gained by revealing the truth. Although she tried to keep her patience and allow Nick the time to make his inquiries, the subject of Michael Winters was never very far from her thoughts. In fact, its domination of her waking moments kept her constantly preoccupied.

Elyn and Nick held a party the second week after their arrival. Consuela naturally made all the arrangements, everything from the evening's menu to the invitation list. Elyn found Nick's friends an odd group, considering the way of his former politics. Most of them were in government or some other form of bureaucracy, ministers, subministers, and police and army officials and their wives and daughters. Though many of them spoke English, few spoke it fluently enough to make any sense to Elyn. Again, as long ago, she had the feeling that she was an alien being, unfit for life in this slow, languid, tropical country. Nick, on the other hand, seemed relaxed and easy. But then, he was at home wherever he went.

The party began in a large room, not quite a ballroom, that had been cleared of furniture. Later the guests moved out into the cool of the veranda and courtyard. When there was some small problem to oversee, Nick turned more often to Consuela than to her, and, not for the first time, Elyn had the strange feeling that she was the outsider, that she was the mistress and Consuela was the wife.

The entire evening would have been a dreadful bore had it

not been for one guest. Elyn had insisted that Arthur's friend Patrick Haney, from the capital's British embassy, be invited. To effect that, she'd had to go to extremes, sulking, threatening, and weeping tears that were not false.

Patrick stayed with her for a good part of the night. He was very attentive, dancing when she wished, discussing mutual acquaintances from home, and eating small helpings of the buffet foods with her at one of the patio tables set on the veranda. He was not a handsome man. The foreign service seemed to attract men with rather bland exteriors, but certainly his wit and broad intelligence more than made up for his lack of masculine appeal. Elyn liked him immediately and determined to write to Arthur straight away and thank him for suggesting they be introduced.

So subtly that Elyn almost failed to recognize what he was doing, Patrick had interspersed his conversation with inquiries into Nick's current activities. How was his business going these days? It did seem that he knew all the right people—and in a country of this type, that mattered, didn't it? She would likely be a great benefit to him, though of course it was clear that he'd married her out of love rather than advantage.

Elyn, listening to the questions, began to wonder exactly what Patrick Haney thought Nick's business was. She herself had no idea. For the most part he was home during the day, going out only on occasion in the afternoons to "meet" with old friends—friends, he insisted, who would only bore her. "Why do you think it so important for Nicholas to cultivate these . . . government people, then?" she asked.

The light on the veranda was not bright. Colored lanterns had been hung around the courtyard and an occasional gas-lamppost lit the cool darkness, but as Patrick Haney peered closer at Elyn Rowan's lovely face, he could discern no cunning or sly dissembling. For a moment he was astounded, realizing suddenly that she didn't know what he was talking about. "My dear Elynora . . . has your husband never taken you down to see the factory?"

Elyn didn't want to say it, but the reply came forth before she thought to cover her own surprise. "Factory? Why, whatever do you mean?"

"Ah, well, it isn't truly a factory as such. Rowan Importing, Limited, is actually more of a warehouse. Nothing is assembled there, you see; it's simply brought in and stored until it is forwarded to its purchasers." He looked around at some of the ministers strolling with their wives, and the expression on his pale, bejowled face was definitely one of distaste. "I can scarce believe, my dear lady, that you had no inkling that your husband imports and supplies arms and ammunition to the Mexican government. By heaven, what did you think he did with his time?"

Elyn's first reaction was shock, then disbelief. Nick wouldn't sell arms to the government. Despite the fact that some former rebels held high government positions, nothing had changed so very much. Even if he were destitute, which with her inheritance he certainly could not be, he wouldn't enter into a business that was so at cross-purposes with his ideals. Or former ideals. Suddenly, after the shock and disbelief, anger set in. Patrick Haney had no reason to ask her anything of her husband's business. Under the guise of being a fellow native of her country, he had pried and used her to gain information for . . . for who knew what purposes? She may unknowingly have hurt Nick with some of her answers. No matter what he had done, or was doing, she would remain loyal. But she would find out, before the evening ended, what Nick was involved in—and she would find out directly from him.

Now she was merely angry—at Patrick, who had used her,

pretending with a diplomat's native charm to find her enchanting, and made a fool of her. "Mr. Haney," she said and stood, "if you have questions concerning my husband's activities, I suggest you present them directly to him. I don't care to be duped, I don't care to converse innocently with a . . . a snake in the grass, and furthermore, I shan't see you again or invite you to my home again."

Elyn started away. Patrick stared after her, surprised as much by the spirited defense she'd shown for Nick Rowan as by the absolute naïveté of a woman who must be at least in her twenties. He stood, wanting to find out one more, very interesting fact. "Wait—please. You said I was not welcome in your home again. If I seem to have tricked you, I apologize. I do truly find you the most interesting of companions, and an innocent in all this. That is why . . . I must say, Mrs. Rowan, that—and *please*, do believe me—you are wrong in claiming this your home. You, even as I, are a guest in the Casa de Machado. It is Señora Machado's hospitality we enjoy tonight."

The lady's face was deathly white. Haney was afraid she would faint, and then how would he explain that to Rowan? She was, though, an amazingly self-controlled young lady. Elynora Rowan straightened her posture, tilted her chin high, and asked once more for clarification, perhaps to assure herself that she hadn't heard wrong. "Señora Consuela Machado is the owner of Casa Aventura? Her husband, her late husband, purchased the property?"

Haney hesitated. He'd already done enough. Big as he was, he didn't want Rowan coming after him for some crazy kind of vengeance. "Madam, I've said too much. Your husband, if he hasn't told you of this . . . I shouldn't like to have my diplomatic career ended here."

Elyn's voice was chilly. "You have my assurance, sir. Nick

will not know from whom I discovered this. He may, in fact, not know at all. Now, how did the señora come by the property?''

Haney swallowed hard. The evening had begun so nicely. ''It came to her, Mrs. Rowan, through a gift of deed a number of years back.'' He didn't have to say more. She knew. Rowan had given his mistress the estate. Patrick decided to leave now, before his troubles worsened.

''And, Mr. Haney—the truth, please—how does the señora support the house and staff?''

''You're asking things I can't answer, madam. I can only assume, as others have, that Mr. Rowan is generous enough to see to the expenses. Now, I've said too much. Please forgive me if I've—''

''Leave, Mr. Haney. I should like you to keep this quiet, please. I certainly cannot kick you out of a house belonging to . . . another woman, but if you don't make an immediate exit, I shall tell my husband of our discussion. *Everything.*''

Elynora Rowan wasn't the soft, empty-headed child she had at first seemed. He would leave as quickly as his short, bandy legs could carry him. ''You're assured of my discretion, madam . . . as I am of yours.'' He started into the house and paused to look back over his shoulder. ''Do give my best to Arthur, won't you?''

Very softly, Elyn said, ''Go to hell, Mr. Haney!'' and turned her back on him.

Not long after Haney made his exit, Nick found Elyn seated in the middle of the courtyard. He had looked through the house for her and checked the veranda, then managed to see a figure nearly hidden by the shadows of a thick-branched willow. ''Elyn?'' he called, and nearly turned away because there was no acknowledgment, not a whisper of movement from the female form seated beneath the tree.

He strolled forward, stopping to shake the hand of a *jefe*, a politico chieftain of the old days, a man he once might have shot without blinking an eye. He spoke to the man for a moment, complimented his wife on the beauty of their two daughters, then excused himself from their company.

It was she all right. From ten feet away he recognized her fair hair peeking out from the edge of the black lace mantilla she wore. From five feet away it was impossible not to note how fair and perfect her complexion was, milky white and creamy even though the shadows surrounded her. "Darling, I've been looking everywhere for you. Is something wrong? You're not feeling ill?" Still she said nothing. Nick came to her, sat down, and took her hands in his. They were cold as ice. "You *are* coming down with something," he said, and added almost accusingly, "Why didn't you let me know?" He touched her forehead. It was as chilled as the rest of her. "I'm getting you to bed. *Now.* Don't you *dare* give me any arguments."

"But *our* guests . . . what will they think?" Elyn felt empty inside, devoid of emotions. She was beyond anger, beyond hurt; she wasn't even curious why Nick had chosen to lie to her—about the business, about Consuela. Nothing seemed to matter, not just now, anyway. She was very tired, too tired to think or feel. Later, in her own time, in her own way, she would find out why Nick had lied. She knew, even before he answered, that Consuela would carry on as hostess, that very few at the party would notice she was missing. After all, she was just another guest.

Chapter Eleven

During the next few weeks, though he'd had a physician look at her, Nick could find nothing physically wrong with Elyn. She ate, played with the children, attended parties, went shopping, riding, and even had several new motorcars sent over for inspection. There was nothing concrete that he could put his finger on, but she had, somehow, changed.

When he came near her, Elyn seemed to retreat, to withdraw almost as if she couldn't bear to look at him. At breakfast their conversation consisted of a shared interest in Jackie's activities and, perhaps, plans for later in the day.

She was worried about something or several somethings, and Nick was going mad trying to figure out what. When they'd first arrived, she had been nearly fanatical about finding her father. Now, except to inquire occasionally if he'd heard anything encouraging, Elyn scarcely broached the subject. He knew she was not unfaithful, and yet if he approached her, even gently to touch her shoulder, she seemed to shiver in disgust and moved away. Two weeks of watching Elyn in form-fitting gowns, in her riding outfit, in her negligees . . . he wouldn't last much longer. Had she not seemed so . . . despondent, he would have pressed the issue much sooner.

He *had* heard something about Michael Winters, but it wasn't something he could share with Elyn ... not just yet, not until he knew more. For the past three years he'd been in contact with an American living in Mexico, using his old connections with the Zapatistas to keep tabs on what was happening in the provinces. His contact was a man named Gyp Andrews, a former flier with the escadrille until a crash had injured one of his legs. During the war they'd been stationed together near Verdun, and before Gyp's crash had taken him on to an army intelligence unit, they'd been poker buddies.

Now, with his bad leg, Gyp made his living working for the United States. Officially, there were no American intelligence units operating in foreign countries. Still, there'd been plenty of espionage and underhanded dealings during the war, and in the "interests of peace" it was continuing. It was not innocent, but to Nick it seemed no threat to the rights of other countries. Mexico and South America were the principal areas of concern. The main idea was to keep an eye on the political stability of the governments of the Americas—with a thought to heading off any trouble before it developed into a confrontation.

By Nick's watch it was close to eight. Normally, with their son in bed, it would have been an excellent time to spend an hour or so with Elyn, talking, sharing a drink, perhaps leading up to a romantic rendezvous beneath the covers. Tonight, though, he had an appointment, one that he couldn't skip, one that might give him more information on her father's whereabouts.

Elyn said nothing when he told her he was going out for an hour or two. She seemed not to care whom he was meeting or where they would meet. He honestly believed that if he'd said he had an appointment in a brothel, she wouldn't have blinked an eye. They would definitely talk when he got home.

A half-hour later, Nick was seated in a cantina across town, wondering why Andrews always had to choose seedy dungholes for his "discussions." Aside from the fact that he, in a clean white suit and panama hat, stuck out like a sore thumb, the stench that pervaded the still air of the saloon made his gut clench in protest. Across the room from his table, close to the rough-hewn planks that served as a bar, the proprietor was thoughtfully sifting another handful of sawdust over the evidence left by a previous customer.

This sure as hell wasn't part of the job, Nick thought and lifted his brandy, drawing hard on the smell and taste of the liquor to dispel the stale air around him. Over by the bar, a whore who'd been old before the revolution was trying to interest a poor young campesino, fresh from the countryside, in what she had to offer. Rustic and young as he was, he wasn't interested. In fact, he had the boldness to tell her that he knew of a she-goat back home who asked a higher price and received it! The whore had been insulted too many times to worry about what a *peon* thought. She told him to go home to the country and see if the goat would take him.

Andrews usually was punctual, but this time he was more than thirty minutes late. If he didn't show soon...The thought was interrupted as a huge hand slammed against his back, a hearty welcoming slap that could come from only one source. Without looking, Nick said, "You sure as hell took your time, Gyp."

"Sorry 'bout that, son. I come up on the prettiest señorita you ever saw and she . . . well, that's a story for another time, eh?" Robert Horton Andrews, who had early on gained the nickname Gyp because he was as footloose as a gypsy, settled his large frame into the chair opposite Nick's and signaled the barkeep. The man was only halfway to the table when Gyp held up two fingers and called, "Tequila, *por favor!*" then turned back to ask Nick if he'd been waiting long.

"Long enough, thanks." Nick leaned on the table, glowering. "Remind me not to let *you* pick the place next time, huh? Your taste leaves a lot to be desired. In fact, there likely won't *be* a next time, so . . ." Nick raised his glass, "here's to all the good times!"

Andrews smiled benignly. Rowan had withdrawn his services before. He always came around for one reason or another. There was no reason to believe he wouldn't take this assignment—particularly this one. "You was gone quite a while, son," he commented in a soft drawl that betrayed his Virginia origins. "I do hope you left *some* young things intact over there."

"I told you I got married, you S.O.B.," Nick answered with a grin, finishing his brandy just as the barkeep brought Gyp's tequila. "I'm a family man now. That's why—"

" 'Scuse me, son, for interruptin'," Gyp said, then told the barkeep to bring another round, a double, for his friend.

Nick shook his head. "I'm not staying that long, pal. And, Gyp, ignoring me won't work. Nothing you can say will change my mind."

Andrews shrugged, seeming unconcerned. "Have I tried, Nick? I know how you feel, I do. Ain't we been friends for . . . what is it now—nigh on to five, maybe six years?"

"Not quite five."

"Well, all right, son. Y'know someone *that* long, fight the goddamned Huns side by side, and you figure . . . Ah, what the hell, son. Like you said, you got yourself a family now. Mighty pretty little thing, too, your wife. Caught a glimpse of her and the kid the other day at the park. Why, she's more'n pretty, she's downright beautiful!'' Gyp took a squeeze of the worn-looking, yellow-green lime that had arrived with his drink and swallowed hard on the tequila. "Guess she don't know 'bout me, hmm?"

Nick's double had arrived. He paid for it and Gyp's tequila. He didn't want to leave this dump owing Andrews anything. It was a debt to his fellow flier in the escadrille that had landed him in this cloak-and-dagger business to begin with. "No, she doesn't. And it's going to stay that way." Nick sipped his drink and shook his head. "Christ, I'd hate to try and explain it to her. I'm not sure myself why I ever got in it."

"Ah, well—that's easy enough," Andrews boasted, and Nick glanced up, clearly skeptical. "It's in the blood, son. In yours, well as mine. You see some dumb sons a bitches struttin' around, actin' like they don't have to answer to nobody, not even God, by God; pretty near makes your blood boil, it does! And then, without thinkin', see, you're chargin' in, with a mind to settin' things to rights. Why, you helped the *peones*, you helped the Frogs, and, son, all this work you been doin' for Uncle Gyp, all it is is savin' the world from more of them jokers 'fore they get a foothold."

"You have a perverted sense of ethics, Gyp."

"You watch your mouth, son. The only thing 'bout me that's perverted is my sex life. That's the way I like it. Now if you wasn't a newlywed, why, I'd show you the hottest—"

Nick grinned. Gyp never changed. "Even if I wasn't wed, you old gimpy-legged dog, I still wouldn't join you. You make me feel about ninety, but I'll take a nice quiet life, nothing strange on the side, thanks, and no, I repeat *no*, intrigue." He could tell by the look in Gyp's eyes that the man hadn't yet given up. "None. N-O-N-E. I am out of it."

"Then there's a lot of your ol' buddies gonna be dead 'fore the year's out."

"Forget it. It won't work. Whatever's going on in that crooked mind of yours, I'm not falling for it. The world won't collapse if I retire. The import business goes back to you, and," Nick stood up, anxious to leave the cantina and go home, "I am taking my family back to Denver. For good, Gyp. Adiós. It's been . . . fun."

"You can't go."

Nick frowned and sat back down, leaning forward, lowering his voice. "You want to tell me why the hell I can't? The way I see it, there's no way you can stop me." He smiled, though he'd seldom in his life felt less amused. "Unless you want to compromise your cover, friend. They don't much like Americans down here, especially Americans butting into their domestic affairs."

Gyp lifted his shoulders and let them drop in a gesture of innocence. "I'm just a businessman, son. I run a few thousand head of prime cattle but m'ranch is in my partner's name. And *his* cousin, Apolo-somethin'-or-other, has a cousin in Obregon's cabinet. They don't take kindly to bein' hassled, see, and *you're* an American, too." It was a shame to force Rowan's hand, but Gyp needed him on this. He was really very fond of the younger man, looked on him almost as a brother. Still, business was business, and Uncle Sam was an impatient and sometimes unfeeling relative. "Why don't I just order us another round while we discuss my . . . our problem."

"Why don't you go to hell, Andrews," Nick answered through gritted teeth. It didn't matter to him what the problem was. He'd agreed one too many times to Gyp's "little" requests, attended boring luncheons with politicos, danced with too many ugly wives at social affairs. He had even squired the daughter of a cabinet minister because Gyp had wanted to know if her father was involved in a suspected coup—and Elena Margarita Rosa Louisa Sanchez had been a sad excuse for a woman. Now he had Elyn and Jackie to think of. "Look," he said in a calmer but still determined voice, "I'm through playing games. I've helped you more often than I ever had to, and I don't owe you a damned thing!"

"This'll be the last time, Nick," Andrews said assumptively. "You got my word on it, my oath." Had he had a more choleric temperament, Gyp might have taken offense at Rowan's snort of disdain . . . but nothing ever rattled him, because he wouldn't permit it. "No, son, by my honor, you don't *personally* owe me. However, your country needs your help. Correct me if I'm—"

Nick tried to remain calm; he thought of Elyn's face and that helped immensely. "I didn't come here for a lecture on my patriotic duty, Andrews. *I am out.* Period."

"Not till you listen to me a minute, boy. I got myself a problem. Now, in the past you helped me out when I had a problem. On top o' bein' patriotic, that was damned friendly. If you was to help me on this one, I swear, last problem, I maybe could help you out with a problem of yours."

Nick smiled. "I don't *have* any problems."

"Wrong. You got a missin' father-in-law. Dependin' 'pon your bride's temper, I'd call that a real hell of a problem!"

"What's Winters have to do with your operation?" Instinct warned Nick that he was about to get sucked into working for Gyp one last time; but Elyn wanted her father back, and so far he'd done nothing toward that end. Personally, he was sure Michael Winters was dead. It would take Elyn a long time to accept that.

"I ain't quite sure. He's involved somehow, whether inno-

239

cent or not. The group is still formin', but they're drawin' support, plenty of it, from former Villistas and your ol' Zapata buddies. There's enough campesinos starvin' and out o' work to make another ten revolutions." He paused for a drink. "You heard anything?"

Nick shook his head. "I don't have the contacts I used to. You think Winters is a captive? There's been no ransom demand."

Andrews shrugged. "Won't know nothin' for sure unless you decide to cooperate. They're beyond the talkin' stage, though. Juan Benito told me—"

"I thought you were staying *away* from the warehouse." Juan was his inventory supervisor, a man who knew as much about the business as Nick did, probably more. "How's it going to look, a man like you, a 'simple' *hacendado,* hanging around an arms importer? Someone might even get the idea you're—"

"*Can* your sarcasm, Rowan. I told you I'm covered. You just worry about Nick Rowan." He glared for a moment, irritated with Nick—or with himself for reacting to Nick's needling. "As I was sayin', they contacted Benito already— one of 'em did, anyway. He was asking about stock, when any new shipments were due in, could he buy wholesale."

"And what did Juan say?"

"'Talk to the boss.'" Gyp leaned back and stretched his long arms behind his head. "And *that* is why I need you. They want to negotiate. You have somethin' they need—it's enough of a ticket in to see the head honcho. The buyer's name, by the way, is Nauyalcoatl, but all the *peones* call 'im Nauyaca."

Nick frowned. "Sounds familiar—and not in a nice way."

"Name of a snake, a particularly nasty critter who deals

240

out a particularly nasty kinda death. I suppose, by implication, Nauyaca ain't to be messed with.''

"Well, that makes two of us, then." Nick sighed, unconsciously tapping the side of his glass while he considered Gyp's "problem." And the bastard was right—with Elyn's father somehow involved, it had become *his* problem. "So what am I supposed to do—wait around until one of these—what're they calling themselves, anyway?—shows up?''

"In English, they're 'Four-fangs,' Nauyals. Call 'em what the shit you want. They need weapons. You'll be hearing from 'em soon. Don't set any prices—I want you to get into their camp and I want to know where it is and how many's involved.''

"Maybe I should just wipe them out while I'm there?''

Gyp shrugged. "Save a lot of time and fuss, but accordin' to the important people, this is a watch-and-see. We're just coming back off a war, son. We don't need to stir up the natives nor have them *federales* chargin' over our borders again. Observe, report, that's all. And as a bonus, you can find out what your daddy-in-law is doing with a bunch of Aztec revolutionaries.''

"I always was crazy about you.''

"So invite me over for dinner some night, son. I know m'salad fork from m'knife.''

Nick mouthed an obscenity and stood, tossing a coin on the table. "I won't let you know when I'm leaving. You'll know, I'm sure, before me." He turned and started for the swinging doors to the cantina. Without turning he said, in a very quiet tone, "This *is* the last time, Andrews.''

Before returning home, Nick headed for the warehouse. It would be locked for the night, but Juan Benito had a small room on the first floor where he kept a cot and a small wood stove. Nick had several things to ask Juan, the most important of which was who he was working for, Nick or Gyp Andrews.

And at home, at the Casa Aventura, another type of interrogation was about to begin. Elyn had asked Consuela into the parlor, ostensibly to share a cup of cocoa but also because she now had the chance to ask the many questions that had plagued her during the past two weeks.

Consuela was of the *peon* class. Her grandfather had been pure Irish, a blue-eyed adventurer looking for gold, but the rest of her was mestiza, part Indian, part Spanish. She was of the land, but she'd had some education and there was nothing stupid about her. Soon after the two women had settled into chairs facing each other, Consuela broke the awkward silence. "You would like to know what I am to Nick, eh?"

Elyn was shocked by the woman's forthright attitude but admitted that, yes, she wanted to know exactly that. "I . . . I don't believe you have slept with him since we came here, but I know of your past affair." She really didn't want to discuss this: it was embarrassing and degrading to talk calmly of a man with whom they both had slept. "Why?"

Consuela's dark brows wrinkled in a puzzled frown. Was this Anglo woman crazy? "Why, you ask? Señora, that much should be obvious. Nick Rowan is a man, a man's man, a woman's man. Is this clear? Sometimes I do not use the right phrases. He is *macho, muy macho,* a man who can take care of himself and those around him, yet a man who can stroke a woman's cheek as softly as if it were made of velvet. This one, how can you *not* love him?"

"Do you? Because, señora, if you do, I will tell you now that I will keep him. I will do everything in my power, use every feminine wile, to keep him. And I—"

"Need not waste your breath telling me how many ways

you can keep him tied to you. You already have won and do not know. Are you blind, Señora Rowan? You have his son." Elyn looked shocked. "Of course little Jackie is his. But if you did not have the boy, you would still have Nick." Consuela sipped at her chocolate. It had grown cold already but was still rich and sweet, as she liked it. Why was she telling this woman these things? Why should she offer her reassurance that Rowan belonged, not only legally but in almost every other way, to his bride? Perhaps she had grown stupid with age. But no, even had she chosen to fight for Nick, she would have lost. He wanted Elynora. It was obvious. And who but God knew the workings of a man's mind or what made him choose his mate?

"I have loved only one man in my life, señora. He lies buried now in a cemetery not far from here. Fino, my husband, the father of my baby, my lover, my friend. He is gone. I want no one again."

"But you wanted Nick. You . . . you slept with him."

"Why does this anger . . . no, hurt you so? It was before he met you, or after he lost you. Yes, I know of Veracruz and how the boy was sired before Nick let you go. I had no husband, Nick had no wife. We both had bodies, one male, one female. This is the way of nature, no? Even in England . . . ?"

"Yes, even in England." Elyn didn't like the idea that the two had been intimate, perhaps she never would; but there was not much she could do to change it. "And he gave you this house . . . and an income, to support you and the child."

"*Sí.*" Consuela would explain nothing further. Let Nick tell his wife the rest. She had not asked for the house; let *him* say why it was hers. "I tell you now, señora. We will not be friends. You resent me. I resent you. I do not love Nick

243

Rowan. I am fond of him. I like when he touches me, when he makes love—''

Elyn thought she would die if she had to listen to an explicit accounting of the affair. "I don't wish to hear anything about this affair, señora. Doesn't it bother you that he has brought me here, to your home? He has lied, led me to believe that this is our home, when really we are nothing but your guests."

"You are most welcome. I will not say I do not feel desire for Rowan. He is . . . well, he made me very happy. But it is done. You will stay as long as he feels you should remain. If you argue this, argue it with him. As you have said, he is *your* husband." Concluding her speech, deciding she would say no more, Consuela stood and bade Elyn a good night's rest.

"Wait!" Despite her vast confusion, Elyn was clear-minded enough to ask the other question that had been bothering her. "Why does Nick sell weapons? You and I both know his feelings about the *peones*, the common folk; something is wrong with this business he is in."

It was true, but it also wasn't Connie's place to say why. Of necessity, she knew much of what Nick had been doing the past few years. She knew Andrews and several of his other friends. "Ask your husband, señora. Ask him."

Elyn had no chance to reply. When she would have pressed Consuela for more details, the woman turned her back and started from the room. Elyn had no choice but to retire to her own room. She couldn't know when Nick would return . . . or even where he had gone.

It was just past midnight when Nick returned. He had spent the last two hours grilling Benito. The contact from the Nauyals had come again. He knew the "boss" was back in the city. He wanted the meeting very soon. Benito was to call the man; he had a telephone number in some chain of complicated exchange that would eventually get word to the man. The meeting was to be set for ten o'clock the next evening, in Benito's room at the warehouse.

The casa was dark when Nick entered except for a small oil lamp Connie had left burning in the hallway. Nick made his way through the house as quietly as he could, puzzling as he came upon the door to his suite and saw a pale pool of light spreading beneath the door. Elyn should have been asleep already. He had hoped she would be. His clothing still stank from the cantina, and he was too tired to explain where he'd been so late.

With a good deal of trepidation, he opened the door. Elyn was sitting up in bed, a pillow propped behind her as she read the latest issue of *Harper's*. Her smile was sweet. An immediate chill snaked down Nick's spine. She looked lovely. Despite his weariness and the fact that he would have to bathe first, Nick was tempted to take advantage of what was, on her part, an obviously amorous mood. "Hi, love," he said softly. He dared not come too close or she would note the odor of that rotgut brandy from the bar. "Up late, hmm?"

Elyn nodded. Nick looked worn, as if he'd been through some mental strain. What *was* he up to? Somehow, before the lights went out, she would know. "Your business kept you later than you expected. Are you satisfied?" Nick was taking off his somewhat rumpled white suit jacket and paused. "With the outcome of the meeting? It *was* business, wasn't it? I certainly would hope so at this hour." Elyn smiled again.

She wanted something, but Nick was too tired to try to figure it out. For the past two weeks she'd been colder than an iceberg and now, suddenly, he was getting signals of a thaw. Not just a thaw, a heat wave. Nick yawned and politely covered his mouth. "Sorry, hon'—it really was a rough

245

meeting. Touch-and-go over prices, quantities—well, all that business stuff is boring.''

As Nick continued to strip off his clothes, Elyn slipped out of bed and came toward him. She stopped about three feet away, noticing a definite odor, a strong smell that could be nothing but alcohol. ''Where'd they hold this meeting, darling? You seem to have picked up a . . . an appreciable odor.''

''Sorry,'' Nick said and hurried off to their bath before she cornered him any further. ''We had so much to discuss, we sent for drinks. We were at the El Plu—well, you wouldn't recognize it anyway, but it's a large hotel near the palace. I'm going to take a bath now. Otherwise you won't let me in the same bed, hmm?''

It was entirely possible that, even spotlessly clean, she would not let him in the same bed. Elyn waited until she heard the bath being poured, then slipped out of her night robe and came into the bathroom attired only in a dark blue negligee. It was partially silk, partially net lace, and clung to her figure in a way that left no illusions as to what shape she was in. Nick was just settling into the water. He actually paled when he saw her, and his brows furrowed as he considered the reason for her presence. ''Anything wrong, sweetheart?''

''No, I just thought I might wash your back, darling. I haven't been very attentive lately. I know it's selfish of me but I've been all wrapped up in this business of locating my father. And meanwhile, neglecting you, poor baby.''

Elyn took the sponge from him and soaped it and Nick leaned back to enjoy the unexpected pleasure of being pampered. The musk-scented soapsuds were thick and creamy. As she spread them across his shoulders and neck, massaging lightly, Nick relaxed even more. It seemed a good time to ask her what had been bothering her, but he didn't want anything to spoil the mood.

"I had a talk with Consuela tonight."

The statement seemed innocent enough, but a warning bell jangled deep inside Nick's brain. "Oh? She's a nice woman. I'm glad you two are getting to know each other."

"Why shouldn't we—we've so much in common. Two children almost the same age, a man we both find attractive."

Nick turned and looked at her. Elyn appeared calm. "What man?" he asked with an attempted smile.

"Why, you, darling. She really feels you have a way with—"

"Elyn, stop right now. I don't think I like the turn this conversation is taking. Now if you want to talk about some—"

Elyn's voiced was honeyed, increasing Nick's apprehension. "Well, there *are* other things to discuss, but I haven't finished with you yet, darling." The sponge slid over his chest and massaged in soothing circles. "Now—where was I? Oh, yes, Connie and I were comparing notes. She just loves it when you—"

"*Elyn!*"

"What? Does it bother you when women exchange information? It can't harm you, certainly not your reputation, and it can only add to your ability to give me pleasure! What, my darling, is wrong with that?"

"Nothing, except that you've suddenly gone from a shy, retiring English flower to a hothouse orchid. I don't need any hints from Connie to make you—" Suddenly Nick realized that Elyn was teasing him. "You didn't really talk about sex?"

She nodded, though she refused to enlighten him as to the actual extent of the conversation. "We talked about several other things as well. Like the fact that you own a business that supplies weapons and ammunition to the Mexican government. Do you care to tell me why?''

Nick looked at her. She had to find out sooner or later. ''Connie has a big mouth.''

''Connie didn't tell me. Someone else, who shall go nameless, did. It seems everyone in Mexico City but me knows what you do. Mightn't you have said *something*, Nicholas?''

She seemed more upset by the news of what his business was than by the revelation of his affair with Connie. ''A man has to make a living. You do spend a lot on clothes.''

''You just inherited several million dollars from my grandmother, you rotter! I could spend on clothes until I was blue in the face and not spend it all. We're rich, we're bloody, filthy rich, and you claim you're worried over *my* expenditures. You've got *your* gall, Nicholas Rowan!'' Elyn was beginning to sputter, the anger she'd checked all evening threatening to spill over. She stared at him for a full minute, then took the soapy sponge and shoved it in his face.

In the seconds it took Elyn to come to her feet from a kneeling position, Nick had instinctively reached out, caught hold of her arm, and tugged. She slipped, fell sideways into the tub, and landed atop him with a shriek. By then he had the soap cleared from his eyes and was glaring at her for the surprise attack. It would serve her right if he did the same to her, and she saw the thought cross his face.

Elyn struggled to rise, but the water, the enameled tub, and Nick's strong arms impeded her escape. ''Don't you dare!'' she threatened. ''You deserved what you got and I have not yet begun to take you to task!''

''You haven't, have you, now?'' Nick smiled as he caught her by the hair, loosening the neatly coiled bun at her nape.

248

Fortunately, the tub was large enough for such horseplay; still, the water splashed about the tiled floor, making an awful mess. He had a firm grip on her, his arms locked about her in an inflexible hold. "Give me all your complaints at once, so I can get them done with. The feel of your silk-clad bottom perched on my lap is distracting, to say the least."

Elyn's eyes narrowed, then widened in surprise as she felt a familiar prod. Again the blue eyes narrowed. "You have given Maria Consuela Machado this house and grounds and supported her all these years. Why?"

Nick's dark brows drew together to form a line. "Because I owed it to her, to her and little Sera. Serafino Machado died because of me. We were in prison together, one not very far from here, in the city. We tried to escape—it was my plan, my fault we failed. He took the blame. I was tossed in a sweatbox."

"And Machado?"

"First they horsewhipped him as an example, then they hanged him. His body was still hanging there ten days later when they let me out of the box." The memory made Nick's handsome features nearly ugly with bitterness. He turned and looked into her eyes. "Still think I gave her the house because she's a good lay?"

Elyn wanted to cry—wanted to but couldn't. She stared back at him, knowing he was telling the truth, knowing she had dredged up memories that he had wanted buried. "I'm sorry."

"Me too. But that doesn't help Connie, does it? And it doesn't make it easier on Sera, either. I can't bring back her father. I also can't see her live in a hovel."

"You're very honorable."

"I'm very guilty. Now let's drop it, huh? What else is on that active little mind of yours?"

Elyn's head had been down. Now she lifted her chin and looked deep into Nick's eyes. "I want my father back. He's alive—I know it. If you don't do something . . . soon—"

"You'll what? What exactly *will* you do? Leave me? I could find you—easily—within a day. Find him yourself? Not a chance, love. Look, I told you I was trying. You just have to trust me." *That* was a laugh—he'd just told her several lies and now he was asking her to trust him!

"I trust you, I think, but you don't seem to be doing much to find him. I thought the world of him. And he loved me . . . loves me . . . very much." Elyn hadn't realized she'd been speaking in the past tense, as if Michael Winters were, indeed, dead.

Something about the intensity of her answer made Nick wonder. There seemed to be another reason she was searching for Winters, and it had nothing to do with her love for him. He wished he knew the answer, but for now it was just one of those things that would have to remain unspoken . . . like his business with Andrews.

"You believe me about Connie?" Nick asked, and Elyn nodded. "And what I do for a living is up to me, right?" Again she agreed, though less enthusiastically. "You'll understand more later," Nick promised. "Now, unless you let me finish my bath, it's liable to evolve into a very wet, slippery lay."

"Promises!" Elyn looked at him with an arched brow. She started to get up but found the going difficult and slipped back. "You could help me. . . ."

Nick smiled, showing his dimples. "Helping you *out* is not what I had in mind. I never turn a needy lady out of a bath."

"Or a lay?"

"Or a lay. Why not the both while we're about it? You

have, by the way, gotten awfully bold and saucy since I married you."

"Perhaps, love, you should have just made a mistress of me."

Nick shook his head. "Wouldn't have been half the fun. Legally, you can beat wives, you see . . . while—"

Elyn hit him square in the face with the soapy sponge and in seconds they were laughing, directly in the middle of a soap fight.

Chapter Twelve

Nick made himself scarce for the next two weeks. His excuses to Elyn were that he was checking into leads concerning her father's disappearance. Again, for what seemed the twentieth time, he reminded her that matters moved slowly here, that one had to make contacts and pay for information, that many times the informants were the police themselves.

The excuse didn't wash, of course, but there wasn't much he could do to explain where he really was during the day and why he sometimes had to go out in the evenings. Benito had told him she'd called the warehouse several times; he was running out of excuses. Elyn became distant once more. At night when he would reach out and touch her, she would stiffen and act as if . . . as if she had no interest in him until he should give her what she wanted most—her father. He left her alone. There was no sense in arguing, no reason to try to explain that he had little or no choice in what he was doing or that it might just get her her father back. The whole thing would be resolved within a matter of weeks. If Elyn didn't hate him by then, she would understand.

At the beginning of the second week a man named Ruiz came to see Nick. They talked in Benito's room, and the short, stocky supervisor was the only other man present. Ruiz was merely a go-between, a messenger. He knew nothing of the weaponry, of prices, of supply. He was to arrange, he kept repeating in a wooden voice, a meeting between Señor Rowan and his leader.

A meeting was fine with Nick but not strictly on the rebel leader's terms. It would be at the rebel camp, wherever that might be. They could blindfold Nick if they were going to play games. He would talk only with the head man, who was . . . ?

"I say no more, I tell nothing," Ruiz insisted stubbornly. "You will know his name, señor, when you meet him. We pay, you deliver—a very simple bargain, no?"

"*If* you've got the money," Nick added, then leaned forward, resting his arms on his knees. "But if something goes wrong, Ruiz, *I'm* the one with my ass in a sling! I want more of a guarantee. I want to know *whom* I'm meeting and what his particular gripe is. If he's a communist, forget it."

"He is no *communisto*, señor," Ruiz promised. "But he is for the people. You—were you not for the people before the fighting ceased? We know you rode with Zapata. A man does not change in a few years. This means we can deal with you." Ruiz shrugged and smiled, showing two missing front teeth. "It does not mean we can trust you, only that we may be able to deal."

"Thanks for the vote of confidence—it's mutual." Nick glanced at Benito, curious as to what he thought so far. The messenger may have been a campesino but he was not nearly as dumb as he'd made himself out to be at the beginning. "I'll meet you here—no, someplace else—the park, by the zoo entrance, at midnight, one week from tonight," he offered. "I'll provide my own mount, a sample of merchandise, and figures on what I can supply. You lead the way to this camp of yours and we'll see how much firepower we can work into this 'people's' revolt. Until then, friend, I don't want to see your face around here again.''

"*Sí*, I understand, señor. I will meet you, but as you said yourself, once we leave the city you *will* be blindfolded."

"Agreed. Now go, before someone sees you here. Juan, show the man out."

When Benito returned, Nick told him to sit, offered a drink and a cigar, and asked Benito's true opinion of what had just transpired. Juan was a quiet man, an efficient, trusted employee. Had he been wealthier, perhaps the import business would have been his. There wasn't much Nick could do about that. The place didn't belong to Nick either, though only Andrews and, Nick supposed, Andrews's superiors knew that.

The supervisor shrugged, a gesture that conveyed the uncertainty of all things in life. He had refused both the smoke and the drink, preferring to concentrate, to calculate his answer for Nick. "One cannot tell by this man they send. He seemed no fool . . . perhaps his leader is less a fool. There have been so many reasons over the years to change Mexico . . . why not try one more time?"

"Because, *mi amigo*," Nick answered with a frown, "one more time isn't just numbers of rifles, bullets, figures on paper. For all the blood, mestizo, Indio, or Creole, spilled in Mexico, your country should be dead right now. Change will come. Mexico must learn patience."

"You did not talk this way a few years past, señor," Juan reminded him. "For centuries we have waited to be free. Almost eight centuries. A very long time, when it is *up* you look, not down."

For a moment Nick almost corrected Benito. It had been four centuries plus several years since Cortes had come to conquer. Then he realized that Juan was speaking in terms of

255

Aztec centuries, the fifty-two-year periods in the pre-Columbian calendar. As far as he knew, Juan was a mestizo, as Mexican as you could be if you discounted the original native Indians and the Spanish Creole settlers. "I've been there, Juan . . ." Nick reminded him, "looking up."

"Forgive me, sir, for the observation, but you have also been standing high enough to look down. You have seen us from more than one angle. Which will you choose now?"

"You're concerned, Juan. I know you think the government hasn't done enough, moved quickly enough. No government's perfect. You think the U.S. does everything it's supposed to for its citizens? You think our congressmen don't take bribes, aren't influenced by favors? The world runs on corruption—it's just a matter of how bad it gets, how much you can stand."

"We want freedom, señor. That is all. Equality of the classes, some land for the poor to use . . . less for the very rich, more for the poor." Once more, the shrug. "These things, are they so terrible to want? Are they more, perhaps, than what was asked for in the revolution of your forefathers?"

Nick's smile was ironic. "I'd love to claim we were patriots, Juan, but in truth, we—my family—were on the losing side. They hadn't come over yet from England."

"Well, here, sir, the conditions are worse. The wealthy, those in power, treat us as cattle, something not so human, workers to serve. They say we are free; but what is freedom to a man who starves? And to a man who cannot feed his little ones, his pride hurts worse than the rumblings of his belly."

Juan Benito felt more deeply about the common people than he had ever let on. For the first time, and Nick wasn't sure why, he had opened up, bared his soul, and shown how he felt. "Do I pay you enough, Benito?" Nick asked. It

256

seemed a rather innocuous question when they'd been discussing ideals, but he sincerely wanted to know if, in his wanderings, he had ignored the needs of the man who'd virtually run the company in his absence.

"You pay enough, señor. It is Mexico, not me, who could use your help. But I should say no more—for I have stepped over the bounds of courtesy. You have fought for men not of your own race. This alone says much. Now, I must check the warehouse and prepare for my night's sleep. You would not want a sleepy man counting your stock."

"I want you to take a leave." Benito looked shocked, more as if Nick had stabbed him in the back than offered a bonus. "You've done nothing wrong, Juan. I simply want you to take a week off—spend some time with your family. You deserve it. The warehouse, as smoothly as it runs, will not collapse in seven days."

Beneath his dark complexion, Benito had paled. "But, sir, I cannot take the time now, not now. You are too generous and take upon yourself a burden too great! Shipments are due from the north—they must be sorted, checked, counted...."

"I'll see that it's taken care of."

"Sí, señor," Juan replied almost disconsolately. "But what of this meeting with the rebels ... can you concentrate?"

"I'll manage. You start tomorrow. If I need you, I'll find you. If you don't hear from me, I don't need you. Simple, eh?" Benito started to protest again but Nick cut him off. "Look, if I have to fire you to get you to take a rest ..."

"But, señor, *this* week especially, I think I should stay."

Nick's mouth quirked to the side, showing one of his deep dimples. "Should I call your wife and tell her you refused to take her on a vacation?"

Benito crossed himself. "*Madre de Dios*, no, señor! You

have no idea how miserable she would make my life. I will go then, starting tomorrow?"

"Starting tomorrow, *sí*. Wait here one minute." Nick left the loft room and leaded for his own office. He was back in five minutes with a yellow pay envelope. "Your wages for a week, plus a little something to make the vacation enjoyable."

Benito accepted the envelope reluctantly. He didn't quite know how to react to such generosity. "Are you *sure* this is the time to leave you alone, señor? I can—"

"Not wait—because *I* insist you take it now. The seashore would be a good place; a welcome relief from the city heat. Think, Benito, how you'll be a hero to the family. For once in your life, Benito, enjoy. You'll see—you'll come back, and all your lading bills and invoices will be in perfect order."

"You shame me, Señor Rowan. I make you beg me to leave. I hang my head in shame."

"Well, don't. How can you watch the pretty señoritas at the seashore with your head down?" Nick laughed. "Now finish your last night's watch, and I must be going. I have a wife at home who thinks I've been meeting with a dark-eyed beauty."

Benito looked shocked, and Nick told him he was joking. "But we are newly married, and she is waiting. Have a good time, Juan Benito . . . and don't worry!"

"But who will watch the warehouse while I am gone? You know, no one has even attempted to steal so much as a mouse trap since I stay here and watch."

"I'll find someone, perhaps an off-duty *agente de policía*," Nick said. "You know how they're always looking for extra money." Nick stuck out his hand and smiled. "Anyway, this is *my* problem, not yours. You go and relax. I'll need your help next week—and I'll need you sharp, on your toes."

"I understand, señor, I do. I will see you, then, before that midnight meeting with Ruiz. You have my word on it."

"And I trust your word, Benito," Nick replied. "Now, let me go before I find my bride has locked me from my bedroom!"

Juan laughed at the thought. The señor was a handsome and, yes, wealthy man. His bride would do no such thing. If she was wise, she would welcome him with open arms—no matter what the hour. *'Adiós, patrón.* And *gracias, muchas gracias!'*

Nick was home within the hour. Connie had left a light burning in the entry hall. He went immediately to the study and turned on the desk light, then closed the door for privacy and quiet. The call, placed through the exchange, took about five minutes before he had his party, and even then it was only a man in a noisy cantina who took the message for his friend, Sylvano Verrana.

"Have him ring me at this number," Nick said, then added somewhat irritably, "Yes, of course I'll reimburse him for the call back! See that he calls within the hour." There was a pause and Nick frowned at the receiver. "Then give him a potful of black coffee. Tell him it's worth several thousand pesos—*if* he calls me back soon. *And* in a halfway sober condition."

While he was waiting, there was a soft knock at the door and Consuela entered. Nick winked at her and said, "I thought you were supposed to wait for permission to enter a room?"

With a heavy silken robe covering her nightgown, a robe Nick had bought her once on a trip to Paris, Connie sauntered over to the front of the desk and perched her broadening derriere on its edge. She gave him a smile that was lazy and, at once, intimate. "Not so, *mi corazón,* not in my own

259

house. It *is* my house, still, though you have brought back your bride to stay?''

Nick was still waiting to hear from Verrana. ''You know damn well it's yours. And for no other reason than Fino. Let's not discuss it—I'm not in the mood.''

''And what is it you are in the mood for, Nick? I see much lately; I see how your bride turns from you. Perhaps it is lovemaking that you have on your mind, eh? A man cannot go so long without . . . but then perhaps you have not, eh?''

''And perhaps you have too active an imagination, love. I've got other things on my mind. If I wanted you, you'd know it. You wouldn't have to come following me like a cat in heat. It's over, Con. We had good times . . . but no more, hmm?''

Consuela responded with a narrowing of her eyes. They were blue, a heritage of her Irish grandfather, but they had a slanted, feline set, and now she looked furious enough to spit and hiss and let her claws show. ''You are handsome, Rowan. You have money, much money. You make love like an animal, like the jaguar, with power but restraint. I miss that—any woman would. Your wife, she probably misses—''

''Shut up!'' They had been friends for years, lovers, companions, but Consuela had entered a part of his life that was completely his own. ''What I do with my wife . . .'' he took a deep breath; he wanted to be calm when Verrana called, ''whatever we do is our business. Connie, I don't want to hurt you. I'm sorry for the way I took you by surprise, bringing Elyn home like that. You must have known it would end sometime.''

''*Sí, amorado,* but not so suddenly, expecting you to come through the door and into my arms and find . . . her between us. You were cruel; I never thought you cruel.'' Wanting Rowan and not being able to have him was tearing her apart.

260

There were too many memories of warm nights and sweat-slick bodies tangled in the wide bed he now shared with Señora Rowan. "She rejects you. I hear things; the house is not silent. What she does not want, I will take. She need not know. I will never tell, I will never flaunt it in her face. I need you. You need a woman."

"I need a woman . . . yes, but not now, and it's something I can control. Right now I'm waiting for a business call. What you need, Maria Consuela, is a husband, a full-time man to keep you satisfied and help raise that child of yours."

"I thought once . . . hoped . . . it might be you. Sera, she loves you as a father. Perhaps it was me. I am older now—"

She was being dramatic. There had always been a touch of the dramatic in Consuela, a combination of the Irish and Spanish. "You're lying—to yourself, love. And that's the worst lie a person can tell." Nick got up and came around to stand next to her, put out a hand to touch her shoulder. "We were just there for each other. Isn't that what you told Elyn? It's true, Connie. Don't paint me as the world's champion lover. It's flattering, but I'm more realistic than that. There are plenty of men out there who'd welcome the chance to be a father to someone as sweet as Sera, to be a husband to a woman like you."

Connie stubbornly hung her head. "It's *you* I want. The church says I cannot have you, *you* say I cannot, she . . . your beautiful Elyn says I cannot—"

"You may have him, with my blessings." The voice, tight with suppressed anger, came from the open doorway. Elyn stood there, half-shielded by the door, staring at them. She could not have been there long, otherwise she would have heard the rest of their conversation and Nick's denial of Connie's offer. Consuela's face darkened with a flush, with just enough color to make her seemed embarrassed to have

261

been caught in a tryst. Nick . . . Nick only stared. They hadn't been talking loudly, so he hadn't expected Elyn to wake.

Suddenly, after a long and irritating night, he was angry. More than angry, he was furious. He seemed to be the middle of some bargaining session as if he were a piece of meat the women were haggling over. "Right now I don't want either one of you." That seemed to take them both back a step. Two pairs of blue eyes were focused on him. First he waggled a finger toward Elyn. "You—get in here." She hesitated, and he raised his voice to a shout that made her jump. *"Now!"* Then he turned and glared at Connie, who had suddenly turned meek and mild. "And you, your majesty—though I know I'm presently staying in *your* goddamned house, would it be too goddamned much trouble for you to make up the bed in the east wing?"

Connie practically curtsied, as in the old days, before she had become the mistress of Casa Aventura. She slipped away from Nick carefully, for he looked enraged enough to do her bodily harm, then ran the gauntlet of passing Elyn at the door. This she did as speedily as possible, though she still felt a distinctly arctic chill as she passed the younger woman.

Elyn had come through the doorway but she stood her ground, arms crossed, toes twitching as if she were restraining an urge to tap her foot. She hadn't obeyed. She would not . . . after all, *she,* not Nick, was the offended party.

In a deadly calm tone of voice, speaking very slowly and distinctly, Nick repeated his command. "I am waiting for a phone call. You will come here and let me explain, or so help me God, Elyn . . ." He let the threat hang in the air, unfinished, intensifying its effect. "Elynora, I said . . . come here."

Finally, to show him she was not in the least intimidated by his show of leonine roaring, but had chosen of her own accord to enter, Elyn strolled forward. She stopped some five feet in front of him, chin high, staring haughtily from half-shuttered lids. "It is past the hour of midnight, sir. You were away with God knows who—"

"Whom," Nick corrected.

Elyn inclined her head slightly in acknowledgment and continued, "with *whom*, doing God knows what, and *then*, then I find you in the company of that . . . that hot Mexican chili pepper, trysting in the study! Couldn't you find some other, more suitable room—or have you exhausted every one? There's always the garden, of course, but then one must be wary one's bare ass isn't stung by a scorpion." Having finished with a flourish, given it her best shot, and even spoken the word *ass* aloud, Elyn started to turn her back on Nick.

Nick came forward more quickly than she had expected. He caught her arm and, with very little consideration, jerked her body around to face him. Elyn stared at him for a moment. Deep in the blue of her irises were confusion and bewilderment, and almost hiding those emotions were hurt and anger. She glanced down at his fingers tightly grasping her arm and then back at him.

"You are hurting me."

"I hope so. It seems to be the only thing that penetrates that thick head of yours. Elyn, has it occurred to you that you are acting, in the slightest degree, like Lady Anne?"

That stopped her. Nothing he could have said would have shocked her more than the comparison to the woman they both considered the epitome of selfishness. "And how, pray tell, did you come to *that* conclusion?"

"Because all you care about, all you've cared about since we got here, is finding your father. Have you forgotten you have a husband? What is this return to daddy's little girl?"

Furious, Elyn brought up her hand, palm flat out, and

struck his cheek with all her might. The sound seemed to reverberate through the study and Elyn took a step back, not because she was afraid of retaliation but because she was shocked by her own behavior. She loved Nick. He was good to her, kind and protective in a way no one had ever been, and yet he had disappointed her, seemingly lost in his own business affairs, caring little for what she wanted.

She needed him—and he wasn't there. She wanted him, and he was off at some strange-hour rendezvous with God only knew who . . . whom, whatever. What was he doing? If he trusted her, why couldn't he tell her? If he loved her, why didn't they share everything? Suddenly Elyn covered her eyes with one hand, thinking. Something had clicked . . . sharing, everything—they were supposed to share, and she . . . she hadn't told him what it was that was bothering her, this business of her father not being her father . . . the matter of wondering whose child she'd been, what type of heritage she had passed on to their son.

With her eyes still shaded, the tears began to fall. Elyn couldn't keep them from falling and didn't even want to acknowledge their presence. Nick likely thought she was weeping out her jealous frustrations. Oh, God, what an awful mess, mostly her fault, though, because she'd been too ashamed to confide in him. A love child, that was what she was, even though the countess had found her mother a husband in time. And she, not Nick, had erected this wall between them. Even if he had given in to Consuela's blandishments . . . She stopped and imagined them wrapped in each other's arms, Nick being consoled by the voluptuous Connie, then broke out in renewed sobs.

Suddenly she became aware of Nick's arms. They were around her, holding her close and safe. As furious as he had been, he wanted to comfort her, and surely that must mean that he loved her still, as dreadfully as she had acted. She wept all the harder for the realization. It was as though a veritable dam of frustration had burst, and there was no containing the volume of salt water it had held in check.

His hand gently stroked her head, slowly from the crown to her nape. The motion was so loving, so sympathetic. He mightn't understand what was wrong but he seemed to mean to offer what reassurance he could. Vaguely she heard a telephone ring and felt Nick quickly lift her into his arms and carry her to the divan. He left her then, and she lay back with one arm across her eyes. She was calming, even to the point of vainly thinking that her eyes must look awful, all puffed and swollen.

She barely heard the conversation, but she knew from his tone that Nick was speaking with a man, someone he knew well, perhaps a friend from the old days. There was something about trucks and stock and a place called San Giovano's. It wasn't important. What mattered . . . should she leave now and go back to bed with her own problem, or should she share it? How could she tell him she was a love . . . she couldn't even call it that. In the common world she was a bastard, one with royal blood but a bastard nonetheless. Nick wouldn't care. It was people like Alec who would think less of her for it. And of course, no one need know. She heard Nick hang up the receiver. Perhaps she could tell him now, this unbearable burden.

He was quiet for so long that she almost had the feeling she was alone in the room. Finally, wiping away the last traces of her tears, Elyn half-sat and stared across at the desk. Nick was sitting there, both elbows leaning on the desktop, his hands supporting his head as if he were tired, so weary. She couldn't tell him now. It was as he'd said: she was acting like her grandmother, concerned only with herself. She hadn't bothered, really, to probe for what had occupied him these past weeks.

She stood, her legs a bit wobbly for a moment before they carried her over to the desk and his side. "Nick?" He was still for moments before he finally looked up. "I'm sorry. I *did* behave abominably—and I made a scene over nothing . . . it *was* nothing?" He nodded and even that seemed an effort. "I owe you an apology." He suddenly looked more awake, interested, surprised. A lock of his dark wavy hair had fallen forward over one temple and Elyn paused to stroke it back. "You needn't look so . . . so as if you cared to gloat!" Elyn protested, then gave him a half-smile. "I *was* acting like Lady Anne, thinking only of myself—though it did seem awfully as though you'd shut me out of a part of your life. Something's been troubling you—has it to do with Father? Nick . . . has he done something . . . illegal?"

Nick shook his head. He still didn't want to involve Elyn, but she seemed on the verge of telling him something. He took hold of her hand, turned it over, pressing a kiss on her palm. "Elyn, I have to go away next week. I may be gone for about ten days. It's business," he looked up and smiled, *"really.* And a part of it, well, a part of it could help me find your father. Don't ask any more. I won't say, I can't. Be patient, please. Believe me, I'll try and find him for you."

Elyn bent her head and rested it atop his. "I know. It's funny, I do—and I don't want you to find him. Some things are better left alone, the way they stand. Is it dangerous where you're bound for?"

Nick sat back in the chair and pulled Elyn into his lap, nuzzling against her hair. "D'you spend *all* your time washing your hair? Whenever I get close to you, it smells of wildflowers." Now he touched the softness of her cheek with the roughness of his own and she squeaked in protest. "I know—I could use a good shave. I hadn't expected to get this close to you . . . it's been a while, love. I hate to admit this—and I'm probably being presumptuous anyway—but I'm too damned tired to make love. To do you justice anyway. Could I make an appointment with your ladyship for sometime tomorrow night, say after a dinner alone, by candlelight?"

"You may. I accept, sir."

"Well—now that that's settled, what's wrong between you and your father?"

Elyn stiffened. She had been caught off guard. She couldn't bring herself to say . . . but if she didn't, it would lie there between them, tomorrow night, and she didn't want him going away with that invisible barrier up between them. She sighed. How did one put it delicately? She leaned her head against his chest and closed her eyes, sighing once more. "It's been most difficult to phrase, darling, and I . . . I'm not sure I can say it now."

Nick kissed her forehead. "Try. I'm listening."

"All right." She took a deep breath and exhaled, confessing in a soft, breathless tone, "Michael Winters is not . . . he's not . . . not my father. My real father, I mean."

Nick looked down at her face. She was blushing; a rose tint touched her cheekbones with color. Her expression, though, was what pained him. She ached, not physically, but she hurt inside, maybe deep enough so that nothing he said would help. "How do you know, hon'?"

Her voice was lackluster. "Grandmother wrote me a note. Mr. Munroe gave it to me the afternoon he read the will."

"And how did the old bitch put it?"

"She said Michael Winters wasn't worth going after. He

wasn't a relative anyway, and if some wild Indian natives had done him in, the world had lost nothing."

Nick tightened his grip around Elyn's shoulders. He didn't know if it was true, only Michael Winters knew the answer, and *that* was why Elyn had been so eager to find him, to have him confirm or deny Lady Anne's claim. The lousy bitch! How did Elyn feel about Winters? Many men had adopted children and treated them no differently from their own. But Nick knew what really bothered Elyn. She was too damned much a lady to want to be somebody's love-child. There were all kinds of words for it . . . *by-blow,* in the old days, *bastard,* and none of them much accurate except for *love-child.* That one wasn't so awful. It implied more than lust. Poor baby, poor Elyn . . . so that was what had bothered, driven her all these weeks, why it seemed to irritate her that he had found nothing to lead them to Winters. Well, now he had a reason as strong as hers. There was no sense in Elyn's suffering—it would be settled this coming week, at the rebel encampment.

"It doesn't make a difference, you know. I'm sure he loved you." She seemed not to hear him, and Nick firmly but gently clasped her chin and raised it. "*I* love you. All that's bothering you is a past you can't change—couldn't if you wanted to. What matters is now. *I love you.* We have a son, a good boy, and he'll have brothers and sisters soon enough. We're our *own* family, Ellie. We—you and I and Jackie, plus whoever may be in the making—*we* are what counts. I don't give a . . . well, I don't care who your parents were. They could have been beggers, paupers, kings or queens. By God, Elyn, don't you think there are skeletons in every family's closet? My grandfather, good old Gordon, the man I'm supposed to take after, killed a man over my grandmother." Elyn looked up at him in wonder. "I swear it's true. Ask her . . . but wait until you've known her awhile. She likes to pretend we're nothing but civilized!''

"But what if he were . . . what if my real father were some kind of awful man, a thief, a . . . a chimney sweep?''

Nick started to laugh and couldn't stop; try as he might, the laughter just kept coming. "I think chimney sweeps would be awfully offended at being lumped with thieves, darling,'' he finally managed to explain.

Poking him in the ribs with the tip of her finger, Elyn frowned, just a tiny frown. "You know what I mean. Someone mentally deficient or . . . God only knows what. You see *why* I must find out. And if Father—if Michael Winters—is dead, I shall never know. I mean, our children may suffer—''

"How many people, aside from kings and royalty and such, really know who's in their backgrounds? As long as the children come out with their head set on the right end, then I don't—''

"Don't jest!'' Elyn pleaded. "This is serious. You knew who *your* parents were; I want to know about mine, as well. I cannot imagine Mother giving herself to just anyone, the stableboy or the like . . . but she had been terribly sheltered.''

"Not enough, apparently. And now who's being the snob? Who cares if he *was* the stableboy? It could be why Jackie rides so well.'' Nick ducked as his wife swatted at his ears.

"I want to know, I say—and I shall, Nick, I shall!''

"I firmly believe you, love, but that's for the future. Right now I want to know if we can retire for the night . . . just to *sleep*.''

Elyn tilted her nose in the air. "I thought la señora was making up the bed in the spare bedroom? She's likely lying in it now, waiting for you!''

"Then let her wait. I'm sleeping with my wife—tonight, anyway.'' Elyn swatted again and this time boxed his ears. Still, as he turned out the desk light and carried her off to their room, she was smiling.

Chapter Thirteen

The last truck was loaded on Thursday. Nick watched as one of Verrana's men bolted shut the double doors and sealed the bolt with a heavy coating of wax. The truck was ready to be driven tonight to the convent on the outskirts of Puebla where the other five truckloads had been delivered.

The warehouse was now virtually empty. It was dusty and hollow-sounding, a two-story metal and wood building that for the next few weeks, at least, would remain simply an empty building.

"So, you trust me with all this, eh?" Verrana said with a smile. He poked Nick's shoulder and grinned. "How do you know, my friend, that I don't sell to the highest bidder? Or maybe I make my own revolution and become *Presidente* Verrana of Mexico, eh?"

"How do I know? Because you've had the chance to sell me out before—and didn't. And because you would make the worst damned *presidente* Mexico ever had, worse than Diaz. Even you know that. Now take good care of my 'lighting fixtures' and keep an eye on your drivers. You I trust. I hope you can trust them, amigo."

Verrana started to laugh. "I have to, Rowan, they are all my brothers!" The more he considered this, the harder he laughed, and finally his laughter, contagious, made Nick smile.

"Well, then take care. When you return my shipment... intact, Verrana, I'll have a bonus waiting for you."

The Mexican, who had ridden with Villa first and then, in a fit of anger, had changed to Zapata's leadership, grinned and punched Nick's ribs with a sharp elbow. "What—you will have a woman for me, a fat one like the *puta* I found in Santa Rosa?"

"I had more in mind something you could drink from a bottle, Sylvano. A case of brandy."

"Ah, but how cold a bottle is, and hard, while a woman..." Verrana shrugged. "But who am I to argue with a gift. With the case of brandy, I can trade a bottle or two for a woman! *Sí?*"

"*Sí,* amigo—but only if everything goes as we planned."

"The Virgin of Guadalupe shall strike me dead if I fail you, Nick Rowan! A friend, one never betrays, one never fails."

Nick didn't mention what to do with the consignment should he fail to contact Verrana. He didn't want to consider the chance that he might fail.

Later that night, after a dinner with Elyn and Jackie, Nick played with Jackie longer than usual. He had found a small set of cast-iron cowboys and Indians in a shop off the Paseo de la Reforma, and he and the boy chose up sides, fighting a mock battle on the tiles before the parlor fireplace. Naturally, Jackie took the side of the Indians. As he had once told Nick, he thought they had been treated very unfairly. Of course, before Elyn announced it was time for bed, the Indians had routed the cowboys two to one.

Nick waited for a while in the parlor after his son had been put to bed. He was beginning to settle into the life of a family man. Some of his friends, even those who had last seen him only six months before, would have been amazed at the change. He liked sitting home, sharing a quiet evening with Elyn, perhaps retiring early to bed, not to sleep but to play, to tease and see how many sighs he could draw from her lips before they did sleep.

Elyn came back into the room. She had safely seen Jackie tucked into bed and given him a kiss. She was smiling, though, a young girl's blushing smile, pleased but embarrassed. She came to sit next to Nick on the settee and he asked what amused her. "Did your son ask something intimate? He's an awfully curious boy, you know. I don't think it'll be long before . . ."

"Oh, *please!*" Elyn knew what he meant, but Jackie was still her baby, too young, surely, to have thoughts of sex. Still, if he favored Nick, they would have to keep a close watch on his activities. "No, nothing like that, except . . ."

Elyn seemed not quite to know how to phrase what she had to say. "Except what?" Nick pressed.

"Except that he asked, plain as could be, when he might expect a brother or sister to play with."

No wonder Elyn had come back blushing. "Did he ask how we got them . . . or has he guessed?"

"We didn't go into it except that I said we would consider it and . . . let him know."

Nick swallowed the last of his Scotch in a quick gulp, put his glass on a coaster, and grabbed Elyn's hands. "Let's go consider it, then. You know there isn't anything I'd deny my boy. If he wants a brother or sister, let's—"

"Shush! He may not be asleep yet. I know perfectly well where little ones come from."

"Where's that, my sweet?"

Elyn turned to him, all wide-eyed innocence but impish.

273

"Why, they're to be found in cabins, sir. Shepherds' cabins, preferably at high elevations." She turned and smiled at him as they reached their bedroom door. "Didn't you know that was how I found Jackie?"

He went along with her teasing and swept her up into his arms. Clearly, Elyn was in a playful and amorous mood. It was in the back of her mind, as well as his, that he would be leaving very early the next morning. "And how do you account for the growing population of Mexico City, ma'am? We're not on top of a mountain."

Elyn laughed as he deposited her in the middle of their canopied bed. "Ah, but we are at a very high elevation! It must be height, then, and not shepherds' cabins. Oughtn't we try to find out . . ." she made a very serious expression, "just for—strictly for—scientific observation?"

Nick was already stripping off his shirt. "Of course, madam . . ." he teased back. "Wouldn't consider it for any reason but the advancement of theory. Now, if you don't move quickly, m'lady, that rather expensive dress will need repairs—or possibly be beyond repair."

Elyn raised a brow. "Promises, promises. I think there must have been a pirate somewhere in your family history. You seem to think I am a prize just captured off a brigantine!"

Bare to the waist, Nick made an elegant bow and came up with a smile that approached a leer. "My lady, my blood boils to be at you—and you are a prize no matter where I've gotten you from. Now, strip, or be ravished among the shreds of your finery!"

Elyn lay back, arms set beneath her head, smiling. "Go ahead, then, ravish. I never did care for this dress. And I've always wanted to see what ravishment entailed."

The dress did end up in the trash bin. It was not salvageable after the pirate had subdued and taken his prize. When

Elyn finally woke, late the next morning, and found Nick gone, she retrieved the torn dress from the waste bin and smiled very briefly at the memories it called up. Then she lay back and the smile slipped away. This trip of Nick's scared her. It was strange and somehow unlawful. Though he would not confide in her, she knew it had to do with those late-night meetings of his. Though he had promised to bring her word of her father, she worried more that it was Nick, not Michael Winters, who was in danger. And she could not live without Nick.

It wasn't even light when Nick arrived at the park zoo. He wandered about for a while, listening to the nocturnal sounds of the animals, some of them very close in timbre to the remembered sighs and moans of last night's lovemaking. Elyn had been insatiable and more, it seemed, without the benefit of a drink or any aphrodisiac; she had pushed aside her usual inhibitions, those ladylike pretenses, and made love as if . . . as if it were their last night together.

Suddenly he realized that she may have feared that. It made him almost want to go back and wake her, to assure her that nothing was wrong, that he was simply on a business call and would even see old friends from his days with Zapata. But there wasn't time to go back for that moment of reassurance. She would see, when he returned.

The sun was just beginning to paint the sky in the east with pink when a single man approached him, a hat drawn down over his face, a foul-smelling cigar hanging slackly from his mouth. This was Ruiz, but where was Benito?

"This vacation you give him, señor, it seems his wife insisted he stay another day. What could he do? Women are impossible to live with—and without, as well. We should go now, before the *policía* sees me. We have far to go, very far."

Soon after leaving the city, Ruiz stopped his trusted Model

T truck and blindfolded Nick. They headed south, then east, and Nick was sure they were aiming for some isolated archaeological spot, a dig at Monte Alban or perhaps even the huge mounds at Puebla. He listened closely, occasionally hearing a voice as they passed through a village, or a songbird or some other sound of nature. By late that afternoon, he was almost sure that Ruiz had doubled back and they were going north.

The number of times Ruiz had to shift gears indicated that they were climbing higher into foothills, and the land southeast of the capital was a low plain, at least until one came to the Yucatán highlands.

Nick slept off and on, with nothing to do but listen to the rumble of the engine. It was out of tune, misfiring. Night came, and they ate. Not even once was he allowed to remove the blindfold. It became a nuisance, interfering with every normal bodily function—eating, sleeping, relieving himself. He couldn't wait to get to the camp, make his observations, his "false" negotiations, and get the hell back home. But of course that would entail another needless journey with the blindfold.

A day and a half later, they arrived. Ruiz parked the truck off the road, lifted Nick's blindfold, and told him to get out. There was nothing around them but trees, firs, pines, scrub, and some flowering cactus. "Up the road and a way yet, señor, is the camp." Nick must have looked at him as though he doubted his sanity. Ruiz smiled and made a sweeping gesture toward a bare path leading to the woods. "One does not advertise a camp of the rebellion. We cannot put up the sign saying, 'This way, *por favor,* to the rebellion'!" Nick shrugged. It was true but a damned nuisance. "Watch where you step. The snakes here are sleepy in the heat of day, but on occasion . . ."

Nick watched as he walked very carefully, making sure that it was solid ground he was putting his feet on. When finally they emerged from the woods, his mouth dropped open. Whoever was running this operation knew what the hell he was doing. The camp was a compound, a resurrected Aztec city like the one they were excavating at San Juan. This one, however, couldn't have been in too bad a state of disrepair, because the restoration was nearly complete. It *looked* like an Aztec city from the past, as if some power had either preserved it perfectly or . . . or as if he had stepped back into the past.

The place was huge, with several pyramidal structures, a large plaza and ball court, and even a rectangular, colonnaded building where the women were housed. There was also a strange serpent building oriented to the west.

The high priest, a tall fellow done up in a costume that could have been a picture plate in a book on ancient ceremonial dress, came down the steps of the serpent building to greet him. He spoke in fluent Spanish, but for some reason Nick suspected that it wasn't his native language. He wore a mask, quite as elaborate and as horrifying as any Halloween mask Nick had ever seen. It was a mix of feathers, brightly colored, mosaic pieces of turquoise and silver, the face of a skull with the eye sockets built up and, emphasized, a grinning mouth.

The rest of his clothing was an elaborate loincloth, a long, wide, sweeping robe that tied across one shoulder, and sandals with laces that crisscrossed his calves to below the knee. His armbands were of beaten gold inlaid with mother-of-pearl, and earrings, obviously heavy and pendent, swung on either side of his head as he talked.

His name was Miguel. He was, he said with some pride, the high priest of Texcatlipoca, lord of the night, the magician, the dark god. Nick was invited up the steps and into the temple of Nauyalcoatl. Here he, along with his benefactor, Texcatlipoca, were held in the greatest reverence. Would Señor Rowan care for refreshment after his long journey?

"I would, sir, but I'd also like to get down to business. I am assuming that there's someone higher than you I'm dealing with? If so, I would like to see him, as soon as possible, please."

Miguel clapped his hands. A servant appeared immediately and the priest spoke in Nahuatl, apparently ordering a drink or food. When the man had left, Miguel turned back to Nick and nodded. "You are correct, my friend. I may call you this, may I not? You have come so far to help us, you must be our friend. There are many, many of your old comrades in this place we call Aztlan. They speak of your courage in the time you spent with the rebel Zapata; they say there was no one who could shoot with more deadly an aim, who could spy better than the Americano. You have feelings for us; this I know because most Americans despise us as dogs or take our labor and discard the used workers as garbage. You will have to speak with our leader, the Lord Nauyaca, but I first must know if you are *sympatico* with our ideas. We will soon return the land of Mexico to its former glory under the rule of an Aztec king."

Nick arched a brow. "Nauyaca?"

"*Sí*. And with my guidance, he will make us again proud princes of civilization. But to do this, señor, we need weapons, modern weapons. I can work magic, but none of my spells can call up a rifle to match those in the hands of the *federales*. You have a storehouse full of these weapons, and you have the bullets that fit these guns. I cannot ask for the old days that you give us the materiel, but I say to you, your name will be honored if we can agree to a price that assures us of victory."

"There are a few things I'd like to know first, Miguel." The refreshments arrived and were placed on a small marble table between their chairs. From two goblets the color of gold—Nick couldn't believe they had been formed of so precious a metal—they drank pulque, the milky fermented product of the maguay cactus, the "drink of the gods." "Like, for instance, have you got a man in your camp, an Englishman named Winters? He was digging near Teotihuacán about nine months ago when he and his party disappeared. I heard—I understood—that he was here."

Behind his mask, Miguel whispered a sigh. "We do not like foreigners here. You—you are tolerated; no, this is not right—you are welcomed because you fought with us against the government in the revolt. No Anglo is here. This man, if he has been gone so long, must be dead. Many things can kill in the desert, señor. Why, if I may ask, do you seek him?"

"For a friend. A lady who cared for him. I'm sorry you have no more heartening news, sir. Now, though, perhaps we should talk business. Though your king is the 'leader' of this little coup, I sense you are the power to deal with."

"You observe well. I am older and Nauyaca listens to my counsel. I can tell you now what we can give for each weapon and the ammunition we will need. For a rifle, seventy-five hundred pesos, and for a round of ammunition, two hundred."

The terms amounted to eighty dollars for a two-hundred-dollar rifle, and twenty dollars for a box of ammo that cost him thirty. "We're talking business here, friend, not charity. I have import duties to pay, fees to the government, not to mention the fact that if I get caught running guns to you, I'm

279

a *dead* importer of weapons. I just got married recently, and thank you, but my wife would like to keep me awhile yet.''

Miguel shrugged. He was not going to rail at Rowan when there were still several days to come to an agreement. He had little doubt it would be arranged to his satisfaction. That was the only way it could be. ''You must talk to the Lord Nauyaca, then, and he cannot see you.''

This whole deal was nothing but a runaround. He'd traveled two days in a damned uncomfortable truck just to hear this Halloween figure from Mexican history make an offer that would have insulted Christ! ''Exactly when this afternoon can I see him?''

''Not this afternoon, señor. According to the astrologers, the king cannot meet with you until tomorrow, after the sun has set.''

Great, just great! He'd have a word or two to scorch Gyp's ears when he got back to the city. ''And what do I do until His Highness grants me an audience?''

Miguel gestured with a wide sweep of his hand. ''Señor, you are our honored guest. There is a tower room above the women's quarters. There you will be able to rest and take your ease. Anything you wish will be provided, within our means. Ask anything—we will try to be accommodating.''

''Then send me a bottle of something strong and a couple of your best virgins.''

''Señor, you are serious?''

''About the bottle, yes. Now, I *am* tired, so I'll go and rest, if you'll excuse me.'' It was difficult to hide his impatience and as hard to hold back his sarcasm. ''You could do me one more favor—have the astrologers recheck their calculations. I'd like to get back home as soon as possible.''

''This I will do, though they never err. Anything you wish

is at your disposal, señor. We want you to relax during your stay.''

''I'll have great fun, I know.''

There was nothing to do. The tower room had only one small slit of a window, facing east. After the sun had passed its zenith, a lamp was brought to the room by a quite lovely young girl. Nick eyed her as he would have in the old days but kept his hands to himself. You couldn't get shot for thinking. As he'd promised, Miguel had supplied an earthen jar of pulque. Nick had a drink and fell asleep, dreaming fitfully of Halloween masks and snakes' heads.

Finally he awoke. It was dark outside. At the door, an open portal covered by drapes, stood a burly guard with a huge chest. Nick smiled and waved; the man remained stony faced. It was going to be fun all right. An hour later, after he'd eaten a meal of tortillas and chicken molé, he was escorted below and allowed the luxury of a bath. It was amazing, the amenities one could find in a mountaintop camp.

He had no idea of the time. Once done with the bath, there wasn't much to do but have another drink and rest. Suddenly there was a sound at the doorway. Nick looked up to see Miguel standing there.

''May I enter?'' he asked formally, and Nick stood, making a wisecrack about his humble abode being Miguel's humble abode. A good deal of Nick's humor seemed to go over the head of the priest, but it made Nick relax to feel he could poke a little fun, especially with everyone so solemn around here.

Miguel came in; behind him was a girl of about thirteen. She was short, not really petite, just short. Her black hair was parted in the middle and braided. She gave off a heavy floral scent that seemed to radiate from her oiled braids. The girl kept her face downcast but she was *not* a beauty. Even by

281

Aztec standards this one was homely. Miguel gestured to the girl and introduced her by some unpronounceable name.

"Before, you asked for pulque and a few virgins. I have supplied the pulque and hope it is to your liking. This child," he turned and caught her hand to bring her forward, "is a virgin. In keeping with your preference for them, I have selected the finest, most pure of our young women. You will enjoy her. She will please you."

He turned to go, his voluminous robes sweeping around in an arc. Nick held out a hand and touched Miguel. "Wait a minute—I was only joking! We're like that, we Americans." He took another look at the girl and smiled, a sort of sickly smile. "I can't take you up on your offer, no matter how generous. Really, it's too much to ask. . . ."

"I do not think you understand. This girl has been chosen, of all the virgins, to be sacrificed at dawn. She will be dedicated to the honor of your visit, sent to the arms of Texcatlipoca in your name. If in the morning she is found to be . . . no longer a virgin," Miguel shrugged, "she will not be deemed good enough to sacrifice. Now, Señor Rowan, you understand?"

Nick swallowed hard. "I think so. This *is* against my religion. I'm a married man. I really think maybe some other guy . . ." Miguel shook his head and continued, on his way out, "She speaks Spanish, by the way. You should have no problem communicating your desires. She will do anything you wish."

The girl looked up at Nick and smiled shyly. If she was the best of their virgins . . . Nick had a feeling that this was a joke and he was at the center of it. Yet, he believed Miguel. She probably *was* the morning sacrifice. These bastards had really gone the route, all the way back to paganism.

In Spanish, he told the girl to have a seat. She obeyed

immediately. He sat and asked her about the sacrifice, and she admitted quite calmly that yes, she was to be killed in the morning. But if she wasn't a virgin? Then she would serve the temple in some way: the priests sometimes needed women, or she could cook and sew.

What it amounted to was that if he didn't make love to her, she would die at dawn. Ugly as she was, he didn't want that. Still, he was married. To a gorgeous, long-legged beauty who loved him. Elyn wouldn't know, but . . . all he was doing was making excuses. He simply couldn't find a thing about the girl that aroused him. They had a problem.

This was not Nick's only problem. At the door, the giant of a guard was staring, glowering at Nick as if he wanted to break him in two—like a toothpick. When Nick asked the girl why, she explained that Juan Maxtla had written her love poems. He was, most certainly, jealous. Nick smiled. Would she give the guard a message for him? Anything, she answered; she was here to please him. Nick grinned.

An hour later, Nick returned from a stroll around the complex. He had the benefit of a moonless night, but it was the layout of the place he wanted to memorize. By the time he returned, he had a mental map etched in his head, with the location of every building and the number of guards posted at night. That was enough. He'd done his duty. As soon as he spoke with this puppet-king Nauyaca, he was going home and taking Elyn back to Colorado, Andrews be damned!

The next morning, to Miguel's surprise, an examination of the girl proved that she was no longer a virgin. The priest congratulated Nick on putting aside for one night his own beliefs and morals. Nick modestly accepted the praise and found that, indeed, the astrologers had changed their minds. His audience with Lord Nauyaca could begin immediately.

The disagreement over price remained a sticking point. The

negotiations were in no way final, though. Nick stated that he would return to the capital and reconsider. They could contact him again, using Ruiz, through his assistant, Benito. He had greatly enjoyed his visit; and though he hated to seem an ingrate, he did have an anxious wife waiting for him.

Nauyaca understood perfectly. When one loved a woman, the earth seemed a paradise. He offered his hand to Nick. "We will be friends, but more . . . we will be allies, Rowan. This I know, this I have seen in dreams. We will meet again soon."

He would have to leave blindfolded again, an unnecessary convenience, but until he was one with their cause . . . Nick insisted that he understood—anything to get out of the camp.

When he was gone, Nauyaca spoke to his priest. "Take off the mask. No one will see you here. It is forbidden to enter unless I decree it. What do you think, then? How will he cooperate?"

"Well, my lord, when we have his wife, he should be most happy to do anything we ask of him. The price for the weapons will be the return of Señora Rowan, alive, untortured."

Nauyaca smiled. He had had dreams of this woman. He had swallowed the sacred *olioquiliu* seeds and had had visions of such perfection . . . visions that he had kept from Miguel. The priest was sometimes a bother. He seemed to want to bargain honorably with this foreigner, while Nauyaca would have him eliminated once he had the rifles . . . and the woman. "Has it begun?"

"Yes, my lord. Our man even now seeks entrance to the house, to offer the distressing news of Señor Rowan's 'accident.' His wife will come immediately. I understand they were wed only recently. She will come, yes, at once."

Chapter Fourteen

For some reason, tonight Elyn paced the parlor like a caged lioness. Nick wasn't due yet for a week, but she felt something awful had happened. Where was it he had gone? He hadn't even confided what city, she had no way of reaching him, and . . . oh, she was being silly. She simply hadn't been apart from him since their wedding, and she was being the nervous bride. She always felt so secure when he was around.

Jackie had been in bed for the past hour. He was just getting over some strange malady. The doctor had said it was some sort of mild influenza, nothing to be concerned about. For one night he had raged with fever, then his temperature had dropped to near normal, and today he had seemed recovered enough to play awhile with Sera.

More than likely, his illness had added to her feeling of unease. Still, she wished some miracle would bring Nick home sooner than expected. She and Consuela scarcely spoke. Though there were no open hostilities, there was still a feeling between them that the issue of whom Nick belonged to had not been settled. Elyn felt—or had been made to feel—that she had somehow enchanted Nick, stolen him directly from beneath Consuela's nose.

"May I get you anything before I retire?" Consuela's

voice was chilly, barely civil. She could have sent a servant to inquire. Instead, by appearing herself she emphasized the fact that she ran everything because Casa Aventura was hers.

Elyn had never felt so like a cat who wanted to spit and hiss. This woman, who had definitely shared a past intimacy with Nick, who had known him in times before Elyn had met him, who, Elyn could even admit, might love Nick, was radiating poison. "You needn't concern yourself with my welfare, señora. In fact, within the day, Jackie and I shall be moving to a hotel. I do not intend to stay in the same house alone with a . . . with a woman my husband has slept with!"

"You may do as you please, señora, but if you lie and say it was I who drove you to this act, I promise you, I will make you regret it. Though he married you, Nick shares with me many fond memories—of matters other than sex. Do not turn him against me because you are jealous."

"I—jealous?" Elyn was incensed. "You're the jealous one. . . . Why, you've been like an alley cat in heat ever since we arrived! If I cared to define the term *flaunting,* I should look to your behavior as a fine example. I happen to love my husband, Consuela, and I don't intend to lose him—to you or any other woman."

"You will if you do not control your raging. A man does not wish to hear about such matters." Connie shrugged. "Oh, perhaps at first he finds it flattering. After a while, the angry remarks seem like insults. You will remember this or lose him. And if you lose him, I shall be there—or if not I, some other woman. Nick is a most attractive man. If you look past your spite, señora, you will see that he is a man of much independence. He chose you. If you do not see what this means, I pity you."

At the last moment, after all her venom had been spewed, Consuela had offered a phrase of solace. Even in her anger,

Elyn recognized it. "Wait! I—Consuela, I am . . ." It was difficult to say, "I am sorry for the way I've acted. I am. I have said things to you that I never would have dreamed of saying." She held her hand to her head, ran her fingers through her hair, and shrugged. "I don't know why. I am so nervous tonight."

For a second Consuela felt an odd, maternal concern stir within her. The girl was only ten years younger than she, but she had been sheltered and now . . . could be excused. "I will fetch a headache powder. Sit. More than likely, the child's illness makes you see terrors where there are none."

Suddenly the door knocker banged, making both women jump. They looked at each other before Consuela crossed to the door and peered through the peephole, calling out to ask who it was. Then quickly she opened the door. Juan Benito stood there, hat in hand, looking exceedingly nervous. "Come in, come in, before you bring the mosquitoes!" Connie said impatiently. "What brings you here at this hour?"

"Bad news, I am afraid. Is the . . ." He broke off as he caught sight of Elyn standing in the parlor, hands folded tightly together. He turned to her, wringing his hat until it was crumpled beyond repair. "Señora, there has been an accident." Both women gasped as they stared at him. Elyn's eyes widened until they seemed nothing but large blue orbs.

It was Connie who impatiently snapped the question they were both most curious about. "This concerns Señor Rowan, sí? If you have alarmed us for no reason . . ."

"No, I would not. The señor was driving a rented car in Cholula and it was raining. The car, she spins off the road. The doctor says to find the Señora Rowan, to bring her."

Elyn felt herself slipping into a kind of numb shock, that deadly calm that precedes hysteria. "How badly is he hurt?"

287

"His left arm, it is broken, I think. He was thrown clear. He is unconscious."

Elyn turned to Connie. She put her hand to her head again. Consuela wanted to go to Nick herself but knew it was not her place. She turned to Benito and ordered, "You will wait. I must fix the señora a headache powder, then fetch her a sweater." To Elyn she added, "The children will be fine. I will go every hour to Jackie's room and look at him."

Elyn suddenly felt weak. She reached the nearest chair and sat, still holding her hand to her head. "He isn't . . . he's not . . ." She couldn't bring herself to ask if Nick was dead, and perhaps Benito was afraid to tell her.

He felt sorry for the señora. "No, señora, Señor Rowan will survive. He is strong and the doctor says he recovers quickly."

With amazing speed and efficiency, Consuela returned and dropped a powdered substance into a glass of water. She made Elyn drink it, then maternally arranged a sweater around the younger woman's shoulders. "I will say a prayer. Nick is tough. You must be, also."

Then Benito escorted her out the door and down the walk to the gate. She walked automatically, without thinking, entering a dark car, staring straight ahead as Benito shifted the gears and turned on the headlights. He said something to her about the rain stopping, but Elyn was a thousand miles away, thinking about the time she had met Nick. If she should lose him . . . It was unthinkable.

The rhythm of the car as it rumbled along the city streets and the action of the powder combined to lull Elyn into a troubled sleep. She rested her head sideways against the car door, woke several times, then slept again.

When she woke the last time, the sky was just beginning to lighten. Something was wrong, but she couldn't quite put her finger on it. They were headed for a mountainous area. The road angled sharply, and the sun, just rising, struck her eyes from the right. Cholula lay southeast of the capital, and the sun should be directly before them or slightly to the left. "You have taken a wrong turn. . . ."

When she looked at him, Juan Benito had a gun in his hand. It was pointed at her, wobbling in the hand that wasn't on the wheel. "I am nervous, señora. Make no sudden moves. I do as I am told, and they say bring you, I bring you."

"There's nothing wrong with Nick?" Elyn felt simultaneously relieved and apprehensive. Nick wasn't hurt; he was well and healthy, still on his business trip. But who were the people who'd ordered Benito to lie, to pretend in the middle of the night that there'd been an accident? "Benito, why is this happening?"

"I can say nothing, señora. Others, perhaps, will be able to answer your questions." He took his eyes from the road for a second and said, "They will not hurt you, señora. I swear."

She had so many questions, but it was clear that Benito was only a hireling. Again, for no other reason than weariness, Elyn slept. She woke when the stillness around her seemed to shout. Still half-asleep, she rubbed her eyes, trying to clear the fog from her brain. Benito, a gun—and yes, Nick was safe. That was the most important thing of all.

Benito was not beside her. She looked across the road and saw him standing next to a tall, rough-looking man dressed in traveling clothes. Twenty feet behind them stood two Indian guides, holding the reins of several animals, mules, five in all, if you counted one small, fragile-looking creature that was weighted down with supplies.

Benito pointed to the car, and the man with him looked up. Elyn shivered. She didn't care for the look of him at all. A low, broad-brimmed hat was lowered across the upper half of his face, giving him the look of someone who wished to avoid being recognized. Together they walked toward the car, and Elyn panicked, nearly opening the door on her side to bolt. But where would she run, where was she? A quiet voice deep within her said, *Cooperate . . .*

The man leaned in the driver's window and looked at her. Again Elyn shivered. His eyes had raked across her. She'd seen men look at women like that before, but it had never happened to her. Then, thankfully, he straightened. He was speaking to Benito in Spanish; she saw a wad of pesos change hands and frowned to herself. Someone was paying to have her abducted. It did seem that in Mexico she had more than a usual chance of being kidnapped. This time, though, she could not hope that her kidnapper would be as good or as gentle as Nick had been.

Chapter Fifteen

It was dusk of the second evening when the party of four paused to make camp for the night. Elyn was too tired to know where she was or to care. She had only the vague idea that her captors had taken her higher into the mountains north of the capital and that in the morning they would continue their ascent.

Nick wasn't hurt, nor had he been wounded. The entire story had been a ruse to kidnap her. By now he was most likely back at Casa Aventura, listening to Consuela's account of Benito's distressing nocturnal visit. Rueben Brady would tell her nothing. She gathered that he had been partially paid for his work and would receive the rest of his reward when they reached whatever godforsaken place they were heading for. She doubted that he would harm her. Whoever had arranged for her abduction wanted her alive and in good condition.

They had traveled by mule for two days, but since she had no way of calculating how far a mule could travel in a day, she wasn't sure how far they had come from the city. On the first night out, Brady had come to the spot where she lay tied and covered with a blanket, and had lain down next to her, reaching out to catch her close and roughly brush his mouth against hers. His breath smelled of stale food and cigar smoke, and he needed a shave, and when she was free for a moment she told him he needed as much and a good bath to complement it. It was silly of her to speak so carelessly, but though she was tired and weak, she stubbornly refused to show any fear before so ignorant a creature.

Perhaps just to show that he cared little what she thought of him, he had rolled atop her then. Somehow, for once, God was listening to her prayers. She brought her knee up hard against his groin. Since then he had ignored her, though now, as he helped her down from the mule, it wasn't by accident that his hands brushed her breasts. Had her hands been free, she would have striped his face with her nails or, at the least, smacked him hard for the insult.

But her hands weren't free, and there was little likelihood of their being so in the immediate future, so Elyn chose to ignore Brady. She would have preferred to refuse the drink he offered from his canteen, but thirst would not allow her that dignity. She let him hold the canteen to her lips, then jumped back and glared as the water he had purposely spilled wet her thin cotton blouse, clearly outlining the shape of her breasts and nipples. "Go ahead, stare!" she snapped. That was all he could do. "You can't hurt me, lest the man who hired you refuse to pay you the rest of your lucre. He *might* even have you killed." Elyn was treading on thin ice, but she felt spiteful enough to want to repay in some measure the humiliation he had dealt her.

He did nothing, proving that he *was* impotent, unable to possess her even though that was clearly what he wanted. He was afraid, then, of his employer. Good. Whoever the man was, at least he'd helped her *that* much! She turned away now, still unable to cover herself or the outline of her torso revealed by the damp, clinging material. "Whatever these people are paying you, my husband can offer you a hundred times more," she said, then glanced over her shoulder to see if he reacted with greed. "For my release—unharmed—in the capital." The ploy wasn't likely to work, but anything was worth a try.

Brady was gnawing on a piece of beef jerky. He found a particularly tough piece and spit it out to his left, smirking at her offer. "Honey, I learned a long time ago: only make one deal at a time. This one's to . . ." He'd almost given away the name of his employer but caught himself in time and grinned as he tossed off an oath. He threw the unfinished jerky to the ground and took several steps toward her. She wasn't afraid of him, and he found that fascinating. He didn't have the best reputation for treating women like ladies, but she didn't know that, did she? Maybe, just maybe, it was time she found out.

Even though she had believed he wouldn't hurt her, Elyn saw his eyes harden. They turned flinty, narrowing just before his wide, calloused palm came smashing across her left cheek. The slap knocked her senseless; for moments she lay on the ground, her head ringing from the hard, driving blow. She tasted blood, but there was nothing to do but let her cheek bleed. The cut would clot soon enough; certainly she would not die from the loss of a little blood. Suddenly there was a cloud of dust next to her face. Elyn coughed and narrowly opened her eyes to see a pair of worn, dirty boots next to her.

"You ready to shut up and do what *I* want?"

She was afraid he might kick her, and the idea of being struck by his booted foot, directly in line with her face, sent a shiver rippling down her spine. She nodded, though the motion made her feel as if her head were spinning. Elyn shut her eyes and kept them closed. "I shall say nothing more, Mr. Brady, you've my promise on that." She would not, however, promise to do anything he wanted. God only knew what *that* might include! She rose on one elbow, glaring until he finally reached down a hand to help her to her feet. Elyn tried her best to suppress the sarcastic remark that came to mind.

"Are we to be allowed to rest now?"

"I'll be damned if you ain't got the prettiest way of talkin'!" Brady commented and then nodded. "Don't travel after the sun goes down here." His eyes widened and he looked around, shrugging as if he had shivered. "All kinds of things to get you in the dark. Ever hear of the dark god? The one who roams the roads at night, heart beatin' all open so's you can see it pump? He'll tear you limb from limb unless—"

"You're brave enough to reach in and take his heart, for which you are rewarded with any wish. His name is Texcatlipoca." Brady was staring at her open-mouthed. He had meant to frighten her, perhaps enough for her to draw close to him for protection. She looked thoroughly collected, even with the scratch on her cheek. This was some woman Rowan had married.

"I bet, be I a bettin' man, that you'd meet up with Tex—whatever his name is—and you wouldn't be one bit scared to try and get your wish. Bet also, I know what you'd wish for."

There was a worn boulder about a foot away from where she was standing; Elyn moved toward it and sat wearily. "You win—on both counts, sir. I should be most delighted to meet the dark god tonight." She smiled to herself for the first time in several days, imagining herself ordering Texcatlipoca to tear Mr. Brady slowly limb from limb.

Brady took his hat and swept it from his head in a mocking bow. "Rowan's sure got hisself some first-class piece of . . ."

For some reason he left off his description and continued, "You from over there in England, ain't you?"

"London. May I ask where you are from?"

"You may ask all you want, ma'am, but I ain't tellin'. Folks in my line, we don't give out with a lot of information. Let's just say I'm an American."

"That says a good deal in itself."

Brady glowered. "That supposed to be smart-mouthed? 'Cause if it was . . ." He took a threatening step toward her.

Elyn leaned away. "Please! I meant nothing. My own husband is American. The Americans helped save us in the war. Noting the type of man you are, so capable of taking care of yourself, I'm sure you fought overseas. You *were* in the war?"

It didn't matter if he lied a bit. "Course I was. I helped save your womenfolk from gettin' raped by them fuckin' Huns!"

"Truly, Mr. Brady, I can't think we were ever in danger of *that*. What I can't understand is how you can abduct me now, when so recently, for the good of humanity, you helped women like myself." She stared up at him, knowing that the scratch on her cheek and the innocent look in her eyes might have an effect on this moron of a man. "I know, at first, I was sarcastic—but how many ladies are pleasant under the duress of an abduction?" Elyn's lashes fluttered. "I beg of you, sir . . . you must have had a mother, perhaps a sister? I wonder—under the same circumstances, could you see them treated so callously?" It was a maudlin appeal but she was not dealing with a normal human being here.

Brady scratched his head, thinking. "Ma'am, Ma, she run a brothel in Saint Louis, and my sis, the youngest, anyway, turned tricks on a streetcorner in New York."

Tricks? What on God's earth did he mean? A brothel she

understood—they were houses of ill repute, for ladies of the evening, a universal blight. It had not been the best of beginnings for a young boy, but that wasn't her problem. "I know you've principles, sir. If, after you have finished this 'job' for . . . whomever it is who's hired you, might you see your way clear to allowing my husband to hire your services?" She let this sink in and then casually mentioned that their combined fortunes amounted to several million American dollars. "Whoever hired you, I assure you, cannot have access to that type of payment."

He scratched his head again. Either this was a part of his thinking process or head lice were a problem. Either was a distinct possibility. "I can see my way clear to that bein' a honorable act," he said finally. "As long as I deliver you and finish up m'first job, I'm free to take on anythin' else that comes my way." He seemed pleased, satisfied morally, and even eager to get on with it.

"There is *one* stipulation, sir," Elyn said firmly. "I shan't be inclined to recommend your services to my husband if I've suffered at your hands. I shan't mention the bruise on my cheek; however, I do expect you to keep your hands to yourself and be more considerate in your care of my person. Do we understand each other? You would be able to retire on the sum my husband will pay you for my *safe* return."

"I understand you perfectly, ma'am, and I wish now that I had not been so crass as to strike you. It won't happen no more. Nor will I touch any of your private parts—unless it should be accidental-like."

"*Do* be careful," Elyn emphasized. "My husband is very jealous of all my parts."

"Such as it's worth, ma'am, you got my word." Brady turned and shouted at one of the native guides, speaking to him in Spanish and some type of local dialect, apparently telling him to settle in for the night. He turned backed to Elyn when she called his name.

"One more thing, please," she said and gestured to her bound wrists. "I'm not going anywhere—I don't even know where we are. Couldn't you untie me . . . please?"

Brady considered this, shuffling his feet, trying to decide if the act conflicted somehow with his first deal with the Indians. She was right—even if she got away, she would be lost. She would never find her way out of the mountains. "Okay. You gotta promise to behave, though."

"I shall be an angel." Elyn thought she would have promised anything . . . well, almost anything, to be free again. Even now, as Brady untied the ropes, there seemed to be little feeling in her wrists. She rubbed them, chafing the skin to get the blood circulating once more. Brady was staring at her, almost as if he'd changed his mind. "An absolute angel, Mr. Brady, I swear it!" Elyn said to reassure him. She despised being nice to a man of such low moral caliber, but it seemed she had no choice. If Nick rescued her, which he had better do, she would personally borrow one of his handguns and dispatch this crude excuse for a man.

Despite her flippant attitude and an air of bravado, Elyn was scared to death, certain she was never coming back from wherever it was Brady was taking her. For some reason that had to do with Nick, she had been kidnapped. Would they hold her until he paid a ransom? Would she be a captive until he gave them something else, something more valuable than money? Who were "they" and what, in this godless place, was more valuable than money?

Elyn tried to think, but weariness made a muddle out of any attempt at logical thought. If she knew who "they" were, she would have the other answer—and vice versa. Brady wouldn't tell her anything unless she played up to him, and that she could not do. The idea of leading him on, of letting him think, even briefly, that there was a chance that she might offer herself for the knowledge of what lay ahead, was repugnant. Damn Nick anyway! Where was he?

The man named Juan Benito had worked for Nick. But he had led her into this trap... with Consuela's help? No, Connie wasn't a part of this. If she wanted Nick—and she likely still did—she would have used her body, her feminine wiles to win him. No, Connie had believed Juan Benito's claim that Nick had been hurt. And so it was Juan who had lied, Juan who worked, not for Nick, but for this mysterious person who had ordered her abduction.

Suddenly Elyn realized what had more value than money. Guns, rifles, ammunition, weapons to fight another revolution. My God, *that* was what Nick had gotten himself into—but which side was he on? He had partied, socialized, played to the hierarchy of the Mexican government; would he now supply weapons to those who wanted to overturn the government?

And because of his involvement, she was a part of it, and perhaps even her father was too. What had he gotten them into? Suddenly she was furious with Nick. If he loved her so, he should never have allowed himself to become involved once again in a rebellion. God help him the next time she saw him... if, indeed, she saw him again. But of course she would, she would survive... it was part of her nature.

Brady had gone so far as to make her a bed of blankets near the fire the guides had built. They had started to warm their supper of beans and tortillas; but the spicy smell only turned Elyn's stomach. She hadn't eaten much since leaving the casa, but she had a distinct feeling that if she tried, it would not stay down long.

Behind the higher elevations of the mountains above, the

sky had turned a pale yellow, then mottled with purple and streaks of orange. The morning would be hot, Brady informed her as he brought his tin cup full of hot, bitter-smelling coffee close to the spot where she rested. Did she not want something to drink or to eat? She would grow weak if she didn't take some nourishment.

How solicitous he had become since she had mentioned how much money Nick could pay him. It didn't matter; she needn't be polite or socialize. He was, after all, a criminal. Suddenly in the fading light she saw a movement to the left of Brady's legs. She stared, trying to make out what it was, praying it was none of the awful creatures Brady had mentioned earlier.

Brady was just considering a change of heart, as he drank his coffee and stared down at the Rowan woman. She was beautiful. Lucky Rowan, the bastard would have her his whole life long. Would he miss one hour of pleasure she spent with someone else? "Maybe we ought to amend that...." She wasn't listening, hadn't heard a word he had said, and Rueben Brady turned to glance in the direction in which she was staring.

It was the movement of his head that made the snake strike. Coiled some five feet away, the serpent resembled a rattler. It was a member of the rattlesnake family and had the same rattle shape to its tail, but there was no warning sound from the tail, only a bright flash of its yellow belly and throat as it launched, uncoiling like a tightly wound wire that had sprung.

Brady's hand had just touched the butt of his gun when the snake struck his leg. Everything was a blur of movement. Elyn Rowan screamed and scrambled sideways, as far away as she could get from the repeatedly striking fangs of the serpent. The guides had recognized the reptile but stood watching in awe, though an arm's length away, near their saddlebags, a rifle lay in its scabbard.

The snake was what the white men called the fer-de-lance, but to the two Aztec guides it was their sacred symbol, a representation of their god-king who bore the same name, Nauyalcoatl, the Four-fanged Serpent. To kill this wondrous beast would have been a blasphemy, for surely their leader, who knew all and could see the future, had become displeased with the American. He had not liked the man's treatment of Rowan's woman, and now his displeasure had been satisfied.

Brady hadn't gotten off a shot. The snake, a viper, had struck six times, releasing the poison from the sacs behind its fangs, fully emptying them before it drew back, reared its lovely, deadly head high, and slithered back into the rock outcrop from which it had come.

Elyn was still staring at Brady. After the first scream, after fear and loathing had instinctively sent her out of danger's range, she had gone into a kind of dull shock. She knew Brady was in pain. Agony was a better word for it. He writhed on the dusty ground in anguish, holding onto his leg, his howls sounding much like a woman's screams, knowing he was dying.

Finally Elyn shook off the feeling of lethargy and scrambled toward Brady. The snake was gone. She sensed, rather than knew, that it wouldn't return. The guides were still standing near the fire, arms crossed over their chests, still and silent as the night. She didn't know what to do. In his pain, Brady struck out, his arm slamming against her shoulder and sending her flying backward. For a moment she was dazed, her scalp bleeding from the spot where her head had struck a sharp rock. Finally the Indians moved, but it was to her they came. One of them lifted her easily and carried her over to the fire, dampening a cloth to wash the blood from her pale brown hair. The other stayed near, watching Brady's torture.

Brady had lived most of his life as an animal. She had even imagined such a fate for him at times during the past two days, but to sit and watch, to listen and do nothing while he died . . . Elyn wasn't sure the guides could understand her, and she knew only a few words of Spanish, but she tried to tell them to do something, anything to help Brady.

The one holding her tightened his grip around her shoulders. They were to deliver the woman to the Aztec compound. This man Brady mattered as little as the rocks and dust surrounding him. For a while he had been useful, but he had clearly overstepped the bounds of what their leader, Nauyaca, had requested. Let him die. Nothing they knew of could save the being who had been touched by the powerful poisons of Nauyalcoatl.

In a kind of daze, Elyn watched the stages of Brady's final hours. It took hours, nearly till dawn, before he finally gave in and there was no more movement. It was the most horrible of deaths imaginable. Not soon after he had been struck, the mercenary had begun to sweat. Blood seeped from his mouth after the first forty-five minutes. Elyn believed he was hemorrhaging. The sweat continued to pour forth but took on a rose hue, then turned scarlet. He looked, in the reflected firelight, as if someone had sprayed him with a fine mist of red water. His leg, from the knee to the thigh, had swollen to three times its normal width, straining at the material of his pants. Elyn closed her eyes at last. Some people lived awful lives. Knowing Brady for the short time she had, she knew he had spent his time on earth in less than kindly pursuits, perhaps even in purposeful cruelty. Still she could not imagine such a hellish death. It seemed that no one deserved it, but then she was not sure of anything any longer. She slept then, cradled in the arms of one of the Indians, covered by his blanket, zealously guarded and watched over the night through.

When she woke, the sun was just rising. It sparkled in her eyes, causing her to draw up her hand to shade them. Her head hurt; she raised a hand to touch the spot and remembered, then, why and how she had come by the bump that had bled and still ached. She glanced almost timidly toward the spot where Rueben Brady had suffered his agonies—and saw nothing. He was gone, his mule was gone, and only a few of his belongings—his gun and saddlebags, resting on one of the guide's own mules—showed any sign that he had been with them. Had she dreamed of Brady? The entire trip, with his crude remarks, the bargain she had made with him . . . it could not all have been a dream, a hallucination. She felt faint. The ground suddenly seemed to rush toward her, the blue of the sky to fall away.

The taller of the two guides caught her before she touched the ground. She was unconscious. The trip would be over within two hours. It would be better if she remained unaware. The brave mounted, cradling the limp woman in his arms, ready to leave this night camp where Nauyaca had made his will manifest. Brady's body, tossed over the cliff before dawn, would begin to molder soon. None of the animals would touch it, not the predators or the scavengers. Nature recognized poisoned food far more astutely than did man.

The party arrived at the compound later than Nauyaca had expected, and this displeased him. Also, when he saw the still, limp form of the woman in the arms of one of his warriors, Huitzal, he feared. Of the Americano, Brady, there was no trace; only his other warrior guide, Tochtli, the "rabbit," rode behind. Beside Nauyaca, arrayed in his finery of jaguar skin and feathered headdress, with the frightening mask of Texcatlipoca covering his features from the populace, stood the high priest, Miguel. Together they slowly descended the steps of the pyramid. It was safe to do so now. Some years back, when it had been reclaimed, the complex had lain in ruins, covered by dirt and scrub, brush and fir. Now it was again a capital worthy of one so holy as Nauyaca. He owed much to Miguel, Nauyaca did. His dreams of glory would be dust in his mouth had the older man not made of him what his destiny had decreed.

There was a quick explanation of what had happened. The young king heard his high priest suck in his breath as the woman stirred and began to wake. Miguel quickly suggested that she be taken to the women's quarters and be given comfort. Blood still matted the fair, ash-brown hair at her crown, and the scratch across her cheek had broken open and was bleeding slightly once more. She opened her eyes, eyes that despite a look of bewilderment, were a clear, vivid, velvety blue. Nauyaca stared at her for a moment, then smiled. The *olioquiliu* seeds were ever true. Aside from the shock of what she had witnessed and the wear of travel, she was as he had dreamed. Now the rest, in time, would come to pass. As Miguel had suggested, he ordered that she be taken to the women's quarters and tended.

It was still early. There were ritual ablutions to perform: the caste of priests under Miguel's control were to prepare a sacrifice to honor the destiny fulfilled in Nauyaca's dream. Neither of them had eaten yet and so, after dismissing his warriors and the girl, Nauyaca, the god-king of the Aztecs, and Miguel, the high priest of Texcatlipoca, shared their morning meal.

"Rowan should be home by now. He will be furious when he realizes we have his woman." Nauyaca was practically preening with confidence, so well were his plans fulfilling themselves. "Now he, who thought surely that he held the

303

upper hand, will beg to give over his store of weapons for my . . . our cause. How well it is working, is it not, my friend? He may stall, but he will bring me what I want. Oh, the power fills me—I feel, priest, I feel more than a god, more than a king. Creation fills me." He chose a fresh mango and peeled it, then ate carelessly, as does one who has no one to answer to for his manners. "You are strangely quiet. Why? Are you keeping any secret from your king?"

Nauyaca was at times exceedingly arrogant, annoyingly so. And yet, for him to succeed, for the Aztec nation to rise from a remnant to an image of its former wonder, he had to be arrogant. For centuries, the people had worshipped a meek and mild man who spoke in platitudes and of patient change—this was the Christ brought to Mexico by the invaders. Christ of the otherworld promised peace and plenty and wonder of wonders but in some other place, after this existence of pain and poverty.

Miguel wanted the Aztecs to take back what was theirs, now, in this life. Paradise or dreams of it were for fools. Too long had the people believed in later. Paradise was coming and soon. But there had to be one uniting force; and young Nauyaca, with his beauty and charisma, was that force. He was tall, taller than the average Aztec by at least six inches.

His complexion was light—a superstitious tie to the old Feathered Serpent, Quetzalcoatl—but still darkly tanned enough to make him one with his fellow Aztecs. His nose was a proud aquiline beak above full, sensual lips. A strong, determined chin, a broad and noble forehead. Dark, mesmerizing eyes that could capture imagination and make it real, as real as an artist blending colors to paint a picture into which one could step.

His physique was a model of perfection. A heavily muscled torso slimmed down to a flat belly and narrow hips. He was lean and powerful, as good a specimen in body as in mind. He was the savior—and salvation was not far in the future.

"I am only tired, my lord Nauyaca. The night was long and filled with dreams. I was afraid Brady would be the wrong man to send. If the woman has been harmed, she will be of little use in bargaining with Rowan. If she should die . . . all of the demons in the other worlds would not keep him from our throats."

"You are growing older, my friend. I fear no one and certainly not this man Rowan. His woman was in shock only; she saw a violent death and it surprised her. Everything is simply explained. You worry too much, my mentor. Nothing else troubles you?"

"No. Only later, I want to see her. I must know if she is recovered."

Nauyaca frowned. Miguel was getting old. He knew so much, and yet . . . age was decay, and it had begun to file the sharpness from a once-brilliant mind. "This I grant. Even now, she probably eats, for the men said she nearly starved herself on the journey. Once she has bathed and rested, she will be as I saw her in my dream."

"Yes, my lord. Now—if you will excuse me, I must see to the sacrifice. The hour will come soon enough, and the drug must be administered to take effect."

With a regal nod, Nauyaca permitted Miguel to take his leave. The old man had been bothersome anyway, and Nauyaca had other things to consider, many things he could no longer share with Miguel.

At first Elyn moved like a doll, a limp body, conscious but without volition. She allowed herself to be handed over to several women who took her into the cool interior of a recessed stone building. There was an odd scent in the air, something floral and intoxicating. Just as she was beginning to come fully to her senses, it made her feel languid, without care.

The women, some of them young girls, one an older and clearly more powerful individual, crowded around her, remarking in their strange language over her complexion. They stripped her of her thin cotton blouse and skirt, wrapped her in a thin, finely woven sheet of something like linen, and paraded her off to a warm room that contained a large, almost Romanesque bath. That same fragrance hung in the air but was stronger here, and as Elyn stripped once more and entered the warm, waist-deep waters, she found herself wondering why she had ever felt upset. A man had died—but he had not been nice to her. He had not been nice to many in his life. It seemed only logical for him to die, then, and most certainly it had been no fault of hers. Still she felt vaguely troubled. Someone poured a fragrant, pinelike-scented oil on her hair and lathered it, then another of the girls helped to rinse away the suds. She felt pampered, secure. Nothing was wrong.

Later, reclining on a soft padded couch, the women and girls took a certain delight in feeding her. She *was* famished, hungry enough for two people. Elyn in no way felt threatened. She was a guest, an interesting divertissement for these secluded and sheltered ladies.

She slept. There was no drug on earth quite as tranquilizing as a luxurious bath, a full belly, and much-needed rest. It was early afternoon before she woke, and then, finding herself alone, she sat up, stretched—and remembered. Now everything came back with crystal clarity, the death throes of Brady and the implacable, immobile Aztec guides watching him die as if he were a fly.

Suddenly she heard chanting and a strange, resonant sound rather like a horn blowing. Finding her way out to the hall and toward the lighter section of the building was not difficult. She met no one. Everyone was gone, attending some sort of service outside. She came to the front portal and shaded her eyes against the brilliant sun. The chanting had ceased, and now in its place came a shrill reedlike piping and the sound of a drum, a steady beating of a hollow drum.

For the first time, Elyn realized how immense the complex was. It was an old Aztec compound, with a double-pyramid temple like the one in Tenochtitlan and several other, smaller pyramidal structures still in the stages of reconstruction. They were in the process of reclaiming a part of their heritage, and only God knew how much acreage extended into the forest surrounding the cleared compound. How her father would have loved to see this, to discover something like it on his own. She didn't know enough of archaeology to date it, but it was very ancient, at least seven hundred years old, or older if the Aztecs had built on the site of an earlier culture.

Everywhere, on every building, there were signs of ongoing renovations. Freshly painted images of birds, animals, flowers, all in colors so vivid that any artist might have wept to learn their secret composition. There was an *ocelotl*, the jaguar, and a *chapul*, the grasshopper, the image of which made up part of the name of Chapultepec Park, and of course butterflies. Aztec art at its height had been beauty in form, a celebration of life, an odd contrast with and yet a part of their use of ritual sacrifice.

From what she remembered, her father had taught her that the Aztecs had believed that the afterlife was as real and existent as life on earth. Death, therefore, even before one's time, made little difference. It was an entrance to a different realm of being. Their "flowery wars," the mock battles used to gather sacrificial victims, the almost reverent kinship between the death dealer and the victim, the fierceness of battle juxtaposed against the gentle and courtly behavior of a warrior who would scribe poetry to his love and bring her a flower . . . these seemingly opposite values were melded in a society that was as mysterious in its way as were the cults of the Far East. Always evolving and yet set with absolutes.

Elyn turned to her left and froze. Some twenty-five feet from her was a building unlike any she had ever seen, certainly never in her father's drawings. The building itself was circular, much like those usually dedicated to the wind god, Ehecatl. There were something like twenty or thirty shallow steps leading up to the main entrance, which was— and this was what awed Elyn so—a depiction of a snake's head. The height of the entrance seemed to be at least six feet, possibly another half-foot. At each corner of the snake's mouth, a large fang projected, and there were two more facing downward from the roof. The image was done to scale, perfect down to the colors of the reptile's throat and the gradations of its scales. She had seen it before. It was very possible that she would always dream of it, for this *was* the snake that had so viciously killed Rueben Brady.

The serpent had always been a part of Amerindian cultures. Especially the winged serpent, the plumed or feathered serpent, the god of goodness and light, of all things gentle and beautiful, Quetzalcoatl. This serpent, though, she had never seen or heard of its worship; it had to be a type of serpent worship but she knew, sensed rather, that it represented not good but evil.

Suddenly the drums ceased beating. They had become so much a part of the atmosphere surrounding her that the silence seemed disruptive. She turned back toward the twin pyramids. There, high above an assembly that must have numbered at least seven hundred, possibly eight hundred natives, stood a tall, robed figure wearing a grotesque, distorted mask. Next to him was a younger man. He wore a mask as well, the image of the serpent building, the face of the deadly snake that killed in silence.

There was an air of expectation. Elyn craned her neck. From her vantage point, she could hardly see those two strange figures and what seemed like servants with them. The drums beat again, steady and sure, then abruptly stopped. The tall priest bent, a murmur rippled through the crowd, then suddenly he straightened, holding in his hand what appeared to be a red lump. Elyn knew what it was; and her scream and those that followed spoiled the "beauty" of the sacrifice. The victim's still-beating heart was burned, offered up to Texcatlipoca to make strong his ally, the redeemer serpent, Nauyalcoatl.

Royal guards dressed in eagle-cult costume surrounded Elyn. She didn't see them. All she saw was the heart, dripping its life blood, held in the hand of a man. Her mind repeated a phrase over and over. *They don't do this anymore, they don't do this.* . . . Again, faintness overcame her. One of the guards caught her before she touched the paved ground.

Before him appeared the king, the Lord Nauyaca. The guard bowed, a difficulty with his charge but well acquitted. "Take her back to her chamber in the women's quarters. And bring to me the man who should have stood guard at the same building."

Later that night, when Elynora woke, the room was half-shadowed. One wall sconce burned with some sort of scented resin. Across the room, a man sat in a chair. He had remained motionless for the past two hours. Now that she stirred, he moved. Elyn rose, leaning on one elbow. "Who's there? Who is it?"

The figure rose and came forward into the pool of light. It was a young man, an Aztec. He wore a finely woven green robe and a type of loincloth that banded his waist and covered only the most essential parts of his male anatomy. He had worn sandals; the strap marks still showed on his calves but now he was barefooted. For longer than she wished, he stared at her. His eyes, dark and hypnotic, roamed over her body. Elyn felt . . . strange, almost as if they had given her a drug. She was trapped, like a caged animal; this man, younger than she but so self-possessed, was her captor. Her skin tingled; she shivered and goose bumps freckled her arms. She wanted to reach for the thin coverlet but something, his presence, his "hold" upon her would not permit the move.

He probably couldn't speak English. Spanish was possible, but she was dreadful at it. Certainly the ancient tongue of Nahuatl was out of the question. He solved the dilemma finally by speaking—in English that was nearly as perfect as her own.

"I," he announced with a slight inclination of his head, "am the king, Nauyalcoatl. You are safe here, as long as I choose to keep you safe. You will *not* cause a scene—as you did this afternoon in the plaza. You will remain quartered here unless sent for by royal command. You do understand?"

His arrogance was appalling, though he did seem to have the qualities to carry it off . . . on any ordinary person. Not so, Elyn. "You, sir, king or not, are a murderer. The priest acted at your command. In any civilized country you should both be given death sentences for what took place this day. As for obeying you, I shall not. And I think you may threaten me with sacrifice all you wish. I am a hostage . . . a *valuable* hostage, at least until you make my husband aware that you have me." Elyn lay back, wondering how far she could push this strutting cock of a false aristocrat. "Do *you* understand?"

At first her attitude infuriated Nauyaca. No one, not even Miguel, had ever spoken to him so haughtily. Then, because it was unusual to meet anyone, man or woman, who had the courage to speak so, he smiled. She was unlike any woman he had ever met, and she was desirable as well. Just as in his dreams, only more so. "We both understand. But I am still the king, while you . . . I have other sources for procuring the guns your husband will trade for you. If I wanted to I could make love to you and then sacrifice you at dawn's light."

She didn't believe him, at least about the weapons. He needed Nick's cooperation and he surely wouldn't have it unless he was able to produce a healthy hostage. And he wouldn't sacrifice her. The problem was keeping him at arm's length. He wanted her even now; that much was difficult to disguise due to the manner of his attire. "But you won't. Not any of your threats frighten me, sir. Now, I am tired and wish to be left—"

"What if I kill your husband? After he delivers the weapons, he is as nothing." Nauyaca folded his arms, enjoying the reaction he had finally gotten from this woman. "I might save him, I might cut out his heart and—"

"Stop it!" Elyn covered her ears. The Aztec youth who thought himself a king was mad. He was cruel as well, and she would not listen to such awful talk, especially concerning Nick.

Nauyaca started to laugh. He had her now. This one who seemed so self-possessed had a vulnerable spot when it came to the mention of her husband. "You care for him?" She glared at him for a moment, then glanced away. "You love him . . . you actually *feel* something for Rowan, do you not?" He laughed all the harder, mocking the emotion, and with his amusement the spell was broken. If he had ever seemed to fit the role of king, it was impossible now to see him that way. He was a man, just a man who sweated and made mistakes and could die, as any other, as the victim had on the pyramid altar. As so many others had done before him, he was attempting to lead a resurrection of the old ways. But he was no different. Like those before him, he would fail.

"I will have him killed as soon as we have the guns and ammunition," he taunted, and reached out to touch her cheek, to stroke the scratch that marred the perfect, flawless complexion. She shivered at his touch, and Nauyaca mistook her revulsion for excitement. "I am not without mercy or compassion. These things too a king must have. You will not have to watch as he dies."

"You'll need him. He can supply you with more bullets, more rifles. . . ."

Nauyaca shrugged. "I will need nothing more from Rowan. The gods favor a return to the old ways, to the magic and the blood. We go back along the true path, not the one chosen so long ago by the fool Montezuma. He and his Quetzalcoatl, with his soft preaching so close to that of the Christ of your people. We were betrayed, but the time comes to return the betrayal. Once more in glory, the Aztec nation will rise."

He had charisma. She could imagine his speaking to his people, firing their imaginations, telling them of how, after four hundred years of being the lowest of the classes, they would retake their heritage.

"When he is dead, your man, I will keep you as one of my women." The king came closer. He had a certain animal virility, an attractiveness born of confidence, power. But he was mad, and before he could possess her she would fight. She caught the hand that would have slid down her cheek and along her throat, that would have gone on to explore her breasts and thighs, caught it and dug in deeply with her nails, not satisfied until she had drawn blood. Then, as if it were a bothersome insect, she pushed away his hand.

He stared at her, measuring, it seemed, her expectations

against his own feelings. She thought he would hit her. His hand was bleeding, striped as if the she-jaguar had struck. Nauyaca smiled. He wanted her more, claws extended, spitting like the cats one had to conquer before they could be pets.

Suddenly they both became aware of a presence. There was no sound to announce the arrival of the high priest, but Miguel stood at the draped portal to the hallway. His figure was tall, robust, half-shrouded in shadow, and more menacing because of the power that emanated from him. He was in charge here, at least until the revolt began, and then he would remain the power behind the throne, for as long as he could control Nauyaca.

He ignored Elyn as if she didn't exist, addressing his protégé in a flurry of Spanish, in a tone of utter denunciation. Elyn watched the young king for his reaction. The air seemed to crackle with a tug of power, a struggle of wills. The younger man stiffened, seemed to offer a weak defense, then glanced back over his shoulder with an expression the priest could not see. He meant to have her. Whether the priest held the power now or not, Nauyaca would do as he pleased—and the time was not far off.

The high priest entered, holding the drapery to one side for his lord to exit. As Nauyaca, head held high, strode across the room, the priest bowed his head. Strange, their relationship. He commanded, the older of the two, and yet he seemed to serve as a mentor to the young man.

Finally they were alone. The man came toward her in strong, sure strides. Elyn stared, transfixed, more frightened of the priest with his robed figure and terrifying mask than she had been of Nauyaca's threat of physical possession. He was faceless, a terror yet to be reckoned with, one of many she had endured these past days and perhaps the worst of all.

313

For a while he stood close to the bed, staring down at her, as quiet and still as when he had entered the room.

Elyn closed her eyes. She was dreaming. Yes, surely that was it—she had caught the fever Jackie had had and was hallucinating. None of this was real.

"It may seem so, my child, but you're not hallucinating." The priest had spoken, not only spoken but in English, not only in English but in her father's well-remembered, beloved voice. Elyn opened her eyes and stared. The mask came off and there stood Michael Winters, not quite smiling, but for all the world looking as if he'd just come to take her for an afternoon stroll in the garden.

Chapter Sixteen

Instinctively, without thought, Elyn sat up and held out her arms. Michael Winters came down on one knee and pulled her into his arms, holding tightly, as if he would never let her go. Elyn was crying, though the sound of weeping seemed to come from a great distance . . . and to belong to some other distressed soul.

It didn't matter that he wore a strange and ancient costume or that he smelled vaguely of the overly sweet copal incense used in the Aztec rituals. For minutes there was nothing more important in the world than the fact that she had found him. Her father held her; what could be wrong in the world if his strong arms were around her?

Then, after those minutes when he held her and stroked her hair as gently as he had when she was a child, Elyn remembered that he was not her father, really, and she drew back, staring at him through a blur of tears.

Physically he'd changed little. The hair at his temples was a bit more silvered; a few more lines etched the outer corners of his eyes. There was still a vigor about him, a strength she'd always felt as a child. He no longer smelled of his special brand of tobacco, though, and for some silly reason that she could not explain, that made her begin to cry anew.

"I . . . I cannot th-think what to say, Father," she managed to stutter. "How can it be that we're in this strange, awful place? How can *you* be the man who leads Nauyaca to such atrocities?" She paused then and seemed to draw away from him, to shrink back, though she stayed within the circle of his arms. Her voice sounded dazed, puzzled, when she spoke again. "But it *can* be, because so many things are not what they seemed to be." Elyn looked up and her blue eyes met the gray of Winters's. "For all my life, you were my father, and now . . . now you are not. You're some strange man, plucked from God knows where, to marry Mother and save the family honor. You pretended all these years to be my father, and, sir, performed most convincingly. I applaud your acting. Tell me, were you paid well?"

Michael's face was darkly tanned. Years in the tropics had given him a complexion close to that of a native. But for the light color of his eyes, he might have been one. Now, though, he paled, and then a moment later reddened. Elyn had struck a nerve with that cynical inquiry. She had always been a girl to go out of her way to avoid hurting anyone. Yes, he'd taken Anne's money. Hadn't everyone she'd ever wanted anything from done the same? He wasn't proud of it, he was ashamed, but he had loved the child his "marriage of convenience" had produced, loved her then and still. Certainly he had loved her more than he loved her mother. "I deserved that, I imagine. However did you . . . no, you needn't say, it must have been Anne who told you. She would take joy in revealing such a shocking bit of news. Tell me, did she make it seem an accidental slip of the tongue? That's your grandmother's way, y'know."

"Lady Anne is dead." There, again she had shocked Michael Winters. She *wanted* to shock him, even to hurt him if she could find some vulnerable spot to wound. For all her life, Michael had listened to her fears, consoled her for her

316

losses, cheered her on for small victories, held her when, in the damp sleep of a tropic night, she had wakened with a nightmare. Now it all seemed a lie. The comfort, the compassion—how much had been real, how much pretend? She felt bereft of emotion. "Actually, she wrote me a note. Her solicitor saw to it that I received it after the funeral."

"Even after death, the venom, eh?" The statement was bitter and resentful. "So, you came searching for your father who wasn't your father—why? To make me pay up for the lie?" His smile was acrid, ironic. "I'm sure it wasn't to inform me I was named in her will."

"Neither was I, really, Fa... what shall I call you, then? Mr. Winters is it, or perhaps, seeing our long acquaintance, perhaps Michael?" Still holding her with his left arm, Winters drew back his right hand and smacked her full across the face. The idea that he had struck her was at once horrifying and gratifying. In all her life, whenever her mother had insisted she deserved physical punishment, Father had been unable to strike her. Now he had, and it was because she had found and struck that nerve, that vulnerable spot within him. This all-powerful man, who could call one of his guards in a second and have her killed, had hit her and was as shattered by the act as she. They stared at each other for minutes, then Michael pulled her close to him again.

"You will listen to me now, Elynora, I insist. I have never, never struck at you in anger, and now I am sick of myself. Anne was so powerful. She reaches now, from beyond the grave, to slip between us."

Elyn sighed. Tears quietly slipped down her cheeks, unheeded. She could hear Michael's heart beating rapid and strong.

"It wasn't enough for her to take your mother from the man she loved and make her marry me, nor to keep you from us for so long; no. She had to lend her viper's tongue to this

317

'truth' and confess. I could have lied, Elyn.'' He drew back a bit and glanced down at her face. Her eyes watched him but they were nearly swollen shut with weeping. "I could have lied and said I *was* your father. In God's most holy name, I swear, my darling, I felt as if I were the man who had sired you. You were mine more than your mother's."

Elyn sniffled. She felt like a child again. Michael Winters was telling the truth. She had sensed it all her life, a distance between herself and her mother, a vague feeling of resentment emanating from the pale English lady. Even, on an occasional visit, a look of animosity. She had thought she had imagined it, but it *had* been there. Resentment. "She didn't want me, did she?"

"Oh, it wasn't so much not wanting as . . . as being her mother's child. Alice wanted her own way and she was denied it. She was mad for your real father, but he, poor blighter, never had a chance. Anne saw to it that they were separated, found a suitable substitute, and married off her pregnant daughter. Hoping all the while, I'm sure, for a male heir. All it meant to Alice, being pregnant, was that she'd lost her love."

"Is he alive?"

"I don't know. And don't ask who he is, either. I shan't say, ever. Let it be, after so long. Did I not always treat you as mine? I felt you were. Are you not still?"

Elyn shook her head. "How can I be? I'm married, and your young pretender to the throne of the Aztec kingdom wants to do my husband in."

"Rowan? That *is* a problem. I had no idea until I saw you brought into camp. . . . You see, as his wife, you are the bait, the reason he'll deliver the weapons we need. If he loves you—"

"He does. Father, you haven't asked about Jackie."

318

Michael's eyes brightened. He'd seen the boy twice, once as a babe in arms and once when he'd just begun to walk. All that, his old life, seemed distantly behind him now. "How is the little fellow?"

"Just recovering from a fever, and not so awfully little, Da." It amazed them both, Elyn calling him by that familiar term, the same she had used as a child, before she'd grown into a young lady and taken to calling him Father. "He's six now and . . ."

"Yes?"

"Looks amazingly like his father. Rowan *is* his father. That surely must change your plans. He is the man I love with all my heart, the father of my son, *not* his stepfather."

"What the devil d'you mean, that *he's* the one . . . ?"

Elyn nodded. Her father could not have forgotten the incident leading to her divorce, or how she had sought him out and found comfort in his arms, still marked by the bruises Alec had left upon her cheek. "You cannot kill him, else *I* shall die. Would you leave Jackie an orphan?" With what other means could she appeal to this once-gentle man who had suddenly turned into an advocate of violence? She was frightened, of him, of what would happen to Nick, to Jackie.

"Why have you taken up this cause, Father? I know you, better perhaps than Mother ever did. You're a gentleman, a man who's always lived honorably, a scholar. This revolt has no chance. It can only mean death for the Aztecs, whom you obviously love, and for others, innocents. Will you order your warriors to slaughter every non-Indian in the country? What of the mestizo? How shall you choose, like a Solomon, which parts of their bodies are Spanish, which are Indian?" Elyn placed a hand on either side of her father's face, forcing him to look directly into her eyes, praying that it was not too late for him to understand. "This rebellion is doomed. The

319

Aztec peoples are a minority. You cannot win. All you'll do is force the government to move against the Indians and, finally, exterminate their race. Is that what you want? Is it?''

Michael pulled away her hands. He couldn't be swayed by such arguments. Years of planning had gone into this. It would succeed; it had to. "Nauyaca was meant to lead his people to victory, Elyn. It's you who do not understand. I've seen it myself, written in the stars so plainly. We do everything here in the old way, the pure ways. We will return to the days before Cortes vanquished Montezuma.''

Elyn was suddenly, chillingly afraid. The man so close to her was Michael Winters in appearance, but his words and the dangerous fervor of the fanatic that shone in his eyes belonged to a stranger, a man she could no longer reach or influence. "Who is Nauyaca? Where did he come from?" She hated to ask, but thinking back now, it was so clear. "He's your son, isn't he?" Winters looked away, across the room, toward the door, as if he wanted to leave. *"Isn't he?"* Elyn almost screamed the words the second time. "Your son, the son Mother never gave you. Who was his mother? Did my mother approve of your choice or was it simply a discreet—''

"You're overstepping the bounds of what is proper, Ellie." Winters sounded cold and distant as he put her away from him and stood. "He is my son. His mother was a woman named Xochitl, and yes, your mother knew about it, and she couldn't have cared less. Xochitl was of pure Aztec blood. . . . She disappeared into the mountains soon after Nauyaca was born. Only his name then was Miguel. He doesn't know, Elyn. Say nothing to him. It would be a mistake, I assure you.''

"Why have you never told him?"

Winters snorted, impatient with the question. "Why? Because he would not believe me. It's essential that he believes his blood to be pure Aztec. He will lead his people to resurrect a civilization that was bright and modern when garbage and filth ran through the streets of Europe's major cities.''

Suddenly Elyn understood. Her father, somewhere in the loneliness of his work, in the isolation of his profession, had drifted toward the fine edge of madness. He believed in this scheme of his, that it would succeed and that his son would rule over a vast, revived Aztec empire. Somewhere deep within herself she was glad that some nameless man had slept with her mother. Such madness, if it had been hers to pass on to her children . . . She could not think of it, not consciously. "You'll not like this, Father, but I am going to test you."

"How so, my love?"

"I want you to choose between the girl you raised as a daughter—raised, mind you—and the boy you never saw until he had grown to manhood. Your love for me is a lie if you choose this violent upheaval. It is doomed to fail. Everyone you love will die. Do you think Nauyaca will spare Jackie?" Michael's head came up sharply, jerking toward her. "Do you think he'd spare another child of mine?" The older man's dark brows, threaded with gray, came together in a childishly puzzled frown. "Yes, Father, I'm pregnant. What will happen when the baby is born? Nauyaca will have his way and make me one of his women, but do you think he would tolerate my baby, Nick Rowan's baby?" It was a lie, the only lie she had ever told her father in all of her life, but she was desperate. "Do you honestly think you can control him once he's started? Why would he need you after all of it's done? If it's revealed that you, the high priest, are a white man, the enemy of his people . . . Oh, Father, what in the name of heaven have you started?"

"I'll protect you—and the children. As for Rowan . . . I

can't promise anything. Nauyaca is the sum total of my life's work, in flesh. Everything he knows of his heritage, I have taught him. He is my son. The only way to stop him now is to destroy him. Would you have me do that, Elyn?''

"Yes! If you can . . . if you still can.''

Michael looked at her with a puzzled expression, then turned and quickly left the room. Elyn's shoulders slumped and she lay back. Had she had any effect on him whatsoever? Were they all doomed? Nick was walking into a trap, one from which neither of them would escape. Poor Jackie, that was all she could think. He had just found his father, and now, because of events that had formed before he was born, before *she* was born, he would soon be an orphan. A very wealthy orphan, but what on God's green earth would that mean to him? She prayed. For the first time in years, Elyn asked God to forgive all of her trespasses, whatever she had done, and save everyone. She couldn't think of another power that could alter what seemed to lie ahead.

Nick wouldn't let her down. He must already know she was a captive, and he was obstinate when it came to his possessions. He wouldn't let her die—and he wouldn't die himself. She knew that, believed it, and for the first time she felt hope. Even now, he was planning, doing something, perhaps contacting old friends who would help rescue her. He loved her too much to let her be taken from him so soon after they had found each other again. He loved her.

Of course he did. And at the very moment when Elyn was praying for a savior, he was back at Casa Aventura, one hand gripping Gyp Andrews by the throat, threatening him with a prolonged and painful death unless he had Gyp's cooperation in locating Elyn. As big as Andrews was, Nick had the advantage of five inches more height, a good twelve years of youth, and the anger of an animal whose mate has been captured.

"You goddamned, stupid son of a bitch! Why the hell did I make a point of telling you to watch the house? I didn't ask much of you in five years. This time, I said, 'Watch the house, see that nothing happens to Elyn or my son.'" Gyp gurgled a reply, his collar choking off any intelligible answer. "I ought to hang you up on a maguay cactus. You ever see what happens to a man crucified on one of them? Come morning, he's got three-foot thorns sticking through parts of his body he never knew he had."

He let Gyp drop, let him fall into a wing chair by the fireplace in his parlor. "You tell me *why* they got away with this. Do you realize yet, in that liquor-fogged, befuddled old flier's brain of yours, what the hell you've done?"

"W-well now, they got her, son," Gyp muttered hoarsely. "Seems t'me they got you by the balls. You either give 'em the guns or . . . or they . . ." He couldn't say aloud that Elyn's life wasn't worth a plugged nickel if the Aztec rebels didn't get what they wanted. And now it seemed, they didn't need a peso's worth of credit.

Nick had been pacing the room. Now he stopped by the arched portal leading to the entry hall and whirled on Andrews with an incredulous look. "No, Gyp, it ain't *me* they got by the balls!" In his entire life, very few things had worried Gyp Andrews enough actually to scare him. The look in Rowan's eyes did now. He had a crazy streak in him, Nick, and he'd lived and fought with Indians. That threat about the maguay . . . Gyp had heard of it. The torture was one of Zapata's favorites, reserved for captured *federales* or informers. During the night, in the growing season, the cactus thorns, spikes really, would grow two or three feet, piercing the body of the man tied atop it.

"I did what you asked, pal," he insisted now. "I watched the house, I swear I did." Sweat beaded his forehead, running down the sides of his temples in rivulets, wetting his armpits and the creases of his elbows. "How was I supposed to know it was Benito? I thought... well, I thought you'd sent him...."

Nick glowered and stalked across the room again to pour himself a drink. He dismissed Andrews's presence, crossed to the fireplace, and leaned an arm against the mantel, thinking. He had suspected Benito. More than half of this was his fault—he just hadn't expected Juan to be back in town yet. For whatever reason, Benito had turned; and he wouldn't get off easily ... in fact, he wouldn't get off at all. He had, no matter for a short or a long period of time, endangered what Rowan loved most in all the world. Depending on one's viewpoint, that had been either a very brave or a very foolish thing to do. Above, in the center of the room, the ceiling fan whirled, doing little more than blowing the hot, humid air around the room.

"You got a plan, Nick?" Gyp said it hopefully, anxious to redeem himself.

Nick was almost sorry for Gyp now. It wasn't his fault that Elyn had gone off with Benito. Even Consuela had known and trusted the little bastard. They wouldn't harm Elyn; she was their payment, in place of gold bullion, for the guns he could supply, guns that had vanished from the warehouse and were now stored in a safe spot only he knew of.

He bellowed for Connie. She wasn't far. In an instant she silently entered the room and came to him. Despite the fact that she still cared, there was sorrow in her eyes. Nick loved his Englishwoman ... and Connie was afraid of what would happen should she not come back. For his sake, she prayed to the Virgin that Elyn Rowan would be safe.

Nick spoke absently, as if he were repeating things to

himself, reaffirming actions he wanted taken. "In the morning, I'm calling my brother Stephen in Colorado. I want you to pack, take Jackie and Sera and get them on the train for Chihuahua, take it as far as San Antonio. Steve'll meet you there; he'll take Jackie back to Denver until this is...finished."

She didn't care for the way he said that. Nick was always confident, he was capable, a man of qualified talents. He knew what he could do, how far he could push himself. In this situation, there were too many variables, too many things he could not control. He would do what he had to, but Connie sensed for the first time in all the years that she had known him that he was unsure of the outcome and scared of failing. The boy, though, must be safe from the same type of abduction. Nick was thinking; this was a good sign. "I will, you know...anything you ask. I make no excuses for Señor Andrews, Nick, but Juan Benito...his acting was most real. I, too, though it was not my place to go to you, thought you had been hurt. I will pray, Nick. The señora, she will return."

Nick inhaled a deep breath and let it out slowly. "I know, Connie. Elyn's a survivor. Now go pack a couple of bags for Jackie. Don't wake him—I'll talk to him before you leave." Consuela went off, always helpful but this time in particular, eager to alleviate the anxiety Nick was experiencing.

"You got a plan, don't you?" Gyp realized he had repeated himself, but it made him nervous to sit around doing nothing.

"I do," Nick said. "And you're a part of it. Fail me this time, you S.O.B., and I'll personally hang you up by your—"

Andrews held up a hand. "No need to get graphic, son. I goofed once. I won't do it twice. I owe you, I'll pay. What do I do?"

"Find me a man named Alesandro Guillermo. He should be in southern Sonora. I don't want to hear how hard it's

325

going to be. He's a six-foot-five bastard with two gold front teeth. Tell him, when you get past his henchmen, tell him to remember the Day of the Dead. He'll know what you mean. And tell him I need a small group, *compadres,* along with him. I'll meet him here in a week." He consulted his watch. "I'll see him at seven in the evening."

It wouldn't be easy, what Rowan wanted, but Gyp owed him. Aside from any debts, real or imaginary, he didn't want Nick as an enemy. "I'll find your Guillermo, but what if he won't come? He may even be dead."

"He owes me one. And he wouldn't dare not come," Nick answered confidently. "You'll find him—or once he hears you're looking for him, he'll find you. He's not dead . . . too mean to die." That brought a smile, briefly, to Nick's mouth. He reached into his pocket and brought out a cigarillo. He didn't bother to offer one to Andrews. Until Gyp had redeemed himself, he was an acquaintance only. With calm deliberation, he lit up and inhaled. "I told you I didn't want to work this one. Now you know why." Nick pointed to the hall with the cigarillo. "Door's that way. I'll expect to see you in a week."

Chapter Seventeen

Nick stared at Benito, letting his feelings speak in his expression. He hadn't lived in Mexico for so many years without learning that the native people were sensitive to honor and loyalty. Juan Benito had betrayed Nick in the worst of ways—he had sided with people who were Nick's enemies, and he had delivered over Nick's wife, his beloved, his heart.

Benito was in the warehouse. Every soft whisper of sound in the empty building was magnified, every tiny rustle; the patter of mice feet seemed to Juan Benito the sound of stalking jaguars. He had hidden, after leaving Elynora Rowan with the man named Brady. Afraid of what he had done, he had been deeply ashamed that in obeying one master, he had betrayed a man who had been only kind and generous to him and his family. Now that man wanted an accounting, not only of Juan's reasoning but of his faith to the Lord Nauyaca.

At first when they had found him, Señor Andrews and another man, Juan had wanted to die rather than go with them. He had been in hiding since the morning after the kidnapping. Somehow, it did not matter how, he had been discovered. And now he must answer for his crime against the man who had treated him so kindly—the man he had betrayed.

"Why?"

When Rowan asked the simple question, so softly, as though he had been sacrificed and his heart had already been torn out, Benito could not think immediately what to answer. He had been drawn into the movement by his wife's cousin, José Maria. It was time to let the world know how the land had been stolen, how the once-great heritage had been mocked as savage and pagan. They were Aztecs, once rulers of Mexico and Central America. No one was going to give back what had been stolen; it had to be taken back. But they had needed, for centuries, the right leader.

Now, or so José Maria had insisted, that man had been recognized. Like Christ, he had come of age and would lead. He spoke and the people listened. In his words they heard a message of hope. They would have their day, though not without bloodshed and violence; but Mexico had never been without blood on her soil—violence seemed to pulse through her veins. It had to be now, this year. The anniversary of the death of the last Aztec king was coming in August. Four hundred years had passed since the foreign dog Cortes had laid siege to the city of Tenochtitlan, the city the Spaniards had leveled to build their colonial capital. On the steps of the merchant market, halfway up the pyramid at Tlatelolco, Cuahhtemoc and his brother warriors had died. With them had died Aztec resistance. Pride and resentment had slept together for centuries in the breasts of the true Aztecs.

But how could he tell this to Rowan, who wasn't Mexican, who knew nothing of degradation or suffering? Yes, Rowan had fought with Zapata, offered his life for a cause not his own . . . but could he know, really know, how princes-made-beggars might feel?

"I . . . what can I say? You will, before the night is through, have your friends beat me. Perhaps I deserve it. You would

328

prefer, for I know you have a heart not so hard as these others, that I tell you what you wish to know. Sir, I cannot. My friends, my relatives are there, in the camp of the Aztec king. The hour to strike is soon at hand. The priest ordered that your wife be brought there, to make you turn over the guns to help us in our victory. She was not harmed. I know this order was—"

"You *don't* know! You know what you were told, that is all," Nick snapped, losing his patience. He had thought that guilt would make Benito turn and help him. It wasn't going to work. As Juan had said, his friends would use force, and even that would not work. When a man of personal honor, one such as Benito, made a pledge to an ideal, there was little that could sway him from his position. Idealism many times had proved an anesthetic against torture. So it had once for him in prison.

Nick sighed and shook his head. "Like Judas, Benito, you have little understanding of what you do. They, your Aztecs, cannot win. There are far too few of you left to rule a nation the size of Mexico. It has reached a different stage, so different from the one in which Cortes arrived. Then there were millions of your people; *then* they should have resisted. Now . . . how are a handful of Indians, right or wrong, going to manage a country with millions of citizens? You base your plans on race. Most Mexicans are mestizo, mixed. Will they be second-class citizens? And the whites, do you intend to kill them off, or force them into common labor as a revenge?"

"I am committed, Señor Rowan. And sorry, too, that they asked me to betray you. If I could help, but I cannot. . . ."

"You can. Tell us the location of the camp. We're not taking it by force, for God's sake! I'm not calling out the army and insisting on a mass attack. I want my wife, Benito. I know she would be killed if I asked for help from the

government. My friends and I will rescue her. Just tell us how
to get there, the number of guards posted, the routine . . . all
we need to make a raid. Look, I don't give a damn what your
group does! This is personal. I want my wife. You made a
mistake when you brought her into it, friend, a big mistake."
Nick sighed. "I ask once more: tell me what I want to know.
After Elyn is free, I don't care if your revolt begins."

Benito shook his head, though in his heart he ached for the
pain he knew Señor Rowan felt. "I cannot, señor. Honor
for—"

"Bring her in," Nick ordered, interrupting Benito's plea
for understanding. The man stared at him, puzzled. Suddenly,
from the end of the warehouse, two footsteps echoed. There
was a soft whimpering sound, magnified by the hollow
building. Then Juana was standing in the room, her arms held
behind her by the Texan. She was short and plump, his Juana.
After the birth of so many little ones, her breasts sagged, but
they were plump now, filling for the expected child who made
her belly swell slightly. She was five months' pregnant. The
two, husband and wife, exchanged a look. She was scared; he
was . . . puzzled, still.

"I want . . . maybe I should change the way I'm saying
this, Juan Benito. I need to know that information. I will use
it only to save my wife. Your wife is here, in our hands. It
seems we have the same situation, except, regrettably, your
wife is carrying another child. If I do not have the information from you now, without your protests of loyalty, your
woman is dead. She'll die in front of your children, Benito,
her throat cut by an unknown assailant. It happens all the time
in the city, often enough so that the police cannot expend
much energy to find the killer. This means, of course, that
your children will be orphans. I couldn't let you live, hating
me. Decide."

330

Benito looked at Juana, so vulnerable in her pregnancy. Rowan's wife had been vulnerable as well, pregnant or not. He had done wrong, bringing in Rowan's woman, and now, Juana . . . it was his fault. He would cooperate; he nodded his assent. "*Sí*, I can give myself for the cause, but not Juana. I will tell you what you want. Please, if she could have a seat, my wife. The baby . . ."

"Of course." Nick gestured to the Texan, pointing to an upholstered chair that would be more comfortable than the plain wooden ladderback to which Benito was tied. "Gently, if you will." In Spanish, Nick assured Juana that all would be well, that there had been a misunderstanding only. If she would wait, while he spoke with her husband . . .

It was a while after they had untied Benito before he could use his hands. The circulation came back slowly, then finally, with pen in hand, he began marking a map of the area north of the capital. Once he looked at Juana, then at Nick and nodded. "I am making a true guide for you to follow, señor. I know I can trust you. You must believe that I, too, can be trusted."

"I believe you, Benito. I hope also that we will have your prayers. Even with these to show the way, God will have to walk with us."

"God is already with you, señor. He would not have made me turn traitor unless that was so." The map was finished. Clearly marked were the guard locations, the women's quarters, the "palace," the serpent building, and the plaza with its twin pyramids.

Next, Benito was handed a blank sheet of lined paper. Again he took up the pen, and, as Rowan asked, he copied both the questions and the answers in his clear, legible handwriting. How many warriors were in camp? How many had modern weapons? What was the daily routine? How often

331

were ceremonies or rituals performed at the temples? Where would they keep Elyn? How many guards at the women's quarters? Finally, what were Rowan's men's chances of getting in and out without being observed?

"This was the easiest of all the questions, señor. Your chances, I am sorry to say, are next to nothing. It is possible to get in. To take back your wife unnoticed, escape, and not be seen . . . with all my heart, I say to you, I am sorry."

"I don't think the gentleman has given us enough credit." This came from Gyp, who had suddenly, almost silently come through the warehouse. "I've found the plane you want, Nick. She's not in great shape but she flies. She'll get me south and back in plenty of time. Now . . . how many of these damn things did you say you wanted?"

Chapter Eighteen

If, and it was a damned big *if*, everything worked out according to plan, Nick would have Elyn out of the Aztec compound within two days, three at the most. Gyp had found Guillermo in Sonora and brought him back to the capital. Alesandro had wanted to throw a celebration in honor of their reunion, but when he learned that Elyn had been kidnapped, the huge ex-Villista immediately abandoned his plans. "When she is safe and back in your home, *mi amigo*," he said, "then will we celebrate."

Alessandro had brought five of his best men. Nick remembered two of them from the old days, but the other three were of the same cut. They wouldn't be with Guillermo if they couldn't be trusted. Every one of them was a hard-drinking, whoring thief who earned his living as best he could. For an hour Nick and Alessandro argued back and forth over whether money would change hands for their services. No, he would not accept anything for helping to save the wife of an old friend. But this expedition had nothing to do with friendship, Nick insisted. He was hiring them to help stop a revolt that would kill women and children. For Elyn, he would pay them nothing. For the other work, for helping to squash this Indian pretender to a nonexistent throne, he would pay well.

When the offer was put in those terms, Alesandro agreed.

There were no pure Aztec heirs, as far as he knew, to the throne of Montezuma's family. In the later days, soon after the conquest, the nobles and aristocrats of the royal court had all intermarried with Cortes's men and the new Spanish settlers. That made them mestizo. There were still pure Aztecs, but none of them could make the claim to royal blood that this young whelp had made.

Nick had hired a car and borrowed a truck from Verrana. It shortened by half the time it took to get to the mountain retreat, though the vehicles had to be abandoned some kilometers from the road that would take them up to the compound. Several mules were to be brought along, and the men, unfortunately, had to share the truck with them.

Gyp wouldn't be going. He had another job. An important one that Nick very quietly, very calmly informed him had best be handled with as much skill as he could call up. "Fail me this time, Andrews—"

Gyp wanted to live. He had, in fact, a certain little lady in mind to settle down with back in Fairfax, Virginia. One could only give so much of one's life to patriotic duty, and his time to give it up had come. This one last job was not for his country, not for Nick or himself, but for Miss Lily Ann Sherrill. He would do it to the best of his abilities. "I swear on my honor . . ." Nick looked dubious, "on m'fiancée's life, Nick, I *will* be there, just when y'all want me to."

"I choose to believe you."

Gyp let out an audible sigh and took out his pocket watch. "I now have the time of ten-o-three on my timepiece, which, given to me by my grateful government, keeps excellent time. I'll see you—or more rightly, son, you'll be seein' me—at seven A.M., come sunup Friday."

Nick's watch showed a difference of five minutes. He adjusted it to match that of Andrews's watch, then looked up.

"Don't forget to keep it wound, 'son.' A stopped watch could be fatal, for either one of us."

After Gyp left, Nick was alone for a while in the study. Guillermo and the boys had gone to Mass, to confess and receive absolution. One had to be prepared for the end, always. Still, none of them wanted or expected to die, and they had already reserved an entire whorehouse, all to themselves, for the following Monday.

Consuela came in. As Nick had requested, she had delivered his son to Stephen Rowan. Stephen looked enough like Nick to reassure Jackie, though he had been unusually quiet during the trip and had asked nothing about his mother until it was time for Connie to take Sera and board the return train to Mexico. "She's all right, my mum? Nick . . . my dad, he wouldn't let her, let her . . ." Connie's heart had gone out to him then; and because she was not sure herself what would happen, she had bent and taken him into her arms to hug him tightly, insisting that of course his father would not let his mother come to harm. Jackie would see her soon, see both of them soon.

"Can I get you anything, *querido?*" Consuela asked Nick now. She had to repeat the question before he heard her. He was staring into the fire, eyes glazed over, thinking, remembering, perhaps even praying.

Finally he turned and looked at her, shaking his head. "No, there's nothing I need, except—"

"Except to have your Elynora home safe, eh?" Nick stared at her, his eyes suddenly shiny, suddenly squinting before he covered them with a hand and rubbed, as if he were tired. She wasn't fooled. A woman knew more of emotion than a man could guess at in his life. He loved Elyn so much. Nick, who was always in control, who never showed emotion except to blaze in anger, was as close to tears as he could allow

335

himself. It wasn't manly to cry, this was almost universally taught, in Latino countries, in Anglo countries. She sensed fear, too. Not for himself, never that, but fear of failing, this one time when he couldn't fail, when failure meant death for Elyn. Consuela loved him more at that moment than she had ever loved anyone. To see such love for another woman did not make her jealous. It filled her with wonder. Such love belonged in tales of romance, never in life. Life was harsh, sometimes dull, and occasionally beautiful enough to go on. "On Monday, when the two of you return, I will have a flan prepared. You like this dessert, I know. The señora likes it even better."

Nick took away his hand. Connie believed Elyn would be all right. As jealous as she had been of Elyn, the woman was generous. He wished there were some way to show his gratitude. "I'll tell her, Consuela...her mouth will be watering the entire way...home. You have a good heart, *querida*."

"This I know. And I can cook and clean and bear children. And often in the night, I wonder why there is no man beside me who appreciates all these fine qualities!"

"You haven't looked for him," Nick replied.

Connie shrugged. "I thought I had him." The statement was bittersweet, not meant to wound. "You can do this for me, if you would. Should you come across a man who looks like you and is in many ways like you—and if he should be looking for a woman who would take good care of so fine a specimen of manhood, you send him to me, eh? I will know what to do with him. Such a man should not be wasted on a woman who is less than his worth."

"Thank you." Connie looked puzzled for a moment. She didn't understand, couldn't conceive of what she had given him. She had reminded him of what he'd done in the past, when he'd had to, how at that certain moment when the mind thinks it cannot, the body takes over, to do what has to be done. He was certain now that he would bring Elyn home.

Connie woke Nick in the middle of the night. It was close to three but it was time to shave and to bathe; for what might be the last time in days, and to dress. He went over the plan again, for what seemed the ninetieth time, looking for error, flaw, anything that would turn success into failure. He couldn't find a thing. There was nothing wrong with the plan, and only one minor detail could cause problems: timing, a human variable, not only in those accompanying him but in the reactions of the Aztecs at the compound.

The car was ready, with extra fuel cans stacked in the rear, food for the road, and space enough only for Nick and Alesso. The mules, five of them, had been loaded onto the truck the night before, and Guillermo's men complained bitterly at having to ride as their companions. Alesandro left the car for a minute to speak with them, lecturing in a low, hard voice. This was the way it would have to be. If they did not like it, they could not return and visit the night through with the *putas*. One of the men made a ribald comment, something about hoping he returned *with* something with which he could visit the *putas*. "*Mi compadre*, Raphaelo," Alesso replied with a grin that flashed the moonlight on his gold front teeth, "I have known whores with whom you spent the night who smelled worse than these poor beasts. Now, we go. Anyone who doesn't want to, get out, now."

Tense as they were, the men grinned at their leader's observation, and no one, not even Raphaelo, chose to stay behind. They had survived worse and would more than likely find worse in their future. Especially riding with Alessandro, for Alessandro was a madman. It was good to be his friend. Certainly none who knew him would want the giant for an enemy.

The roads were empty at night and they made good time out of the city. A farmer's cart, loaded with produce for the open-air markets, passed, but the farmer was nearly half-asleep, letting his horses follow the familiar path on their own.

Travel was rougher once they were off the city's thorough-fares. Mexico was just emerging into the twentieth century and had just been through a devastating rebellion of over ten years' length—there were higher priorities than smoothly paved roadbeds.

After a day's travel into the mountains, the truck and car were left off the road behind a stand of thick firs. They were not likely to be spotted for some time, if at all, since the rebels came down from the mountain at night or at dusk. Several mules were loaded with enough food and ammunition to last Alesso and two of his men for the next three to four days. Nick and Raphaelo each took a mule, secured several wooden boxes of rifle bullets atop one, food and camping supplies on the other, and began a trek up the road. Before they parted, though, Alesso gave Nick his cross to wear. While Alesso and his two companions would take a more circuitous route and try to enter the complex unnoticed, Nick was purposely walking into the enemy's hands. With any luck, he'd be spotted the next morning and, he hoped, would be taken in to the high priest for questioning. Nick was counting on the likelihood that anyone entering the sacred area would be questioned instead of shot on sight.

He was right, fortunately. Close to ten-thirty the next day, fifteen Indian guards surrounded him and Raphaelo. They "surrendered" almost immediately, though Raphaelo had thought it better to make at least a token show of resistance. For this he was prodded in the upper arm with the tip of a very sharp lance. Nick glowered at him, primarily for not

338

listening to orders, and whispered that he'd better follow them from this point—or he *wouldn't* make it back to the capital for that celebration.

It was late, nearly dusk, when the two captives were marched into camp. Lord Nauyaca was resting, but the high priest, Miguel, emerged from the open mouth of the Nauyalcoatl building and gestured for the two to be brought up to him. Apparently he had given an order to break open the wooden boxes. Again, he spoke in the Nahuatl tongue, and Nick could only guess that he was angered by the report that the contents were rifle bullets.

Within the camp, Miguel separated the two. Raphaelo, as had been arranged, insisted that he knew nothing, that he had been hired by the señor to help carry the equipment up the mountainside. He didn't know why, or who had given the señor his travel instructions. Nick hoped they wouldn't use force on the man. Though he wasn't the brightest, he might pull it off by sticking to the story.

Nick had a different problem. He knew from the first second Miguel motioned him up the steps that the high priest meant to concentrate on him. He ordered Nick tied to a pillar tiled in a bright red mosaic pattern, checked the ropes that bound his wrists behind it, and then dismissed the guards. When they were alone, he removed the mask he'd worn before in Nick's presence, exposing the fact that, though darkly tanned, he was no native Indian. Nick raised a brow, questioning the reason for exposure.

"Come, come, Mr. Rowan," Michael Winters said in his crisp native English, "you know perfectly well who I am."

Nick wasn't giving anything. "Oh? And how would I know that, Miguel? So you've suddenly developed a great British accent...illusion is part of a high priest's act, isn't it?"

339

"I don't appreciate your brand of humor, Mr. Rowan. Or should I call you Nick. We are, after a fashion, related."

"Let me guess how," Nick said with a smile. "You can't be my great-grandfather—he's been dead awhile. Could be someone on my grandmother's side of the family. D'you know a May Burney, by chance? No? Well, on the other side we're all Americans. We speak regular English, you know—like saying clerk instead of clark and schedule instead of shedule. I never could understand how you fellows got Lester out of Leicester. Goddamned strange way of screwing up the language, if you ask me."

Michael tossed his mask onto a chair and circled Nick, hands locked together behind his back as he contemplated this brash young American whom Elyn claimed to love. "You're trying to bait me, son. It shan't work. You *are* my son-in-law. Like it or not, we share a common love for a wonderful young woman named Elynora. My aim is not to hurt her but to protect her."

"Sure. That's why you had her kidnapped, right? A father's love knows no bounds."

"I believe you did the same once yourself—resulting in the birth of my grandson? The pot calls the kettle—"

"Save your excuses, Winters. I had my reasons for what I did, and they didn't include hurting Elyn. And Jackie's not your grandson. Elyn knows it, I know it, and by now you probably do too. He's safe in the States, by the way—in case you had any plans that included him."

That statement stung. For the briefest moment, the look in Winters's eyes was nakedly revealed. He was waging a war within himself, half-worried that what he'd started would be the beginning of the end, half-believing that it was a destiny fulfilling itself. "I did not know . . . when I sent for her, I could not in my wildest dreams imagine that your wife and

340

my daughter would be one and the same. You must believe that."

"Why? Why should I? I can't see how my opinion would make a difference. If you were an honorable man, which my wife once claimed you were, you'd have let her go immediately as soon as you knew. Save your confession for God, Winters. He's far more generous and compassionate than I."

The older man seemed to shake himself visibly as if throwing off the old and renewing his identity with his alter ego, Miguel. "So, we shall drop the subject of relationships. Why, Rowan, did you appear at my compound with only several small boxes of ammunition? I know the stores of rifles and even handguns stocked in the city. By now, *you* know that Benito is with us. Why have you not brought what was asked? What would you have me do with these rifle bullets?"

"They don't work as well this way as when they're shot out of a rifle, but they do make a nasty lump on someone's head—if you're close—"

His sarcastic reply was cut off as Winters's palm smashed across his mouth. Nick's head was knocked to the left by the hard blow, but he came back smiling. The reserved-English-gentleman facade was gone, finally. Winters was now more Miguel than Michael. There was a trickle of blood at the corner of Nick's mouth but he seemed stronger for having withstood the blow.

"I have been questioned—and tortured—by men better equipped than you, Winters." He touched his tongue to the spot that was bleeding. One of his incisors was loose. It occurred to him to have it fixed as soon as he returned to Denver, and then, only then, did it hit him that the chances of making it back to Denver were a little slim. "Come now, do let's be civilized about this, old chap," he said, affecting the

341

accent only to irritate in return. "You actually expect to get
what you want out of me when I don't even know if Elyn's
alive?"

"You may take my word—"

"Your word's as good as goose shit with me, 'sir.' Until I
see my wife, unharmed, you're not getting anything out of
me. To use an old, colonial colloquialism, sir, 'fuck you'!"

"I cannot, for the life of me, see what Elyn sees in you,
but then her mother had rather plebian tastes as well,"
Michael replied with an affected sigh. "I shall have her
brought here, briefly, to reassure you of her health, and then
we shall resume our little discussion. You may even, if you
answer truthfully, spend the night with her. By the way, not to
spoil the surprise, old chap, but it seems your virility exceeds
your general level of intelligence. You have gotten her with
child again." That should make him think, make him consider the wisdom of cooperating.

The mask returned to its place, and a servant was dispatched
to fetch Elyn. It was five minutes before the man returned
with her. She paused in the entrance to the serpent temple,
the blue sky innocently outlining her figure while the four
fang protrusions menaced her. The servant was dismissed and
Winters approached her, speaking to her for a minute in a
low, soothing tone. Finally, he kissed her forehead and looked
back over his shoulder.

"I shall leave you two in private for five minutes. I suggest
you say whatever is important, as if it were your last chance
to speak. Not that it must be, of course."

They were alone. Elyn approached him slowly, stepping
out of the reflected sunlight and into the semishadows of the
recessed room. She paused, as if she were hesitant to come to
him, and for a moment Nick was afraid she'd been given

some kind of drug to make her docile to Winters's will and suggestions.

"Elyn?" Nick strained at the ropes binding his wrists, succeeding only in rubbing a raw spot with the rough hemp ties. "Honey . . . are you all right? I know you must have—"

She couldn't believe he was here, that he'd come. Even if he had refused to deliver the ransom, her father wouldn't have harmed her; but then, Nick had had no way of knowing that the priest and Michael Winters were one and the same. Elyn came closer, wincing as she saw the drying trickle of blood by the corner of his lip. She was at once furious with him for the entire business of being mixed up in this world of intrigue and rebellion and, at the same time, so glad he was alive and seemingly unhurt, except for the cut by his mouth.

At any other time, Elyn would have thrown herself into his arms or, seeing that he was tied, thrown herself at him. Her mouth was set in a way that had become familiar to him over the past month, a mixture of stubborn anger and pouting. Her eyes were luminous, though, with tears. "You could say hello, anyway," he said at last.

"Hello, then."

Nick rolled his eyes, about to curse, but it took extreme impatience for him to curse before a woman—any woman, but especially this one. "I understand . . . Winters said something about a baby?"

Finally she stepped forward and was only about two feet from him. "That's a lie," she said in a whisper, "something I made up because—" Elyn couldn't finish, couldn't tell him about the worry and fear of the past week and a half, about lying to Michael Winters so that he would be more protective of her, about seeing Brady's horrid death, about the skulls hanging on the skull rack outside, one of them with a camera hanging by its strap on the same post. Or the sight of the priest holding up the bloody heart and the realization later that it was the man she had always loved as her father who had torn the beating heart from the victim's body. None of it could she repeat. If she started to speak of any of it, she would go mad, scream and scream and, perhaps, never stop screaming.

Elyn bowed her head and covered her mouth and nose with both hands. She felt confusion radiating from Nick, but at the moment she could feel little sympathy. She was furious with him, livid with anger that his . . . his "game playing" had not stopped after all these years. Whatever, however he had been drawn back into the dissent, the weaponry, the tug of war between ideas, she wanted no excuses from him. Before she could love him again, she had to hate him, just for a moment or two.

"Look, we don't have that long. And I can't say too—" For the second time in the past half-hour, he was struck. Elyn hit him, open-palmed, with all the might she could muster and then took a half-step backward, staring at her reddening hand, at the streak of blood that had come from Nick's lip. "You may not *be* his, baby," Nick snarled in return, his eyes as hard as the emerald stones they resembled, "but you sure share a family talent! What the hell was that for? I came here to get you *out*."

"From a place I shouldn't *be* if not for the enjoyment you derive from *your* adventures, Mr. Rowan! I'd like to know, I'd bloody well like to know, before I go, just why you're involved in this . . . this minor cultural revolution! I'm sure it must have satisfied a certain masculine need for violence seven or eight years ago, it might even have been a lark to pillage and whatever else you did with your rebel friends then, but you're a grown man, for God's sake! You've a son—and, at least for now, a wife."

"What the hell's *that* supposed to mean?"

"It means, sir, that after they get the rifles, they're going to sacrifice you. Have you ever witnessed a sacrifice? It is a nasty way to go out of this world, Rowan, and I shall likely have to watch. Then, would you care to hear the rest—or perhaps you don't want to know what Nuayaca plans for me?" She was working out her fury, slowly running out of steam and beginning to shed those tears that had made her blue eyes seem like glass. She wiped at them absently. "He will not tolerate whites, except I suppose he must save some for the servant class. Nauyaca will not let our son live. I, on the other hand, am to be accorded the honor of becoming one of his women." Elyn stepped closer; perhaps six inches separated them. "Do you suppose, you damned, selfish bastard, that I've any reason to be upset?"

She was right, of course. He couldn't say a word in his own defense; and if he hadn't stayed in touch, been involved with the rebels, the mercenaries from the old days, neither he nor she would be in this mess. At least he'd had the sense to send Jackie north. He was safe. "Jackie's in Denver, with my oldest brother, Stephen. For the past week. Connie took him up to San Antonio; Steve met him there. He's a good man, Steve. You'd like him. He's been grown up a long time."

Suddenly she was sorry. Even though he had deserved every word she'd said to him, for as long as they both breathed, she loved him. Elyn reached up, touching the corner of his mouth cautiously and wincing as he did. "It hurts?"

"Not as much as what you said." Nick hung his head, missing the flicker of pain his statement caused her. He hadn't meant it that way . . . it was simply a statement of fact. The truth was all she'd said, and the truth, dammit, hurt. "I'm sorry, love. There isn't much I can say. It isn't over yet, you know." He couldn't say much aloud. It was a strong possibility that the room had a peephole or some spot for listening. "Winters said I might be able to spend the night with you. I guess he doesn't know how you'd feel about that."

"Neither do you." Elyn's hands settled on either side of his face; she stood on tiptoe and gently kissed him, careful of the soreness of his lip. "Wherever we are, to whatever place we go, Nick Rowan, I shall never stop loving you. You know that, don't you?"

He knew it, hadn't doubted it even through the tirade. It couldn't end here, whatever it was they shared. This kind of love was once-in-a-lifetime, fairy-tale love. And fairy tales always had a happy ending. Always, happily ever after. Nick sighed. "Trust me. I know I said that before. Please?"

Elyn nodded, then put her head against his chest. His heart beat strongly, more vigorous and healthy, more youthful than her "father's." She took that as a sign. Nick loved her too much for it all to end here, uselessly. Otherwise, he would never have found her in London.

Suddenly she felt a tug on her arm, and felt Nick stiffen as he would if he'd seen something menacing, like a snake. It was Winters. He was gentle enough, holding her arm as he pulled her away from Nick, but firm. "Time for that later, Elyn, after your Nick's told me what I want to know." He called for the servant again, and Elyn followed. Nick watched her go. There was a spring in her stride, a lift in her walk that hadn't been there before. She'd be all right and she'd hold up okay when . . . if the action started popping.

"Now, as you see, I've held to my word. Elynora is well, and she'll stay that way as long as you cooperate."

Nick smirked. "You wouldn't hurt her even if I don't cooperate."

"True, most likely, but then Nauyaca might. I am not

346

always in control of the young man, and though he admires your wife's beauty, he admires his cause much more.''

"Which he wouldn't have unless you'd filled his head with nonsense. Why couldn't you let it be, Winters? I thought you liked digging in the dirt, looking for pieces of old civilizations. You probably found this place. What turned you from a scholar into a kingmaker?''

"I am at one with these people, Rowan. Have you never come to a place and known that you were there before, have you never felt so at ease with the customs and faces of another people that you knew you were one with them? I have known that. A great injustice was done to my people long ago. Now it must be put to rights.''

Winters was mad. Suddenly, and he was sure Elyn shared his feelings, Nick was very glad she was not this madman's child.

"You can't wait four hundred years to right a wrong!" Nick protested, knowing even as he did so that it would make little difference. Elyn had had time to give him the same arguments and had not succeeded. "In my country, we did a great wrong by buying and selling human beings. We fought a war to change that, but we couldn't go back and try to repair the damage done for three hundred years. All you can do is correct a wrong, Winters, and see that it's not repeated. You say you love the Aztecs, that you're one with them. Don't lead them to destruction. D'you want to succeed with what Cortes started? Revive their culture, yes; it's started even now. They're reopening excavations at San Juan, in Puebla, Monte Alban. Mexico isn't Aztec anymore. Winters, for God's sake, there are not enough of them to hold power even if they overthrew Obregon!''

"You're a persuasive speaker. Had I had you on my side, we might have begun this years earlier. Now, though, I must ask you again, where are the rifles we were to receive from you?''

"I hid them. They're safe—from you and the government. And as far as I'm concerned, if I get out of this, they're being shipped back to the U.S. They aren't even *my* goddamned guns!''

"Whose, then, would they be?''

"Try Uncle Sam, alias the United States of America. I am a front, Dad . . . I can call you Dad, since, after a fashion, we're related? I don't own the import business. If you checked the records, you'd discover that I don't own anything in Mexico.''

"The house where you were living in the capital?''

"Deed's in the name of an old friend, Señora Maria Consuela Machado. I bought it for her as partial repayment of an old debt.''

"But you know the location of the guns that were in the warehouse. Unless Benito was lying . . .''

"Benito wasn't lying. He was a good supervisor, a little untrustworthy, but as an employee I couldn't fault him. He turned on you, by the way, only because I threatened to slit his wife's throat in front of the kiddies.''

"Not the most civilized of acts.''

"Tit for tat, Dad. He was responsible for endangering *my* wife. He told me how to get here, then he went on a little trip. He may return; then again . . . But I'm sure you couldn't be bothered with the life or death of one comrade in arms. After all, it's the cause that counts.''

"We *will* succeed, you know, even without your petty arms consignment,'' Winters asserted. "There are other ways to get weapons, more dangerous, but ways can be found. Unless you tell me, now, their location, you have signed your death warrant, and that would make my Elynora a very sad but beautiful widow.''

"You'll kill me even if I tell. Right?"

Winters sighed. He was too tired to pretend, to act convincingly. "Yes, but if we have these rifles, I may be able to convince Nauyaca that you could be valuable to us, in obtaining more. . . ."

"Forget it. Your boy wants Elyn and I'm in the way. If you were God, which you are far from being, you couldn't persuade him to let me live."

There was no use in discussing the matter further. Winters knew many details of Rowan's past with the Zapatistas. The man had survived the prison of Tlatelolco. There wasn't much he could do to him to make him talk. He would allow Elyn her one night with he man she loved, and then, in the morning, Rowan would die.

"Tochtli!" He called the servant again and had Nick's bonds cut. "Take him, under guard, mind, to the baths and let him be cleansed. Then he is to be allowed to spend the night with his wife, in the tower above the women's quarters."

Nick was rubbing his wrists and looked up with a sardonic smile. "You really know how to send a man off to heaven, don't you, Winters?"

"To my knowledge, Rowan, that is not where you shall be bound."

Later, in a room several stories above the women's quarters, Nick lay with his head in Elyn's lap, staring up at her, half-amused, half-amorous. He still didn't believe he would die at dawn. No one ever believed he was going to die; even born with the knowledge, it was a message rejected. "So, after they rip out my heart and chop off my head, Winters says I'm bound to be heading for hell. Earlier you would have agreed, hmm?"

349

Elyn handed him another piece of spiced orange and shook her head. "No, even when I was furious, I wouldn't have sent you there. And, since your heart is mine, they shan't have it. By morning, my love, we shall have thought of something."

Nick ignored the fruit, tossing it aside to reach up and hook a hand around her neck, tumbling Elyn down beside him on the padded sleeping mat. "At the moment, morning is the farthest matter from my mind. I missed you, darling. And worried that some Indian bastard would get his hands on you."

"Nauyaca tried—and changed his mind."

Nick frowned, then the expression slipped, altering to amusement. "I can imagine what you did to change his mind for him, love."

"I striped his hand with my nails. He rather seemed to like that, though, and left me with a look of anticipation. I daresay, he can't wait for you to pass on. Now that you know about him, might I ask you a question, sweet?"

"Of course. In anticipation, I can say with complete confidence that nothing happened between Connie and me. She's very worried about you. In fact, she told me to tell you that she expects you back Monday—in your honor, she will be baking a flan!"

"How sweet. I shall make you taste it first, to make sure it contains no—"

"*Elyn!*"

"Actually, it wasn't Connie I was concerned with. You have been here before, have you not?"

"You know I have, not that long ago."

"And, while you were waiting for the king's stars to permit an audience, were you treated as a guest?"

350

"Well, truthfully, I can say they were nicer to me the first time around. Why?"

"Because, darling, there are the most titillating rumors going round amongst the women—those who speak enough Spanish and English made sure I understood—that you were given a young virgin for entertainment. That if she remained a virgin at morning's light, then she would be sacrificed. And that the outcome pleased everyone. Upon careful examination the next dawn, she was found to be no longer intact. Could you . . . would it be an imposition to explain how this hospitality was handled?"

Damn, but women were gossips! No matter where you went, the problem was universal. And if the subject was sex, they were worse than men. The problem here was, would Elyn believe him? He was innocent. How many men, faced with the same situation, would have solved it as he had? To tell the truth, he deserved a medal for that one. "I, though you won't believe me, was *not* the deflowerer of the poor girl. You see her lover—well, he obviously wasn't her lover yet, but he did love her—he was the guard at the door. A great hulking beast he was, too. At any rate, I, refusing the invitation, still could not let the girl die. She had to sleep with someone . . ."

" . . . And you felt such pity stir in your heart that her plight made you—"

"Now, Elyn, let me finish. At the door, this huge oaf was glowering, looking as though he wanted to skewer me with his knife. To make a long story short, I asked him in, let the two have a go at it, and satisfied everyone." Nick beamed. The solution *had* been brilliant.

"And you stayed there while he . . . while they . . ."

"Give me some credit for good taste, love!" Nick complained. "I left the room, went exploring a bit, to see the

351

layout here, and when I got back, the deed was done."
Actually, as he remembered it, the sounds the couple had
made in the dark had been more of an incentive to take a
walk. "I never touched the girl. And she was damned
good-looking, too." Let her think about that one!

Nick had told the truth. Elyn had heard the entire story
firsthand, through an interpreter, from the spared virgin
herself. The only thing the girl had not added was the fact of
Nick's nocturnal stroll—but then she had been otherwise
occupied. He had lied only on one small point. The girl,
virginal as she may have been, had not been in the least
good-looking. She had a dark, mottled complexion, a broad,
flattened nose, and several missing or discolored teeth. Elyn
wondered how well Nick's fidelity would have held up under
the temptation of a truly beautiful young maiden.

Elyn had been silent so long that Nick glanced up at her
his eyes deep green and innocent-wounded. "You believe me,
don't you, darling? Elyn, I swear, I haven't wanted another
woman since I found you again in London. And I've had
chances, I'll admit. Not out of vanity, you know, but a man
sometimes . . . well, sometimes it's practically thrown at you!
Anyway, I haven't broken my vows."

Should she tell him? "I believe you, darling. And I want
you to know that I have been as faithful."

"Of course you have. You haven't had much chance not to
be, hmm? Still, I know if you had the chance . . ."

"The king did run his hand along my shoulder . . . he
moved it lower and it was obvious, quite obvious, what his
intentions were."

It was, was it? How did she know? "Since when are you
an expert on arousal in men? I hope you did more than stripe
his hand, the dirty beggar!"

"Well, a woman alone, in a strange place . . . there's only so much one can do. I'll show you what I didn't do."

Nick's voice was offended. "What was that?"

Elyn snuggled closer and ran the tips of her fingernails along his cheek, then lower, across his bare chest. She traced light circles in the wiry curls that covered his flesh, then slid her hand lower, to touch his belly just above the bulge of his genitals. She smiled to herself, feeling him react, sensing a pulse of movement beneath the light caress of her fingers. Then she stopped, took her hand away, and lay back on the mat, one arm pillowed beneath her head. She pretended indifference as she heard him move restlessly and half-rise to lean over her. She pointed with a long, oval fingertip and said, "That is how I knew, darling. One needn't have a convent up-bringing to recognize an alteration of size and shape. It's a matter of arithmetic, geometry, and addition. One . . . plus—"

". . . One equals one," he finished, leaning over with a smile as he touched his mouth to hers.

"That wouldn't get you an A for addition, darling."

"Bet I could earn one in another subject. Let's see. . . ." Nick started at her neck, kissing a spot just behind her ears that always brought a giggle from her. It was an especially erotic zone for her. He moved on to another and another, until very soon her clothing was gone, tossed across the room; his was lying in a pile nearby and he was lying atop Elyn. Moonlight shone into the room through a narrow slit of a window; it fell across the blend of their bodies, mellowing the flesh until it seemed that one and one had become one.

Chapter Nineteen

The time was just after dawn. The priests had saluted the coming of the new day with incantations and ritual salutations to the cardinal points. Among the populace there was both an air of expectation and a feeling of unease. For years since the Aztec tribes had been converted, they had blended their old ways and rituals with the new religion, creating their own practices tied to and yet not wholly dependent upon the Catholic Church. For centuries the great Aztec gods and goddesses, veiled beneath Christian names and identities, had existed, revered by all, in reincarnated form.

Many people could not accept this revival of the blood sacrifice. They could find nothing in their new religion that advocated the taking of a life and the dedication of human flesh and blood to their gods. The commandment "Thou shalt not kill" was to be honored. How then could they rebuild their empire and found it upon a system of sacrifice? Whose daughter would be next; whose child would be taken to honor the God of Growing Things; who would lose a husband to the knife?

There was growing dissension within the assembly. In the old days, no one had known of the Church and its *santos*. They, the old ones, had been ignorant of the true way and therefore were forgiven. But would the present Aztec people be forgiven? Could they be, if they knew the commandments and disobeyed? Everyone was afraid, for there was much magic afoot, and evil happened to those with whom Nauyaca or his priest disagreed.

Today, the victim of the sacrificial rites was a man, a foreigner. Certainly foreigners had died before; the skull of one of them, the one who had been a taker of pictures, hung on the rack, fleshless and staring.

But this new man, was he not someone important? Would his death not bring retribution from his friends and relatives, from officials in the capital? The people trembled, and yet there was not one who could conquer his superstition or his fear and deny Nauyaca what he considered his right.

The victim's wife stood atop the pyramid, hands tied, watching as her husband, bare except for his *maxtli*, the loincloth, two wide flaps of material suspended from a belt of embroidered flowers. She had been crying—even those at the bottom of the pyramid could see that her eyes were swollen and red—but now with dignity she stood quiet and still. This was not right for so young and beautiful a woman, Anglo or not, to lose so fine and healthy a husband. Diablo, the devil, was behind this work, no matter how Nauyaca claimed it was the power of the great Texcatlipoca.

Nauyaca, standing next to Elyn, watched as the four masked priests stretched the victim over the altar stone. Spread-eagled, with nothing between his bare skin and the rough stone altar, was not a comfortable way to spend one's last moments on earth. Inside the cane-and-thatch hut that served as a devotory above the pyramid, Miguel chanted, making the final preparations, cleansing the sharp knife that would slice open Rowan's chest cavity and expose his beating heart. He wished that his daughter did not have to watch. The

356

work was better done quickly and, these days, with as little flourish as possible.

The king-pretender could not help approaching the victim to toss a taunt in his face. "To deny Nauyaca what he wants, this is your sin, and soon your punishment will follow. You should have told me where you hid the weapons, Anglo."

Even in his strange, uncomfortable position, Nick managed a smile, a cynical smile. "And you would have released me?"

"Of course not, but I would have given you the drug that makes one feel courage at the sight of the knife blade, that sends one soaring to the sky before the heart ceases its beat." He turned and gestured to Elyn. "Now your lovely wife must watch as you suffer. First comes the slice," Nauyaca grinned as he illustrated with a long, almost feminine fingernail, "so. Then Miguel, he reaches within, under the ribs, to pull the still-beating heart from its place. Your eyes may still be open to see the red pulsing muscle that once caused your blood to pump life to your limbs."

Nick only smiled. He figured it was the only thing that would get to the bastard.

And it did. Nauyaca wanted Nick groveling, begging for his life, humbling himself before his woman and . . . *Before his woman!* Nauyaca suddenly realized that a major mistake had been made. They could not torture Rowan; he only became more stubborn under pain. But what of seeing his wife in agony? They need not kill her, really; just a pretense of it and Rowan would babble the truth in his fear for her life.

The king ordered that the victim be brought to his feet. The four priests reacted sluggishly, as if they hadn't understood; Nauyaca glared. The priests of Texcatlipoca were trained to respond instantly to any command given by king or high priest. A vague sense of apprehension settled over Nauyaca.

357

Was he imagining that one of them had grown taller? Or that another was more portly than any of them had been before? So much of the ceremonial costume covered individual features.

It was difficult to concentrate. The excitement of the moment had affected him, altering his judgment. No one from the outside could penetrate the security of the well-guarded camp unnoticed. He commanded the tallest of the four to seize and hold Rowan, speaking in Spanish to make his commands clear. Nauyaca himself grasped Elyn's arm and drew her toward the bloodstained altar where her husband had lain.

When Nick realized what Nauyaca was doing, he let out a bellow that drew the crowd's attention. He struggled against the hold of the priest and another came to grab his right arm, securing it behind his back. He cursed Nauyaca in every Spanish oath he knew, and called Winters words he hadn't used since his days with Zapata, when everyone used them.

Elyn, of all those on the surface level of the pyramid, was calm. She had watched Nauyaca, seen his plan develop in his expression, and noted the latent desire that still smoked his eyes. He was using her to make Nick confess. And Nick— Nick wasn't thinking. He was reacting, a furious tiger trying to protect his mate. *Think, oh, please, think, Nick,* she prayed silently even as several guards spread her back across the same stone where Nick had lain.

That morning the women had dressed her in *enaguas*, a length of cotton material as fine as linen, wrapped several times around as a skirt, banded by a *faja*, a wide sash to secure it about the waist. She wore also the *huipil*, a loose cotton blouse embroidered about the sleeves and neckline with brilliant garlands of red, yellow, and purple flowers. The rock now abraded the fine material; chafing her back, though she tried to remain as still as possible to communicate her calm to Nick.

Now Nauyaca ignored her, turning to face Nick with a grin. "Tell me now, where are my rifles? So beautiful a body this is." He gestured flippantly toward Elyn. "It would be a crime, even against my gods, to waste it. Speak, quickly or I will draw down the *huipil* and bare her body for the sharp blade of the *itztli*."

Inside the sanctuary, Miguel was finished. He had heard the last of Nauyaca's speech and raised his head, suddenly tired, an old man who had dreamed one dream too many. Turning, he cradled the *itztli* in his hand and emerged from the sanctuary.

"No, the woman shall not die. No one shall die anymore." Miguel spoke loudly and clearly for the crowd. Nauyaca was so stunned by what Miguel had said that he simply stared. Miguel removed his mask. Few in the community had ever seen him without it, and though his years in the tropics had turned him sun-dark, it was clear to all that he had no Indian blood or features. He tossed the knife down the steps and watched it roll, then spoke again.

"Listen, Oh my people, for I have led you down a false and dangerous path. Even with the rifles, with all the rifles in the world, we could not bring back our empire. I am not Miguel, the high priest of Texcatlipoca, but Michael Winters, an old man from across the sea." He turned and looked at Nauyaca, gesturing disdainfully. "This one, whom I have supported, he is no king, he is not even a pure-blood Aztec."

"You lie!" Nauyaca had gone white, the blood draining from his face as if he had been the decided victim of the sacrifice. "Do not listen, people. It is true, I have hidden the secret of his blood. He knew much of our lore, but I have it now. *I* will lead us on to victory and glory once more!"

"He does not lie." The voice came through the crowd, feminine and clear, sure of its purpose. "I am Xochitl, 'Flower.' Long ago, when he brought his wife to our land to study the old ways, I loved this man, Winters. Nauyaca came of our union. He is half-Aztec . . . half, only. He leads you astray. At birth he was called Miguel. It was only when he came to see his father that he suddenly became Nauyaca, Nauyalcoatl, the serpent of evil." The crowd parted and a still-pretty woman came to stand at the foot of the pyramid. She looked up at Winters, her expression a mix of love and dislike. "You, Winters, have done wrong. Right it now, before it is too late."

Winters nodded. "Again, I tell you, this boy is no king, and he has no kingdom to own. Keep to your faith, people. It is old and true."

Nauyaca's eyes blazed with an unholy fury. He had been betrayed. Miguel could not be his father, even if his mother had lied for some reason. He *was* king, and nothing, certainly not the old Englishman, would stop him. He turned abruptly, grasped a lance from one of the guards, and threw it. His father, standing not five feet away, facing the people, went down, the lance piercing his back and exiting just below the heart. His body tumbled down the steps, breaking the wooden shaft of the lance. Three-quarters of the way down, it rolled to a stop. As if she had expected his death, Xochitl began a mourning keen, draping herself across the body of the man she had not seen for over twenty years.

The men holding Nick loosened their grip, drew off their masks, and were revealed as Alesso and his cohorts. Another of them had held Elyn's left ankle. He helped her to her feet now, and Nick came to her, to hold her and shield her eyes from the sight of Michael Winters's death.

Everyone had forgotten Nauyaca. He backed away stealthily, watching for resistance. He stepped back, one foot into the sanctuary, and suddenly screamed, and screamed again as all eyes turned to the temple door. Nauyaca, the Lord King Nauyalcoatl, was as good as dead, though he still breathed and moved. His eyes bulged in pure fright. Clinging to his leg, fangs pumping their poison, hung a large nauyalcoatl, the fer-de-lance. One of Alesso's men, who had borne the sacred ax used to sever the heads of the dead victims, used the weapon to strike at the snake. It sliced through the serpent's throat, leaving the head gruesomely attached to the nearly severed calf of Nauyaca's right leg.

From the east there came a loud, buzzing drone, as if a thousand angry bees had suddenly decided to descend. Nothing appeared to produce the noise, though it continued for minutes and then faded slowly to a low hum.

Suddenly, again from the east, a flock of birds appeared in the sky. Against the brilliant blue and the white mists of the clouds, they were a bright green and long-tailed, almost like a small parrot. Some settled in the trees surrounding the complex; one circled the area of the twin pyramids and flew to the peak of the one where Nauyaca lay dying. Already the deadly flush had begun; he was pale and sweating, moaning in pain. The bird landed nearby, seeming to cock its head in consideration and then dismissal, before waddling over to pick at the freshly severed body of the snake.

One of the priests, not a member of Alesso's men but an Aztec, fell to his knees, bowing his head low in reverence. He seemed to worship the bird, and all the Indians seemed in awe of the rest of the flock perched in the trees, preening.

Close up, the bird had a small head and body. Its wings were a vivid scarlet, and, most lovely of all, its long sweeping tail feathers were an iridescent green.

Nick looked at the bird and at the others in the trees and

counted perhaps twenty in all. They were rare these days. He wasn't sure how Gyp had managed it, but somehow he'd gathered up the birds, probably in Honduras, and flown them here. He was a little off time but he had come through. The appearance of the Quetzal, the ancient symbol of the Aztec god of light and goodness, symbol of the plumed serpent and the Mexican Hermes, had awed the assembled Aztecs. Except for the calling of the birds, the compound was silent.

In Nick's arms, Elyn trembled. The plan had worked, but with Nauyaca's change of victims, it could have failed. Elyn had been through enough. He was taking her home, first to Casa Aventura, then to Denver. And he was pretty sure that, at least for a long time, they wouldn't come back to Mexico. It would survive without him. He had barely made a dent in its fortunes, seen it wounded and recovered, and still it would go on. It always had, it always would. Mexico was . . . Mexico. And he was a grown man, at last, with a wife and a son, and maybe, if they spent some time on it, another one to love.

Epilogue

"He was possibly the most handsome man I had ever seen, so virile he took my breath away," Pamela Rowan said. "And I shouldn't have cared if he'd been a dirt farmer—or remained one."

It was an amazingly candid confession for someone of Pamela Rowan's age. Usually, at eighty-two, one expected to hear memories of long-dead friends or incidents dredged up. Nick's grandmother was spry and youthful; intelligence sparkled from her green eyes, making her seem all the more attractive. Elyn adored her, just as Nick had predicted she would, and since he had brought her back to Denver three years before, she and Gran had become fast friends and almost constant companions.

Their feelings for each other were mutual. Pamela thought Nick had redeemed himself by marrying Elyn. She'd told him this so often that he'd teasingly accused her of becoming senile, but she was not and never would be. She saw in Elyn a younger version of herself. A woman of high courage, a woman who could stand up to some difficulties, though since their brief sojourn in Mexico, Elyn's life had been relatively easy. Soon after their arrival, she had announced that she was expecting, and Leah had been born seven months later. Now she was to have another and the time was drawing close.

For the past several weeks, Nick had been away on a buying trip—he had settled into the "legitimate" business of ranching—and Elyn had spent her time here at Rosehill. Jackie was in day school, and, for the first time, because of the pregnancy, Leah was under the supervision of a nanny. So the days passed quietly, with the two Rowan women sitting on the terrace overlooking the gardens, talking of the past, of the future.

"Although you know I hate to disagree with you about anything, Gran," Elyn replied with a half-smile, "I beg to differ over the subject of whose husband—yours or mine—is the most handsome. I've seen the portrait of Grandfather Gordon, I know how Nick resembles him, but you've forgotten something important."

"What's that, my dear?"

"Nick was an improvement on *your* model. He has your eyes, Gran, and those eyes . . . I could melt when he looks at me in a certain way." She glanced down at the huge mass of her belly and smiled wryly. "Why do you think I'm carrying another Rowan? We were supposed to stop at Leah. One boy, one girl."

Pamela smiled cheerfully. She wanted more; children were life's blessings. They made her feel young, most of them. "You may possibly be right about the mix of Gordon and me. Anyway, love, it was sweet of you to say so. We are both lucky women, you to find your Nick, I my Gordon. Such luck is rare, as rare as the roses Vallen grows."

Elyn straightened in her chair, peering over the terrace balustrade down into the garden at the young man who knelt, toiling in the early summer sun. She had never met him and thought him awfully young to be a gardener, looking more the age of an apprentice, but he seemed to work miracles with the extensive arrangements of flower beds and shrubs. He was working hard, digging in the moist earth and loam, indeed working miracles with the skill of his hands. Jackie was a little like that: a green thumb they called it. She liked the look of Vallen, what she could see of him. His shoulders were broad, and though he bent over his flower beds, his posture was straight and somehow confident. "Vallen, did you say his name was? I don't think, in all this time, that I have met him."

"Then you shall, after lunch." Elyn grimaced at the thought of food and Pamela amended her idea. "Something light—perhaps some fresh fruit and a cool, iced drink? You need your strength, my girl . . . especially now." Pamela knew of what she spoke—she'd had five children of her own and all of them at home, without doctors and nurses fussing about. "Be a good child, Ellie. I promised Nick I should take the best of care with you."

"And you have. I wouldn't be with anyone else at so unnerving a time. You have a calming effect on me—I feel at peace. I can understand why you and Gordon chose to build here." The house, mansion really, stood on the side of a mountain. In the distance the Rockies were snow-capped, jagged peaks despite the thaw of several weeks past. The house rather resembled her grandmother's in Belgravia except that it was even larger, more grand, and somewhat more graceful. The gardens especially were lovelier than anything Grandmother had known, and she had always made a point of employing the best.

It was strange to think of her now, beyond the ability to hurt anyone, perhaps beyond retribution. She had done her last bit of mischief in that private note to Elyn, and now even that was done with.

Elyn's expression suddenly seemed so pensive that Pamela's heart went out to her. "Darling—are you not feeling well?

You seem so . . . depressed. Lord knows, when mine were due, I would sit and cry for hours on end!''

Elyn smiled, reaching out to touch Pamela's hand. It was a fragile hand, made frail by age, and thin but strong. "No, actually I was thinking of my father."

Ah. Nicholas had told her of the death of Michael Winters. She knew a little of the violence of those days but not all of it. There were things, Nick had said, that Elyn would not discuss with him. Perhaps now, just the two women alone . . . "If you want to talk of him, Elyn, I am always here, to listen."

"Did Nick say why it was so important for me to find my . . . Michael Winters?"

Pamela shook her head. "Only that you were worried for his safety."

"It was more than that, Gran. You see, he was not . . . my father, not my natural father. Grandmother made sure I knew that—it was her last message to me."

Pamela Rowan frowned. "She always was, if you'll pardon the expression, a bitch!"

Elyn's mouth dropped open, then she started to laugh. She continued for several minutes, holding her rounded belly, unable to stop because it was true, because it had to have been stated by so cultured and well bred a lady. "You're right, darling. She was. Anyway, I kept it from Nick, the real reason. I wasn't sure of my parentage, of who I was. You know my mother's stock, but my real father . . . only Michael Winters could tell me who *he* might have been."

"And did he?" The old woman's eyes, a brighter green than Nick's, were wide with interest and gentled by compassion.

"No, there wasn't time. Had there been time, I don't think he'd have said. He did say it was a fine jest on grandmother, something that had truly set her back on her heels. I assume

366

that Father—Winters—was found and deemed to be a suitable husband for my mother. He was paid, I believe, a stipend. Because she was so awfully rude to him, and to my mother, whom she never forgave, they stayed away from her—and me most of my life.''

''That sounds like her. I will now tell you something no one alive knows about Anne Fitz Morough-Whyte. And as *I* witnessed it, I assume I'm the only one who ever knew of it. I came to an afternoon tea one day—this was before I left for America—and in going through the house, I happened on the wrong room. Your grandmother was kissing her father. It was *not* a daughter's kiss. He didn't see me, the earl, I know, or he should have stopped it immediately, but she did. Anne saw me—and kissed him all the harder. Needless to say, I stayed no longer than I had to. Now, I am no one to tell tales, especially upon the deceased, but *that* one had no right to act righteous with anyone.'' After she thought over what she'd said, she was sorry she'd confessed it. ''I shouldn't have told; she *was* your relative. I shan't repeat it again, ever, love.''

''I know.'' Elyn couldn't believe that her grandmother, who had always been more Victorian than Victoria, had done so awful a deed. It surely hadn't stopped with the kiss. The fact that her mother and grandfather had shared an incestuous relationship was shocking enough, but it had happened—and in families of older names than hers. It shamed her, though, before Nick's family, to have such good people know it was a part of her background. Well, only Gran knew, and she had promised. . . . Still Elyn felt diminshed, as though *she* had committed the offense. ''I'm sorry you had to see such a thing, Gran.'' Elyn thought of her mother, then. How had she ever grown up as decent as she had, with Anne for a mother? Had she ever known a moment's happiness, married to a man out of necessity?

Pamela guessed her thoughts. "Your mother was a sweet girl, Elyn. I remember her well. She had you, and that part of the man she loved will always be. In you she had images of him, just as Nick has my eyes and his grandfather's stubborn ways!" Pamela rang for the butler and ordered iced tea and a fruit plate for Elyn and the same for herself. After he was gone, she smiled at Elyn and patted her hand. "I have to care for myself almost as if I were carrying, too! One gets that way with age. It would be awful—getting old—if I hadn't had so wonderful a life."

The baby moved, striking out something—a fist—against the wall of Elyn's womb. She shifted uncomfortably. She wished that Nick were home. It was very close to her time and she wanted him; he had promised to be with her. "This one's a boy," she said. "It must be—he's so like Jackie when I carried him."

"When *is* my baby due back from school?" Pamela asked. Of all her grandchildren, Nick was the favorite, and of all her great-grandchildren, she favored Jackie—and for obvious reasons. Except for his wavy blond-streaked brown hair, he was the image of Nick.

"He isn't a baby any longer, and don't say so in his hearing," Elyn warned. "Why, just the other day he came to me to ask, seriously as can be, might he please escort a girl named Maria Martin to an afternoon social! Can you imagine? He's not yet eleven; won't be until October."

"The Rowans, the males anyway, mature early, dear. Did you say he could go?"

"I told him to wait and ask his father. Nick still has to talk to him yet, you know, father to son, so that he behaves properly."

Pamela gave a laugh and slapped the arm of her chair. "Nick's not the one to do that, my girl, though I recall several times he seemed almost . . . monkish. One time, when he decided to join the seminary—heavens, his mother had a fit!—and swore off the opposite sex.''

"And the other time?"

"When he returned from Mexico in . . . when was it . . . in fourteen, I believe. He had something bothering him, driving him so that even *I* couldn't get him to tell me what the matter was. Finally I told him to either go join the priesthood or come back to life!''

"He came back to life . . . as usual, I assume, with enthusiasm?''

"No, if you mean seeing other women. He went off to France and learned to fly an airplane. He had some sort of energy to rid himself of, and apparently fighting the Germans helped. He was himself when he came home. There were girls every . . . well, not everywhere, but he was Nick again.''

Their lunch arrived, and Pamela insisted that Elyn try to nibble on what she could. "You haven't any pains?'' she asked finally.

"My back aches but I've no contractions. Still about ten days to go.'' Elyn sipped at the tea and stared out at the mountains. She loved Denver. It was high and clear, and the air was as fresh and clean as Nick had once told her, so many years ago. How had time passed so quickly? Could Jackie really be almost eleven? She loved Nick now, if it were possible, even more than in the beginning. Again the baby kicked, perhaps protesting how long she had been sitting. The doctor *had* said to exercise.

She waited until Gran had eaten and then suggested a stroll. "We're both about up to the same speed today . . . slow!'' she said, laughing, and Gran agreed. Down through the garden, with Gran cautiously using her walking stick, they strolled, stopping here and there to admire a particular flower or grouping. For a while they paused on the first level of the terrace and stared at the view—it seemed as though they were on top of the world, as high, perhaps, as heaven.

"Our gardener came here from England to tend . . . to create, really, the Rosehill gardens," Pamela said. "His name was Arthur Vallen. He died only last year." The old woman pointed below to the young man who'd been working so diligently. "That's his son, Andrew. He has his father's flair for working with plants and nature. Come . . . I shall introduce you."

It was a slow progress downward, each of them, for different reasons, taking the broad steps carefully. "Arthur—the father—once worked at your grandmother's Belgravia estate. He left—I never knew why—and went to work for my sister, May. You know May, of course you do. She was sweet, always, my sister, but never bright. Then soon, for May's gardens weren't extensive enough, Arthur came here and married a local girl. You can see what magic he created for us—and how well his son continues it. I cannot imagine Rosehill without him."

"Andy! Andy, I should like to introduce you to someone," she called, and hearing her, the young man rose and dusted off his hands, straightening to his feet. He was tall, something like six feet two, and wiry despite his very broad shoulders. The first thing Elyn noticed was his smile—it was sweet, but not in any way unmasculine; it was simply gentle and full of peace. She liked him immediately.

His hat came off as they approached, and as he briefly bowed his head, the sun lighted strands of gold among the ash-brown of his hair. He could not have been more than twenty-four or -five. She thought for a moment, as he looked her full in the face, that there was something very familiar about his features. But it must have been the sunlight, that and the height. Ofttimes the higher altitudes affected one's perceptions.

She wasn't sure why, but she had expected a British accent. When he spoke, Andrew Vallen was as American as Nick—in fact, as they had grown up in much the same place, their speech was quite similar.

"You're Nick's wife," he said, and something in his tone indicated that such was an admirable position. "Of course, I've seen you around—you and the young ones. He's a lucky man, Nick Rowan. I've always said so, haven't I, Mrs.?" Clearly, there was a bond of affection between Vallen and the old woman—almost as if he were one of her vast, extended brood.

"You're quite a marvel with the gardens, Mr. Vallen," Elyn said. "I daresay, I can't recall many in England—and we're renowned for them—to equal these."

"You're too kind, ma'am," Vallen answered with humility that in any other man might have seemed false. He asked that she call him Andy, as everyone did, and thanked her again for the compliment. "Your name—it's Elynora, isn't it?"

"Why, yes, it is—but everyone calls me Elyn. I do wish you would, too."

"I will, then, thanks." He turned to the older Mrs. Rowan then and smiled that special smile. "Should I show her the rose, ma'am?"

Pamela nodded. "Aside from meeting you, it was the reason I brought her down here."

Andy stepped between the two women and gallantly offered each an arm. There were two broad flagstone steps to negotiate before coming to a well-tended bed of rose bushes. Before each bush was a small, hand-carved sign that gave the name or type of rose. Vallen bent and dug in his pocket for a pair of clippers. He took a cutting and offered the long-stemmed white rose to Elyn. "It has no thorns—bred that way. See the center?" Elyn looked, and her lips parted in a kind of awe. The color was a pale, pale lavender-blue, surrounded by creamy, off-white petals. "It's called the Elynora."

Elyn's first thought was . . . what a strange coincidence. Then she bent, or dipped as her belly would allow, and glanced at the sign before the bush. It spelled, very clearly, ELYNORA. She nearly dropped the flower she was holding. She looked at Pamela, who seemed to wear a very secretive, very pleased smile, and then back at Andy for some explanation. "You said your father bred the rose—how strange that he should call it by the same—"

"Not strange at all, if you knew him, ma'am," Andy interrupted. "It's called the Elynora for his mother, my grandmother. He loved her very much, Father did."

Suddenly Elyn knew why he looked familiar. His hair color was close to Jackie's, streaked by the sun in the same way. His eyes, though not as light as hers, were as blue as the heavens. His father had worked at the Belgravia estate. For the next few moments, long moments that seemed endless, the sun's heat intensified, and its brilliance nearly blinded her. She felt vaguely drowsy and heard as from a distance Pamela's shout for Andy to catch her. A pair of strong arms easily lifted her and carried her away. There was a soft, firm bed supporting her, and in and out of dreams she heard voices mentioning hospital and nurses round the clock.

Through it all she tried vainly to tell them that she was fine, but somehow her tongue failed to coordinate with her thoughts. She knew pain, but it was a familiar pain—the same she had experienced giving birth to Jackie and Leah. The baby was coming, but it would be hours yet before he arrived. Elyn was sure it would be a boy, and as sure that she wanted to give him the name Vallen.

After five hours of intermittent contractions, she was sedated. The anesthesia was just beginning to work when she heard Nick's voice. He was there; she could feel the strength in his fingers holding hers, grasping her hand tightly as if they were one and the same body.

She spoke, going on about roses and a gardener named Andy. And through it all, she smiled. It was clear that Elyn was contented even though each succeeding contraction stiffened her lower body with arching pain. The contractions came closer together, parted only by a minute or so of relief. She heard the doctor mention Caesarian and grew frantic at the thought that she could not bring her own child into the world unaided by surgery. She cried then, despite her unwillingness to show any weakness, and drew Nick close. No operation . . . she could, would do this by herself.

It was another fifty minutes before the baby was born. With no scale available, the doctor hefted the swaddled boy and proclaimed him at least ten pounds. The doctor finished his necessary work, the nurse helped Elyn into a clean gown, and finally she and Nick were allowed time alone with their new son.

"I want to call him Vallen. Can you guess why?" Nick nodded. He knew from his grandmother's description what had happened. He'd known for a long time, most of his life, of a rose named Elynora. She and Andy looked enough like brother and sister that their paternity couldn't be denied.

Nick reached forward and moved the light blanket away from his newborn son's face. The child had dark hair, like Leah, and so far his eyes were blue. He had a very soft upward curve to his lips that suggested the Vallen smile.

"I can't think of a better name," he said, and reached down carefully to take the baby, cradling him in the crook of his arm before he laid Vallen in his bassinet. Then he came back to sit beside his wife. "I wasn't sure how you'd react. It was enough of a blow to learn that Winters wasn't really your father. Seeing who you are, how you were raised, I could hardly tell you the gardener was the man your mother had loved."

"What a snob you are, Nick Rowan. Does it make a difference to you that I'm the gardener's daughter? I would trade all the king's blood in me to have been completely theirs, his and my mother's. Arthur Vallen did a fine job rearing his son. I wish . . . I only wish I might have known him. What was he like?"

Nick smiled. "Andy is a copy of Arthur. Only he smiles more often. I would imagine, knowing now what I do, that Arthur had less reason to. He had loved—and for no reason, lost." He leaned forward and kissed Elyn on the mouth with a certain reverence, as though she were a sacred object. "Thank you for my son."

Elyn's eyes narrowed, and her mouth rounded into a protesting O. "There wasn't supposed to be a . . ." She paused and looked over at the bassinet, happy that there had been a "this time" and knowing now, as she turned back to stare into those mesmerizing green eyes of Nick's, that there would be another time, and perhaps even another. She could have a half-dozen or more children by him. The pain was forgotten soon enough, leaving only the pleasure. The Elynora roses were indeed lovely, and bred without thorns, rare roses born of love.